MARY CELES

The Solved Mystery of a Ghost Ship

"Based on very real and very interesting people, is not only full of twists, but it has a heart full of compassion."
— Sandee Curry, writer, editor, sandeecurryeditorial.com

"No ordinary family,
...a surprising twist near the end of this wonderful saga transports the seafaring heroes to dimensions filled with mythical wonders."
— Genie Gabriel, author, www.GenieGabriel.com

"Rich in detail,
with all the sea lore and all its customs. I particularly enjoyed the parallel narrative highlights of the political, social, humanistic and moral issues of the 19th century."
— Jose Marques

"Captivating,
from beginning to end. Based on true events, it is filled with characters and imagery that took me on a time-traveling adventure. Creating points of reference by bringing historical elements into the story's timeline was extremely clever and kept this imaginative mystery-thriller authentic."
— Nancy McDonald, Indelible Mark Publishing

"A rollicking sea-faring tail of adventure,
that spans oceans of time and sensibilities with daring ramifications for all of us living today."
— Laurence Overmire, author and poet

Mary Celeste

The Solved Mystery of a Ghost Ship

Dr. Veronica Esagui

Library of Congress Control Number: 2023900646
ISBN 978-0-9826484-7-6
First Edition: May 2023
Veronica Esagui
Book Cover: Genene Valleau

PAPYRUS PRESS, LLC
West Linn, OR 97068
www.veronicaesagui.com

ACKNOWLEDGMENTS

I would like to thank Captain Briggs and his wife Sarah for allowing me to watch their beginnings, hear their thoughts, meet their family and friends. It was because of their ongoing support and encouragement that I can now share with you their story, the true story of the Mary Celeste's passengers and crew as I came to know them better 15 years later or what some may consider a few seconds in time.

CONTENTS

PART II: AT SEA

PART III: LIMITLESSNESS

Map of Massachusetts (1870's)

Records show that the Briggs and Cobb families originally from England, settled in Massachusetts in the early 1600's.

The following family trees are a condensed version of Sarah Cobb and Captain Benjamin Briggs (Benj) closest family members.

Cobb's Family Tree

Reverend Oliver Cobb (1770-1849)

Sarah Everson (1773-1819) (m. 1795)

Hannah Burgess (1788-1860) (m.1820)

-- Children --
Sophia Matilda Cobb (1795-1803)
Nathaniel Cobb (1800-1878)
*Leander Cobb (1801-1872)
*Sophia Matilda Cobb (1803-1889)
Maria Cobb (1805-1828)
George Washington Cobb (1809-1853)
Elizabeth Lothrop Cobb, (1810-1895)
William Henry Cobb (1812-1849)
Edward W. Cobb (1823-1895)
Sophronia Handy Cobb (1813- 1830)
Hannah Burgess Cobb (1825-1907)
Oliver Cobb (1828-1918)

*Reverend Leander Cobb (1801-1872)

Julia Ann Scribner (1808- 1849) (m. 1831)

Selina Bacon (1816-1905) (m.1850)

-- Children –
William H. Cobb (1831-1837)
Harvey S. Cobb (1834-1837)
Edward A. Cobb (1836-1876)
Harriet M. Cobb (1838-1917)
**Sarah Elizabeth Cobb (1841-1872)
Mary S. Cobb (1843-1923)
William H. Cobb (1846-1876)
Julia A. Cobb (1849-1876)
Maria Cobb (1852-1943)

Briggs's Family Tree

Captain Benjamin Briggs (1755-1826)
(m. 1787) Elizabeth Spooner (1764-1831)

-- Children --
Stetson Briggs (1788-1811)
Spooner Briggs (1791-1839)
Weston Briggs (1792-1854)
Thomas Briggs (1794-1813)
Elizabeth Briggs (1797-1873)
*Nathan S. Briggs (1799-1870)
Sarah Briggs 1801
Cornelius Briggs 1803

*Captain Nathan S. Briggs (m. 1830)
* Sophia Matilda Cobb
(Better known as Mother Briggs)

-- Children --
Nathan Henry Briggs (1831-1855)
Maria Matilda Briggs (1833- 1859)
**Benjamin Spooner Briggs (1835-1872)
Oliver Everson Briggs (1837-1873)
James Cannon Briggs (1839-1922)
Sophronia Briggs (1841-1843)
Zenas Marston Briggs (1844-1870)

**Captain Benjamin Spooner Briggs (Benj) †

**Sarah Elizabeth Cobb (m. 1862) †

-- Children --

Arthur Stanley Briggs (1865-1931)

***Sophia Matilda Briggs (1870-1872)†

† Sailed in the *Mary Celeste*

PREFACE

Since coming to the U.S. in 1963, I faithfully wrote every week to my parents in Portugal, until they passed away in 1996. Four years later, I found myself longing to write once again in Portuguese, my native language, and I began eagerly looking on the internet for pen pals in Portugal. I still had one family member in Portugal, my brother Max-Leão, but he hated writing.

Mid-spring 2000, I was delighted to receive two responses from the north of Portugal. One from Paula, a lady who looked forward to chatting with someone in the U.S., and the other from a widower who was having a difficult time after losing his beloved wife and needed a friend. He wrote that his name was Fernando, but he signed Artur Barros.

Paula was happily married and had a 10-year-old son. She and her husband owned a very successful frozen food company. Our writing of one page or less was mostly about our daily lives and what each day brought along, much in contrast with Artur's emails which could be five to six pages, mostly about how hard it was for him to deal with today's society's lack of morals and how much he loved his deceased wife, whom he considered a saint. I sensed he was going through some form of emotional hell after losing the love of his life, and being that he had been born in 1948, I presumed he was an old-fashioned man trying to find his way in a modern world. His website presented him as a writer and artist with several published books, paintings and ceramics. I felt extremely privileged to have a Portuguese writer and artist so interested in what I had to say. He called me a prolific poet after he read my description of a spiritual experience I had as a child when I encountered an old, broken-down brick wall with tiny pink roses sprouting from its innards. I told him my mother was a famous Portuguese poetess who was featured in the "Dictionary of Famous Women" right along with Mother Theresa and Queen Elizabeth of England, but I knew nothing about writing poetry. Still, I thanked him for the compliment.

For Christmas that year I received from Paula, a card and three romance novels by well-known Portuguese authors. Artur sent me pictures of himself with Leonardo, his grandson, and his house and office as well as the latest book that had just been published, "The Mystery of Saint Eulália." He also sent me a request, "Since I know that prior to being a chiropractor, you were a music teacher, I would be very happy if you could write the music for the lyrical poems I have enclosed. Yours truly, Artur."

I was glad to do that for him, since it sounded like fun. I also read "The Mystery of Saint Eulália" from beginning to end, just in case he asked my opinion, which he did. I didn't want to hurt his feelings, so I told him I had found it interesting. A kind word I learned from a friend, who used it to describe something dreadful, without hurting someone's feelings.

Early spring of 2001, I received "Arts Encounter of 2000," a Portuguese anthology of poetry and short stories, which included Artur and 17 other authors. He must have liked my story of the roses more than I realized, because he had put his name as the author of "Roses on the Wall."

"As you can see," he wrote. "I simply rearranged your writing into a format of shorter lines and thus became a poem. Now you know you can write poetry." Odd way to teach, but I accepted his explanation.

It took me a few months, but I finally finished writing the music for Artur's lyrics. I wrote the music on staff paper, made a tape playing my acoustic guitar and singing, and mailed it to him.

He kept mentioning in his emails that he was planning on rewriting the Bible, which to me sounded like reinventing the wheel, until one day he piqued my interest when he told me about a manuscript, he had started a few years back about the *Marie Celeste,* an American ship found near the Portuguese Islands with no one onboard. "I wonder what happened to the crew and passengers," he wrote. "You're the only one who can help me finish this book. I can't think of anyone more creative than you, and it would be a great honor if you would consider writing this book with me as co-author."

I was thrilled, to say the least, and the first thing I did was look on the internet for *Marie Celeste* and found that the name was *Mary* and not *Marie*. I asked him to send me what he had written, and I would see what I could add to it.

I received attached in Word, the file *Marie Celeste*. And he wrote, "… I can see from the email you sent me that you already acquired some knowledge about the ship. That helps a lot. Here are some of the ideas I have for our book. Feel free to explore them, like how to get the passengers and crew transported to the world of Atlantis, maybe? And how do you think the men of that world were able to transport everything that existed in Atlantis to a different world. But where: another planet, another universe? I don't know which to choose. I also don't know how to define the transport used. I only know that it has to be something completely new and different from what we are familiar with. Possibly a door is open to that world where sometimes humans get sucked in? I created a sailor named James. He is a bit of a rebel but yet the most educated and clear-headed. I believe that description needs to be explored further. There's also a young Italian sailor, Luigi, who suffers from terrible problems, and that can help add some drama to the story. There's another sailor who spies on the captain and his wife, but I didn't have a chance to introduce him or the others into the story. The idea is for you to use these characters to create romance, jealousy and hate toward the captain. I don't have much of anything else to say since that's when I stopped writing except for some more thoughts I had, but I didn't write them down. Don't forget to come up with something like what happens to the crew after they get to the other world. Some of them should die on the way there — at least one or two. Maybe Luigi or James. What do you think? I don't know. Think about all these details. There's no rush, okay? Ah, the file is going on Word 2000. If you don't have Office 2000, let me know, and I'll send it on Word 97. A big hug from your friend, Artur.

The *Mary Celeste* reminded me of "The Mystery of Saint Eulália." The characters were as evasive as the story, with super long paragraphs of philosophical non-explanatory ranting about life, death and God, that reminded me of his usual emails. What had I gotten myself into? I was terrified. Of the 80 pages he sent, 12 were about a wise old man who invited him for tea, and after a long philosophical conversation about death, handed him an old sachet envelope containing the truth of what happened to those aboard the *Marie Celeste*. But Artur didn't elaborate in any of the pages about the acquired knowledge he received from the old man. He described Captain Briggs as a man of high morals, and his faithful wife was devoted only to him. He had forgotten to mention their two-year-old traveling with them. Everybody was happy, and everybody got along great while going about the ship discussing the mysteries of life and talking about the weather and how nice and calm the days were, until one night they awoke to some strange sounds that he couldn't describe, and that's where he stopped.

Artur lived in Portugal, and I was in the extreme west side of Oregon. I knew it was the coward's way out, but once I read his manuscript, I had no intention of going any further with our pen pal relationship. It was one thing to write emails and another to write a whole book.

I told Ralph, my older son, the dilemma I faced, and he said, "Just finish the end of the story and don't worry about what he wrote."

It was easier said than done. How could I write the end to a story that didn't exist?

After a week of not answering Artur's emails, not sleeping well and being stressed out, I decided to grab the bull by the horns. So what if it was going to be a challenge. Life was a challenge! I was ready to take on the project but needed permission to make changes starting from the very beginning.

He wrote back, "I trust you, as my co-author."

From that day on, I still wrote to Paula and Artur, but my emails were short and only once a week. My early hours in the mornings were spent with the *Mary Celeste,* and the rest of the day treating patients and office work. I also had met someone, and the precious gift of romance had entered my life.

September 20, 2001, the *"Mary Celeste"* manuscript was completed. I copied it onto a floppy disk and mailed it to Artur. After several emails asking him to let me know if he had received the disk, and not getting a response, except for short emails about his daily experiences with traveling to Spain, I re-sent the manuscript as an attachment with an email. Still, I got no response, and I figured he didn't like what I had written and instead of letting me know how disappointed he felt, he had decided to ignore me.

Three months later, Artur let me know in a matter-of-fact way about our book being in his hands, but he had been too busy to read it, the reason he had not responded.

Mid-January, of the following year, he wrote that he had finally read it and was surprised I had not incorporated the character of the *old man* that he had told me about, who had provided him with the story of the *Mary Celeste*. He was too busy to take care of it and was on the way to Columbia to meet a woman he had met on the internet. The one he met in Spain had not worked out. He would get back to me when he returned.

There wasn't a single positive or even negative word of acknowledgment about the writing I had done. I decided to ignore his request to do any further writing. As co-authors, he needed to start doing his own part. If he wanted the *old man* in the story, he could go ahead and write it himself.

Time moved on, and the emails between Artur and me become sporadic. I felt that the *Mary Celeste* had been lost forever in his hands just like the music I had written for his lyrics that he never acknowledged.

Late April of 2003, I sent an email to Artur that I was getting married and planned on going to Portugal for the honeymoon in September. I wrote, "I look forward to meeting you and your new wife from Columbia. And since you told me about your plans to have the book published in May," I added a hint, "I look forward to seeing our book in print."

A month later, I received an email from Artur. "You won't believe how busy I've been. Just want to let you know the book was launched and it was a huge success. Many of my political friends attended the event. I sent you a copy of the book by mail weeks ago, but it looks like you did not receive it. In relation to the book, I had told you a long time ago I intended to use our names (yours and mine) as authors, but I found out it can't be done because of taxes, since you are not a resident of Portugal. I would have to register you as contributor and, as such, you would be obliged to make yearly declarations of moneys received, and that would be complicated and embarrassing. Therefore, I had to opt to put my name only, but inside, I made an author's dedication to your encouraging friendship …"

I immediately sent a copy of his email to Paula and followed up with a call to The Portuguese Society of Authors in Lisbon, Portugal, and read his email to them. I was devastated to find out that Artur's excuses for not using my name as co-author were false. They wanted his name, address and phone number, and would make sure the book would be taken out of circulation. I also received a fax from Paula, who had found a lawyer who was willing to represent me and charge Artur with plagiarism.

Two weeks later, I received a copy of "The True Story of *Mary Celeste,*" by Artur Barros. Lucky for me, Danny, my brother-in-law and a child psychologist, was in town. I shared with him Artur's deceit. I felt betrayed and confused and really didn't know how to proceed.

"You need to evaluate what's most important to you and follow your heart," Danny told me.

I thought about it for about two minutes, and that was enough for me. I was going to Portugal for a honeymoon, not to start legal procedures toward someone who had done me wrong.

I sent Artur a short email, "I thought we were friends and trusted you. Instead, you lied and stole my work. Since the book is more important to you than our relationship, everything is over between us, including my intention of translating it into English. As of now, our friendship is over forever."

An email arrived the next day. He was sorry about what he had done and confessed that he had done the same to others who had meant a lot to him, and that he had lost them as the result of that. He had self-published *our* book and promised to remove the few copies he still owned from the market. He finished the email by apologizing once again and begging me to forgive him and to remain his friend.

I did not answer.

Fifteen years went by since parting ways with Artur. But on November 7,

2018, I experienced a most peculiar vivid dream. I found myself standing by a waterfall where a small group of people dressed in white tunics gestured for me to cross the water and join them. A young woman with long dark hair and holding a boy's hand announced with a pleasant smile, "We're the people who traveled on the *Mary Celeste*. Would you like to come with us?" Funny how the mind works even in dreams, but I suddenly remembered my mother saying that when one dreams about dead people, we should never follow them, because they can keep you there forever. I answered quickly, "If you don't mind, I'd rather stay on this side." I awoke in a sweat.

The dream haunted me all day, but that evening, I purposely went to bed earlier. I was no longer scared. If anything, I was very excited about the possibility of seeing them again. It took me a while to fall asleep. Then, it happened. I stood by the waterfall once again as if that was the front door to their home. It crossed my mind that I might be intruding, and I was about to leave, when from the same group I had met the night before, a man and a woman stepped forward and introduced themselves as Captain Briggs and his wife Sarah. They looked quite different from the way I had imagined them originally. The few solemn black-and-white pictures left behind had not done them justice. They were beautiful, healthy, joyful people.

"You're alive!" I clapped my hands, and a smile from the little girl next to them made me feel ecstatic. "And this place I once described is not in my imagination — it does exist!" I crossed to the other side.

They had been the ones who had brought me over, and before parting, Captain Briggs said, "Think of our collaboration as a personal gift for keeping us alive in your heart all this time and now in the minds of your readers. Sarah and I will make sure to project to you the images of our past. Just have fun writing the true story of the *Mary Celeste*." I awoke and couldn't get back to sleep. It was five in the morning. Two hours later. I was sitting in front of the computer in my office. A soft tune played over our sound system. My fingers typed, "*Mary Celeste*."

I waited patiently. Then, like a bird looking down from high above, my vision opened like a wide-angle lens, and I saw the *Mary Celeste* anchored at an old pier. I was there.

Staten Island, New York Harbor

Thursday, November 7, 1872

The 282-ton American brigantine *Mary Celeste* set sail on its way to Genoa, Italy, carrying in her hold, a cargo of 1,701 barrels of denatured alcohol.

Captain Benjamin Spooner Briggs and his wife Sarah stood at the helm, facing the vast ocean ahead. She took in a deep breath of chilly salt-laden air and gazed up at the sails fluttering in response to a moderate yet gentle northeast breeze. "Benj, they're like angels' wings."

"Yes, my love," he wrapped his right arm around her shoulders, bringing her closer to him. "And Lord willing, it's going to be an auspicious voyage, for all of us."

PART I
Massachusetts

CHAPTER I

Wareham. – The Briggs family. – Mother Briggs gives birth. – Opium's side effects. – A sea captain's wife. – Angel Sophronia.

Friday, November 11, 1842

"Come on Benj," said Sophia Matilda Cobb Briggs, who went by the name Mother Briggs. "It's been two weeks since your Cousin Sarah's baptism. Now stop fiddling around and write a proper note to your Aunt Julia Ann and Uncle Leander." She was a loving mother, but her children knew better than whistle, laugh or "kick down the leaves" during Sabbath. A religious but outspoken woman, she ran her home like a tight ship, much like her husband Nathan Briggs, a successful and well-seasoned merchant captain. She grasped the large worn-out oak writing box from the center of the kitchen table and placed it next to Benjamin. His father had used it at sea for the last 14 years, until he decided to acquire one with a screw-down mechanism that kept its contents secure when the ship had to contend with the usual crescendo and diminuendo of the ocean waves. Besides the extra compartments and drawers, Captain Nathan's new writing box even boasted enough space to store candlesticks and a reading stand.

Benjamin was only 7, but he already knew that someday he would follow in his father's footsteps, and he would be the captain of his own ship. Deeply involved with a pencil in hand, he drew such a ship on oil-stained brown paper while methodically erasing any errors with a piece of crustless bread.

Mother Briggs smacked him gently over the forehead with the back of her hand. "Do as you're told!" and she rushed to check on Sophronia, her 3-month-old daughter, who she kept wrapped in a wool blanket inside a wooden cradle next to the crackling blaze of the open hearth in the kitchen.

Maria Matilda, two years older than Benjamin, stopped reading the Bible to their 3-year-old brother James who had been sitting on her lap, staring wide-eyed at her, mesmerized by his sister's storytelling. She gave Benjamin a gentle elbow poke and gestured her chin toward him and then to the box. "I already did it; it's not that difficult. Now, stop being so lazy," and she went back to reading aloud about Adam and Eve being banished from the Garden of Eden, after being told not to eat the forbidden fruit from the tree of knowledge.

"But Mama, I don't know what to write," Benjamin did not stop drawing.

"Fine," she removed a large loaf of freshly baked bread from the stove. "Your choice, but you're not getting any breakfast."

The next meal of the day, dinner, would not be served until early afternoon, and supper, a piecemeal late in the evening, was nothing to count on, since most of the time, a cup of hot tea was all that came about. The aroma of a snug breakfast of chicken fixins, eggs, ham-doings and even slapjacks on the iron pan provided the motivation he needed.

Inside the box, he found a wad of small writing paper with matching cream-colored envelopes tied neatly with a blue silk ribbon, two dip pens, a half-filled inkwell glass jar and a mini pouch with sand for sprinkling over the wet ink — a lot cheaper than blotting paper. Paying particular attention to his calligraphy, he wrote, "Dear Aunt and Uncle, Sarah is nice, she does not cry all the time like other babies. Your nephew, Benjamin."

Benjamin had his share of stories about babies crying and waking him up at all hours of the night. The birth of his sister Sophronia had more than captured his imagination, when in the middle of the night, he heard his mother's piercing voice calling from her bedroom, "Maria Matilda! Maria Matilda!" Then followed by an agonizing, "Jesus Christ and Mother Mary, is anybody awake?"

Benjamin and his siblings sprang out of bed simultaneously, looked at each other for a split second, and then ran upstairs. They found their mother lying in bed, her long disheveled dark hair covered in sweat, and a single bedsheet covering her parted legs.

"Nathan," she pointed to her oldest son. "You run and fetch Mrs. Hoyle, the midwife on Sunset Street." He remained like a soldier at attention. "Boy, stop staring and run like the devil, do you hear me?" He ran out in the rain, barefoot and in his nightshirt.

"You, Benj, take Oliver and James back to your room and stay there until you're told to come out," she took a deep breath in and out, and with a stoic grin, she added, "Maria Matilda, get the largest pot you find in the kitchen, fill it with water, and set it on the hearth to boil. When you're done, come back as fast as you can."

Her husband had been gone for four months, and she did not expect him for at least another two, but she did not mind. Men were of no use during this critical time in a woman's life. If anything, his absence provided her the freedom to cry out words most unfit for a God-fearing woman. The birth process sometimes could take hours or even days, and once in a while could be less than an hour, but either way, the pain of giving birth was reserved for women only.

Opium, known as laudanum, was the only relief known for pain control but was rarely used since the church believed women were destined to suffer during childbirth, as the Bible decreed. It was also believed that experiencing relief of pain during childbirth caused the mother to lose her maternal instinct, which could only be attained from suffering. The fact that laudanum produced a condition similar to intoxication, and it made its use a serious immoral act, there were other well-known ill effects attributed to it, like epilepsy, convulsions and insanity. But if Mother Briggs had been able to get some laudanum at that very moment, she would gladly have traded her soul for an ounce of it.

Sophronia arrived three hours later, a sickly scruffy little thing, under six pounds. The silence that followed Sophronia's barely audible first cry caused Benjamin and his brothers to think that their mother and the newborn had perished. Maria Matilda found her brothers huddled together crying in one corner of their bedroom.

Captain Nathan was only 15 years old when he started his life as a sailor, primarily as a cook and deckhand on a sloop, a small, square-rigged sailing ship. Six years later, he took on his first voyage bound to Marseilles, as master of the 90-ton schooner brig the *Betsy and Jane,* and by age 26, he had become a shipmaster of merchant sailing ships on regular ocean crossings.

When first married, Mother Briggs accompanied him on many of his sea voyages — but when she became pregnant with their first child, they decided it was in the best interest of the family that she take on the responsibility of motherhood on land, something she took on keenly since she found life at sea to be quite boring.

As the wife of a sea captain, she was no different from all the other women in her family who were married to sailors and had become accustomed to sometimes waiting a year or more to see their husbands. In the case of Oliver, their fourth child, Captain Nathan came home and met their almost one-year-old son for the first time.

Nathan, their oldest, born in 1831 and named after him, had

been followed by a new sibling every two years, take away a few months here and there. One did not have to guess when Captain Nathan was home from his seafaring.

He had missed the birth of all of his children, but was home February 26, 1843, when Sophronia was called to the Lord. Mother Briggs would later explain to her children, while reasoning with herself, that Heaven needed another baby angel.

A week earlier, Sophronia had awoken feverish and refused to drink her milk. When she developed problems breathing, Mother Briggs borrowed the neighbor's horse and buggy to visit her father, Reverend Oliver Cobb, who lived in Sippican, six miles south from Wareham. She remained on her knees until the end of his sermon and waited with her head down for him to approach her.

"Father," she kissed his hand. "You're the closest to God. As the grandfather of my child, I beg you to ask Him not to take Sophronia. He'll listen to you."

Mother Briggs awoke the morning of February 26 and told her husband that it was odd that Sophronia had slept through the night without crying. He went to check the cradle at the foot of their bed. It was the first time she witnessed her husband weep as he snuggled the inert body of their daughter in his arms.

The loss of Sophronia may have played an important role in the Briggs decision to leave Wareham. The Briggs and the Cobb families were related by several intermarriages and shared the same family values and religious beliefs. Being closer to each other was a dream come true for the women in both families, who through the years, had built a common bond of sisterhood.

Two months after selling their home, the Briggs moved to Sippican where their closest relatives lived.

CHAPTER II

Sippican. – 1843 – 1844. - Plotting a bath. – Breaching party. – Little Johnny. – Cousins Sarah and Benjamin.

Sippican, a prosperous seafaring town situated between Bird Island on the east, Converse Point on the west, and New Bedford, the busiest whaling port in the world, just 14 miles south, thrived with seamen who sailed on whale ships, coastal schooners and Liverpool Packets. There were about 80 sea captains and their families living in Sippican. With more than 15 years as a ship merchant, Captain Nathan and his wife had saved enough to afford building the home of their dreams alongside the other prosperous families like the Luces, the Delanos and the Gibbs, who owned magnificent homes.

The Briggs found a wooded lot on the far side of Pleasant Street, just a few blocks inland from the harbor and within walking distance from their relatives and Mother Briggs's father's church, the Congregational Church of Sippican.

While their new home was being built, Mother Briggs and her five children, Nathan, Maria Matilda, Benjamin, Oliver and James moved into her father's modest sized home, where her brother,

Father Leander, his wife Julia Ann and their three children, Edward, Harriet and Sarah already resided. They managed to live together for a year, and later in life they would reminisce about "the good old days," and their delightful experiences under such a tiny roof. Reverend Leander and Julia Ann's room barely fit their small, narrow bed. The boys shared two wood cots nestled side by side in their grandfather's bedroom, and Mother Briggs shared her bed with the girls. Captain Nathan came home once that year and quietly submitted to sleep the two weeks' furlough on a rocking chair in the kitchen.

Along with everything else she considered of value, Mother Briggs brought from Wareham her most prized possession, the family tub. It was diligently put away in the backyard, behind the doghouse, out of her father's sight. The older generation at that time leaned on old-fashioned medical theories involving the balancing of humors and the elimination of bile through the skin, and thought submerging oneself in water was a sure path to weakness and ill health, therefore a religious conflict for her father and many other clergy members. On bathing days, someone in the household made sure Reverend Oliver Cobb was kept busy with church matters and away from home long enough to allow the whole family to bathe. The ritual was always the same — since there was no inside plumbing — they carried the tub inside the house, and patiently filled it with water one bucket at a time. After bathing, the water was taken out once again bucket by bucket, and the tub was scrubbed and cleaned of all the slime and grit, before taking it out into the yard and hidden.

One blessed day, thanks to Elizabeth, Mother Briggs's sister, they learned about a most innovative idea — by lining the wood tub with thick linen before pouring the water in, it acted as a strainer and helped the tub walls from getting too much grime. Mother Briggs and Julia Ann gladly took turns washing the linen afterward with lye soap and hot water, and then hung it outside to dry.

For a family to take a bath in the 19th century, it made the most sense to take once a month and share the same water. Out of respect for their oldest family members, they were usually given priority when it came to using the tub first and then they finished with their youngest — most likely the origin of the German proverb: "Don't throw the baby out with the bathwater."

The average household in the United States had — usually in their bedroom — a water jug and a small basin for washing the face, neck, hands and more intimate parts. That was fine for other folks, but Mother Briggs, Julia Ann, her husband Reverend Leander and the children bathed once a week, and they took much pleasure in plotting the event.

"Perfumes and powders were created on'y to cover smelly body odor," Mother Briggs liked to make a strong argument over perfumes being an evil affliction to her senses, and sneezing was her nose's job for fencing out disturbing smells.

Julia Ann considered herself lucky for not suffering from the same affliction as Mother Briggs, who would go into sneeze attacks after breathing anything other than fresh air.

After finishing their daily household chores, both women liked to sit and chat while mending socks and other clothing items. By the end of that summer, they turned their creative sewing interests into stitching thick square layers of fabric to make different size quilts to cover the winter chill that came coursing through the doors and windows of the old house. Julia Ann told her that while living in Charlestown with her husband, they kept their tub next to the kitchen stove, and on cold days, they heated a few bricks and put them inside the tub to keep the water heated a bit longer. The bathwater was used over and over again, and all they had to do was add more as needed. It could last a month before they had to change it.

Mother Briggs figured she would do the same when she moved into her own home — but go a little further with its use.

She ordered a copper tub she'd seen advertised in a catalog as being the best material for maintaining the water warmth. She intended to put it in her kitchen next to the stove and use it for bathing as well as for washing clothes. She felt an intense joy imagining larger items like bedsheets and covers being stirred inside the tub and beaten with the plunger as usual, but all in the comfort of her kitchen.

Her brother and Julia Ann were thrilled when she promised to leave them her wood tub.

In those days, it was quite proper for very young boys who had not yet completed potty training to wear skirts or dresses. Even though such attire was associated with girls' wear, it provided straightforward access when nature called.

Benjamin and his brothers had completed their potty training at 2-and-a-half years old, but James had accomplished that task at 2. The family was ready to celebrate, but they had to wait three more months for Captain Nathan to come home since he insisted on being part of all his sons' rites of passage. When the joyful day came, the Briggs and the Cobb families gathered to sing their praises at James' breeching party as he modeled for everyone the handmade breeches Mother Briggs had sewn. At this point, a father would usually become more involved with the raising of his sons, but considering Captain Nathan's profession, it would remain a scarce relationship until James reached the proper age of 15 and became a deckhand on his father's ship.

But as James grew up, he never shared the enthusiasm of his father or his brothers for the sea. He preferred to keep his feet on firm ground, as he made it clear more than once, when, even on a balmy day — while on a river cruise with his siblings, he became seasick. Everybody agreed he had more of an inclination toward fixing things, especially animals. When he was 9, he came home carrying a sparrow with a broken wing. He asked his brother Nathan and his mother for help, and when they told him nothing could be done to save the dying bird, he concocted a sling made from two twigs and a piece of cloth to hold the wing in place. The bird lived but couldn't fly. He carried "Little Johnny" on his shoulder everywhere he went, except to church where no animals were allowed.

While living together, the Briggs and the Cobb children bonded more like siblings than cousins. They slept and played together, and every morning Julia Ann, with Mother Briggs as her assistant, held a mandatory two-hour homeschooling in the kitchen. Anyone 3 or older was expected to participate. They were instructed in English grammar as well as French, Latin, geography and arithmetic.

Julia Ann enjoyed taking the children for hikes into the woods. She introduced them to the various plants growing in the wild and showed them which were safe to touch or eat and which not to even brush against, like the giant hogweed with pretty white flowers that could cause skin blisters, or the poisonous pokeberries with such appetizing grape-like clusters.

Reverend Leander and Julia Ann were firm believers that literacy was the only way to ensure the reading of the Bible, but the Webster's American Dictionary made them just as enthusiastic. The more their children learned, the more prepared they would be to fend for themselves later in life.

Even though Sarah was barely 3, she showed to be exceptional at picking up languages. In class, she always sat next to Benjamin, and when walking outside, she held his hand.

December 6, 1843, Julia Ann gave birth to another girl. Mother Briggs took care of baby Mary, the family, and the household, while Julia Ann recovered for the next two months.

CHAPTER III

**The best birthday gift. – Zenas, last one out of the old fort. –
The Rose Cottage. – Sea battles between brothers. – Captain
Nathan. – Sarah's parents. – Sarah. – How to pull out a tooth
and survive.**

April 24, 1844

The Briggs moved into their new Victorian style home, and
Benjamin considered that to be the best birthday gift he could ever
wish for. No more listening to his grandfather snoring and other
insulting sounds or having to push and shove to turn over, while
sandwiched between his siblings Nathan, Oliver, James and cousin
Edward. His only roommate now was his brother Oliver. But he
didn't mind since they shared a mutual interest in seafaring and
they had separate beds.

July 6, Mother Briggs was consoled in giving birth once again. As
she strained to push the newborn into the world, she shouted, "God
taketh away and God giveth back! Alleluia!"

Her husband arrived three days later. Still wearing his
captain's garb, he entered their bedroom carrying a tray with a

bowl of hot chicken broth.

"Your sister Elizabeth is down in the kitchen," he couldn't help noticing her amused smile. "She told me you had a difficult time and are in much need of nourishment." He put the tray on the bedside table and stood admiring her and Zenas, their new baby boy, whose eyelids were held tightly closed and his tiny button lips held firmly, like a suction cup at Mother Briggs's nipple.

"Good to see you, husband o' mine."

"The feeling is mutual, my dearest," he kissed her forehead, and then pointed to the baby, "Looks like we got a healthy one there."

He sat on the side of the bed, stirring the broth with the spoon, "Let's get you to eat now. Your sister didn't think you were going to make it. I'm so glad you're doing better today."

"I couldn't have done it without her," she pulled Zenas away from her nipple and began tapping his back gently. "Close the door. I need to tell you something very important."

He put the bowl back on the tray, closed the door, and sat back on the bed.

"Here," she handed Zenas to him. "I'm done bearing children!"

His mouth fell open and then reasoning with himself that she might be joking, he laid Zenas gently in his cradle and remained next to it, staring silently at her, hoping he had misunderstood what he heard.

"He takes the place of Sophronia as it should be," her voice rang with a strong tone of authority. Then she pointed between her legs. "As of now, I'm closing down the old fort."

He couldn't help raising his voice. "Are you cutting a shine on me?" Then he shouted even louder, "No more children?" Zenas started to cry. He picked him up from the cradle and began rocking him steadily while pacing back and forth. He looked at his wife's face and knew her answer but went on, "You can't be serious. No more ...?"

"No! No more!" Then softening her voice, "Husband, I'm 41 years old!" she sighed loudly. "My body has had enough. I want to live and get old with you. Besides, raising more children than what we have already been blessed with will take me away from taking care of our new home and property."

She was well aware of God's wishes to be fruitful and multiply and also her moral obligation as a wife to bear as many as possible to make up for all the ones lost at birth and other circumstances, but Mother Briggs stuck to her final decision and...

Three months later, she immersed herself into the landscape and planted so many roses that in less than two years, their home became known as the *Rose Cottage.*

But it was far from being a cottage. The outside colors a two-tone of light ochre and taupe with russet beige trimmings blended well with its surroundings, but it also helped to enhance its large structure. It boasted three Rumford fireplaces, appreciated for its tall classic elegance and heating efficiency, five bedrooms upstairs, and downstairs a kitchen large enough to accommodate "the tub," and a pine wood table that could seat up to 14 people comfortably. The pantry featured lots of shelving that extended into the cellar. The pine wood floors were laid in random widths and, except for the kitchen, all the rooms had an area rug that complemented the colors of the wallpaper in each room. When entering the front door, one could not miss the parlor to the right, with its whimsy flowery wallpaper and the four tall windows facing the front yard. When open, the windows created a cool, delicious airflow throughout the rest of the house, and the natural sunlight made the room, with all its dainty but sturdy French furnishings, ideal for year-round use while having tea with family and friends. In the corner of the room, a Brazilian rosewood square grand piano and a matching stool with a hinged, padded blue top created what Mother Briggs described as a perfect gay touch to an otherwise gloomy room. It was a beautiful expensive piece of furniture, and the children knew better than to play on it.

Across the hallway to the left was the dining room with its blue and white nautical-themed wallpaper. Two elegant bronze candelabras holding seven candles each sat in the center of the long mahogany dining table that, when extended out, could accommodate up to 20 people. A matching, intricately carved mahogany cabinet displayed a well-organized assortment of Mother Briggs' silver platters and bowls, a blue and white porcelain set of dinnerware with English country scenes and another white set with red borders and a stamped bouquet of flowers in its center. Six bronze sconces with their respective snuffers hung in pairs on the walls by the front window, the doorway and on each side of a Venetian glass mirror that Captain Nathan had brought from Italy. The dining room was only used when Captain Nathan was home, and meals were a family celebration between the Briggs and the Cobbs. Its access led appropriately through a butler's pantry and into the kitchen.

A U-shaped driveway extended up the sides of the property and around the back of the house. Four conical fieldstone pillars flanked the driveway's front entrance, giving it a grand look that complemented the wide covered porch around the house.

Another advantage of being in their new home was that Benjamin and his brother Oliver no longer had to worry about their grandfather catching them bathing. When they behaved exemplarily, Mother Briggs rewarded them with being the last ones to use the tub. They remained in the water until it went cold and used the lye soap sparingly, since they liked to play games like who could hold their head underwater the longest. They always finished by playing out a major sea battle with their toy boats. But they were very good at refraining from splashing at each other, unless they wanted to clean the floors afterward. That happened on one occasion, and it had been enough.

Mother Briggs did have more than one washing rule for her children; their feet were to be scrubbed clean in the foot basin in their bedrooms every night before getting into bed. "Mark my word," she only had to say it once. "The day I find the smallest particle of dirt in your bedsheets, that week you'll be doing the entire household wash for the family."

The water from the foot basin was discarded by adding it to the chamber pot usually kept under the bed. Each member of the household was responsible for getting rid of its contents the next morning. Captain Nathan was the only family member exempt from such menial task. Mother Briggs took care of it, but in exchange, she expected that upon returning from his long sea voyage, he would bathe.

No one was to bother Captain Nathan until he yelled out for a towel.

The relationship between the Briggs's and Cobbs families once they no longer lived together, continued to be nurtured as planned by Mother Briggs and Julia Ann. Once a week, the two families gathered for dinner at the *Rose Cottage* and called it family day.

When Captain Nathan was able to join them, it became an informal yarn session about the legends of the sea. No one stood after the meal ended — all eyes on him. Still, he waited until someone asked something like, "how was your voyage?"

His passionate storytelling always enlightened the romance

and excitement of his multiple sea adventures. Many of them had to be repeated since they were too good to hear just once. While at home, he liked maintaining his role as the Captain and took a serious delight in carrying sea terminology with his family. When he called out for his children to go "aloft," they knew he meant upstairs to their bedroom, and when he said go play in the "quarterdeck," he meant the front porch. His love for the sea carried out by the poetic view of a true salty dog, produced an overall excitement in the young minds of his three sons, Nathan, Benjamin, and Oliver. They couldn't wait to be 15 and join their father, who had assured them that once they worked up through the ranks and became accomplished sailors, they would be able to get their master's certificate and be in command of their own vessel. The boys were not afraid of the ocean's vastness or the possibility of capsizing and being devoured into its dark monstrous depth. They were not afraid of pirates or sea monsters. With God on their side, fear was nonexistent. Nathan, the oldest brother, was already scheduled to join their father the following year.

There was only one sea item that they did not look forward to, "pilot bread," a cracker-like bread made from flour and water. Their father introduced it to the family saying it was great at sea because of its long shelf life. Mother Briggs soaked the crackers in an inch of salted milk for about one minute, and then fried them in a buttered skillet. The children ate it since they had no other choice.

The prevailing atmosphere in the Briggs home was one of order, duty and propriety as cardinal virtues, and being the daughter of a minister with high puritanical values, Mother Briggs did not "spare the rod" when it came to instilling those virtues into her children. They quickly learned at a young age that before being allowed to go out and play, it was in their best interest to finish their homework and memorize by heart, the daily Bible teachings she had chosen for them to read.

Playing outdoors helped offset many of these strict rules.

Benjamin and Oliver became fond of climbing on the narrow stonewall that ran the full length of their front yard and walk on it as if on a tight rope.

"The day we can run on top of this wall with our eyes closed and not fall," Benjamin told his brother, "It will mean we can hold steady on the deck of any ship and not lose our balance when it gets hit sideways by a huge, huge wave."

Mother Briggs had several siblings, but the one who made her the proudest was her brother Leander, four years her junior. At a very young age, Leander had shown a profound religious inclination, and when he turned 16, their father, Reverend Oliver Cobb, invited him to do a sermon at the Congregational Church of Sippican, where he received considerable praise from the parishioners.

Leander went on to attend Boston University, and upon graduation, moved to Indiana as a Protestant missionary for the American Home Missionary Society (AHMS). As the new pastor in the city of Charlestown, he vehemently encouraged his churchgoers to do right by the Bible and follow his personal favorite, the Golden Rule, "Do unto others as you would have them do unto you." His passionate and inspiring sermons soon became the talk of Charlestown.

He was 29 when he met 21-year-old Julia Ann Scribner in the early spring of 1829, at a private political soirée at the home of young George Washington Julian, who served as an attorney in notable fugitive slave cases. Years later, George became a U.S. Representative (1861–1871) demanding recognition of slavery as the cause of the Civil War, while promoting rights for formerly enslaved people who had been released from slavery, usually by legal means. He proposed constitutional amendments granting suffrage regardless of race or sex, "equality, without any distinction or discrimination."

Reverend Leander and Julia Ann shared the same political views and a mutual intolerance toward bigotry. They were sickened when they learned of President Andrew Jackson signing the Indian Removal Act on May 28, 1830, which gave the federal government the power to relocate all Native Americans in the east, to territory west of the Mississippi River, under the excuse of opening "new" land for settlement to citizens of the United States.

After making several appeals with the help of George Washington Julian and other lawyers, they realized they couldn't do anything to change President Andrew Jackson's mind, and they became involved in at least one Underground Railroad operation as far as Kentucky, to help with the escape of slaves. Bonded by their strong beliefs in equality, freedom and justice for all, they made the perfect pair.

They were married that same year.

Their first two sons, William, and Harvey, respectively 6 and 3-years old, died a few months apart. Their third son, Edward, just one-year-old at the time of his siblings' death, had been staying with Julia Ann's mother, and luckily didn't get exposed to the smallpox epidemic.

September 8, 1838, Julia Ann gave birth to Harriet. As a busy wife and mother, she ended all major humanitarian endeavors to focus on her family needs while using her organizational skills to help her husband with church matters.

In the summer of 1841, Reverend Leander received a letter from his father. "... I can feel my age crawling steadily upon my old bones. Son, I really need you here with me, as my colleague. How soon can I expect you?"

They arrived in Sippican, October 20, just in time for Julia Ann to give birth to a healthy baby girl. They named her Sarah Elizabeth, after her deceased grandmother, the wife of Reverend Oliver Cobb.

During the next five years, the relationship between Reverend Oliver and his son grew noticeably stronger. They shared the same religious and political views, and at the end of the day, church business came home with them.

Julia Ann enjoyed listening to the two men discussing the interpretation of some of the Bible's passages and/or reading to each other their newly written sermons, while seeking each other's approval. If their discussions ran late into the evening, she would bring them some tea, light a few candles and then sit quietly mending clothes in need of repair.

Two years later, Julia Ann gave birth to William, named after her firstborn who had died at 6. This was an ongoing practice, a way of bringing a child's memory back into the living world. It was considered an honor to be named after a dead sibling, principally if such child had been loved or gifted. As such, the newborn would also assume the day of his or her sibling's birthday and discard his own.

Even though with each child bearing, Julia Ann's health diminished considerably, abstaining like Mother Briggs did not fit her role as the wife of a pastor. Fortunately, for the next three years, she did not bear any children, and her health seemed to improve as she went about with her household chores.

April 24, 1847, reinforced the bond of friendship between Benjamin and Sarah. Even though Sarah was only 6, she was aware of Benjamin's interest in seafaring, and for his 12th birthday, she made him a mini boat out of cardboard.

"Look," she pointed to her white embroidered handkerchief attached as a sail. "When you put it in the water, it will float nicely with the help of the wind."

Impressed with her navigation skills, he asked if she would like to be his second mate. Brother Oliver remained as his first mate, and the three became inseparable, as they played in "their" pond, just two blocks from their homes — making up stories about cruel pirates and young damsels in distress. He put her in charge of scooping their handmade boats, with a stick he made from two old brooms with a hook attached at the end. The two brothers swam around the models, blowing at them and using their hands to move the water that carried the boats forward. Sarah always remained on shore and raced to see which one arrived first to the other side of the long but shallow pond. She took great joy at scooping out the winning boat and cheering for the winner.

Sarah's parents' contempt for wealth as the sole pursuit in life had a marked influence in her developmental character. She appreciated things like keeping a caterpillar inside a box and waiting patiently until it morphed into a butterfly. In her backyard, she would remain still for as long as it was necessary to observe a hummingbird take in the nectar from a flower.

"They look like fairies," she said once to her siblings, but they laughed at her. She began sharing the interpretations of her life experiences with Benjamin; he never made fun of her.

She loved holding ladybugs in the palm of her hands and then blowing softly on them to watch them fly away. In the summer, she enjoyed sitting alone on the ground by the shade of the stone wall in her backyard, where the wild sweet peas, large violets and deep crimson flowers let out a sweet fragrance that she found most dreamy. Her ease with languages made her the favorite of her French maternal great-grandmother, who barely spoke English and was more than happy to teach Sarah a few favorite French songs.

Sarah always looked forward to playing outside with her siblings and cousins, particularly with Benjamin. He never played tricks on her or pushed her down, like the others did.

Being the family's matriarch came with certain obligations, and Mother Briggs held the honor of being sought out for pulling out teeth, usually from those between 6 and 11 years old. She tied a thin string to the base of the tooth and the other end to a doorknob, then slammed the door closed. She had it down to a science, but there were times when she had to use a pair of pliers.

After watching her brother Edward screaming and then

fainting after having a molar pulled with what seemed to be a brutal looking instrument of torture, Sarah confided her fears to Benjamin, and he was more than happy to share with her his reliable technique for taking the easy way out.

"As soon as you feel a tooth going soft at the bottom, use your fingers to loosen it, every day like this," and he showed her the back-and-forth motion that had proved to be a great success for him.

With adults, it was a bit more complicated. The roots were deeper and most of the time rotten or chipped. On those occasions when the pain imposed an immediate response, they had no other choice but to visit the closest barber.

Barbers cut hair, applied leeches and even performed embalming. For extracting teeth, they used a ratchet wrench, and most of the time, all it did was break the tooth. More in-depth dental procedures were beginning to be performed by general physicians who were able to scrape out the "junk" in the cavity and create a filling of sorts with beeswax, lead or tin.

Considering there were no toothbrushes in those days, the Cobbs and Briggs possessed beautiful, healthy teeth. The Briggs felt they owed it partially to Julia Ann, who had shared her knowledge of dental hygiene, during the year they had lived together. To remove stubborn stains, chalk, powdered sage or salt on a small cloth, proved to whiten old teeth. She had also shared with Mother Briggs her homemade mouthwash blend of vinegar and mint she kept in the kitchen pantry along with a few glass jars with cloves, cinnamon and sage for chewing on such occasions when after a meal, the smell of garlic or onions lingered on.

CHAPTER IV

Julia Ann and Selina. – Reverend Oliver Cobb's last words. – Reverend Leander's first sermon. – The Indian Removal Act. – Sarah loses Grandpa Oly and her Mama. – No, nothing really dies. – Reverend Leander and Selina take on the vows of matrimony.

Mid-January 1849, Julia Ann knew she was pregnant once again when the smell of stew made her run out and into their backyard. Sarah, now 8-years-old, followed her outside. She watched her mother bent over on her knees spewing a coarse, brownish fluid that marred the once pure white snow covering. The foul odor forced her to back away as she prayed that her own insides did not come out too. Julia Ann finally stood, her face white as chalk, her hands trembled when she used the apron around her waist to wipe her face. "I need to go lie down and rest just for a little while," she told Sarah, as she slowly climbed the steps to her bedroom.

Sarah sat by the kitchen window and caught view of old Joe, the street cleaner, who used a shovel to scoop the snow off the street and threw it inside his one-horse pulled cart. He wore a dingy black apron that reached below his knees and covered the front of his worn-out brown pants and black leather boots. The dark brown hat and overcoat didn't seem warm enough for such harsh, cold weather, but she could tell he was sweating even though his bushy brown beard covered most of his face. "That's such a sad, hard job," and then her thoughts turned toward her mother.

By the end of March, Julia Ann lacked the strength to take care of her family, including her father-in-law who had become bedridden with what seemed to be an ongoing chest cold since the past Christmas. Mother Briggs invited her niece Selina, a single 33-year-old, to move in with the Cobb family. Room and board and a modest compensation were offered in exchange for taking care of Julia Ann, Reverend Oliver, the children and all household duties. At first, Julia Ann didn't want to hear about it, but one morning she fell after getting up from bed, and became concerned with suffering a miscarriage. She accepted Mother Briggs' offer. As the days went by, Julia Ann became more dependent on Selina, and a sisterly bond quickly developed between the two women.

Considering the health issues Julia Ann went through each time she gave birth, the family voted to have her enter a hospital when close to the due date, so she could receive the best of care from a real doctor versus that of a midwife.

"I leave in peace, knowing that our flock is in your hands, and you'll continue to teach them how to redeem themselves and into the arms of salvation," those were Reverend Oliver Cobb's last words to his son Reverend Leander, on the early morning of June 23.

Reverend Leander's first sermon as the official pastor at his father's church, addressed the Indian Removal Act and its devastating effect. He took his time to describe why the forced march deserved to be known as the "Trail of Tears." He finished the sermon with an exulting alleluia for God's love and how much of that love the congregation should share with those they met who were less fortunate. Then the church choir sang "Glorious Things of Thee Are Spoken" and "Amazing Grace" by John Newton, whom he greatly admired. Sarah was the youngest member of the choir, but it wasn't rare to hear comments from the parishioners regarding Sarah's voice standing out as the loveliest of all. Being a choir member gave Sarah the benefit of listening to her father's many diverse sermons.

"We, the people of Sippican, should always show respect for the ground we walk on," he would proclaim, waving his hands above his head and with an added exalting tone, "We owe it to those who once lived here with their families and were murdered just a century-and-a-half back, by the white European colonists." They knew he was referring to *their* ancestors, and everyone took it personally, as if they were as much responsible.

According to his nephew James Briggs, no one ever fell asleep, including him, during his uncle's sermons since Reverend Leander liked to emphasize his words by stamping his feet on the podium and hitting his fists on the lectern.

Three months after Reverend Oliver's death, Julia Ann was admitted to the closest hospital to start her "lying-in" under the care of a doctor. Thirty days later, she gave birth to a healthy baby girl, but a relentless fever wouldn't go away. Many of the causes of death in the 19th century were due to prolonged birth, bleeding and/or infection and fever. Her doctors couldn't offer much hope, except to tell the family to remain strong since they had done their best and now it was God's will if He wanted to take her into His kingdom.

Reverend Leander held a heated religious debate with the two male doctors who had attended his wife, and after accusing them of *evil practices*, wrapped her in a blanket, and with the help of two other family members, took her home and called in the midwife they had always used. But Julia Ann continued to get worse with each day.

On the evening of October 5, she requested a heart-to-heart

talk with her husband and Selina.

They sat one on each side of her bed.

"Dear husband, I know you love Selina as much as I do. And you really need to listen to me — I don't have much time left. After I'm gone, our children will need you both. If you truly love me, you'll marry her," she put one finger to her lips, when he tried to speak, and then turned her head to look at Selina who could no longer hold her tears. "You have been my dearest and kindest friend, and I know you'll also be a kind mother to my children," she took hold of her husband and Selina's hands. "I give you my blessings toward your union." Before losing consciousness, she murmured, "Remember ... I love you."

Sarah awoke to wailing coming from her mother's bedroom. She recognized the voices of her sisters Harriet and Mary and brother Edward. "Mama is dead, Mama is dead," Harriet's lamentation could be heard over the others. She knew her Mama was very sick but to be dead meant forever gone, like it had happened to Grandpa Oliver, Oly as she used to call him. Panicking fear and disbelief took over her as she had to force herself to gasp for air. She purposely walked slowly to her mother's room. Perhaps by the time she got there, she would wake up from such a horrible nightmare. *Yes, it's a nightmare. This is nothing but a very bad nightmare.*

She found her father kneeling beside the bed, holding Mama's inert hand in his. His praying was barely audible, but she recognized the words as Latin. Mother Briggs and everyone else in the room stood around the bed crying softly. Their white kerchiefs held against their faces were stained with tears; Mama's pale white skin was marred by purple discoloration. She put a hand on her father's shoulder and kneeled beside him, closed her eyes and brought her hands together. "Dear God," she prayed silently. "Please don't take my Mama away; my new baby sister needs her. You can take me instead. I'll be very thankful if you let my Mama live," she kept her eyes tightly closed and waited to be stricken by lightning or the darkness of death, whichever came first. She waited and waited. She heard, "Sarah, come with me." To her disappointment, it was Selina's voice. "Come, Sarah, come to the kitchen with me. I'll make you some hot tea."

How dare Selina interrupt her pleading prayer to the Almighty. She pushed her angrily away. "No! No! Let me be, leave me alone. I want my Mama back."

"God has taken her to a better place, where there is no more suffering," her father turned to hug her, but she pushed him away.

"No, that's not true. You're lying! You're going to bury her deep in the dirt like you did to Grandpa Oly, and I'll never see her again." She hit his chest with both fists in an uncontrollable fit of anger, "Do something!" she yelled. "Tell God I want my mama back."

"Everybody thinks that God listens to me. If he did, no one would ever die. Child, you're too young to understand, so I forgive you," he stood and grasped her by the back of her neck as if she were a chicken to be plucked. "Selina, please, take her out of the room."

Sarah crossed her arms defiantly across her chest but followed Selina out of the room. "I understand how you feel. I lost my father when I was close to your age," she handed Sarah her handkerchief. "You can keep it to wipe your tears. Come, let's get you dressed, and then we'll have an early breakfast. Doesn't that sound good?"

Sarah allowed Selina to help her get dressed without uttering a word, but when Selina turned to the dresser to get a hairbrush, she ran out of the room and didn't stop until she reached *her* pond, two blocks away from home. It was her very special place where one could feel safe away from all the hurt that came from living and dying. She sat under *her* large red oak tree and stared at the water, which seemed to absorb even the faintest glimmer of light from the moon above, like a multifaceted mirror reflecting back a hundred times brighter. Twice, she took in and out a deep breath, savoring the aroma of the sweet cool air and then closed her eyes to better immerse into the early morning protective shadow of *her* tree. The humming sound of its branches moving caught her attention, and she listened attentively to its sweet murmuring. "I hear you," she whispered. "So ... nothing dies? Really? And ... Mama ... is here in the very air I breathe and ..." she opened her eyes. "Oh, within this tree and everything that's alive. I see ..." She stood, put her body flat against its trunk and opened her arms. They were not long enough to give it the big hug it deserved. She cried.

"Let me help you." She recognized Benjamin's voice and stopped crying. She did not even wonder how he had known where to find her. "I'll stand on this side and you on the other," he stretched out his arms around the tree trunk. "If you hold my hands from your side, you can do it."

November 21, barely two months after Julia Ann's death, Reverend Leander and Selina took on the vows of matrimony. Only their immediate family attended.

The ceremony was done without much celebration other than having an almost somber dinner afterward at the *Rose Cottage*. But Mother Briggs broke the severity of the occasion at the end of the meal by bringing a platter from the kitchen with everybody's favorite dessert, a Bakewell pudding.

"On'y those that smile will get a piece," she said brightly.

CHAPTER V

The Call of the Sea. - Moby Dick. - Reverend Leander's fiery sermons. - Auspicious family changes. - Farewell to Sippican. – Books and seashells, but please no sewing.

APRIL 24, 1850

Captain Nathan was home to witness Benjamin's 15th birthday. Upon blowing the birthday candles out, he said, "Father, if you'll have me, I'm ready to join you." His older brother Nathan had been working as a sailor for the last four years with their father, and Benjamin looked forward to working alongside him.

Sarah sat in the parlor doing her homework when she heard a knock at her front door. She looked out the window and saw Benjamin with a book under his arm. She knew he was leaving that week, but the mere idea that he considered her important enough to stop by, meant a lot to her. She was 9-years-old and closer in age to Cousin Oliver who had just turned 13. But it was Benjamin with whom she was smitten. If anyone was to ask her why she felt that way, most likely she would have shrugged her shoulders and said he is my best friend.

She opened the front door. Someday when he became the captain of his own ship, she would ask him to take her along to see the world. Her thoughts were interrupted when he said, "I came to say goodbye and lend you my favorite book," he handed her <u>Moby Dick</u>, by Herman Melville. And then as if he had read her mind, "Because you also love the sea, and someday maybe you'll be a sailor, like me." They laughed.

Selina came in from the kitchen, her hands covered in flour, but that didn't stop her from giving him a strong boisterous hug. "We're going to miss you. You take care of yourself, Benj. Do ya hear me?" And she went back to making bread.

Sarah stood on the front porch waving. When she could no longer see him, she closed the door and sat on the windowsill of her bedroom to read the first chapter of <u>Moby Dick</u>.

Captain Nathan didn't give his sons any special privileges. If anything, he made sure they knew right from the start that he expected them to work as hard if not harder than their fellow mates. He expected them to become proficient at handling the steering wheel, standing watch, going aloft to reef and furl the topsails and to put their hands into tar and slush right along with the other sailors.

Besides being adamant about following Christian doctrines, work ethics and strict discipline, he also expected them to study daily, and that meant reciting passages from books on navigation skills, geography and history. Literature was part of their curriculum, and he encouraged all his men to take advantage of his prized book collection aboard.

Benjamin enjoyed reading <u>The American Practical Navigator</u> by Nathaniel Bowditch, a renowned mariner-mathematician. Later, when he became captain of his own ship, Captain Nathan gifted him a copy.

The loss of his father and wife did not put a damper on Reverend

Leander's fiery convictions — once home, he continued his debates with his newly devoted wife Selina. Besides reading passages from the Bible to each other and analyzing each paragraph carefully for its concealed meaning, they agreed on one thing, all men were created equal in the eyes of the Lord. Slavery was an abomination created by the greed of rich plantation owners, and the sooner it was abolished, the better it would be for mankind.

"President Zachary Taylor is a southerner and a slaveholder himself," Reverend Leander told the family before sharing his opinion that morning with the members of his church. "I don't expect him to do anything to help those poor souls out of their misery." He used the money gesture by rubbing his right thumb over the tip of the index and middle finger. "Oh no, that would mean less profits in Mr. Taylor's pocket if he lost all the free labor."

Reverend Leander made a point every morning of faithfully reading the Herald Extra and the New York Herald. As such, his family was the first to hear the latest news, followed by his congregation, who looked forward to his heated sermons while being informed of the outside world. Attending church was a prerequisite to salvation, plus some added benefits for those who couldn't read. Or, if they did, they saved a few pennies, by coming to church.

Reverend Leander never realized that he provided above and beyond the usual local gossip, the only live entertainment in the almost solemn town of Sippican.

July 9, 1850, President Zachary Taylor died suddenly from a stomach-related illness, making Millard Fillmore the 13th president, better known as "The Accidental President."

For Christmas, Reverend Leander elaborated to his congregation — as he did every year, the miraculous story of baby Jesus being born to the Virgin Mary. And then, not to anyone's surprise, he finished his joyful sermon by bringing up what was really on his mind, President Millard Fillmore.

"Our president stated that he personally opposes slavery and the slave trade, and it is now prohibited in Washington, D.C.," he shook his head and laughed wholeheartedly.

Such rare display of emotional joy from their reverend could not go unnoticed. The parishioners were not quite sure what the laughter was about but joined in anyway. Sarah stood quietly as she watched the choir members also participating in the contagious informal hysterics. She knew her father well enough to know that his laughter was a painful cry of disparity. It didn't take long before he raised his right arm and opened the palm of his hand at them, with the look of a father grieving for his foolish children. The room went silent.

"I apologize for my laughter. I should have explained that Mr. Fillmore is a hypocrite, a man with no scruples, like so many other politicians. Sorry, but I was laughing out of disgust. If the slave trade is prohibited, how come slavery is still ongoing, of all places, in Washington?" He waited a few beats. "He's using federal force to carry out the return of slaves to their masters under the Fugitive Slave Act, and we must get involved and help these unfortunate folks. What are we going to do about it?"

Nobody offered a solution; they knew Reverend Leander would find an answer.

The Fugitive Slave Act, originally designed to curb slave escapes, had now created the opposite effect. Escapes from Kentucky increased 53 percent after 1850. The south gained by the strengthening of such law, and the north gained a new free state, California. Within a short time after the passing of the new law, news reports compared the exodus of slaves as a stampede, and Kentucky slaveholders met to discuss heightened security.

Reverend Leander and Selina knew their marriage had been blessed for the purpose of keeping the family together, but they also believed Julia Ann watched them from above, guiding them to do right for those in need.

Reverend Leander's earnings were meager to say the least, but thanks to the monetary donations from some members of his church and family, he was able to cover the cost of creating 200 posters warning black people to beware of watchmen and police officers who were legally allowed to kidnap them due to the Fugitive Slave Act of 1850.

He paid a trusted carrier to take the posters to Boston and into the hands of liberator Frederick Douglass and Theodore Parker, who were also active in the antislavery movement.

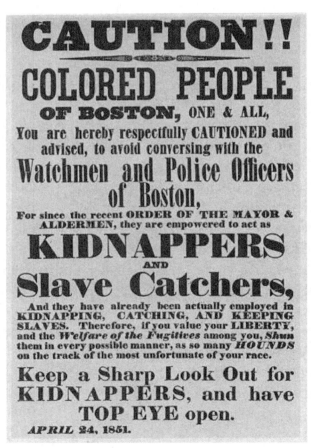

1851 was a non-eventful year, or as Mother Briggs liked to say,

"No news is better than evil news."

The following year brought some auspicious changes. Selina wasn't as fruitful as Julia Ann, but she did give Reverend Leander one child, Maria.

Nathan, who had become a seasoned seaman, quit working on their father's ship and took a better paid position with a large shipping company in the Gulf of Mexico, and their brother Oliver, now 15, joined his father and Benjamin, as a novice deckhand.

During the spring and summer months, the people in Sippican took full advantage of the fresh seasonal fruits and vegetables, but by the end of the summer, the women in most households were busy with the task of properly preserving and storing foodstuffs for the cold months ahead. Meat was easily preserved by drying, smoking or salting, and legumes placed in the sun or near a heat source. Fish and seafood, their main staple year-round, was always available and could be bought from the local fishermen or at the fish market. Sippican's one and only grocery store, run by Mr. and Mrs. Addington, a middle-aged, ill-disposed couple was not to be relied on. They had the bad habit of waiting until they ran out of "dry" goods and then they would close without notice, except for the small handwritten note pinned to their front wood door, "Come back when we are open."

At least twice a year, Mother Briggs invited her sister Elizabeth and Selina to go to Wareham in her open horse wagon. They left as early as 7 in the morning and took their time visiting old Mr. Stanhope. They called him Stan, for short. Stan kept his grocery store the same way as when it was a trading post. He sold not only dry goods but also clothing, furniture, household items, tools and other miscellaneous merchandise.

The women knew better than to rely on the Addington's lack of business sense, and before returning to Sippican, they made sure to stock up on baking soda, dry beans, flour, sugar, whole grains and rolled oats.

On their last outing to Wareham, to pick some little fixins like malleable materials from one of the milliners, Selina also brought home two live chickens and kept them fenced in her backyard to be fattened up for the holidays. But when the time came to kill the gentle creatures, Sarah and her siblings made an uproar against such cruel behavior toward their pets. The birds became their source of fresh eggs, and Selina went back to getting their chickens from the local butcher.

In addition to the usual preservation methods, people were now starting to use ice. Harvested in the winter from snow-packed areas or from frozen lakes and stored in icehouses, it was delivered domestically to families that could afford an ice box or what some called a cold closet. The large ice chunk delivered by the iceman lasted a little over a week, and neither the Briggs nor the Cobb women enjoyed the chore involved with cleaning the melting mess. Besides, they much preferred to shop for their families on a daily basis — it gave them a chance to get together and socialize.

The villages of Sippican, Rochester, and Mattapoisett had been bickering with each other for over a decade concerning the different grants issued to each one.

Besides feeling entitled to their own larger grant, certain Sippican villagers also felt it was about time they gave their beloved town a prominent place on the map with a more dignified name. They formed a committee and traveled back and forth the 50 miles north to Boston, seeking the help of a powerful political ally to petition that the town of Sippican be incorporated as Marion, in honor of General Francis Marion, the Revolutionary War hero from South Carolina.

What had started in the early 17th century as a friendly association between the white settlers and over 30,000 Native Americans, members of the Wampanoag tribe that lived in the Sippican region, soon turned into a major calamity when more puritan settlers arrived and began to push them out of their way.

By the end of the 17th century, nearly 90 percent of the Native population had been eliminated from the diseases brought in by the European colonization and ongoing massacres.

No one in Sippican wanted to be reminded of the past, and this was a great opportunity to put on a new face and act as if history never existed. They got their wish on May 15, 1852.

Sunday, the following day, Sarah's father read a few passages from the Bible to his congregation and then left after telling the choir there was no reason for joyful singing that day.

Sarah came home to find her father and Selina seated in the small parlor by the unlit fireplace.

"Father," she said. "Are you well?"

"Sippican was a beautiful name — the only thing that was left of them." He cried shamelessly.

She knelt next to him and laid her head on his knees.

Benjamin's sister, Maria Matilda, now 20 and engaged to be married, volunteered to teach appliqué, a sewing technique used to lengthen the life of clothing, to her cousins Sarah and Harriet.

Selina felt that learning to sew was a vital part of being a good housewife and insisted that her daughters take advantage of Maria Matilda's offer.

Only three years older than Sarah but a lot more of a homebody than her sibling, Harriet took on the idea of learning to sew with great delight.

"It's too tedious," Sarah pleaded with Selina. "I'm only 12. I should be outside playing."

"An hour a day won't kill you. You'll learn to like it."

Much later in life, Sarah would take great pride in her sewing skills and even owning a sewing machine.

Besides school, sewing, playing the piano, singing and helping with her younger siblings, Sarah had developed a love for reading. She read Moby Dick twice, but she also took on seafaring through the books she eagerly borrowed from her Uncle Captain Nathan's home library. Walter Scott's The Pirate and The Pilot by James Fenimore Cooper drew her to read by the same author The Red Rover, Afloat and Ashore and Edgar Allan Poe's, The Narrative of Arthur Gordon Pym. The latter being her least favorite because of the abrupt ending as well as her doubt in the truth of the events portrayed. She was bothered by the author's description of the black cook and the skin color association, which made him evil and bloodthirsty, as well as the dark-skinned men being described as savages and animals. All it did was augment the reason they were not to be trusted, and as such, it was acceptable to mistreat them.

She brought her concerns to Selina, whom she loved and respected, and was surprised when told that no book should be censored for its contents. "It's up to the reader to make an opinion based on their beliefs to either agree or not," Selina said. "Your father has taught you well. You learned to differentiate between good and evil, and as such, you have developed a conscience. Someday, it will be your job as a mother to teach your children, so that when they encounter a split in the road, they'll know which path to choose." She smiled and added, "By the way, I'm curious why do you read so many books about the sea?"

"When Benjamin comes home, we have a lot to talk about."

The fact that Sarah saw Benjamin for a few days only two or three times a year when on furlough made him seem that much more mature and appealing. He always brought her a present from his travels; sometimes seashells, sometimes a starfish he had found on a sandy beach. Each gift proved that when he was far away, he still remembered her as his best friend.

CHAPTER VI

The lightning rod. - Captain Nathan's whales. - A testimony of faith for brother Nathan. - Cotton socks. - Benjamin's poetry. - Benjamin's first brig, the _Sea Foam_. - A growing nation. - Mother Briggs' pot roast secret. - Political turmoil in the chamber of the United States Senate.

Mother Briggs had a personal list of people dead and alive that she looked up to, but in her opinion, none could compare to Benjamin Franklin, who had invented bifocals, the Franklin stove, and, in her opinion, the most outstanding of all his discoveries, the lightning rod.

As a young girl, she had witnessed the deadly result of an uncle being struck by lightning while on the field as well as a neighbor's home in Wareham being burned to the ground with the mother and two children inside.

Mother Briggs and her husband hardly ever got into an argument except for when it came to installing a lightning rod on the roof of their house.

"Why do they put 'em atop church steeples, if they're useless?" she argued her point.

"Woman, when was the last time you heard of a church getting hit by lightning? God would never allow that to happen. If you ask me, it's a complete waste of money to put a rod up there."

"We have such a nice home; I hate to think we could lose everything." Noticing he wasn't paying attention, she implored, "What if we get hit while we're inside the house?"

"Woman, stop worrying. Captain Morris' home is on a lot higher than ours. If lightning were to fall around here, I promise it will hit him first. And that would serve him right," he made the cross. "Not that I really wish that to happen to his family."

Once, Captain Morris and his wife Anna, invited him and Mother Briggs for dinner. The two captains went over their heads in an overheated argument before they even finished their meal. Captain Morris had been a whaler for 40 years and had no regrets killing them. "Like any other fish, they possess no intelligence. God created them for the benefit of mankind." He ate the last piece of fried cod from his plate.

"Well, I never heard anything so absurd in my life," Captain Nathan remained seated but had no intention of finishing his meal. "I've had the opportunity to watch many a whale from afar. They travel close to each other, like a family going to church or to a picnic in the summertime." Since the response from their hosts was an incredulous look accompanied by complete silence, Captain Nathan decided to take advantage of the situation to further speak his mind. "If it's alive, it can feel pain. If it can take care of its family, it has a heart and feelings. I cannot even imagine how much they suffer when a family member is harpooned and taken away."

Mother Briggs's attempts at getting his attention with her eyes failed, and she began to nudge her knees against his. He turned to her, "Woman, stop banging at my knees," and he went on even more passionately. "Mankind benefit, eh? That's a crude, unforgivable blasphemy to even state that's God's intentions. You must mean personal profit benefits. Right now, New Bedford has 329 registered whaling ships, plus the ones going out from our harbor, right here. I'm afraid that with such large scale of killing, whole families of whales will soon be extinguished. Done. Kaput!"

Everyone felt Captain Nathan was getting soft with old age, including Mother Briggs, but she didn't express her opinion.

Captain Morris and his wife didn't invite them over again, which was a good thing, since the Briggs had no intention of inviting them over either.

October 23, 1855, Benjamin's brother Nathan, only 24-years-old, succumbed to yellow fever onboard his merchant ship sailing out of Galveston, and was buried at sea, in the Gulf of Mexico.

The family gathered at church for the service in his memory, and Benjamin gave a testimony of faith on his brother's behalf. Afterward, the family gathered at the *Rose Cottage*, where Benjamin read a poem he'd written for Nathan when they were sailing in their father's ship. It spoke of the good times they had experienced while growing up and how much he admired him. It was a happy poem, but everyone cried.

With so many seamen in their family buried at sea, it was accepted as the result of their profession, but it didn't make it less painful. Nathan's death was hard on everyone, especially on his parents, but as always, one went through mourning and then on with life. And as previously planned, two weeks later, Benjamin followed the rite of passage with his very first trip around Cape Horn as mate on the *Hope*, a ship commanded by his father. Until then, Benjamin had served as a deckhand.

Before he left, Sarah gave him a small package neatly wrapped and tied with a bow, with instructions not to open until at sea.

He found a pair of cotton socks she had knitted and a little note, *"I hope they will keep your feet warm on cold nights. Be safe, your cousin Sarah."*

Sarah was familiar with most, if not all, of Benjamin's poetry about the gospels, the sea and nature. Those he gave her, she kept in her *treasure* box with her diary, the seashells, and other small keepsakes he had given her through the years. She kept the box in the bottom dresser drawer, hidden from her sisters Harriet, Mary and Julia, who slept in the same room with her.

Reading Benjamin's poetry awoke her desire to read the poetry of Emily Dickinson and Walt Whitman. She became gifted at citing long passages of poetry from memory, which always amazed her family. But after reading Edgar Allan Poe's works, she confessed once again to Selina, "Edgar's poetry drags me down as if death is inevitably approaching me. I stop breathing when I read it."

"That's because you're very young and have never really suffered, but you must agree that he's a great writer because his words reached your core and made you feel the weight of his agony."

As part of the choir at her father's church, Sarah also developed an interest in politics, but her conversations were refreshing due to her quick sense of humor and positive attitude.

After finishing his apprenticeship onboard his father's ship, the *Hope,* Benjamin did what most seafaring sailors in the 19th century hoped to achieve with a master's certificate. They either worked for a shipping company or purchased their own ship. He put all his savings into a brig, the *Sea Foam,* and started doing his own commercial runs.

Mother Briggs felt most righteous for not only being the daughter of Reverend Oliver Cobb but also the sister of Reverend Leander, and when Benjamin was home and gave testimony at prayer meetings, she went out of her way to assure that those attending the service were welcome to her home where she served them a hearty, homemade dinner.

Her famous pot roast and delicious corn bread were always a hit. When no one was looking, she carefully inserted small pieces of bacon into the meat to enhance the flavor. She shared the secret of her roast with Sarah, but made her swear to complete secrecy, even with Selina.

Reverend Leander rushed into his church with long, energetic steps as if every second away from his parishioners detained them from hearing the latest word from Moses himself. That particular morning, he carried under his right arm two newspapers, which he slammed on top of his lectern. The congregation sat up and gazed attentively in his direction.

"I brought these for anyone interested in reading them," he took a step sideways to his left, to better face the center aisle. "Meanwhile, I'll summarize the most important news content. Two weeks ago to be exact, Thursday, May 22, Congressman Preston Brooks of South Carolina savagely beat Senator Charles Sumner, leader of the antislavery forces in Massachusetts, with a walking cane, right inside the chamber of the United States Senate. Why, you may ask. Well, I'll tell you why. Senator Sumner made a speech against Southerners who sympathize with slavery, and Congressman Brooks didn't like that. So much for free speech, eh? It's 1856, for God's sake. You would think it's the Middle Ages!" He put his hands on his hips and paced back and forth. "After hearing that the cane used to beat Senator Sumner into unconsciousness had broken, Southern sympathizers sent Mr. Brooks several new canes. Now the members of the Senate are going into the chamber carrying knives and pistols for self-defense, while our good-for-nothing, alcoholic president, Mr. Pierce, has nothing to say, including the nation's Chief Executive, James Buchanan." Some stared at him with their mouths open, others made the sign of the cross, and most accompanied their gestures of dismay by vocalizing the usual, *oh no*.

"We need to pray," he went on. "If something happens to our president, since he's drinking himself to death, Mr. Buchanan will most likely become our next president! Can you imagine?" He felt a need to repeat. "Can you imagine?" and then went on. "Our nation is in serious harm's way. We must pray, pray very hard for God's intervention to reject evil and bring in what's just and fair." He took hold of the Bible, "Let us open our good book to 1 Peter 3:9."

CHAPTER VII

Maria Matilda. - French literature. - Gifted musician and piano teacher. - A growing nation. - The dress pin. - Benjamin's new ship, the *Forest King*. - Lokum. - Mother Briggs' new ironing board. - Hygiene and the Farmer's Almanac.

After the proper engagement length of three years, Benjamin's sister Maria Matilda married cousin Captain Joseph B. Gibbs, on September 29, 1856.

The local newspaper announced that the bride looked absolutely lovely in her best Sunday dress with an embroidered tulle veil held by a circlet of orange blossoms. They wished the very best to the young couple.

While away on her honeymoon, no one missed Maria Matilda more than Sarah, who by now enjoyed the once a week, one-hour appliqué sewing lessons, as much as Maria Matilda's amazing gift as a storyteller.

Except for the appliqué lessons, Sarah's interests were far off from her sisters or girlfriends of the same age, who were more inclined to dream about finding a handsome and financially secure man to take care of them. Sarah dreamed about the sea and visiting faraway lands, and in those dreams, she stood beside Benjamin.

Knowing her love for French literature, every time Benjamin traveled to France, he would bring her a new book. Her expanded collection now included <u>Kernock le Pirate</u>, <u>Atar-Gull</u>, and <u>Le Négrier Aventures de Mer</u>.

It took a bit of penny-pinching, but Sarah's parents finally saved enough money to purchase, for her 15th birthday, an old pianoforte from Mrs. Stewart, whose husband had died two years prior and had left her penniless. She was more than happy to sell it. Having spent so many years at her father's church as a member of the choir and playing the organ whenever Ms. Robertson, their organ player, was out sick, Sarah had earned enough expertise in playing and reading music that she started giving piano lessons at home.

Shipping along America's coasts had become vital to the nation's economy. Many American cities were dependent on bulk cargo ships to supply them with grain, corn and other dry foods, including cotton, lumber, coal and bricks, from different parts of the country. Limestone quarried in Maine was made into mortar and shipped to New York and Boston and used in building construction. Quarries in Maine were also busy supplying granite to complete the Treasury Department building in Washington, D.C., and matching stone to New York and Philadelphia for their new Grand Central post offices.

A steady rapid twirl of inventions had been happening since the early 1800s: the steam locomotive, the steamboat, Morse code, and the telegraph, and now thanks to Walter Hunt, an American mechanic, the safety pin, which he called a *dress pin*. The *dress pin* hit the charts before the end of 1857 with every mother who, until then, held her baby's nappy, — a large handmade diaper-like flat piece of flannel or muslin, folded into a triangle — with straight pins that were prone to jab into the little bodies mercilessly, unless of course she was handy at sewing buttons onto the nappy. The *dress pin* became useful for all kinds of wardrobe problems, including the security it provided by fastening the small but bulky handmade cotton or flannel towels that women inserted into their bloomers during menstruation.

Benjamin sold the *Sea Foam* and purchased the three-mast schooner *Forest King* from his brother Oliver. Benjamin then used the new schooner for his first long commercial run to Greece and Turkey. Before leaving, Benjamin hired Albert G. Richardson from Prospect, Maine. Only 15 years old, he had already acquired one year of seafaring experience from sailing with his oldest brother, Captain Lyman. According to Albert, who preferred to be called Richardson, his brother was a fine captain, and they got along swell, but he wanted to travel more than just along the coast and looked forward to doing transatlantic crossings.

Benjamin returned eight months later and the family gathered at the *Rose Cottage* to hear his stories and check out the gifts from such exquisite far away countries. Mother Briggs was delighted with the six-piece set of tiny white Greek coffee cups, and the small pouch of Turkish saffron. He gave his father a bag of Turkish coffee beans, and to Uncle Leander, a Greek komboloi chain of wood beads, which he said reminded him of the rosary. Selina fell in love with the colorful pattern of tiny flowers of the small, wool Turkish carpet, and made plans to hang it on her bedroom wall, since she couldn't even think of having anyone step on such a beautiful work of art. Olive oil soaps were distributed to the girls and some Greek and Turkish coins to the boys. He handed Sarah a large, rectangular box made of thin strips of wood. Everyone wanted to see what was inside, and she obliged. "It's lokum," Benjamin said. "From Turkey, the sweetest confection I have ever tasted."

By the time they all took one piece, there was only one left, covered in powdered white sugar. Sarah's 8-year-old sister Julian Ann, who had been standing by her side, waiting for her turn, pointed to it, "Can I have it?"

Unanimous laughter rang in the room followed by a slight sense of guilt as they stared at Sarah holding on her lap an empty box except for the leftover powdered sugar.

Benjamin took from his coat side pocket, a much smaller version of the larger wood box. "This one is for her," he addressed the family, and then to Sarah, "Unless you want to share it again with these famished people."

Once in her room, she opened it and, to her joy, she found seven small cubes made of semisoft jelly-like texture with the interesting aroma of roses and studded with her favorite nuts, pistachios. *How thoughtful*, she considered. *One for each day of the week*.

She hid the box behind some blankets on the very top shelf of the bedroom armoire.

Selina counted on her daughters Harriet, Sarah, Julia and Mary to do many of the daily chores. They all had several appointed duties, except for Mary, their 4-year-old sister, who even though a bit too young, still came in handy with dusting and sorting the dirty laundry in two baskets. Sarah saved Monday mornings to stop by the *Rose Cottage* and check on Mother Briggs, her favorite aunt, who thought of Sarah as a rare gem, and a precious breath of fresh air in her life. Every time she came over, she couldn't help thinking, *Lucky is the man who marries her*, and as Benjamin crossed her mind, she smiled and crossed her fingers.

That particular Monday, Sarah found her singing in the kitchen while ironing. Captain Nathan had surprised his wife with the latest innovation for making a woman's domestic work less of a drudgery. A wood ironing board! He'd purchased it in New York City while on one of his merchant's runs.

"Gone are the days of using the large clumsy kitchen table; this ironing board is the perfect size and light enough that I can move it around." She was more than happy to demonstrate how easy it was to fold and put it away. Then she opened it again to continue her ironing next to the stove, where she could easily reach out for the flat cast irons, close to nine pounds each. She always used two, one on hand while the other was being reheated on the wood-burning stove. The metal handles were as hot as the cast triangle below and had to be gripped with a thick rag. No matter how careful, no one could brag they had never been burned while ironing. A girl under 7 wasn't allowed to iron, but she was expected to help by keeping the irons sand-papered and polished, followed by slightly greasing them to avoid rusting.

Mother Briggs switched the iron she had been using with the one on top of the stove, then turned it over, and spit on its bottom. It produced a swift sizzle, and she nodded approvingly. The temperature was perfect for ironing her husband's white shirt, about to be starched.

By now, health experts were in agreement that a brief plunge in cold water helped relieve congestion of the brain as well as fight anything from cholera to whooping cough. But the same experts were not so keen about hot water. A hot bath promoted relaxation, and with that came the danger of making the bather prone to being lazy, and since its warmth also provided an inexplicable feeling of pleasure, its use fell into the category of being a wicked, immoral act.

British domestic engineer J.H. Walsh warned, "However pleasant a long-continued bath may be in hot weather, it is by no means to be recommended," His advice was very explicit, "Parents should yank kids out of their baths, lest they dabble too long in the water and thus do absolute injury to themselves by carrying to excess what is otherwise a most valuable adjunct to health."

Besides these conjured images about bathing, it was also a social taboo to openly discuss personal hygiene. With no home plumbing available for most folks, outhouses made the most sense to the American populace.

It sounded like a great idea when Joseph Gayetty, a New York

City entrepreneur, invented aloe-infused flat sheets of manila hemp, dispensed from Kleenex-like boxes. But his toilet paper invention was a complete failure. It simply made no sense to pay the super inflated price of 50 cents for 500 sheets when most people, even in the cities, used old newspapers and the usual catalogues that came in the mail for free. The Farmers' Almanac, just sixpence (about 4 cents), even came with a hole through the corner so people could hang it on the wall hook in their outhouse, but some people preferred corncobs. Dried corncobs were softer on tender areas and considered quite efficient for cleaning.

CHAPTER VIII

Crude oil. - Who needs education when young whalers are
needed? - Teachers' guidelines. - Sarah's birthday. - Come a-
courtin'. - Baby Henry Nathan is born.

August 28, 1859

Seneca Oil Company, formerly the Pennsylvania Rock Oil
Company, announced that Colonel Edwin L. Drake had
successfully struck oil at 69 feet, off a piece of leased land a couple
of miles just south of Titusville, Pennsylvania. Such finding
created the beginning of the end of commercial whaling in the
United States. Kerosene distilled from crude oil could be produced
in abundance and at a third the price of whale oil. Everyone agreed
the smell wasn't the most pleasant, but the cost couldn't be beat,
and kerosene started quickly replacing the use of whale oil in
lamps.

Marion's old whalers weren't going to stand for it. They
immediately called for an action plan and formed a committee
under the guidance of Captain Morris, to fight tooth and nail for
the commercial whaling to continue full force against the "new" oil
found in Pennsylvania.

"There's plenty of whales out there, we just need more men and boats to do the job," called out Captain Morris at the town's committee meeting.

His buddy, Captain Norton added, "School is a waste of time. We need to stop what they call education and get those young men to the sea, instead!" An ironic statement, since in 1852, Massachusetts had been the first state to enact a compulsory education law.

The old timers now spent most of their time and energy trying to close down the school system and even went as far as getting several teachers fired for any small infraction from the 13 rules in the guidelines all teachers were required to follow.

1.   Teachers, each day, will fill lamps, clean chimneys (lamp globes), and trim wicks.

2.   Each teacher will bring a bucket of water and scuttle of coal for the days' session.

3.   Teachers will make their pens carefully. They may whittle nibs to individual tastes.

4.   Male teachers may take one evening each week for courting purposes, or two evenings a week if they go to church regularly.

5.   After 10 hours in school, teachers should spend their remaining time reading the Bible or other good books.

6.   Women teachers who marry or engage in uncomely conduct will be dismissed.

7.   Every teacher should lay aside from each pay a goodly sum of his/her earnings for his/her benefit during his/her declining years so that he/she won't become a burden on society.

8.   Any teacher who smokes, uses liquor in any form, frequents pool or public halls, or gets shaved in a barbershop will give good reason to suspect his/her worth, intentions, integrity, and honesty.

9.   The teacher who performs his/her labors faithfully and without fault for five years will be given an increase of 25 cents per week in his/her pay providing the Board of Education approves.

10.   Teachers will maintain a garden on school grounds to provide additional food for themselves and students.

11.   Teacher candidates must be at least 16, be able to read and write, do simple arithmetic, and have a clergyman's letter in hand attesting to their sound moral character.

12.   Teachers must attend a house of worship every Sunday.

13.   Teachers must keep the school clean, haul any necessary wood to keep the stove going, bring water from the well, and start a pot to boil in the morning, so students who bring their mid-day meals can heat it if necessary.

A female teacher was called school-ma'am, or school-marm, and as long they could read and write and do basic math, at the age of 15, they were qualified for the responsible position of country school ma'ams.

Sarah's sister Harriett, now 21 years old, had been a school-a'am since she was 16.

Mother Briggs and Selina decided to make Sarah's 17th birthday more than just a family gathering. They knew Benjamin would be home during the month of October. They also knew that even though neither he nor Sarah spoke of their feelings for each other and kept their relationship as "good cousins," there was no doubt in their minds that they were childhood sweethearts, and as such, meant for each other.

Maria Matilda was of the opinion that Sarah needed a glamorous dress for the occasion, and she immediately called for a meeting with the women in the family. They gathered for tea at the *Rose Cottage* and spent a good part of the afternoon looking at French engravings illustrating the latest fashion in Paris.

They were shocked to find a lot had changed in the last eight years. Skirts were now worn a lot fuller with the use of flounces (deep ruffles) with three or more tiers gathered tightly at the top and stiffened with horsehair braiding at the bottom, which made it quite cumbersome to move around. The bodices were fastened in the back by means of several hook-and-eye closures, but there was also a new bodice fashion that could be buttoned in front and worn over a chemisette.

The sleeves were wider and bell-shaped and worn over false under sleeves or engageantes of cotton or linen, trimmed in lace, *broderie anglaise,* or other fancy-work. Even though they felt a little overwhelmed with how much the style had changed, they couldn't help being excited over the task at hand.

Mother Briggs, Selina and Maria Matilda took an all-day trip to Wareham just to pick the proper cloth and sewing materials. They settled to have the dress with the bodice buttoned in front, and the sleeves would be bell-shaped just like in one of the French engravings. They also felt that Sarah would be a lot more comfortable if her skirt wasn't bulky, and they voted instead on using a steel cage crinoline. Introduced into the fashion world two years prior, it was a clever way to help expand the skirt further without the need for flounces and tiers. Its spring steel hoops provided flexibility of movement and enabled the wearer to walk and sit gracefully.

They recruited Sarah's sisters, Harriet and Mary to do the broderie anglaise, and everyone took turns meeting in secrecy at the *Rose Cottage.* They labored close to five weeks and finished two days before Sarah's birthday.

Sarah was invited to join them at the *Rose Cottage* under the pretense that they needed her to try on a dress being fit for one of her cousins. Puzzled as to why they had to blindfold her, she decided to go along as she was taken into the kitchen and then asked to stand on a wood crate and remain very still for the fitting. The request didn't last long. She knew they were up to something with all the giggling going on.

The dress was a deep claret, a popular color for misses and young ladies, that complemented Sarah's fair skin and dark hair. Her birthday gift moved her to tears of joy.

Selina made a point of clearing her small home to make space for all the family guests attending the birthday gathering. Usually, any large gathering of both families would be held at the *Rose Cottage,* but it was Sarah's birthday, and it felt right that she should celebrate her special day in the home where she had been born. The dining table was covered with a white lace tablecloth and the blue and white English dinnerware and silver eating utensils, thanks to Mother Briggs' prolific heirloom. The seating had been appropriately arranged with the names of each family member elegantly written with black ink on a mini white card by Sarah's brother Edward who was known for his perfect penmanship. It wasn't that they didn't know each other; the "matchmakers" just weren't taking any chances. Sarah's name tag lay next to Benjamin's, along with two silver spoons.

While the Briggs and the Cobb families were busy talking in the small parlor, waiting for the birthday girl to join them, Selina was busy upstairs styling Sarah's hair in an updo fashion that required her to use some spit for curling adherence. "Selina, please," Sarah protested, "No matter how much spit you use; it's not going to keep the curls in place."

After several failing attempts, Selina agreed and settled for combing each side up and holding it in place with two matching ebony combs. Before she allowed Sarah to join the guests waiting patiently downstairs, she pinched Sarah's cheeks on each side. "Ouch," she cried out, and backed away.

"Sorry," Selina shrugged her shoulders. "It just makes your cheeks a little rosier, that's all."

Sarah walked with effortless grace into the parlor. Benjamin couldn't take his eyes off her. He had not seen her for over six months. He took a deep breath in awe of her presence and hurriedly walked up to her. "Happy birthday, Cousin. You look beautiful," he kissed her hand.

"If you're trying to make me feel like a queen by kissing my hand, you have succeeded," she responded coquettishly, lowering her thick, dark eyelashes.

Oliver, who had followed Benjamin, gave him a light buddy punch on the arm and then pushed him delicately away. "Sarah," he said. "Getting older really becomes you. Will you grace us with your talents by playing the piano?"

"Yes, Cousin Oliver, and I'll do my best not to bore you," she swept one foot behind and bent her knees for a quick curtsy. Just then, Selina announced that dinner was ready and everyone should find a seat. Oliver maintained the smile, and added, "Hopefully afterward?"

It was a perfectly cooked meal, with delicious conversation between all present, a family gathering of simple folks who knew each other well and valued their time together. No one mentioned anything, but Sarah and Benjamin were very much aware of the two spoons *accidentally* put together between their sitting places, and their romantic meaning.

"I wonder who set the table," Sarah laughed softly and exchanged a playful look with Benjamin who nodded at her. They caught Selina glaring at them and then whispering something into Mother Briggs' ear, who responded with a giggle.

Sarah whispered to Benjamin, "Those two are always up to some skilamalink mischief."

Reverend Leander controlled himself from bringing politics to the table, and Captain Nathan didn't speak of his perils at sea. Sarah's oldest sister Harriet, known for her culinary talents with making <u>olykoeks,</u> oily cakes, and fairy cakes — small little cakes covered with frosting — was overjoyed that after the meal, everyone took a sweet and sat holding a cup of tea on their lap, waiting for Sarah to play on her pianoforte.

She played the upbeat tune of "Camptown Races," and everyone, including the younger children, joined in singing.

> Camptown ladies, sing dis song,
> Doo-dah! Doo-dah!
> Camptown Racetrack, five miles long,

Oh, the doo-dah day!
I come down dah wid my hat caved in,
Doo-dah! Doo-dah!
I go back home wid a pocket full of tin,
Oh doo-dah day!
Twine to run all night! Twine to run all day!
I'll bet my money on the bob-tail nag,
somebody bet on de bay.

Then she sang and played, "Come Where My Love Lies Dreaming," and that's when the children left to play outside.

Selina sat next to Benjamin. "How do you feel about Sarah?" she asked. He fumbled, caught off guard. "On second thought," she added quickly. "She has stopped playing and old Uncle Edward is not going to leave her until she listens to all his military stories. Why don't you save her and ask her to take a walk with you?" Noticing that he was still stunned with her forwardness, she whispered in his ear, "Down from Spring Street the road is lovely at this time of the year, with the green pine trees. And … it's still daylight."

"You think she would go?" he stood.

"What do you think?" she winked at him.

She watched Benjamin approach Sarah. He said something to which she responded along with a smile, and then ran upstairs. In her room, Sarah put on her brown-tiered wool cape-jacket and matching deep bonnet and gazed at the tiny round mirror above her small dresser. Then she reached inside the top drawer and unwrapped a piece of soft cloth, displaying her most valuable and only piece of jewelry she owned, a coral cameo brooch inherited from Sarah, the great-grandmother she never met. More than once, she had wondered if the beautiful face on the brooch resembled her great-grandmother when she was young. She would never know, but she knew they had something in common — that brooch once had felt her great-grandmother's heartbeat, and now it heard hers, as she came down the staircase to join Benjamin.

They strolled away at a slow pace, and then they stopped and faced each other. They seemed to be speaking. Then Sarah reached for Benjamin's hand, and they continued to walk until they disappeared from Selina and Mother Briggs' view, where they stood on the outside porch.

The next morning, Benjamin came to Sarah's home. Her sister Mary opened the door and very politely asked him to follow her into the parlor. Sarah's parents sat on the couch obviously expecting him; Mary left hurriedly upstairs.

Reverend Leander and Selina remained seated and motioned at the same time for him to take a seat on the single chair facing them. They sat with their hands lying flat across their laps, their faces showed no emotion, their eyes steadily focused on him. He smiled at them, but there was no response. He gazed around the room from one corner to the other wishing Sarah would come to his rescue, but he knew it would not be proper for her to be there. Finally, he concluded that the longer the silence lingered on, the harder it would be for him to speak. He stood from the chair and faced them.

"Uncle Leander and Selina," his voice came out a little scratchy and he cleared his throat. "I'm here because I have very strong feelings toward Sarah, and I would like to ask for your permission," he cleared his throat once again. "To come a-courtin' … when I'm home, of course."

"And your intentions are?" Reverend Leander's face couldn't be more impenetrable.

"Once I attain some financial security, which I expect may take two or three years, I would like to ask for your daughter's hand in marriage."

His answer brought a smile to the couple's faces. They stood and hugged him.

"Benjamin, we would love to call you son," Father Leander said. "But as Sarah's parents, you must understand that we cannot take the liberty to speak for her. She must be the one to accept or reject your offer. I'll call her right now." He shouted, "Sarah, please come down!"

She must have been close to the bottom of the stairs listening because before her father finished calling, she was by their side.

Long engagements were a common practice since it wasn't considered proper for a young couple to marry until the man could support his wife, and she had established her trousseau, which included such important items as bedding, linens, curtains, kitchenware and so much more. He wasn't that far off with his predicted date; it could easily take close to three years.

Sarah and Benjamin visited a local artist to have a small pencil drawing of each other done.

Benjamin left two weeks later in his new brig, the *Forest King,* on a merchant voyage to Havana, Cuba.

November 26, 1857
Maria Matilda gave birth to a healthy baby boy, with the help of the family midwife and Mother Briggs. They named him Nathan Henry after his two grandparents.

CHAPTER IX

Another sea fatality. – Pony Express. – Nathan Henry joins his parents in Heaven. – Abraham Lincoln. – Civil War. – "Godey's Lady's Book." – The end of the Pony Express. – Wedding date. – Quilting Bee frolic.

Maria Matilda asked her mother if she minded watching Nathan Henry for a few weeks, so that she could accompany her husband on his next merchant voyage to North Carolina.

"Just look at my grandson, have you ever seen such a sweet, well-tempered child?" Mother Briggs responded. "I don't even know he's here. No, I don't mind, you just go ahead, my dear, and enjoy yourself."

Nathan Henry, just a year-and-a-half old, could play by himself for hours seated in the corner of the kitchen floor with any kitchen utensil.

The worst possible news arrived at the *Rose Cottage* a month later on a cold, snowy morning. Maria Matilda and her husband, Captain Joseph B. Gibbs, had perished at sea, November 16, 1859, when their ship collided with another vessel off Cape Fear, North Carolina.

At church, the choir sang "Jesu, Lover of My Soul," and

"Abide With Me." Sarah could barely speak. Instead of singing, she played the organ for the choir. Then she played a solo, the "Dead March," by Handel.

Eight months after his parents' death, Nathan Henry developed a rash, fever, and vomiting. Two brothers, a three-and a four-year-old down the street had the same symptoms. Mother Briggs recognized the deadly signs of scarlet fever. She prayed for little Nathan Henry day and night at home and at church, and when she found him dead in bed, July 20, she stopped praying. Another angel needed in Heaven wasn't her first thought. Anger took her into a raging fit, and she cursed the mighty God that had taken away little Nathan Henry.

The two children on the same street survived, maybe because they were older or maybe because they were too nasty, and God didn't want them. Mother Briggs took to wearing black for the rest of her life.

Until then mail across the U.S. had to be taken overland by a 25-day stagecoach or spend months inside a ship during a long sea voyage. But on April 3rd, 1860, William H. Russell, William B. Waddell, and Alexander Majors started a mail service, which would become known as the Pony Express. It boasted of being able to deliver messages, newspapers, and mail between the Atlantic and Pacific coasts, in just 10 days. To achieve such remarkable speed, they set up a string of nearly 200 relief stations across the nation. Lone horsemen would ride between stations at a breakneck pace, switching mounts every 10–15 miles and then handing their cargo to a new courier after 75–100 miles. Letters were being delivered faster than ever before, and ads for riders read "Wanted: Young, skinny, wiry fellows not over 18. Must be expert riders willing to risk death daily. Orphans preferred."

The riders were as young as 11-years-old and weighed less than 125 pounds.

Monday, March 4, 1861, Abraham Lincoln, a self-taught attorney, was sworn in as the 16th President of the United States of America. The press described him as 6'4" tall, thin, with a "squeaky," voice and lacking in style. They failed to mention that his unsophisticated appearance concealed a magnificently brilliant mind, and that his firm principles, immense self-discipline and political knowledge had been what propelled him from relative anonymity to the presidency.

At the concluding paragraph of his First Inaugural Address, he declared, "We are not enemies, but friends. We must not be enemies. Though passion may have strained, it must not break our bonds of affection."

Friday, April 12, 1861, the Civil War also known as "The War Between the States" was officially announced between the United States of America and the Confederate States of America, when the Confederates opened fire on Union soldiers at Fort Sumter, South Carolina.

It should be noted here that "Godey's Lady's Book," one of the most well-read and influential American women's magazines of the 19th century, for its attempt to try and halt the Civil War was being read avidly at this time by over 150,000 subscribers, thanks to Sarah Josepha Hale.

It all started when Louis Godey bought the "Boston Ladies' Magazine" and hired a new editor to revamp the publication. He made it clear to Sarah Hale that he did not want his magazine putting its nose into politics. But his argument did not stop her. She was intensely patriotic and found plenty of ways to present her views.

When the country approached the verge of civil war, she carefully chose mournful poetry about dead soldiers and lost sons to bring about the potential of war hitting home — without being pegged as a political view by Mr. Godey. She regularly made pro-union political statements and then validated them through the letters she wrote to the editor that lent credibility to her statements. By putting seemingly unsolicited letters next to editorials, Sarah Hale successfully "created an illusion of proof" that her ideas were highly supported by everyone. Once Selina caught on to Sarah Hale's not-so-well-hidden patriotism, she brought it to her husband's attention. He became an avid follower of Sarah Hale's two columns, the "Literary News" and the "Editors' Table," where she expanded on the moral role and influence of women, their duties and superiority, and also the importance of women's education. When it came to slavery, Sarah Hale described it as "a stain on our national character."

Meanwhile, what had started with such high hopes to make the Pony Express the way of the future when it came to being the speediest mail service in the U.S. the company took a serious dive by the end of 1861, as a result of the transcontinental telegraph line being completed.

Wells Fargo purchased the Pony Express, but it no longer made sense to run it, and it turned into a romantic legend of the old West.

Sarah spent two afternoons a week at the *Rose Cottage*, learning how to cook the dishes Benjamin had grown accustomed to. The day she was putting together a Three-Layer Huguenot Torte and Meringue, Benjamin stood watching from the kitchen entrance the two women he most loved. Sarah was busy straining the apricot jam she had just finished cooking, while Mother Briggs was cutting thin slices of peeled apples into a bowl

"Would my ladies need any assistance?" He couldn't help smiling when they acted startled. He wasn't supposed to come home for another week. His mother ran to hug him, still holding the paring knife, as Sarah quickly grabbed the side of her apron to wipe away the possible vestiges of apricot jam on her lips. As his mother came closer, Benjamin put both hands up, "Mother," he took a step back, "You need to put that knife away unless you intend to kill me." They laughed as they hugged. "I'm going to put everything away and clean up the kitchen," she told him. "Meanwhile, you two go in the parlor and wait there for me. We need to talk."

Sarah and Benjamin sat on the new fainting couch, a furniture piece Mother Briggs couldn't resist ordering from a New York catalog.

Benjamin got busy telling Sarah about his latest trip to Florence, and also about Richardson, his new second mate, now 17-years-old, who had proven to be a dedicated hard-working crew member since he had started two years prior.

Mother Briggs came in the room and sat tautly between them, her head the only thing turning inquisitively from one to another, and then she went straight to the point. "Tell me, when is the date?"

"What date?" Benjamin bent over to look at Sarah, who looked at him and shrugged her shoulders.

"Dear Lord Almighty!" Mother Briggs raised her hands up as if asking God for enlightenment. "Are the two o' you slow in the head? Benj, the date of your wedding!"

"Two years ... I can expect to afford a home ..."

"A home?" Mother Briggs' voice came out a bit abrasive. "A

home?" she repeated in the same manner. Then her voice mellowed down. "Benj, this is your home. You two get married next year," she reached in her apron's pocket to take out her handkerchief and wiped a few tears. "You'll be making an old lady very happy."

Benjamin couldn't recall the last time his mother had cried. "Please," her voice rang painfully and she cleared her throat, "Our *Rose Cottage* is horribly silent, it needs the sound o' children."

"Aunt Sophia," Sarah kissed her wet cheek. "I would feel much honored to live here with you and Benj when we get married next year."

The two women hugged.

Naming the month for the wedding was deeply steeped in ancient traditions: "Marry in September's shine, and your living will be rich and fine. June comes with the arrival of Lent and warmer weather, time to remove winter clothing and partake in one's annual bath. Marry in May and rue the day," went the proverb.

For the days of the week: Marry on Monday for health, Tuesday for wealth, Wednesday the best day of all, Thursday for crosses, Friday for losses, Saturday for no luck at all and Sabbath was out of the question.

The color of the wedding gown was thought to influence one's future life: white - chosen right; blue - love will be true; yellow - ashamed of her fellow; red - wish herself dead; black - wish herself back; gray - ravel far away; pink - of you he'll always think; green - ashamed to be seen.

Sarah chose the color white, and the wedding date, Tuesday, September 9, of the following year.

A Quilting Bee frolic was immediately organized by Mother Briggs and Selina, who called on some of the most talented women in both families and a few friends who had also experience in quilting, to assist Sarah in a once-a-week family social event. It brought the women together to enjoy each other's company as well as create a loving piece of labor for the bride and groom and later to be passed on as an heirloom for many generations to come.

CHAPTER X

Death doesn't discriminate. - Wedding essentials. - Wedding bells. - Provençal quilting and French desserts. - Emancipation Proclamation. - The Yankee ships. - Mother Briggs's yearn.

Thursday, February 20, 1862

President Lincoln was seated in his office over the East Room in the White House when he heard the anguished cries from his wife Mary at the East end, where the family bedrooms were situated. Willie, their 11-year-old son, had succumbed to typhoid fever.

Their second son, Eddie, perished from chronic consumption 12 years prior. A week after Eddie's death, an unsigned poem entitled "Little Eddie" was printed in the "Illinois Daily Journal."

> *"... Angel boy — fare thee well, farewell*
> *Sweet Eddie, we bid thee adieu!*
> *Affections wail cannot reach thee now*
> *deep though it be, and true.*
> *Bright is the home to him now given,*
> *For "of such is the*
> *Kingdom of Heaven."*

Authorship of the poem remained anonymous, but many believed that one or both of Eddie's parents had written it. For Willie, there was no poem published, but Mrs. Lincoln banned all flowers from the White House because Willie had so loved them. She also put an end to concerts on the lawn because as she told her sister, she no longer could enjoy any gay music.

She took to shopping; one might even say she became addicted to shopping sprees in New York City. Most likely it brought her the comfort that there was something in her life that she could keep.

Assisted by all the women in the family, everyone took a serious part in shopping for the material and help to sew many of the personal items needed for Sarah's trousseau. Things like petticoats, corset covers, nightgowns, and nightcaps. They also consulted a few issues of "Godey's Lady's Book," for ideas on the latest fashion, before starting to sew the wedding dress and two more dresses everyone agreed she would definitely need as a married woman. They turned Mother Briggs' extra bedroom upstairs into a sewing room, and as they finished each project, they covered it with a bedsheet to protect it from possible contact with dust or flies.

There were five good-luck objects a bride considered an absolute necessity to carry on the wedding day, if she wanted to guarantee a happy marriage. Derived from an Old English rhyme, it was the kind of tradition that no bride dared to break. "Something old" represented the past, particularly the bond between the bride and her family; Sarah decided to wear her grandmother's cameo brooch. "Something new" represented the couple getting married and their future together; and the wedding ring would definitely be the newest thing in her life. "Something borrowed" was the link between herself and her family, and it had to come from a happily married woman in order to pass on marital happiness to the new couple. Instead of the usual bouquet of flowers, she decided to use her mother's silk folding fan, with exquisitely painted birds of paradise, and borrow Selina's rosary. "Something blue" meant the bride's faithfulness and loyalty. As such, she would attach a tiny cluster of dried blue Quaker Ladies to her white veil, a symbol of her innocence, namely her virginity. The end of the rhyme ended with, "and a silver sixpence in her shoe," and she knew she could count on her father for that. His wish for prosperity in her marriage then would come true.

Even though it was in style to wear low sloping shoulders that flared out into wide sleeves, she opted for a modest tight bodice with high neck and long sleeves for her wedding dress, a plain-woven white and blue fabric that would later be tinted dark blue and reused. Having a dress to wear for just one occasion was extremely impractical and costly. A thin strip of white lace, crocheted by her sister Harriet adorned the neckline and cuffs. The skirt followed the ongoing style, full and bell-shaped.

The hair would be arranged in the latest fashion, parted in the center and tied into a chignon at the nape of the neck.

Her sister Julia Ann, now 12, and Victoria, her 11-year-old second cousin, were very excited to be the bridesmaids and would be wearing similar dresses, which were also to be dyed after the wedding. James and Zenas, the groomsmen, and Oliver, the best man matched Benjamin's mulberry frock coat and vest, white shirt and lavender doeskin trousers. Their hair would be worn parted in the center, with facial hair present, since being clean shaven wasn't in style.

The idea of including bridesmaids and groomsmen in a wedding could be traced to Ancient Rome, when the law required witnesses to be present, but through the years, it had grown into a superstitious belief, that if the bridesmaids and groomsmen wore the same clothing as the bride and groom, the evil spirits would be confused and leave them alone to live happily ever after.

Tuesday, September 9, 1862

The Congregational Church of Sippican — Reverend Leander refused to change its name to Marion — was filled to capacity with family, extended families and friends. Mother Briggs held Benjamin's arm as they entered punctually at 11 a.m., followed by Selina and Sarah's oldest brother Edward and the bridesmaids and groomsmen. Mother Briggs sat next to Selina in the front row, and Benjamin stood alone at the altar waiting for his bride.

Traditionally, fathers gave their daughters away to their future husbands, since females were their property, but in Sarah's case, her father would be performing the ceremony. Captain Nathan Briggs, her uncle and soon to be father-in-law, walked Sarah down the aisle. They walked to the pace of Mendelssohn's "Wedding March," played slowly and smoothly on the organ by Sarah's sister Mary. Sarah wore Selina's rosary wrapped around the left wrist and her mother's fan open against her heart, her right hand trembled slightly around Captain Nathan's forearm.

Everyone in the procession sat at their assigned seats, and Sarah and Benjamin stood at the altar, facing her father, Reverend Leander.

"Don't our children look handsome?" Mother Briggs used her tiny white lace handkerchief to dry a tear that had escaped.

"Yes, they do," Selina drew an audible sniffle. "Weddings and birthdays are the best times of our lives. They give us such high hopes for the future."

Mother Briggs lent Selina her handkerchief.

As was customary, there was only one wedding ring being used, a simple gold band with the couple's initials and the wedding date engraved on the inside. Sarah would be the one to wear it. Oliver made sure to drop the ring on the floor before giving it to Benjamin, thus all evil spirits were shaken out.

Reverend Leander was visually moved as his voice broke down a few times while he read from the Bible, and finished, "... the two shall become one flesh." [Genesis 2:24] He stopped a few seconds to stare at the newlyweds with an awed look of pride, "You may now kiss the bride."

The meaning and origin of the ceremonial kiss that traditionally concluded the ceremony had also come from the Roman era, when a kiss sealed legal bonds and contracts, including marriage — a type of lifelong contract between two people. But with time, the ceremonial kiss had attained quite a different meaning, as it was believed that it allowed the couple's souls to blend into one.

Before leaving the church, they wrote their names on the parish register. As tradition dictated, she signed her maiden name, Sarah Elizabeth Cobb.

They stepped out of the church, and raw rice came flying at them from all directions. They ran to their one-horse carriage. Once seated, they waved back and blew kisses. The family and their closer friends followed them in their carriages.

Selina, Mother Briggs, the other women in the families and their friends had gone out of their way to decorate the *Rose Cottage* inside and out. The stair rails on each side were covered with stalks of scarlet and chocolate brown bearded iris, ornamental grasses, orange and gold lilies and a variety of pink and orange sedums carefully pinned at the uprights with white bows. Glass jars held wild asters, and crowned the fireplace mantel, the top of the piano and all the window sills. On the center of the dining room table was the much-celebrated fruitcake used for weddings, except theirs had the shape of a boat with a tiny white flag embroidered with the couple's initials tied to several mini wood sticks glued together to make it look like a mast. There was an array of dainty sandwiches on four large silver plates with thinly sliced ham, tongue and cheese between thinly sliced buttered biscuits, and stewed fruits spread over sliced square-shaped buttered white bread. Several large meat pies and a large white terrine with creamy clam chowder sat on a side table.

The guests arrived, carrying wrapped gifts, but no one offered congratulations to the bride — as it would be considered rude to imply that the bride was "lucky" to get married. No entertainment would be provided at the reception: It was tacitly understood that the guests didn't need it as it was an honor just to have been invited to share such an auspicious day. But an old amusing custom carried over from England involving male guests still came into play. Five young men were to break into the bride's chamber and steal her stockings. They came running back, after having gone to Sarah's house two blocks away, and raided her bedroom. She had kindly set four pairs of stockings on top of her quilted bedspread just for such an occasion. Whoever landed their stocking on the groom's nose would be the next one to be married. The last one to throw the stocking was Sarah's 16-year-old younger brother, William, who won when Benjamin tilted his head sideways to catch it over his nose.

Sarah, Benjamin and their closest family members sat at the dining table. Everyone else found themselves seated in the kitchen and in the parlor.

For dessert, since no one was allowed to eat the wedding cake at the reception, Captain Nathan at Mother Briggs' hand signal, brought into the house a large wood bucket containing a metal canister surrounded by chunks of ice. Inside there was enough vanilla ice cream for everyone.

At the end of the evening, the fruitcake was cut, each piece carefully wrapped in a small towel and passed out to the guests to take home, as they prepared to leave. Superstition dictated that the bride could not bake or taste the wedding cake, otherwise she could lose her husband's love. But, if she kept a piece of the cake for after the wedding, it ensured that he would always be faithful to her. Mother Briggs wrapped a small slice of the cake in a linen cloth and showed it to Sarah, "Don't you worry, I'll keep it safe in the pantry until you and Benj return from your honeymoon."

No one asked where the newlyweds were heading; it would have been in bad taste. Only Mother Briggs, Selina and Oliver, the best man, knew, and they had sworn to complete secrecy.

Benjamin and Sarah planned on leaving the next day to Marseilles, in the *Forest King,* with a crew of seven men.

The days and nights at sea went by quickly for the young honeymooners in love. Even the ocean played its part by remaining calm and discreet throughout their voyage. One particular night, while they sat snuggled up on deck and the full moon was so bright that its glare reminded them of the sun, they swore to be away from each other as little as possible.

"I've always wondered," he said, "have you ever felt a little jealous of my ship taking me away as much as it does?" "Not at all. The sea has always been an important part of your life, and as such, it is mine, too. Besides, no matter how far you go, I know in my heart that you'll always return to me," her voice softened even more. "But perhaps ... whenever possible, I can travel with you. That has been my dream since I was a young girl."

"Well, my love, it has come true for you and me. I love the idea of always having you by my side," he kissed her neck.

"I choose to be your wife on land as well as at sea, and anytime you want me, I'm yours."

They stood, and their silhouettes melted into each other, as the moon hid behind the clouds.

In the south of France, Sarah discovered Provençal quilting, a distinctive white needlework with raised, exquisite stitched patterns like pineapples, bunches of grapes or flowers sprinkled liberally over the whole fabric. It more than grasped her attention. She bought four quilts, one for Mother Briggs, the other for Selina and two for herself. She had become a good seamstress, from simple garments like pantaloons to intricate ruffled dresses, and her creative mind played with the idea of cutting the quilts to transform them into dressing-table covers, and some fashionable waistcoats. They spent three days in Paris, and Benjamin introduced Sarah to Louis Ernest Ladurée and his wife Jeanne Souchard. The last time Benjamin had seen them, a little over a year ago, they were planning to open a bakery in Paris. Oddly enough, the day Benjamin and Sarah arrived, Louis and Jeanne were having their grand opening at 16 Rue Royale.

Sarah became addicted to their desserts, and she bought a box of their pastries and macarons to take home as presents, knowing well in advance that most likely they would never reach their destination.

Sunday, November 23, Reverend Leander wore a triumphant smile as he faced his morning flock.

"Alleluia, and praise the Lord," his bolstering tone was immediately mimicked, like a bouncing echo. Such rare expression of joy from their Reverend could only mean a high degree of good news. But there were those who made the cross and held their breath in anticipation.

"We've been truly blessed by the Lord," he paced back and forth, holding his hands behind his back while nodding his head. Possibly due to the aging process in the last few years, he had developed a noticeable kyphosis of his upper back, which caused him to carry his head way forward and down. "We finally have a president that's doing something for the benefit of all people. As of July 17, as you know, since I have been keeping you all informed," he stopped pacing and faced his congregation, who stared at him, trying to recall his past announcement as well as be prepared to receive what he was about to declare. "The Congress passed the Second Confiscation and Militia Act, freeing slaves whose masters are in the Confederate Army," he sighed with strong enthusiasm. "If it is accepted, the war goal for reunion of our nation will turn into a crusade to end slavery." A few more made the cross and sat upright in their seats.

He went on, "Here in Massachusetts, we feel like we're a separate country, safe from the horrors of blood shedding, but trust me when I say, we need to pray now more than ever. Remember, both sides have much to lose. The men serving in the Confederate army are also our brothers in the eyes of the Lord, so let's pray for their souls too."

It was the most ridiculous request they had ever heard, but since they did love the old man, and no one had the courage to tell him how divided they really felt about slavery ending, they knelt and brought their heads down.

Mother Briggs finally got her wish. Plumbing was installed in the *Rose Cottage,* and it worked quite well in conjunction with a flushing toilet upstairs and the one downstairs.

For several months afterward, many members of the family and friends came a-calling for tea and the use of her new superfluities.

ABE LINCOLN'S LAST CARD; OR, ROUGE-ET-NOIR.

Not everyone appreciated Lincoln's views of the proclamation. The country was more divided than united, and a large percentage of the people considered it the dangerous act of a desperate president willing to instigate slave revolts to save his position in the government.

With the declining number of white volunteers and the increasingly pressing personnel needs of the Union Army, the president reconsidered the ban of former slaves from serving in the Union as soldiers, and began emphasizing the need for enlisting black soldiers into the Union Army to help protect their home state — building, maintaining, and also defending coastal defenses in Massachusetts. January 1, 1863, President Lincoln issued an Emancipation Proclamation to free all slaves in territories held by Confederates.

The newlyweds arrived at the *Rose Cottage* on December 25, and Benjamin carried Sarah over the threshold to ensure the bride did not stumble, which could bring bad luck.

One week later, Sarah accompanied her husband on his subsequent merchant voyage.

In May, while anchored off Galveston, Texas, Benjamin and Sarah were able to watch at close range from the *Forest King*, the Yankee ships taking target practice. Being a merchant ship helped, and they were welcomed by the Union Navy.

Later, they boasted to Mother Briggs and other family members how, while on the deck of the *Forest King* and close enough to the front lines of the Civil War, they had observed as civilians some loud fiery naval maneuvers.

Selina was of the opinion that if Sarah had been born a man, she would have made a great captain, but Mother Briggs was quick to respond that for the sake of her son, she was glad Sarah was a woman and hopefully soon, the mother of her grandchildren.

Benjamin and Sarah continued to enjoy their blissful time at sea as well as at home. One evening, after Mother Briggs had retired to her room, they filled the kitchen tub with hot water and he diligently got in. Using a loofah and soap, she gently rubbed his back, while for a short while, he delighted with the pampering received.

"My dearest, how can you expect me to enjoy this delicious experience without you?" he took hold of her arms and pulled her into the tub with him, just as Mother Briggs walked in. She made a swift, silent exit. *Soon I'm going to become a grandmother*, she smiled confidently.

CHAPTER XI

**War's turning point. - A man's world. -
Richardson joins the Union Army. - Another massacre. -
Plumbing in the *Rose Cottage*. - Arthur the bark and the price
of sugar. – Our president is dead. - The life toll of war. – Baby
Arthur. - The Briggs at sea. - Benjamin meets Fanny.**

July 3, 1863

"Victory! Waterloo Eclipsed!" Was the headline in the *Philadelphia Inquirer* after the Union victory and the war's pivotal three-day Battle of Gettysburg, Pennsylvania. Sadly, it involved the largest number of casualties of the entire war, but it was still considered the war's turning point.

January 16, 1864

Activist Anna Dickinson, known for questioning Lincoln's policies, generated a presidential smile during her speech in the House of Representatives when she stated that she supported the president despite his faults. Her speech sparked the following editorial comment in the New York *Geneva Gazette*, "Among the excrescences upon the body politic is one which may be best described by its Greek name Gynaekokracy, which manifests itself in the absurd endeavors of women to usurp the places and execute the functions of the male sex. A moral and social monstrosity and an inversion of the laws of nature."

That did not stop her from going on a national tour as an abolitionist speaker. While giving one of her heated antislavery lectures in Marion, before heading to Boston, she met Reverend Leander, who was so impressed by her fiery belief in equality that he put her in touch with the escaped slave abolitionist orator Frederick Douglass, still living in Boston. Anna had been born a century too early, a time when women had just started surfacing for equality and such times dictated for their submission as homemakers, and nothing more. Men had the final word.

Richardson, now 20 years old, came to Marion to say goodbye to Benjamin and Sarah, who they had befriended while traveling on the *Forest King* to Marseilles.

His smooth olive-skinned complexion, thick dark brown hair, blue eyes and a handsomely fit figure made him quite a ladies' man. He had decided to give up seafaring to muster in for coast guard duty in the Union Army, also known as the Federal Army.

Benjamin feared that he might never see Richardson again, but remained supportive of his friend's decision.

Richardson was assigned to Company A in Belfast, Maine,

March 18, under Captain Charles Baker, primarily serving in the garrison coastal fortifications in Maine.

The war wasn't going well, and some were even of the opinion that if the Southern armies could hold out just a little longer, until the election, negotiations for Northern recognition of Confederate independence might begin. But when General Sherman seized Atlanta on September 6, the war effort turned decidedly in the North's favor.

Two months later, Lincoln not only won the popular vote but also the Electoral College by 212–21. But as much as people loved him, he still had many enemies to contend with, like some staunch opponents in Congress, and the news media who did their best to provide negative hostile coverage whenever possible.

Early 1865, Benjamin sold the *Forest King* to his brother Oliver and took command of *Arthur*, a larger sailing ship with three masts. It was Sarah's first voyage to the Caribbean Islands. They would be transporting sugar from the Island of Jamaica to New Bedford.

On the way south, they docked in New York City for three days. His crew took turns going into the city, and Benjamin and Sarah had the opportunity to act as tourists.

They visited the famous Barnum's American Museum, but after

witnessing the exploitation of humans and animals for the sake of entertainment, they agreed not to tell anyone they had even been there.

The next day, they stopped at Lord & Taylor on Grand Street, where Benjamin bought Sarah a paisley Kashmir shawl. They were excited to have gotten the last two tickets available at the Winter Garden Theatre, where they watched Edwin Thomas Booth, the famous American actor in his critically acclaimed performance as *Hamlet*. While having breakfast the next morning at a small deli before heading out to sea, Sarah commented, "It's hard for me to believe that while we sit here, in this big city, with modern buildings, theaters, fancy shops and such display of civilized manners — the Wild West is still being won — the Civil War is tearing apart our country — and the Native Indians are at this very moment being persecuted and massacred."

"I know, it's such a beautiful country, but sometimes I feel as if everyone has gone mad."

"Now I understand why you love the sea so much; it's your refuge."

"Yes, my love, you know me well. But it's not the same without you, anymore. I miss you so much when we're apart. You are truly the sunshine of my life." He kissed her hand, and then they held hands across the table. Even though they were married, kissing in public was an act frowned upon.

They were supposed to stay a week in Jamaica, but Mr. and Mrs. Scofield, the sugar plantation owners, were starving for what they called, "white, civilized company," and convinced them to stay two extra weeks. By the time they left the island, Sarah had developed a better appreciation for what she had taken for granted until then — the production of sugar.

She wrote home ..."It's very difficult for me to witness the perils of the black slaves cultivating sugar canes under the eyes of whip-wielding overseers. From my bedroom window, I can see the sugar canes, some reach nine to ten feet high and tower above the slaves who work stoically all day, no matter how hot it is. They use sharp, double-edged knives to cut the stalks, but it's still a very hard job. I will never be able to eat sugar again without thinking how it came about."

It took close to a year for the sugar canes to ripen. Once cut, the stalks were taken to a mill, and the juice extracted. Once a batch of raw sugar was refined, it was called a sugarloaf. The best sugar came from the first boiling. The sugar loafs varied in size. Then it was packed in large wooden barrels called hogsheads. The larger the loaf, the lower the grade of the sugar, as the size determined the price. About 1,000 pounds of sugar fit inside a hogshead. The slaves rolled the barrels to the shore and then loaded them aboard. *Arthur*'s hold was filled with 500 hogsheads containing sugarloaves wrapped in blue paper to enhance their whiteness.

Back in the U.S., the profitable cargo of white sugar would be sold in tall, conical loaves, from which pieces would be broken off with special iron sugar-cutters (sugar nips). Sugar, a most-needed item in just about every American household, guaranteed merchants to grow rich quick.

April 9, 1865

Robert E. Lee surrendered the last major Confederate army to Ulysses S. Grant at Appomattox Court House in Virginia. The Civil War had finally come to an end. Five days later, on the evening of April 14, President Lincoln, his wife Mary, and a young army officer named Henry Rathbone and his fiancée Clara attended the performance of *Our American Cousin,* at the Ford's Theatre in Washington, D.C.

During the second Act, John Wilkes Booth, a confederate sympathizer and actor, but not as well-known as his brother Edwin Thomas Booth, entered the presidential box above the stage and fired his .44-caliber single-shot derringer pistol into the back of President Lincoln's head. Henry Rathbone tried to stop Booth from fleeing the scene, but Booth stabbed him with his dagger and leapt onto the stage shouting, "Sic semper tyrannies! The South is avenged!" He ran across the stage and out the back door. Being an eye witness to the crime was quite different from just wishing to get rid of their president. A mixture of horrified shock and disbelief ran though the audience and performers, who left the theatre as Abraham Lincoln was carried to a boarding house across the street, where he died the next morning.

Seated in his office at home, Reverend Leander stared at the headlines: "DEATH OF THE PRESIDENT" in *The New York Herald,* and "Appalling Circumstance, President Dead" in *The Herald Extra.* His voice rang with urgency as he called for his family. His sons, Edward and William, were in the kitchen having breakfast with Selina and hurried into his office where they found him seated by his desk, with his face held between his hands. He stood when he saw them, "Our President has been murdered!" He lost his balance but luckily fell backward into his seat. Selina thought he was having an apoplectic attack and started fanning him with one of the newspapers. Once the blunt of reality hit them, they cried with him.

The next morning was Easter Sunday, and Reverend Leander took to his podium like other Christian ministers, to associate the slain president to a second Jesus, who, like the first, had died for his people's sins and rose to immortality.

By the end of the Civil War, roughly 179,000 black men (10% of the Union Army) had served as soldiers in the U.S. Army, and another 19,000 had served in the Navy. But being free from slavery, and the willingness to help with the Civil War, didn't help change the ingrained prejudice the majority of white folks felt toward them, nor had their desire to keep them enslaved decreased.

Two years went by, and plantation owners in the state of Texas "forgot" to divulge to their slaves that, according to Lincoln's Emancipation Proclamation, they were free to leave. It wasn't until the Union soldiers arrived in Galveston, Texas, June of 1865, with news that the Civil War was over and slavery in the U.S. had been abolished, that they learned the truth.

The Civil War had taken the lives of over 620,000 Americans, but disease killed twice as many as those lost in battle. 50,000 survivors returned home as amputees. Richardson received an honorable discharge, and except for having lost an excessive amount of weight, he seemed to be in good health. Since he didn't offer any explanations, no one asked him how he had acquired the two small scars: one on the right cheek and the other on the same side of his neck.

Sarah and Mother Briggs went out of their way to make a special dinner to celebrate his safe return. He stayed two days with them, and before leaving for New York, he gave Benjamin a repeating rifle, known as the Winchester by the Union soldiers.

Benjamin possessed an aberration to guns, which he called instruments of death, but not wanting to hurt his feelings, he accepted the gift. Once Richardson left, he locked it away with no intention of ever using it.

Sarah didn't feel well enough to accompany Benjamin to Cuba once again. When he returned from his voyage, he learned that Sarah was with child.

That night in bed, he whispered, "What do you think? If it's a boy, should we name him Arthur?"

"What if it's a girl?"

"In that case, something of a Caribbean nature ... like Alesha or Naomi."

"It's going to be a boy," she said. They giggled.

September 10, Arthur S. Briggs was born at the *Rose Cottage*, surrounded by all his family including his father, a rare happening, not to count on happening again. No one mentioned the connection of Arthur's name coinciding with the name of their ship.

A week later, Benjamin kissed his wife and son goodbye since he had a load of timber to deliver to Florida. He stood in the doorway of their bedroom watching Sarah nurse the newborn.

They were the closest to the picture of Madonna and little Jesus.

Arthur was the joy and delight of his mother and family. He slept through the night and only cried when hungry or needed his nappy changed. That was until he started teething at five months old. Sarah was now up half the night, rubbing his gums with her fingers for some kind of relief, which rarely came.

"Mother Briggs," Sarah rocked a screaming Arthur. "How did you handle all your children while this was going on?"

"I was too busy to pay attention, and besides," she pointed to

Arthur. "None of 'em screamed as loud as this one."

The only two remedies that Sarah had heard of were rubbing a baby's gums with a small minnow or having the gums lanced, and both sounded barbaric.

Mother Briggs came home one afternoon waving a small glass bottle. "Look what I found at the pharmacy in Wareham! It's called Mrs. Winslow's Soothing Syrup. The advertisement promises that mothers can get some rest once they give the little one a spoonful o' this delightful medicine." She handed it to Sarah. "Isn't it wonderful?"

Sarah held the five-inch-tall glass bottle suspiciously and opened it slowly. She took a sniff and made a gagging sound. "Oh, my goodness," she gave the bottle back. "I can't give that to my baby, it smells awful."

"It does smell a little different, but the pharmacist guaranteed that it can soothe any human or animal, and it effectively quiets restless infants, especially those teething."

"A human or an animal? No offense, Mother Briggs, but I'd rather never sleep than give my baby such remedy."

Sarah had used her innate motherly instinct very wisely. Mrs. Winslow's Soothing Syrup was made with 65mg of morphine sulphate per fluid ounce, a cocktail of morphine and alcohol. True that in 1866, many parents swore by it since babies slept for the most of the day and night, but some never awoke.

After delivering a shipment of salt to New York, Benjamin was about to head north to Buffalo to pick up another cargo, but could not resist docking a few extra hours to visit Richardson, now living in the city.

Richardson had stopped seeing other women, to court one very special girl he had met at a society gathering. "She has completely stolen my heart. She's the most beautiful woman I have ever seen. As my best friend, you must meet her. Her family is having a dinner party tonight, and this will be my only chance to introduce you to Fanny and her family."

Richardson had definitely developed into a chameleon of sorts. He possessed a natural knack for mixing within the sophisticated spheres of high society, as well as in the crude, more basic circle of sailors.

Benjamin sat between Fannie's uncle, Mr. James Henry Winchester, a very successful business man, and Mrs. Morris, an old widow with enough precious jewelry around her neck, fingers and hair to possibly buy a small kingdom.

"I don't care beans for trains and railroads." Mr. Winchester's primary business interest was in salvaging old ships. "No, not a single old red-eyed bean. Give me a ship instead, any ship, and you have my full attention."

Ships and the sea made for an interesting conversation between him and Benjamin throughout the long dinner, and even afterward, when the guests moved to a larger room to drink their cordials, smoke and chat.

Benjamin had to agree, Fannie was indeed as beautiful as Richardson had described her. Her angel-like features were accented by perfectly coiffured golden hair, and her sparkling, long white dress conformed to a youthful, hourglass figure. Benjamin did appreciate beauty, but not her type after she came on to him shamelessly after Mr. Winchester's wife, Mary Jane, took him away to attend to other guests.

"I couldn't help notice the way you look at me," she said, fanning herself flirtatiously with a mini white lace fan.

"Really?" he backed into the wall where she had cornered him.

"Yes, and you should know that I feel the same way about you. Let's meet tomorrow at the new Savoy Hotel and have more of a private time with each other. What do you say?"

He knew Richardson to be a ladies' man who went shamelessly from one affair to another — something he never accepted — but looked the other way because they were friends.

But now to see a woman from a respectable family acting in the same manner as Richardson was the unnatural act of a promiscuous woman. And that's what he told her before excusing himself and leaving.

Benjamin came home to find that Arthur, now 13 months old, didn't acknowledge his presence. He tried to reason that four months prior, when they last had seen each other, Arthur was just a little baby. But that night, he couldn't sleep, haunted by the thought that he had become like his seafaring father and would miss seeing his child grow up. He played with several options. He could take shorter merchant trips along the coast instead of overseas, then he could be home more often, or perhaps it was time to look for another way of making a living — on land and close to home. It was too late to cancel his already scheduled overseas voyage to Marseilles in two weeks, so he made plans to mix business with pleasure. He decided to take his family along, and the following morning, he shared his plans with Sarah.

Two weeks later, Sarah and Arthur joined Benjamin onboard his son's namesake ship to Marseilles, carrying a large freight of textiles, and they would return with French beauty products.

Benjamin played with Arthur every day and attempted to tell him children's stories, but Arthur was still very young, and his attention span only lasted so long. But he did have one story he liked and could hear it over and over again: "The Ugly Duckling," by Hans Christian Andersen.

Sarah gave Benjamin much credit for his patience at attempting to bond with their son. She spent most of her quiet time reading and needlepointing a wool tapestry she hoped to finish by the time they returned from their voyage. She also played the melodeon every day, to the delight of the crew. Old Charlie the cook, whenever he found some free time, sang a few lullabies, which seemed to captivate Arthur's attention to the point of putting him to sleep shortly afterward.

In the evening, Charlie sang on deck from his extensive German and Italian musical repertoire, and Sarah accompanied with the melodeon. Crew members like the brothers Volkert and Boz Lorenzen, and Gottlieb Gottschalk, all from Fohr, a German island in the North Sea, were very appreciative of the German operettas and familiar popular tunes.

Benjamin loved having his family with him, but he wasn't willing to sacrifice their well-being so that he could have them full time by his side. He knew Sarah would have accepted it as a way of life for her, but a ship was no place for their son to grow up. When Benjamin took the next merchant voyage in January on his own, Sarah wrote, "I never heard Arthur say so much about you while you're away. He told me he misses you and hopes you'll be home soon."

Sarah had grown up in a family of preachers and seamen, and much like Mother Briggs, she handled her position as the wife of a sea captain and a new mom with perfect grace. She considered her marriage a dream come true; her husband was the man she loved. While he was away, she wrote him often, since she knew how lonely one could feel without news from their loved ones.

CHAPTER XII

**The *Gift of God*. - Captain Nathan gets struck by lightning. -
Zenas perishes from yellow fever. - Sophia. - B & B Hardware
Store. - *Little Edith*. - Once a sailor, always a sailor.**

January 11, 1869

Sarah gave birth to Everson, but he died nine months later. "Little
Everson" was carved into his headstone, but Benjamin and Sarah
always referred to him as the *Gift of God*.

May 10, 1870

Benjamin and his family left once again for Marseilles, but when
they arrived in France, a telegram from Mother Briggs waited for
them. "Papa Nathan died, please come home."

Except for delivering their cargo and picking up the new one,
they quickly headed back to the U.S. They arrived three weeks
later and found Mother Briggs in better spirits than they expected.

"The newspapers wrote that your father was hit by lightning
while standing in front of our porch, but if that were true, our
porch and our home would have been burned to the ground," her

mind seem to wonder for a few seconds and then added, "You all know how he liked to watch lighting strike, he wasn't afraid. He stood out there," she pointed to the front yard. "I had told him so many times to stay inside at times like that, but he always said, "'Woman, stop worrying so much. If I were to get hit by lightning, it would already have happened a long time ago on one of my ships!'" Well, you know how wicked those summer storms can be, and it was a warm day, Tuesday, June 28 … I was in the kitchen getting ready to make some apple cider when the sound of thunder made me look out o' the window and I saw him, I saw him standing and then … he was flat down on the ground, just like that," she emphasized her words by snapping her fingers together, "I ran out screaming, thinking I could maybe help him up, but he was burned dead, dead and burned." She didn't drop a tear. Turned her face toward the open window and stared out in silence. Then she added in a monotone voice, "The roses ... the roses were fine, and it rained right afterward." Sarah and Benjamin remained silent.

October 12, on a voyage back from Cuba to the U.S., Zenas perished from yellow fever while serving as mate to Captain Oliver, his brother, on his new brig *Julia A. Hallock*.

Mother Briggs heard a knock on her front door and found Oliver on the porch standing next to Zenas' sea chest. She looked at Oliver then briefly at the chest.

"I'm glad you made it home, my son," she hugged him closely and then pointed to the chest, "Please ... bring it upstairs to his bedroom."

Once Oliver left, she closed the door, went down on her knees, wrapped her arms vehemently around the sea chest and cried as quietly as she could manage so as not to disturb anyone.

October 31, 1870

Benjamin arrived from his voyage three weeks too late to witness the birth of his daughter Sophia Matilda. Not that he would have been able to actually witness it, but at least he could have been close by, most likely in the parlor waiting to receive the midwife's word that his wife and daughter lived. Then he would be allowed to see them for about one or two minutes.

After giving birth, the new mother wasn't to talk for a few weeks, or be bothered with anything that might upset her emotionally. Her diet intake would be minimal, no solid foods or drink, and she was to remain in bed on her back for at least a month, since standing before its due time could cause the organs and anything else inside, to plop out.

Benjamin tiptoed into their bedroom and found Sarah propped up on pillows, sleeping. He sat at the foot of the bed watching his new baby daughter sleeping contentedly in her mother's arms.

It didn't last too long; Sarah awoke as if she could feel Benjamin's presence and extended her right hand in his direction. "Benj, you're home."

"Yes, my love, I am," he bent over to kiss her forehead and then her lips. "And I'm here to stay." Seeing the look of surprise in her eyes, he went on, "It took a while, I know, but I've made up my mind. I miss you too much to stay away from you and Arthur for such long periods of time."

"And what will you do for work, dear husband of mine?" she asked curiously.

"I'm not the only one who would like to be close to home. Oliver and I have been talking about this for a long time, and we feel this is the right time to do it. With the money he and I have saved, and with the sale of our ships, we'll have enough money to open a hardware store. We can take turns running the store, and that will allow us to have more free time to do as we like."

"The children and I will appreciate having you home, but are you sure this is what you want?"

"With all my heart."

"Then I'm happy. Here," she handed him the baby. "Meet Sophia Matilda, your daughter. Isn't she a cupcake?"

He slid one hand under her head and neck and the other hand under her bottom. "She's beautiful," he gazed in awe at the baby and then brought her close to his chest, tapping her back softly.

"Of course she is beautiful. She has your eyes."

"Hmm, are you sure?" he squinted his eyes and frowned at the baby. "Well, maybe you're right, but I hope she looks more like you than me." He laid Sophia in her cradle, where she continued to sleep. "Guess what. I also have a present for you, my dear."

"Oh, what is it?"

"It's a surprise. It's downstairs, and in due time, you'll get a chance to see it."

"Downstairs?" she sat up with her feet dangling off the bed and reached for her robe at the foot of the bed.

"Now, now," he took the robe away. "You know you need to stay in bed for a month, and rest until you get strong again."

"Benj, I have been in this bed for three weeks. Mrs. Landbrug's daughter had a baby, and a week later she was back to farming and did fine. Trust me, I need to get out of this bed and this room, or I'll lose my mind." She stood and put the robe on.

A shiny wood melodeon stood next to the downstairs' parlor window.

"Oh my Benj, I love it. It's like a piano but not as big. So beautiful! Thank you so much, I love it!" she sat at the bench and let her fingers run up and down the keys. "No more straps over the shoulders, like I have been using. This is so much better. Where did you find it? It has such a great sound."

"On the way back, I stopped in Buffalo, The Melodeon Capital of the World."

She responded by playing the upbeat tune of *The Melodeon Waltz.*

He was happy to oblige when Mother Briggs came in the room and asked him to dance with her.

"Zenas loved to dance," she cried. "Did you know he loved to dance?"

"Yes, Mother, I know." He kissed her forehead, and they continued to dance.

Oliver and Benjamin had originally made plans to open a hardware store in New Bedford, but after giving some thought to the distance and the time it would take to travel back and forth in the winter months, they opted for finding a place in Marion.

Oliver found a space available for rent on Spring Street, and on January 17, 1871, they held the grand opening of their "B & B Hardware Store." The B's stood for Brothers Briggs.

Their large inventory included all types of knives, scissors, coffee mills, canning supplies, waffle irons, razors and latches. Household hardware for home improvements, fasteners, building materials, tools, keys, locks, screws, nails, hinges and chains. Farm and ranch supplies like cowbells, horseshoes, pitchforks, bailing twine, axes, mauls and all the myriad bits of hardware needed to repair farm equipment and fix barns and fences. Other hardware stores sold guns and ammunition, but they had no intention of carrying firearms.

Except for Sundays, they were open every day and stayed open until the last customer left. If the part needed didn't exist, they managed to create something that worked.

Considering that Oliver and Benjamin lacked experience in sales, it was a profitable year for their new business even though after three months in business, they had lost their enthusiasm. When customers came in, they would rather reminisce over the old days at sea, possibly the reason why, with each passing day, they started carrying fewer household and farm goods and more ship hardware, specifically for sailing ships.

Arthur, now 6 years old, had finally learned to distinguish between Oliver and Benjamin, even though they did look a lot alike.

Sophia always responded with a smile when Benjamin lifted her up, but her vocabulary was one word: Mama.

Mid-December, Sarah complained about being nauseated and a bit under the weather.

"That's because you're with child." Mother Briggs could not be more thrilled.

"You think so?" she yawned. "I'm so tired, I could go to sleep right now."

Mother Briggs took care of the children and the home and made sure that Sarah took as many naps as needed.

But Sarah's baby was born prematurely on June 4 and died two months later. Her grave marker was kept simple: 1872 *Little Edith*.

Benjamin and Oliver did their best to remain focused on taking care of their customers' hardware needs. But all copies of the quarterly periodical, *The Gazette Seafarer*, were kept behind the counter so they could flip over the pages when there were no customers in sight. A lot had developed since they had been at sea, particularly the screw propeller and the triple expansion engine, which marked the era of cheap, safer travel and increased sea trade around the world. But they preferred their older, more familiar sailing ships. On one of those moody days, a scorching summer day in August, Richardson walked into their hardware store.

He had married Fannie, the girl of his dreams.

Benjamin offered him congratulations. But Richardson shrugged his shoulders, "I'm afraid that happiness is not what I got, let's just leave it at that. I'm here, Benjamin, because a few years back, you made a great impression on Mr. Winchester, and he brought up your name. He would like to offer you a share on a brigantine ship he salvaged. Once the major refit is accomplished, which is almost done, he'll need a seasoned captain to transport across the Atlantic all sorts of cargo." And he pointed a finger at him. "He wants you."

"Richardson, my sea days are over ..."

"Are you telling me that you swallowed the anchor, for good?"

Benjamin gave him a friendly pat on his shoulder. "You always had a knack for sea language ..."

"I know, I know. Once a sailor, always a sailor, right? Look, before coming here, I stopped by your house and spoke to Sarah. In the name of our friendship, will you tell me the truth about your work here ... in this hardware store, all day," he pointed to the half empty shelves. "No offense, but is this really what you want to do for the rest of your life?"

Oliver had been listening. He raised his hand. "Neither of us is happy. I would give anything to go back to the sea, and if Benjamin takes your offer, I'm more than ready to close shop."

"I need to talk to Sarah first," Benjamin said.

"Of course, I would not expect otherwise. Then come to New York and take a look at the ship, meet with Mr. Winchester, and see what he has to offer. He's poking for one more buyer. Who better than you? Benjamin, this is a great investment toward your future!"

Sarah's response met Richardson's expectations. Besides, why couldn't she and the children continue to travel with him, once or twice a year? Would be a most pleasant way for the whole family to be together.

The brothers put the hardware store up for sale. Oliver was able to buy back the *Julia A. Hallock,* and Benjamin made plans to meet with Mr. Winchester.

CHAPTER XIII

Reverend Leander's grand departure. - *Mary Celeste's* **history.
- The bad word. - Overseas cure. - Sarah's 31st birthday. - Gal-
sneaker. - New York City, 1872. - The horse plague. - Hot
chocolate.**

Reverend Leander's health had been steadily failing in the last two
years. The doctor's task of getting rid of the offending surplus fluid
through the use of bloodletting, purgatives and mercury, didn't
seem to help, if anything, it left him weaker and far worse after
each treatment. Hacking away through town as he walked to his
church and back, he succumbed to consumption Monday
September 2, the day Benjamin was expected to leave for New
York to meet with Mr. Winchester.

Reverend Leander had made one request: to be buried inside a
simple pine casket. "And please keep it closed," he told Selina and
the family. "No viewing. I hate the idea of having people stare at
me, and I can't tell them what's on my mind."

On his last hour, the family gathered around his bed. One
thing they had in common, they had learned to recognize when a
loved one's death was imminent. Not to anyone's surprise,
Reverend Leander sat up in bed, coughed as if to clear his throat,

looked up and said, "Present!" as if he had just arrived at the pearly gates of Heaven. Then he fell back.

It took all day for family members and the people of Marion and adjacent towns, to walk by the Reverend's closed casket, lying in the center of his church, covered with flowers intertwined with handwritten personal notes left by the mourners as they walked by.

Losing her father just one month after her baby Edith died had been too much for Sarah to endure. Mother Briggs and Selina held her from both sides as they followed on foot the horse-drawn hearse to the cemetery. All the stores in Marion closed, and it seemed as if everyone in town came to participate in the procession, including some dogs silently trailing behind.

The local newspaper posted that they were very sorry to announce the death of Reverend Leander Cobb, and it had been a lovely funeral.

Benjamin waited another week before leaving for New York.

Mr. Winchester took Benjamin to Pier 44, north of Rutgers Street, where the *Mary Celeste* awaited while being fit with new transoms and the replacement of many timbers. Built in 1861 as the *Amazon* on Spencer's Island, Nova Scotia, it had been the first large vessel built in that community. Constructed of locally felled timber and carvel-built, its hull planked flush rather than overlapping. There had been nine owners, which included Robert McLellan, the ship's first captain, who on the first voyage across the Atlantic Ocean to London, transporting a cargo of timber, fell ill and died. Further misfortunes happened when she collided with fishing equipment in Eastport, Maine, and after leaving London, ran into and sank another brig in the English Channel. After that last mishap, she did well until 1867 when at Cape Breton Island, she was driven ashore in a storm and so seriously damaged that her owners abandoned her as a shipwreck.

Acquired as a derelict by Alexander McBean of Glacé Bay, Nova Scotia, he sold it within a month as a wreck for US$1,750 to

Richard W. Haines, an American mariner from New York. Mr. Haines invested $8,825 restoring it, and in December 1868, made himself her captain and registered her with the Collector of Customs in New York as an American vessel, under a new name, *Mary Celeste*. But less than a year later, the ship was seized by Haines's creditors and sold to a New York consortium headed by James H. Winchester, who retained at least a half-share throughout the next three years. Besides the $8,825 spent previously for restoration, the ship underwent a major refit, overseen by Mr. Winchester and costing an added $10,000, which enlarged her considerably. Her length went from 99.3 to 103 feet, her breadth 22.5 to 25.7 feet, her depth from 11.7 to 16.2 feet, and the 198.42 gross tons increased to 282.28.

Impressed with the overall quality of the work still going on, Benjamin told Mr. Winchester that he was interested in the offer and would like to proceed forward as shareholder and captain of the ship.

When Benjamin returned from New York, Mother Briggs took him aside. "Son, I'm very concerned with Sarah and Sophia's health. Their coughing spells remind me too much o' my brother Leander. We need to call a different doctor than the one who treated him. My sister Elizabeth recommended a specialist who lives in Boston."

"We need to get him here as soon as possible. Do you think he'll come over?"

"Yes, but it will be costly."

"Mother, no price is too high for my family's health."

Dr. Jeff Williams, a chubby, well-dressed man in his mid-50's flicked his fancy cane around like a sword while holding on the other hand a shiny black leather bag with a split-handle design on the top. After such a long trip from Boston to Marion, it was admirable that he didn't have a single speck of dirt marring his black top hat, fashionable black suit or shiny black shoes.

"I'm absolutely famished," he announced as soon as he walked into their home. Mother Briggs rushed into the kitchen to get the leftover dinner, still warm on top of the stove, and Benjamin steered him to a seat at the dining room table. Dr. Williams swallowed avidly the first serving of mutton stew, soaking large pieces of cornbread in the sauce and making smacking sounds after stuffing his mouth, already filled, with more food. Mother Briggs was delighted to see that a famous doctor from Boston, most likely used to eating at the best city restaurants, appreciated her cooking enough to ask for seconds.

Benjamin told him about his Uncle Leander's on-going illness, responsible for his death less than two months prior, and now his wife and daughter seemed to be showing signs of the same ailment.

Dr. Williams insisted on examining them without family members being present. Half an hour later, he came out of the room with the stethoscope still around his neck. "Lovely lady, your wife ... and your child too, of course," then he lowered his voice. "Can we talk somewhere privately?"

Mother Briggs brought them hot tea into the parlor, and then sat in the corner, to crochet the start of a brown wool shawl.

"I have seen many patients with the same symptoms as your family, and I'm sorry to say this to you, but ... they suffer from the King's Touch or what I call ... consumption."

Mother Briggs let out a wounded cry. The two long crochet needles and the spool of wool fell from her lap and rolled onto the floor. She went into the kitchen, grabbed a pair of scissors and ran outside to prune her roses.

Benjamin didn't respond to Dr. Williams' death sentences, except stare at him, his chest feeling about to explode. He put his hands to his chest.

"I'm sorry, but I don't have any medicine to stop the outcome," Dr. Williams twirled his fingers around each other.

"How ... long?"

"Well, your wife told me they're not bringing up blood in their cough, but are experiencing weight loss, night sweats and a bit feverish. In my personal opinion, both are in the first stage, so depending on how fast the disease takes over their lungs ... I'm going to guess between six months to two years, could be less ... could be more ... everybody is different."

"I just purchased a brig and planned on delivering a cargo to Genoa next month. I'll cancel the voyage immediately."

"Take them with you, my good man."

"My wife loves the sea. But ... such a long voyage. Won't that be too much for them?"

"Well, maybe ... but the salty sea air is known for its benefits. Not a cure, of course, but can keep the lungs from worsening," he paused to bite off a cuticle from his right index finger. "Come to think of it, there is a well-renowned doctor in France, a colleague of mine ... of course. He has had much success with consumption cases like your family is experiencing. In my professional opinion, it would be worth a visit, since you're going to Italy anyway. He owns a sanitarium in the French Alps, and from what he's been writing to me, the rest and beautiful climate can change the course of the disease if caught at the beginning. If you wish, I can write to him immediately and let him know that you'll be taking your family to see him — that way, he'll be expecting you."

Benjamin left for New York the next morning with one goal in mind, to talk to Mr. Winchester in person regarding his predicament, after the delivery to Genoa. It was most imperative that he take his wife and daughter to see Dr. Jean-Antoine Villemin in France.

Mr. Winchester could not have been more understanding. "I'm a family man, myself. As long as you deliver the goods to Genoa within the time scheduled, I'll be satisfied. You go ahead, Benjamin, and take care of your family; I'll even give you three extra weeks to return after they are successfully treated."

Dr. Williams was supposed to be a houseguest for another day but stayed until the end of the week.

At meals, he liked to talk about the patients he treated at the hospital. Some died and some lived. Once God decided their fate, there was only so much he could do for them.

Before leaving, he auscultated Mother Briggs, Arthur and all the other family members with his stethoscope and gave them a clean bill of health.

Back in Marion, seated in the parlor, with Arthur on his knees, Benjamin listened to Sarah sing "All Things Love Thee, So Do I" while she played the melodeon. With Edith and her father's death so near each other, he knew Sarah was still in mourning. When you have a true soulmate, you know their thoughts, their joys and sorrows. When she finished the song, he clapped vehemently as he always did. His feelings had not changed since he had heard her sing for the first time in the church choir, and had known at that moment that someday he would marry her. If anything, he felt that he loved her more with each passing day.

"My dearest," he stood to kiss her hand. "You sing like a nightingale, such a delight to my ears. Will you bring the melodeon with you onboard the *Mary Celeste?*"

"Oh my God, are you serious, on her maiden voyage to Genoa?" she stood like a teenager at the prospect of a new dress. "Is this an invitation?"

He nodded.

"By golly, Benjamin, you're serious!"

"Of course I am. Come, sit with me on the couch." She did, and hugged him. "It's going to be just one of the many routine merchant trips like I have done in the past," he went on. "But this time, the *Mary Celeste* is the answer to my prayers in more ways than one. Dr. Williams told me the sea air will do you and Sophie a world of good. After Genoa, we'll go to Prey, France, and visit Dr. Jean-Antoine Villemin, who Dr. Williams told me specializes in the illness you and Sophie suffer from. Dr. Villemin will be able to help you both."

"It would be so nice not to feel tired all the time, and lately, little Sophie has not been sleeping well either."

"Don't you worry about Sophie tonight," Mother Briggs had been sitting in her rocking chair, just listening. "I gave her some of the sleepy medicine Dr. Williams left with me. Arthur, get your blessings from your parents. It's time for bed."

Arthur approached his mother, who wrapped her arms around him and then put her hand over his head, "God bless you, my son. Now don't forget to say your prayers before going to sleep," she kissed him on both cheeks. "I'll see you in the morning."

"I want to go with you and Sophia," Arthur had always felt a bit intimidated by his father and preferred to direct his request at her.

"Son, that's completely impossible," Benjamin responded. "You have school to attend," then more softly, "When we return, I promise we'll start making plans to travel to Marseilles, like we did before. Remember the nice time we had together?"

"Yes, but it's too long to wait until you come back. I want to go with you now," he stomped his feet and then cried out, "Mommy, I'm afraid to be alone at night."

"I know how much you're afraid of the dark," she patted his shoulder softly. "But sweetie, I can tell you there's nothing to be scared of. At the end of every tunnel, there's always a light on the other side to guide us through."

"Besides," Benjamin said. "You're 7 years old and not a baby anymore! I want you to promise your mother and me that while we're away, you'll do your best and listen to grandma." Arthur nodded his head. Benjamin put his hand on his head. "God bless you, my son."

Arthur went up to his grandmother who stood by the doorway waiting for him, and took her hand. Before leaving, Mother Briggs turned to Sarah, "You have exerted yourself too much with singing and playing the melodeon. Lie down, and I'll bring you some tea after I put Arthur to bed."

Sarah laid on the fainting couch, but as soon as Mother Briggs left, she propped up on one elbow to listen closer to Benjamin, who now sat next to her. Her once tight bodice, a bit loose due to her weight loss, caused one of her shoulders to become exposed. Her pale skin possessed a translucent look like a rare glass vase. "You're so beautiful," he kissed her shoulder. "I hope you're as excited as I am to be traveling to Italy and then France," he said knowing well in advance that she couldn't be happier.

"Do you remember what I swore to you when we were on our honeymoon?" She didn't wait for his response, "I'll always be your devoted wife on land as well as at sea."

"Yes, my love, I do remember." Their lips met, and then they stared at each other like two teenagers in love. He kissed her lips softly once again, and then she laid back with a sigh of contentment. "*Mary Celeste,*" she said the name slowly. "*Mary*, like the mother of Jesus, and *Celeste* from the Latin word heavenly." She smiled. "I like it."

"By today's standards, she cannot compete with the speed of the steamships owned by large shipping companies, and she's a lot smaller than the ships I have commanded, but after 20 years of hauling all manner of cargo around the world, I feel secure with her size. Besides, while in New York, I made a scrutinizing inspection of her hull, and she's solid."

"I'm sure it will be perfect, much like our first of many ocean crossings," she giggled mischievously, and then with a more serious look, "How are we going to transport the new melodeon with us? It would sure be nice to have something onboard to pass away some of the more idle hours."

"I already made arrangements for it to be picked up tomorrow morning and carefully delivered to our ship. It will be there when you arrive with Sophia."

"So, we're now the proud owners of the *Mary Celeste*. I can't wait to see her. What kind of goods will it be carrying?"

"This time, we're carrying denatured alcohol. Oh yeah, and

we're only partial owners. Mr. Winchester, the New York shipping agent, is the majority shareholder. I only invested a third into it. By the way, while in his office going over the contract, he recommended Richardson as my first mate."

"Richardson? Oh, I'm so delighted to hear that. It will truly be like old times again."

"Yes, my love. I also met our new second mate, Andrew Gillings, from New York. Mr. Winchester introduced him as a knowledgeable and reliable seaman. And Edward Head ..."

"Edward? You mean Charlie, old Charlie is coming too? My goodness, that's wonderful. He cooks such delicious meals, and he's so entertaining too. I can still hear in my head the German and Italian operettas he sang for us. Taking the melodeon with us makes me feel so gay. Thank you Benj," she kissed him on the cheek. "I'll play, and old Charlie can sing. Who else will be joining us, that I might know?"

"My regular mariners, Boz, Volkert and Gottlieb. The others you don't know, but they came highly recommended by Mr. Winchester. I already spoke to them and made sure they understood that I won't allow any alcohol onboard. It will be a peaceful voyage without anyone getting disorderly."

"But you said you're delivering alcohol."

"I know it sounds strange for me to tell you there will be no alcohol onboard. But it's nothing to worry about. The 1,700 barrels we will be delivering contain industrial alcohol. No one, not even a sailor used to drink, would be able to stomach it."

"1,700 barrels! The ship can take that much of a cargo?" "Oh yes, and more. Mr. Winchester invested a lot of money into this brig. He made many changes to it with the intention of making a good profit in the long run. He even had the hold extended enough to be able to haul up to 3,500 barrels for future deliveries."

"That's wonderful, and what were the other changes?"

"Well, let me show you. Imagine two masts towering more than 75 feet above deck," he moved his head close to hers, and with his hands wide open, he used them as if he was opening a large window pane for her to see out. "When they redesigned the ship, they added a fifth yardarm to the foremast and a huge boom about 40 feet long from the mainmast. Even the original windows were filled in and new ones cut. Oh, I meant to tell you that Mr. Winchester was fine with you and Sophia joining me, and he has also given me complete freedom to make the necessary changes to our cabins as I see fit to make you comfortable during our voyage. This is the reason I'm leaving tomorrow morning — not just for attending business, but also to oversee the carpenters with the changes I have in mind. It took me the last two nights to put a plan together, but I believe I finally worked it out." He pulled out a five-by-ten piece of paper and a pencil from the drawer. "Here," he began to draw.

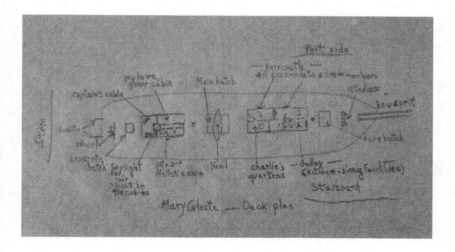

"Once you go down the companionway, there are three cabins. From the largest cabin of the three, where our meals were supposed to be served, I'm taking out the table that can seat up to six people, and moving it into the galley. I know it may be a little crowded there, but you, my darling, will gain a nice-sized cabin with lots of space for two berths, the melodeon and still plenty of space for your trunks and personal items. We'll also be a lot happier having our meals in the galley. It will be nice and warm there, since Charlie, as you know, will be cooking up a daily storm on his stove."

"And his quarters?" she asked.

"In the galley, of course, where he always insists to be. But I'm still having a bulkhead partition built to give him the privacy he'll need," he marked the spot with an asterisk and went on, just as enthusiastically. "My cabin is next to yours, with the usual furnishings, but I'm also modifying it to include a wider berth for when you want to be with me at night," he winked at her and she smiled. "The other cabin here on starboard will be shared by the first and second mates."

"And the crew?"

"They'll be here," he circled the spot. "On the port side of the deckhouse, next to the galley. These two cabins are wide enough to include three hammocks on each, and enough space for their sea-chests."

He did not share with her *Mary Celeste's* foul history. His philosophy concerning an ill-fated ship was nothing but superstitious nonsense. Like everything else, a ship was primarily in God's hands, then its capable captain.

"Time for your tea," Mother Briggs walked in carrying a tray with three delicate, fine-lipped teacups with matching saucers and a plate of butter cookies. "I brought you some too, Benj."

"I'll tell you more later," he whispered to Sarah. He stood and sat on the chair next to a small table covered with a handmade cream color lace doily, where Mother Briggs laid his teacup with two cookies next to it.

"Thanks, Mother. To this day, your butter cookies are still my favorite sweets," he took a bite and sipped some tea. "Mother, I hope Arthur won't be a trial to you as much as when I was his age. I sure didn't follow much of the rules."

"Oh no, dear ..."

"It's very important that he continues to attend school and you oversee his studies. I'm hoping he'll behave while we're gone."

She cut him off, "Arthur is an obedient little boy, and as I told you, I don't mind taking care of him until you all return."

"Thank you, Mother, I know that under your guiding hands and my brother James' supervision, we can leave with peace of mind. I have also made financial arrangements with James so I can pay you for Arthur's room and board here." She raised her hand but he went on, "I don't want to hear you say you won't take it. It's only fair you get paid for the extra expense and work. I'm leaving early tomorrow morning so that I have time to attend the final preparations before taking command of the *Mary Celeste*."

"Son, you're leaving again. You just came home three days ago. You must be exhausted."

"That's right, Mother, but never so thankful as I'm now to the good Lord. Since Sarah has agreed to join me with Sophia, I must return to New York as soon as possible and finish the necessary preparations before they join me," he removed an envelope from his coat pocket. "Sarah, these are two tickets for boarding a Fall River Line steamer to Queens, New York. When you arrive, I'll be there to fetch you and Sophie. I'll be sure to make arrangements for the three of us to stay at a hotel close to the pier. I intend to be with you every evening until the ship is ready for you to board."

"Don't worry, Sarah, I'll help you pack," Mother Briggs said. "It's just too bad I'll be missing Sophie's birthday celebration," she took in one of her usual long sighs when she wanted to emphasize her feelings, and shook her head. "I just can't believe she's almost two years old," she closed her eyes and forced a smile. "I'm sorry you have to go so far away to see a doctor, but you must if you're going to get well," she sat upright and her words were hard to pronounce clearly as she felt a tight feeling across her throat. "I'm going to miss you so much," she finally broke down in tears.

Sometimes Sarah would find her crying for no apparent reason, but she never asked her why. She knew why.

"We'll miss you too," Sarah motioned to Mother Briggs to sit next to her and gave her a hug.

"Mother, we'll celebrate Sophie's birthday in the big city. What can be better than that? She's going to love New York."

"And I promise to write and tell you all about it," Sarah kept her arm around Mother Briggs' shoulders.

"How long do you think you'll be gone?"

"Let's see, 20 days from New York to Genoa, then 20 days back, and if you add our trip to France," he pondered. "I'm going to take a guess of around three months. But I'll keep you posted for sure."

Benjamin left early the next morning.

The following Sunday, the family gathered at the *Rose Cottage* to celebrate Sarah's 31st birthday.

Selina gave her a handknitted wool night-jacket. "For those cold mornings and evenings at sea," she told Sarah. "It will definitely keep the chill away."

Harriet, her older sister had also knitted two pairs of wool booties. "Cold bed, cozy feet," she said.

Her younger sisters Julia and Mary had collaborated in the making of a "blanket sleeper." Even Mother Briggs had gone out of her way by buying Sarah and Sophia brand new socks to take on their voyage.

Sarah understood it was her birthday, but all those gifts gave her an unexplainably off feeling since never before did anyone bring her gifts before leaving on a sea voyage with Benjamin. As always, she confided in Selina who responded, "Silly girl, you shouldn't feel queer about it, these gifts will remind you of how much we love you, and as such, you'll have a good reason to return back to us, safe and sound."

She planned on taking two old traveling trunks and one just as big for Sophia. One of her trunks was her usual old wardrobe steamer trunk with dresser drawers, which she found very efficient not only for keeping clothes on hangers, but also the drawers inside came in handy for storing toiletries, undergarments and small possessions, like pictures, music sheets, a few books and a brand new diary she intended to start anew. With a weakness for plaid patterns, she packed her two favorite bustle wool dresses, the dark brown and soft yellow, and the red and blue. Once onboard, she intended to temporarily hem the skirts at least three inches shorter, so that she could walk on deck without worrying about tripping over ropes and other small deck things or while going up and down the companionway where there was a good chance her skirt might get caught, as it had happened the first two times she had traveled with Benjamin. Long bloomers and pantaloons trimmed with lace were quite in style as well as dress-up clothing ornaments, like floral wreaths, ostrich feathers and pomegranate flowers, but they made no sense for sea traveling. Instead, she packed for her and Sophia homemade heavy cotton bloomers, two large wool shawls, "night clothes," ankle-length nightshirts, wool robes and two pairs of gloves.

Sophia was doing well communicating when she needed to use the chamber pot. Girls seemed to pick up on that a lot earlier than boys. Still, she intended to keep Sophia in breeches during the day and extra wool nappies at night just in case she slept through a mishap.

The final contract concerning the ownership of the *Mary Celeste* was signed on Monday, October 21, at Winchester's office with Mr. Winchester and two other minor investors, showing the remaining being held by Captain Benjamin Spooner Briggs. Afterward, he took a brisk walk to the dock to check on *his* ship. The cabin arrangements had been addressed, and the second deck was close to being finished. That evening, he and Richardson met for a light supper at a hotel to celebrate their new voyage and hopefully the start of many more. "I'm very satisfied with our ship. It's in Bristol fashion," he told Richardson.

While at sea, Richardson was a serious hard-working seaman, but on land, he lost all inhibitions, and it wasn't rare when he went to town with a few sailors on an all-night rampage looking for the delights of female companionship. Benjamin became aware of his friend's lifestyle having not changed when a young woman approached them to acknowledge Richardson's presence and whispered something in his ear, to which he reciprocated. Benjamin had married Sarah for love, and to even think that his best friend did not value the blessing sacrament of matrimony was an unforgivable sin. Benjamin waited for the woman to leave before telling Richardson how he felt.

"Benjamin, my friend, I am not a gal-sneaker by choice. You don't know the details of my marriage. I confess that when I met Fannie, her beauty and charm had me dazzled. I immediately fell in love with her, at least that's what I believed when I asked her hand in marriage. Yes, Benjamin, like you, I long to have a family of my own, and I married her with the idea of settling down. But, within the first month of our marriage, I quickly learned that the idea of becoming a mother was extremely repugnant to her. More concerned with maintaining her figure, she spent her days shopping, and the nights entertaining. Flirting was something she fully enjoyed as if still single. Three months into the marriage, I complained about her spending more time with her admirers than me. "'I love being adored,' she told me while admiring herself in the hand mirror. "Don't you adore me?'" "Anger got the best of me. I grabbed the mirror from her hand and threw it out of the open window in our bedroom. She was nothing but a wealthy, self-indulgent, egotistical girl who believed the world rotated around her. I immediately told her I wanted a divorce. "'The Winchesters don't divorce,' she said. "You go to your whores anytime you want, but remember, as your wife, I'll always be your only one.'" "I asked her why she had accepted my marriage proposal. She mocked me saying I had to be a naive fool to believe I was the only man in her life. She valued her independence, and the more I spent my time away, the more she appreciated our marriage. I began using my influence as a Winchester family member to get any position I wanted in her uncle's company. Being married to Fanny had its benefits, like when I requested to be your first mate on this voyage."

"You should have told me all this a long time ago. I would not have been so judgmental."

"No harm taken, Benjamin. Besides, I have not given up. I'm going to continue searching until I find my soulmate, even if it takes my whole life. You may call me a romantic, but when I find her, believe me, I'll know."

Sunday, October 27, 1872

Sarah and Sophia arrived in fine style on a Fall River Line steamer. But on account of the majority of New York City's horses being sick, Benjamin had to pay the exorbitant price of $5 for a horse-drawn carriage to take them to their hotel. *The New York Times* headline from October 25th read, "The Horse Plague, fifteen thousand horses in the city unfit for use."

The plague, as the news headline called it, was simply a particular strand of equine influenza that sickened nearly all horses exposed, but rarely led to their deaths.

Still, it caused many problems since the city was basically powered by horse-pulling stages and streetcars. Horses were vital for transporting people, raw materials and merchandise, and businesses were struggling with deliveries.

Men were now transporting their goods in handcarts and carriages, and pulling it themselves, like beasts of burden.

Before retiring for the evening, the Briggs enjoyed hot chocolate drinks in their hotel room. Sophia was ecstatic with the beverage and held her sleepy, groggy eyelids half open until she finished the last drop.

New York City was considered the hub of commerce in the New World. With the opening of the Erie Canal in the 1820s, the constant flow of products from the Midwest was causing the Lower East Side warehouses to just about burst at the seams, with merchandise waiting to be shipped to foreign ports and or distributed throughout the country by the new rail lines converging in the area. Ocean-going steamships and steam railroads, developed in earlier decades, took over most long-distance transport, bringing an ever-increasing stream of immigration and industrialization. The *New York Tribune,* the voice of the new Republican Party, boomed with editorials and all the latest news across the nation.

Monday morning, the concierge at the hotel accommodated them once again with a horse-drawn carriage, for half a day at a steep price. All forms of transportation were at a standstill, not only trolley cars, streetcars and horse-cars, but also the omnibus, a large horse-drawn wheeled carriage similar to a stagecoach, which needed at least two horses to pull it. There were a few omnibuses open for service along Broadway, but the unpadded seats caused too much discomfort while going over unpaved roads, and most people opted for walking.

Benjamin took Sarah and Sophia to visit the famous Stewart Dry Goods Store, also known as the Marble Palace, and the Sun Building — one of the nation's first department stores, located between Chambers and Reade Streets in the lower district of Manhattan. A Singer Model 13 Treadle Sewing Machine caught Sarah's eye. Benjamin wanted to have it delivered to the ship, but she said, "Benj, let's be honest, we don't really know how long I'll be using it."

"You may be ailing, my love, but you're alive. And while there's life, there's hope. So, you better get some fabric, right?"

She had packed a small box with needles and different colored threads, but the idea of having a sewing machine onboard to sew anything her heart desired felt like an amazing luxury. She took her time picking fabric and bought enough to make several outfits for Sophia and a skirt for herself. She could not resist buying some white cotton fabric to which she planned to apply the needlepoint she had learned as a young girl from her cousin Maria Matilda. *It will make a lovely tablecloth,* her eyes filled with tears.

Benjamin left them in the hotel room and went to check on his ship and the men. Still daylight, Sarah made plans to take a stroll with Sophia around the block, but when they reached the lobby downstairs, Sophia had a coughing spell and began crying. Experiencing a sudden feeling of exhaustion herself, she opted to going back to their room. When Benjamin returned late that evening, he found them sleeping.

Benjamin was delighted that the next two days, Sarah and Sophia remained in their room, and slept most of the day. *The more they rest, the better chance they have to withstand the long voyage ahead,* he told himself. He made arrangements to have their dinner brought up to their room, and when he returned at the end of the day, they joined him at the restaurant downstairs, but they barely touched their supper. Finally, he made what he felt would be an irresistible proposition: if they ate half the food on their plates, a hot chocolate drink would be the prize at the end of their meal. It worked great with Sophia. Sarah ate just to please him.

For Sophia's birthday on Thursday, they paid once again an *extra* fee to the concierge at the hotel, for a horse-drawn carriage, to take them to the Metropolitan Art Museum, a four-story building at 681 Fifth Avenue.

The museum had opened its doors to the public in February and in May, three months later, reported that over 6,000 visitors had viewed its opening exhibition. Its holdings were a Roman stone sarcophagus and 174 of mostly European paintings by Old Masters. Sophia fell asleep in her father's arms within 10 minutes of arriving at the museum. She awoke bright and cheery 45 minutes later at an ice cream shop where the family tasted ice cream soda for the first time. It was their favorite flavor, chocolate.

When they returned to the hotel, they surprised Sophia with the cloth ragdoll Grandma Briggs had made and a cloth book with the alphabet letters that Grandma Selina had been painstaking stitching for almost a year. Benjamin and Sarah sang to her, "Happy Birthday," "Farmer in the Dell," and "Pop Goes the Weasel."

Later that evening, Benjamin and Sarah laid in bed, her head resting on his shoulder, their arms and legs intertwined. "Will you tell me a story?" she said.

"A story?"

"Yes, like when we were very young. Remember how sometimes we would sit under the red oak tree, next to *our* pond and you would make up a story about some distant and wondrous land we had discovered together."

"You had a favorite one, if I well remember ..."

CHAPTER XIV

**_Mary Celeste's_ seasoned mariners. - Gottlieb Gottschalk goes
missing. - Captain Morehouse to the rescue. -
Helmut Rothe, a more mature fellow. - All aboard. -
Old Charlie. - Carla Maria Nunes da Silva and son Mauricio. -
Slight delay, extra time to write home.**

Friday, November 1, Gottlieb Gottschalk did not show up for the
customary morning call. No one had seen him since the evening
before, when he had gone a-land and waved back saying, "Ahoy,
Mr. Richardson, I have a letter to mail to my wife, I'll be right
back." That was the last time anyone saw him.

Gottlieb had been sailing with Benjamin for eight years and
had always shown to be a conscientious and dependable sailor. If
he couldn't return to the ship in a timely manner, he would have
sent a message of his whereabouts. Benjamin checked Gottlieb's
cabin and found the sailor's belongings were still there and decided
to remain aboard and wait until nightfall.

His men were all seasoned mariners. Second mate Andrew
Gillings, a 25-year-old New Yorker with nine years of sailing for
Mr. Winchester had come highly recommended. He carried a rigid
bearing, accented by impeccable starched clothes, dark bushy

eyebrows and piercing black eyes that matched the upward waxed mustache he groomed daily. His mother had died when he was 3 years old, and he could hardly remember her or recall ever meeting his father. Brought up by an aunt in Chicago, he moved out at 16 and went to New York City looking for work as a mariner. Mr. Winchester took a liking to the young lad and put him under his wing. Andrew went to sea as a midshipman, and rose quickly through the ranks. The sea was his one and only mistress.

Edward Head, better known as Old Charlie, had been born in Brooklyn, New York. The oldest son of Dutch parents, he was 10 years old when his father succumbed to typhoid. Even though his mother worked as a seamstress in a coat factory, it wasn't enough to feed the family anymore. Faced with the financial task of helping his mother and his three younger sisters, he quit school and took a job delivering goods for a grocery store. A year later, his mother died from a heart attack while sewing a coat where she worked. For the following three years, he did janitorial work for several companies, and then looking for a better hourly pay, he found a position as a dock worker, which lasted the next 15 years. His siblings never went hungry. When it came to a homemade meal, he had a natural instinct for mixing the right ingredients. Every night he sang for them, his tenor voice bringing out the best melodies of the times. He sang, but only to his family, with no desire to pursue it as a career. His two main wishes in life were to be a cook on a ship and see the world. At 39, his sisters were by then married. Mary Jane, his younger sister, who had moved with her husband to Boston, wrote to him about the merchant ships off the coast of Massachusetts. He left New York to pursue his dream. Mary Jane, her husband Bill, and their new offspring lived in a small apartment. After a week of babysitting his 6-month-old nephew, he decided to move to Marion where he'd heard there was a better opportunity for getting a cook's job on a ship, without much experience. He found a room for rent at Mrs. Lloyd's home, who told him the ideal place to find the kind of employment position he looked for, would be at Handy's Tavern on 152 Front Street. Built in 1812, it was a popular gathering place for mariners and captains. But he did not drink, and found himself alone in a corner eating deep fried fish and potatoes, the only grub they served at the tavern. He watched seamen come and go, drinking beer and grog, a mixture of water and rum, and exchanging loud sea stories with their buddies. He was about to give up, but one evening, while walking back to Mrs. Lloyd's place, he noticed the lit candles inside the Congregational Church of Sippican on Main Street. Being that it was one of those exceptionally cold bitter evenings, and a long walk back, he decided to go in. Captain Benjamin Briggs stood at the podium giving a testimony of faith, and afterward, he made an announcement, "My ship's cook has come down with a fever and is not doing well. I'm leaving for Florence next month, and I'm looking for a man with cooking experience to take that position on my ship, the *Forest King.*"

"Thank you, Lord," Charlie made the cross and walked up to Benjamin. In the years to follow, when Captain Briggs sailed, so did Charlie, who proved to be not only a great cook but also earned the respect and friendship of his fellow mates. He quickly became everybody's father and counselor.

Boz Lorenzen was 23 years old, six years younger than his brother Volkert, but they looked a lot alike, even their voices, tinted by the same German accent, made it difficult to distinguish one from the other. One might even be fooled to think they were twins, but Boz had green eyes and Volkert's were brown. Boz's deep-set eyes appeared dull until he spoke about his plants, then they lit up and his voice developed a melodious tone. He always brought onboard potted plants, either herbs or some native plant he found at port. This time, he carried a Wardian Case, a portable mini-greenhouse, which had been invented in the polluted dockland area of East London by Dr. Nathaniel Bagshaw Ward. Inside the glass vitrine were two purple orchids. No one asked him where he had acquired the tropical plant, of all places in New York

City.

Volkert smiled a lot, exuding a joyous energy that touched everyone he spoke to, but once alone, his mask came down to show a very melancholic young man. He wrote poetry in his native language for security reasons, and kept it hidden inside his coat. It addressed the end of the world, death and the effect of diseases that took away everyone he knew, including his family. Once night fell and there was no one around, he tore the papers into small pieces and threw them overboard. After going through this nightly ritual of tearing away his thoughts and stabbing his words with a pencil, as he would have described it if he could, he felt a lot better.

The Lorenzen brothers were known for traveling light. They shared one sea chest for all their belongings. And neither spent much of their earnings. Boz's goal was to start his dream nursery where he planned to grow rare plants and then export them. Volkert did it with the intention of leaving it all to his brother. Even though he was younger than Boz, he was sure that he would be the first to die, since he knew he carried several maladies not even found in medical books.

Arian Martens was 35 years old and had also been born in Germany, but at the age of 10, the family immigrated to the U.S. and settled on Long Island, New York. The youngest of seven boys and two sisters, he was the shortest member of his family. His own family members despised him and called him a midget. His mother never protected him from the beatings he received from his father, who made it clear to him that he should have never been born. He was 14 years old when he read "Gulliver's Travels" by Jonathan Swift and realized then, that he had a lot in common with Gulliver. He read the book over and over again, and agreed its genre as prose satire or fantasy, being truthfully labeled, but not Part II: "A Voyage to Brobdingnag". In his opinion, Part II should've been classified as nonfiction, a real tragedy like his own life. He had been born in a world of giants, and Gulliver was his blood brother, one of the main reasons he decided, like him, to go to sea. He walked tall, with shoulders back and chest out. But his height of barely four feet, round body and face, and reddish grizzly beard, caused the crew to think of him as their lucky leprechaun, which had been confirmed as true. With every voyage with him onboard, they never encountered any misfortunes. His fellow mates fully appreciated him and never mocked or made him feel undesired like his family had done.

Tony Esposito and Luciano Marquez, both in their early 20s, had been recommended by Mr. Winchester. They had been working for him for five years and Mr. Winchester described them as well-tempered sailors from good Christian families.

Once night came, Benjamin made the cross over his chest and took hold of the kerosene lamp hanging on the wall, before leaving his cabin. The lamp helped light his pathway at the pier, but he also valued the full moonlight. Before heading to his hotel, he intended to stop at the police precinct — perhaps they could investigate into Gottlieb's whereabouts. He turned around when he heard Captain David Morehouse call his name. He and John Wright, his second mate, were also leaving the pier and walking in his direction.

Captain Morehouse's ship, the *Dei Gratia,* was docked not far from the *Mary Celeste.* A decade newer and slightly larger, to an amateur, the ships looked the same except for the British flag flying from *Dei Gratia's* mainstay. In the past, both captains had exchanged a few civilized words as they crossed paths at different ports but, except for their profession as seafaring merchants, they lacked anything in common. Maybe the good Lord had brought Captain Morehouse his way. Maybe he knew of a sailor who could take the place of Gottlieb at such short notice. Captain Morehouse responded by inviting him to supper at a tavern close by.

"Great food there, nice size steaks," he made a gesture with both hands to enhance their size. "Ye'll be my guest tonight. Come, let's liquor up," he patted Benjamin on the back, who instinctively backed away. "I don't drink and I don't eat this late in the evening either, but I'll join you."

The tavern had lots of strategically lit candles, but the low black ceilings and walls covered with large dark wood barrels of wine stacked up high, gave the impression of a musty dark cave. It was the perfect hangout for noisy drunken sailors chewing tobacco with a rowdy attitude, and where they could let go of their rigid hard-working days at sea and eat large portions of food being served at all hours.

Captain Morehouse's appetite was in proportion to the magnitude of his frame, an imposing figure along with noticeably loud speaking manners. At least one foot taller than Benjamin, he wore his tousled dark brown hair at shoulder length, which contrasted sharply with the darker reddish beard reaching all the way to the third front button of his coat jacket. John Wright, a thin but also tall fellow possessed a comical look, accented by his outdated brown wig slipping sideways possibly due to his bald round skull.

"I completely understand yer frustration," Captain Morehouse took a large piece of the meat into his mouth. "Having to leave so soon, while missing one crew member can be most stressing," he chewed with his mouth open, and as he spoke, it caused some of the food to spit out. "But ye're in luck, my friend. I have just the right person for ye. He lives here in New York, has many years o' experience and is quite trustworthy. I would have hired him myself, but the *Dei Gratia* already has a full crew."

"What's his name?"

"Helmut Rothe, ye should know him. He sailed once with ye. And from what he told me, he thinks ye'r the best."

"I do remember him, about five years ago ... A bit of a troublemaker, and if there was a fight, he started it."

"Five years ago?" Captain Morehouse interrupted him. "Oh, ye'r too harsh on the old chap. Five years is a long time. He's a lot more mature now, ye can count on that. And besides," he wiped his mouth and beard with his stained napkin. "He's the only one I know that's available to leave at such short notice."

"Very well then, I'll take your word that he has become more levelheaded. And when is the *Dei Gratia* leaving?"

"That's yet to be determined. But tell me about yer family. How are they?" he lit a cigar. "Hand rolled in Cuba, one o' the benefits of my world voyages. Would ye like one?"

"Thanks, but I don't smoke."

"John here doesn't like them either. Ye get nauseated, don't ye?" he puffed a mouthful into his face.

John coughed and went pale then stood holding his hands over his stomach. "I'll be back in a minute," he disappeared among the other patrons, most likely out the front door.

"My wife and daughter are in serious peril. They suffer from consumption," Benjamin let out a sigh. "The reason I'm taking them with me."

"If they're sick, isn't that a long voyage in such a small ship?"

"The *Mary Celeste* has been modified to create more space onboard, and I also introduced some modifications to their accommodations, so I'm not worried about the size of our vessel," he paused and took on a somber look. "I only know that I must do everything I can to get them to France as soon as I'm done delivering my shipment to Genoa. The doctor in France who is expecting us has had a lot of success with consumption cases. It's a long trip for them to go through, but I was told the ocean air is very helpful for healing lung sicknesses." He stood. "I must go now," he stretched his hand out to Captain Morehouse. "Having someone to take Gottlieb's place makes me feel a lot better. Thank you."

"I'm always glad to help, but I must ask ye a favor in return," he didn't let go of the handshake.

"Absolutely," Benjamin reassured him with a stronger hold, and then pulled his hand away.

"I happen to know a Portuguese woman, a poor widow who cannot afford to pay the passage across the Atlantic. Come to think o' it, now that ye told me of yer family, she can be a real asset to ye. She's a nurse with years o' experience and will be able to assist yer family. Isn't that wonderful? I'll get hold of her in the morning and give her the news. By the way, her 8-year-old son will be accompanying her." Not waiting for a response, he stood and looked around annoyed, "Where is that good-for-nothing?"

When Benjamin got to the hotel room, he decided not to wake Sarah, and instead wait until the morning to give her the day's news.

Benjamin found Helmut standing at the pier by the *Mary Celeste* with a sailor's knapsack over his shoulder. He seemed older, possibly because he had gained some weight and grown a mustache and beard. "Good to see ye again, Cap'n Briggs," his words rang with joy, "Thank ye, Cap'n, for allowing me to be part of yer crew once again. I'll do my very best not to disappoint ye."

"I'm glad you could make it, Mr. Rothe," he shook his hand. "Thank you for taking on the position at such short notice."

Onboard, they were greeted by Richardson and Andrew, and the rest of the crew stood across from them. Benjamin used the moment to introduce Helmut, "As you know, Mr. Gottschalk is nowhere to be found, and it's imperative that we leave for Genoa according to our schedule. Mr. Helmut Rothe is taking his place," noticing Richardson and Charlie's exchanged looks, he added, "Mr. Rothe did sail with us once, as some of you recall. But I would like to ask you to let bygones be bygones and to treat him with the same respect you treat your other mates. I don't want to sound like a preacher, but I believe all men can mend their ways. Monday, my family will join us, and then we'll leave as planned. Any issues or questions you encounter, I encourage you to speak to Mr. Richardson or Mr. Gillings since they're the best for finding solutions of any kind. Still, if for any reason you need to speak to me, you know I'm always available."

"Any news about Mr. Gottschalk?" Richardson asked.

"The police are aware of his disappearance," Benjamin's voice vacillated. "For those of you who knew him and are concerned about him like I am, let's make a silent prayer to our Good Lord, Jesus."

The men remained in place and lowered their heads. About one minute passed. "Amen," Benjamin said. And he left for his cabin.

After attending the next morning's services at Trinity Church with his wife and daughter, Benjamin wrote to his mother about their upcoming departure and finished by adding, "Our vessel is in beautiful trim, and I hope we shall have a fine passage."

Early that afternoon, Detective Marlon Wakerish came onboard after requesting to see the captain. It seemed that the man missing as described by Captain Briggs had been found that morning. Detective Wakerish needed him to come to the "deadhouse" immediately and confirm whether it was Gottlieb.

Before retiring for the night at the hotel, Benjamin wrote a letter of condolence to Gottlieb's wife. Her husband had drowned in the Hudson River. He felt Gottlieb's wife and three children should be compensated for his faithful years of service and took the sum of a full year's wage out of his own savings. He knew Sarah would most likely understand his gesture, but he didn't feel particularly auspicious about telling her that Gottlieb had been hit over the head with a sharp object and then strangulated before being thrown into the river.

Detective Wakerish had no clue as to who could have done it and why the crime had been committed but would continue to investigate, and if he found any further details concerning the crime before the *Mary Celeste*'s scheduled departure, he promised to let him know.

Promptly at 10 a.m., Benjamin was at the New York Office of the United States Shipping Commissioner and signed the "Articles of

Agreement," and the "List of Persons Composing the Crew." An Atlantic Mutual underwriter initialed the insurance for J.H. Winchester & Co. for $3,400 on the vessel's freight on charter from New York to Genoa, at the rate of 2 ½%.

While he was away, Sarah wrote two letters home: one addressed to both Selina and Mother Briggs. She thanked them for taking care of Arthur and went on with a chatty note about how the women in New York City wore their hair high up with complicated twists and rolls, while others allowed their hair to fall to the shoulders and adorned it with ribbons, bands and decorative combs. "They wear very small hats, tilted forward to the forehead," she wrote. "It makes me wonder, why wear a hat at all, if it doesn't help to keep your hair in place. Meanwhile, we are experiencing a gay time in New York City, and last Sunday, we attended part of the services at Trinity Church, where President Washington and members of his government worshipped long ago. The church is across the Old City Hall on Wall Street, and its 281-foot-high steeple makes it the tallest building in New York City," she described in awe. "You would not believe how big this city has become since the last time Benj and I were here." She finished by adding, "Sophie enjoyed her birthday and loved your thoughtful gifts very much. I miss you both very dearly and can't wait to see you again. Farewell, Your Sarah."

The other letter went to Arthur, asking him to behave, study his lessons and always listen to his uncle and his grandmas, especially Mother Briggs, with whom he lived. She also reminded him not to be afraid of the dark, "... I think if you remember that verse in your 'First Reader' beginning 'I will not fear,' you will not be afraid to go after milk if it is dark. Remember that your father and I love you very much and very soon we will be together again."

Being with Benjamin had always been something she treasured, and if it wasn't for Sophia's failing health and her own, life couldn't be better. She consoled herself with the thought that as a loving mother, she had been right to leave him home to focus on his schooling.

When Benjamin returned to the hotel, he found Sarah already seated in the lobby's round settee with Sophia sleeping on her lap.

A horse-drawn carriage awaited outside the hotel. Two bellboys carried out the trunks and Sophia's small box of toys.

They found Charlie and Richardson standing by the *Mary Celeste's* railing waiting for them, and when Charlie caught eye of Captain Briggs and his family getting out of the carriage, he ran down the gangway, calling out to Sophia. She had only seen Charlie once, but she opened her arms to hug him.

"Uncle Charlie is going to make chicken soup just for you, how about that?" he lifted her up as she giggled and carried her up the gangway. Sarah looked up admiring the majestic ship before her, but she did not let go of her dark mahogany medicine box, which she held tight with both hands against her chest.

Benjamin reached for the box. "I'll have that, my dear," he held it by its large brass handle. "Just hold on to my arm until we get onboard." When they reached the top of the gangway, she was out of breath and coughing. Richardson greeted them, and then added quickly, "Mrs. Briggs, may I bring you a chair?"

"Richardson, you don't have to be so formal with me," trying not to take big breaths that would cause her to further cough, she added softly, "Yes, a chair would be nice, thank you."

Having a captain's family onboard had become such an ordinary component with seagoing commerce that the sailors had a name for ships with a wife and children in the aft cabin: "hen frigates."

Sarah sat and watched her belongings being carried up the gangway, which coincided miraculously with the department store delivering her new sewing machine. Sophia stood next to her mother sucking her thumb and when she recognized her toy box being brought up by a sailor, she clapped her hands. With their most prized possessions onboard, Sarah decided it was time to retire to their cabin.

Benjamin had not overstated about her accommodations being spacious. She surveyed its furnishings with pleasure. A tiny brown basket with a bouquet of fresh violets on the side table caught her attention. She found a handwritten note lying next to it. "Forever yours, Benj." She held the note to her chest and smiled. In the corner of the room stood her beloved melodeon and next to it, her new prized possession, the sewing machine. Sophia sat on the floor next to her toy box, and took out one item at a time, analyzing it carefully and then throwing it over her shoulders. Sarah sat on the red velvet arm chair and opened the medicine box. A cold chill ran down her spine when she reached inside and took hold of one of the two large tincture bottles wrapped in brown burlap, sealed with red wax and marked, "Caution, Poison!" Benjamin had been instructed by Dr. Williams on how to use it if either she or his daughter needed to be alleviated from their suffering, when the final hour arrived. She stood and placed both vials, way in the back of the top shelf of the wall cupboard. Then put the medicine bottles of Vin Mariani and laudanum up front, within easier reach. Vin Mariani was to be drunk rapidly for better effect against fatigue when getting up in the morning and in the evening. Laudanum, a tincture of opium for pain relief, worked as a cough suppressant. She used the tiny hanging key on the shelf to lock the cupboard glass door.

Sophia had found what she had been looking for, a pink ribbon. She held it against her nose, and sniffed it, like a puppy would.

In his cabin, Benjamin was going over some charts when he heard two quick knocks on his door.

"Excuse me, Cap'n Briggs," Helmut took one step into the cabin. "Cap'n Morehouse asked me to tell ye Mrs. Carla Maria Nunes da Silva is coming onboard tomorrow morning and is ready to take on the position of caring for yer wife and daughter. I would like to put in a kind word for the good woman, since she worked for two well-known families in New York City as a nanny and as a nurse to an elderly lady. They were all very pleased with her services. I believe yer family will appreciate her kind and caring nature, and her son, who I had the chance to meet a few times, is a very quiet and well-mannered child."

Benjamin could not be happier with Helmut's introduction, but he had not counted on having one more passenger onboard even if one of them was only 8 years old. *God will provide,* he reminded himself.

Possessing a natural ability for wheeling and dealing, it had taken Charlie two weeks to get all the supplies needed onboard the *Mary Celeste* since quality and keeping the cost down was imperative to him. That afternoon Charlie finished overseeing the final loading of provisions. They had enough food and water supplies onboard to last six months. The water in wooden casks was stowed in the coolness of the hold.

Benjamin had confided in him about his family being in serious need to see a doctor in France after delivering their cargo to Genoa. Not knowing how long they might have to be docked in France, he preferred to be prepared for the worst and intended to make full use of *his* icebox onboard.

Until the mid-18th century, ice had only been transported on ships to be used occasionally as ballast, usually in the bilge, (the lowest part of a ship where the bottom curves up to meet the sides), to help with stability. But by 1869, ships began using ice for shipping purposes like beef carcasses from Indiana and Texas, to New Orleans, Louisiana, and to be served in hospitals, hotels and restaurants. This gave Charlie the idea of creating his own personal icebox onboard. He used a salt-ice mixture for keeping meat frozen but added straw for insulating the box. Knowing how well it had worked on their last voyage to Europe and back, he encouraged Benjamin to have an icebox built in the *Mary Celeste*, below the galley and as such, within his easy reach. The icebox was built with a partition in the middle. One side for frozen food — the other to keep perishables cold but not frozen, like fresh fruit, vegetables, dairy products and pickled eggs.

Charlie had been a blessing since the day he started working for Captain Briggs some 10 years prior. As a cook he wasn't only meticulous with cleanliness but also took pride in serving balanced meals. Ship Fever — a generic term for dysentery, typhoid and cholera — ran unrestrained onboard other ships where overcrowding and unhygienic conditions existed. The diet served to sailors on those ships usually consisted of heavily salted, low-quality meat stored in wood barrels for who knew how long, which the sailors called *bow wow mutton* because of its close resemblance to dog food, and biscuits made of whole meal flour, salt and water that lacked any nutritional value. While working on the docks of New York City, Charlie had the opportunity to see what happened to many young healthy men, that upon being at sea just a few months returned with swollen purple legs marred with bruises, barely able to walk, and the loss of teeth and bleeding swollen gums, made it hard to eat. It was then that Charlie came across a book by James Lind, a Scottish doctor, who in 1747 was of the opinion that such debilitating illness could be prevented through the consumption of citrus fruits and fresh vegetables. Captain James Cook, a British explorer and navigator, had come to the same conclusion and made sure his men had a daily portion of fruit intake. Dr. Lind and Captain Cook had no idea what was the protective substance and neither did Charlie. All they knew was that it worked.

Having Captain Briggs' backing gave him the freedom to purchase a wide range of provisions, such as lard, bacon, salt-cured pork, honey, raisins, vinegar, olive oil, "sour crout," sugar, molasses and suet (great for making puddings, pastry and mincemeat), dried beans, rice, potatoes and onions, corn meal, bran & shorts, rye flour, wheat flour, cornmeal and spices. Besides frozen beef, and pork, he also stored pemmican, a paste of dried and pounded meat mixed with melted fat. He personally packed the flour in well-sewn stout double canvas sacks of 50 pounds. And because coffee beans were sensitive to moisture and could easily rot, he also wrapped them, (about 5 pounds each) in natural fiber to allow for circulation, and stored it tightly inside recycled metal cans. He used the same process for keeping tea leaves fresh. He'd learned from Sifu Wen Kwok, a Cantonese cook and self-made doctor he befriended in New York City, that certain spices for cooking had their own medicinal purpose. As such, he always had in stock extra garlic to help with memory issues and when mixed with ginger and served as a tea, it helped with colds. Thyme was great for coughs, congestion and colds, cinnamon bark helped with nausea and digestive problems, and cloves worked well as an antiseptic and also as a digestive aid.

He loved the usefulness of condensed milk invented by Gail Borden in 1856, which became well known for its practicality during the American Civil War, since it didn't need refrigeration. Great in coffee and to make all kinds of desserts, Charlie figured on using two dozen cans of condensed milk during their voyage. Desiccated vegetables were another important item in his list of necessities, and whenever they docked long enough, he got busy cutting all sorts of fresh vegetables into thin slices, subject them to a powerful press to remove all the juice, and then dried them in an oven. The result was a piece of hard dough almost as hard as a rock. A small piece of it, about half the size of a man's hand, when boiled, swelled up big enough to fill a vegetable dish and was sufficient for three men. If he didn't have enough time to desiccate the vegetables, or ran out of fresh produce during a long sea voyage, he settled for using canned vegetables. He preferred cans, versus glass jars, which at that time came with a handy screw-on zinc cap or with sealing wax, but his philosophy was that metal cans, much like a cat had nine lives, even if they rolled on deck and caused you to trip over them, were a lot safer than broken glass, which made a bloody mess while walking barefoot on deck, as most sailors did.

Eight live chickens came along as part of the provisions, not for their eggs, since it was late in the year and the hens most likely would not be laying anymore. He intended to keep the birds away from Sophia so she wouldn't develop an emotional connection with them like what had happened to his younger sister who, after learning that Minnie, *her* chick, had been butchered for Christmas, became a vegetarian. All fresh produce was scheduled to be delivered to the ship the next morning before departure.

It had rained on and off through the night, and the morning's menacing dark skies seemed to be ready to downpour once again when a two-horse carriage approached the pier and a woman dressed in black, a sign of being a recent widow, and a young boy in long worn-out pants and cropped waist-length jacket were left by the *Mary Celeste*'s gangway. She held a large worn-out brown leather bag with one hand while using the other hand to keep in place a tiny black hat on her head. Her long wavy black hair had come loose from under it, and the wind caused its strands to whip her face harshly. The boy's curly, reddish blond hair also flopped in all directions after his cap flew away. He stood quivering next to her, holding with both hands a smaller bag held together by two leather straps around it.

Helmut caught sight of them and motioned to come aboard. Once on deck, he took them to the main hatch where Richardson was busy in the hold, making sure the barrels of alcohol were properly tied. Helmut cupped his hand over his mouth and shouted down, "Eh, Mr. Richardson, the lady Captain Briggs is waiting for is here."

Richardson came up the ladder diligently but stopped on the last step, not able to hide the effect the young woman made on him. His blue eyes sparkled and she instinctively lowered her gaze.

"Mr. Richardson," Helmut said. "I have a lot of experience

when it comes to storing goods. I can easily take over the barrels."

"Humm …Yes, you go ahead and do that. I'll be back as soon as I can to help batten down the hatch," then to the woman, "Captain Briggs is expecting you, please follow me." He picked up their luggage.

Helmut made a little salute with his right hand and watched them walk away. Once they were out of sight, he walked at a fast speed to meet two sailors bringing onboard a few more barrels.

Benjamin expected a matronly woman and was taken by surprise with her youthful appearance. He stood from his chair and walked up to her. She extended her hand to him, "My name is Carla Maria Nunes da Silva."

"Welcome aboard the *Mary Celeste*. My wife will be most pleased to know that she has a companion close to her age."

"You're very kind to offer me this opportunity …"

"I am quite overjoyed to know that my family will be in the hands of a qualified nurse. Indeed, I could not ask for better fortune," then he turned his attention to his first mate.

"Mr. Richardson," he waited for his attention. "Mr. Richardson, would you mind …"

"Captain …" he said, sidetracked.

He couldn't help smiling at Richardson's enamored look. "Would you mind, bringing my wife and daughter to meet this lovely lady and her son?"

He left and Benjamin resumed his place behind his desk. "What's your name, son?" he asked the boy.

"Captain, sir …" he stood at attention. "Mauricio, sir …" he brushed the hair away from his face. His large, beautiful green eyes gazed in awe around the room then focused on the captain's well-organized desk.

Benjamin opened the top side drawer and handed him a small magnifying glass.

"Here. Take a look through it."

Mauricio brought the magnifying glass to his face, and then

used it to look closer at the palm of his left hand. "Wow, golly gee," he said.

"You can keep it. I have another one."

"Thank you …" he looked at his mother for approval. Just then, Sarah entered the cabin with Sophia.

Carla made a gracious bow. "Mrs. Briggs, it's so nice to meet you. I'm going to do everything I can to make your voyage most comfortable," she smiled.

The smile on her lips does not match the sad expression of her dark eyes, thought Richardson, who suddenly felt an intense desire to hold her in his arms and tell her that he would always be there to protect her.

"It's nice to meet you too," Sarah let go of her daughter's hand. "This is Sophie. Go ahead, say hello to our new friends." But Sophia hid behind her mother's skirt and refused to let go. "This is my son, Mauricio," Carla said.

He turned toward Sophia and imitated his mother's courtesy but tripped over one leg and had to balance himself not to fall. Sophia let go of her mother's skirt to clap her hands then took a few steps forward and pointed to Mauricio's magnifying glass.

"I have to be honest, there's a bit of an issue concerning the accommodations," Benjamin said. "There's only two berths in my wife's cabin."

"Like me, Mauricio is used to sleeping on the floor," Carla put an arm over her son's shoulders. "But if you can spare a blanket..."

"My goodness, we have enough covers to share with you and there's no reason to sleep on the floor," Sarah said. "There's plenty of space in my cabin. Sophia likes to sleep with me, so we only need a hammock for your boy."

Sophia, who had taken a liking to Mauricio, stood next to him, analyzing him. He brought the magnifying glass to his face and set it against his right eye.

"Spider, me like spider," she clapped enthusiastically.

"Come, Carla," Sarah said. "Let me show you our

accommodations," she took hold of Carla's arm as the children followed them, and so did Richardson with the luggage.

"I'm so happy," Sarah went on. "It will be nice to have a female friend to talk to, and the children seem to have already taken a liking to each other. You can't imagine how that makes me feel. Also," she lowered her voice, "having someone to watch over Sophie at night will give me the opportunity to spend, once in a while, a night with my husband in his cabin."

Carla couldn't help giggling along with Sarah.

"Why wait," she said. "Please be with him tonight and any other night you like. My job is to make your life a little more pleasant."

Richardson left and went back to check on Helmut.

"All stowed safe and secure, Mr. Richardson," Helmut stood at attention. "I placed four plank sections over the hatchway, and they're flushed tight with the top of the coaming, as ye can see."

"Great job, Helmut. You're a fast worker, I'm very impressed. I'll give you a hand with the tarpaulins."

They added three pieces of tarpaulins over the hatch cover and attached them to the wedges of the coaming battens. Then they inspected the corners several times, since they couldn't afford to have the tarpaulins ripped off by heavy seas. If that happened, the wooden covers could become dislodged and water could pour into the hold. Instead of having the ship's 18-foot yawl carried across the stern to the davits, they opted for placing it on top of the main hatch and lashed it down.

"Nice and tight," Helmut said. "I dare the devil himself to try and open it."

Benjamin called on his two mates for a meeting in his cabin. "As you know, we were to leave today as scheduled, but I find wind ahead, and I would prefer to start with smooth sailing." They agreed to navigate to Staten Island, the southernmost part of New York and wait there for the weather to improve.

It wasn't until they anchored that Benjamin realized he had missed the chance to say goodbye to his brother Oliver who, as the Captain of the *Julia A. Hallock,* had arrived at the New York harbor just an hour after *Mary Celeste*'s departure.

Sarah awoke early the next morning to find Benjamin still next to her. "Have you been watching me sleep?" she rubbed her eyes with both hands and smiled.

"With each day, you look more and more beautiful," he moved a few curls away from her forehead. "Do you know that when you sleep, you smile? Just a tiny sweet smile on your lips," and he kissed them softly.

She drew herself closer to him, "I don't know how much longer Sophia and I have left, but no matter how long, I consider each minute that we spend together on this ship with you, the most precious time of my life."

"My very thoughts. But I have faith that God will take us safely across the sea and in time for you and Sophia to get the help you need." They laid still with their arms around each other, savoring each second that passed, her head on his chest listening to his heartbeat as he prayed silently for her life.

The morning had come once again with heavily threatening gray skies, and the swells of a leftover storm still active. Benjamin and his two mates agreed once again to wait another day for better weather conditions. When it came to facing violent storms at sea, the level of experience Benjamin had gained from working with his father for so many years, and then on his own had made him a cautious and capable captain.

Sarah took advantage of the delay to write to Mother Briggs. "Tell Arthur I take great dependence on the letters I shall get from him, and will try to remember anything that happens on the voyage that he would be pleased to hear."

PART II

At Sea

Thursday, November 7, 1872

An exuberant feeling came over everyone onboard the *Mary Celeste* as she slowly headed out of the Staten Island Harbor. The chanting of "Oh, Riley, Oh," along with the whistling accompaniment from those that did not sing, could only be compared to a boisterous orchestra's grand finale. One by one the sails unfurled, high up toward the skies fore and aft followed by an uproarious shout among the men with each sail successfully secured. Captain Briggs and his two mates stood on deck watching.

"All-a-Taut for putting to sea," Richardson remarked nodding his head. "These cotton canvases are so much better for sailing!"

"Aye, aye Mr. Richardson," Andrew said. "They're flatter and less porous, a lot more efficient than the old hemp canvas material used by our British competitors."

"Mr. Winchester is a good business man," Benjamin said. "By setting us up with the best, we'll make the delivery of our goods in great time. And after a few days in France to take care of my family, we'll speed right back." He felt overjoyed by the vision his words brought to him.

When it came to being responsible for bringing suitable clothing and other items deemed necessary for being at sea, the crew and sailors on the *Mary Celeste* were no different from those on other ships. Some only had what they wore, and some even made their own clothing, but most of the men onboard the *Mary Celeste* came prepared with their own apparel to face stormy weather, like a hat and a rain cape of canvas duck, made waterproof with a thin layer of tar, or coated with multiple applications of linseed oil and paint. They also brought oil clothes, Guernsey jumpers and sweaters made of tightly knitted wool.

Most sailors wore baggy pants known as galligaskins and made of denim and they were done up by using a buttoned panel or font-fall fly.

Their clothing inventory, even if simple, had at least three black handkerchiefs, a muffler (wool scarf), undergarments such as drawers, singlets, body flannels (full body underwear) and stockings — usually two pairs, knitted wool and sewn cotton. Sailors only wore stockings when they wore shoes, usually on shore or in cold/severe weather. Like in most ships, every member of the crew owned some sort of footwear, but very few owned more than one pair of shoes. Only the captain and his mates owned more than one pair. India rubber boots would have been useful for keeping feet dry except that it wasn't the wisest choice considering how slippery the deck could become during cold winter conditions. Pants were made from a variety of fabrics, duck, flannel and wool.Shirts, much like pants, were usually made of flannel or wool. White shirts were far from practical, and the captain and his mates were more inclined to use them since they were expensive and had to be cleaned more frequently. Collars were also difficult to keep clean and were often purchased separately from the shirt. A collar-less shirt was called a Crimean shirt in the sailor's inventory. The captain and his mates wore a three-piece suit with a waistcoat over the white shirt and braces of leather or cloth straps attached to buttons sewn on the inside of their high-waisted pants.

The braces (suspenders) kept up the pants and went over the shirt and under the waistcoat.

All sailors had one dressing code in common — they all wore a wide brim hat or cap. Besides their clothing, sailors also brought their own blanket (usually two), a pillow, and to the utmost surprise of many non-seafaring folks, books. Sailors loved reading. Being at sea for over 20 years, Benjamin was aware of its importance and made sure to always have a book bin well stocked in the galley, so that his men could borrow books at freewill. His collection included a copy of King James Bible, travel accounts, nautical books, and adventure novels with good representation of authors such as Hester Blum, Jane Austen and Alexander Dumas. There were also a few books in French, German, and Spanish from sailors that brought them from their homeland and once done reading, sometimes left them behind. Avid readers during their quiet time, they willingly traded books with each other, except Old Charlie. He owned one book, The Virginia House-Wife, kept under his pillow along with a large stack of handwritten recipes he had collected through the years. He was in love with Mrs. Mary Randolph, the author of The Virginia House-Wife.   First published in 1824, to the delight of all her readers, it had been republished at least 19 times before the outbreak of the Civil War. It boasted 40 vegetable recipes, and the use of 17 aromatic herbs. It also included the first ice cream recipe published by an American author. Mary's recipes were influenced by African, Native American and European foods, with Southern classics such as okra, sweet potatoes, biscuits, fried chicken, barbecue shot (young pig), and the European influenced recipes for gazpacho, ropa vieja, polenta and macaroni. Six curry recipes were included — the first curry recipes ever published in the U.S. Specialties from other parts of the U.S. included a recipe titled "Dough Nuts - A Yankee Cake." In addition to its 500 recipes, The Virginia House-Wife was also a household guide on how to make soap, starch, blacking (black polish), and cologne.

For the first dinner onboard, Charlie made enough pigeon pies to feed the passengers and crew with double portions. For dessert, he served Wyeth's English plum pudding, a recipe he had acquired from a manuscript book by Virginia Randolph Trist. He had no issues with using the required cup of brandy as recommended in the recipe even though he knew no alcohol was allowed on the ship. He had reasoned long ago that cooking with alcohol had nothing to do with drinking it, and no cook with any self-respect would disregard an ingredient stipulated in a recipe. He kept the wine and brandy inside a locked cabinet over his berth. One bottle was labeled as white vinegar, the other as apple vinegar.

Friday, November 8

The next day at sea was quite pleasant as the weather remained in their favor. The skies of light blue displayed a few wispy clouds as if Mother Nature had been running her fingers through to create just for them a lovely canopy.

Once across the vast Atlantic Ocean, they would pass the Azores Islands, their high peaks a familiar landmark to Benjamin as well as to all other captains with Mediterranean-bound vessels.

Sarah was enthralled by her companion's life story. Carla had been born on the island of Faial, part of the Portuguese archipelago islands of Azores. The youngest sister to seven brothers, she was only 9 when the family moved to the south of Portugal where she had lived an idyllic life growing up on a horse farm, while being privately tutored by a British nanny. She wanted to be a doctor, but only men went to medical school, and she had to settle with becoming a nurse. But she didn't really mind. As long as she could help the sick, that's all that mattered to her. At 19, the family moved back to Faial, and she married Antonio, a devoted

Christian, and the nicest man any woman could wish for. Three years later, she gave birth to Mauricio. But Antonio had one major purpose in his life — save as many souls as he could. She and her newborn son followed him to Manaus, Brazil, where he looked forward to bringing the word of the Lord Jesus Christ and with it, the way to salvation to the sinful indigenous people of the Amazons. Sometimes he would be gone into the jungle two, even three months, but she understood his piety and did the best she could on her own until he returned.

When two years passed without news of his whereabouts, she still felt an obligation as his wife to remain in Manaus and wait for as long as it would take for him to return to her. It was during this time that she took a job with a doctor at a hospital, where she became his attendant nurse. Then one day, a friend of her husband, who happened to be his guide into the jungle, brought her the most unbearable news. Antonio had perished when he met with a tribe that practiced cannibalism, and were not willing to stop their old religious rituals. It took her three more years working as a nurse before she saved enough money to pay for their two tickets on a cargo ship to New York, which happened to be on Captain Morehouse's *Dei Gratia*. "If it had not been for him, I would still be in Brazil. And now that I'm here with you, I feel so complete. Your family enriches my life. Your Christian values and the way you and Captain Briggs care for each other remind me of what I once had when I was married to my Antonio." Tears rolled down her cheeks.

"I'm so sorry," Sarah hugged her. "If I lost my husband, I believe I would die without him."

"I'm strong, for my son," Carla quickly wiped her tears with a handkerchief.

"I admire your strength. But don't you worry, my dearest friend, very soon you'll be home with your family again."

"Yes, thank you, for your support," Carla stood, grabbed a wool cape and put it over Sarah's shoulders. "Come, let's take a walk outside and see what the children are doing." Arm in arm they found them seated on a roll of rope taking turns staring at a seagull feather through Mauricio's magnifying glass.

Mauricio did play daily with Sophia, but he'd rather follow Richardson around or stop by the galley to listen to Charlie's Sea stories while having butter cookies with a mug of hot milk, which Charlie was more than glad to supply, considering Mauricio did not mind peeling potatoes afterward.

Saturday, November 9

Typical jobs on board included a variety of duties such as keeping
watch, handling sails, washing down, scrubbing and swabbing the
decks. These and other chores, together with filling the "scuttled
butt" with fresh water, and coiling up the rigging, occupied the
time until seven bells (half after seven), and time for breakfast.
Then there was also tarring, greasing, oiling, varnishing and
painting. Every ship, no matter how well built, still took on water,
and the *Mary Celeste* was no different; it had to be pumped every
day. Some duties required a lot of muscle, raising the sails,
hoisting the anchor and manning the winches that loaded cargo
onboard when needed. Besides steering, reefing, furling, bracing,
making and setting sail, pulling, hauling and climbing in every
direction, everyone took their turns with four hours of night
watching. During their time off, they read, slept, played dice and
cards, and told some pretty tall tales. A few had a knack for
creating interesting wood carvings, drawings, and model making.
Playing an instrument and singing "sea shanties" — rhythmic work

songs like, "Carry Me Long," and "Oh, Riley, Oh," were heard often when doing repetitive tasks of any kind, especially with teamwork like hauling on ropes. Sometimes they made up the lyrics to the tunes they were already familiar with, and depending on the mood and if there were no ladies about, they could be quite sassy. A strong camaraderie prevailed onboard the *Mary Celeste,* since most of the sailors and crew members knew each other from previous voyages with Captain Briggs.

Charlie didn't like anyone in *his* galley while cooking, unless they were there on his off time to borrow a book or seek his advice, which he was more than happy to oblige. Yet, he never enforced his boundaries, and the men and passengers took it for granted that they could drop by anytime between meals when they needed a hot cup of coffee or tea to warm their innards. Having moved the dining furniture into the galley had made it the ideal place for gathering for meals. Charlie's ongoing stove provided the only place in the whole ship with constant warmth. His sheet-iron stove was set up for baking on the inside and cooking on top of it. The smoke went up through a funnel to the weather deck. He took great pride in keeping the brass galley-stack brightly shined and called it *Charlie Noble.* He always had a large kettle filled with hot water ready to pour into copper hot water bottles cozily wrapped inside a fabric pouch/bag, so no one could get burned on contact. They were regularly distributed among the passengers and the crew, to help them keep warm at night. The sailors went about with tending to the ship's needs while listening to Sarah playing the melodeon, which had become part of their daily entertainment. Sometimes she amused herself by playing lively tunes like, "Tritsch -Tratsch – Polka" by Johann Strauss II, which made them go about faster, and more motivated. Other times, she led herself to performing something soft and romantic like Beethoven's "Piano Sonata No.14" and a few couldn't help being swayed into thinking about love, its rewards and their losses. No matter what repertoire she played, she always finished with "Amazing Grace" just like at her father's church, and a few of the sailors hummed the last verse along followed by "Amen" and made the cross over their heart.

Putting into consideration how hard the men worked, Charlie liked to provide what he called "three square meals a day," since it was served on square wooden platters. For those doing the usual four hours' dog watch at night, he felt personally responsible for keeping them alert, and even though the galley closed for food through the night, he always kept the coffee warm and available on top of the stove.

Breakfast consisted of bread, butter, jam and freshly brewed coffee — a must every morning — but also included fried potatoes and eggs, sometimes bacon, other times, pan fried flat cakes. He also kept a large pot going with what he called Burgoo, oatmeal porridge. "If breakfast does not stick to thou ribs, thou'll be a miserable good-for-nothing sailor," was one of his favorite sayings.

Dinner from 1 to 3 p.m. came with a hearty bowl of beef or chicken soup to which he always managed to add some kind of chopped up vegetables, a sandwich with sliced meat and cheese, and a side of fruit. Fresh produce would be available for the first two-and-a-half weeks, and then it would be down to canned vegetables, dried fruits and nuts. He had already planned on purchasing abroad fresh produce for the return trip.

Supper, usually the smallest meal back home, had become a lot more substantial onboard the *Mary Celeste*. It consisted of stews, beefsteak and kidney pies, and always a side of potatoes or a rice medley. Everyone looked forward to supper, usually between 7 and 9 in the evening.

"Supper without dessert is like having bread without butter," he announced that evening, when bringing out his dessert specialty, parmesan ice cream. Its creamy, salty texture and sweet-like-pudding consistency had become Benjamin and Sarah's favorite when Charlie first introduced it onboard the *Forest King*.

146

Sophia's lack of appetite was an issue, and Charlie could not be more delighted than when she asked for a second serving of ice cream followed by Mauricio doing the same.

"Charlie," Carla said. "Where do you keep the Parmesan cheese?"

"Ah, in my candy stowage, a very special locker that keeps perishables alive." He liked naming items that were useful to him; his candy stowage was the refrigerator component part he had invented to keep things fresh but not frozen.

He did have a pet peeve: bad breath. He attributed his healthy white teeth to cleaning them after every meal with chew sticks (a thin twig with a frayed end to rub away crud stuck between teeth) and made sure everyone had easy access to them after meals. A pair of pliers for pulling teeth was kept in full sight, next to the chew sticks container at the center of the table. It was also a handy tool for cracking walnuts and almonds.

From the first day that Richardson and her son met, Carla had become aware of their growing rapport. Richardson had shown Mauricio how to throw a line to catch fish and tie different sea knots. Sometimes they stood talking at the helm. *It's as if they have known each other forever,* she stood leaning by the side railing, watching them. *He would be a perfect father for Mauricio — he's patient, kind and ... quite handsome.* She suppressed a giggle and turned her gaze back to the sea. Richardson noticed her presence below, and when Andrew came to take his turn at the wheel, he walked up to her.

"A penny for your thoughts, Miss Nunes."

She could not help blushing. "My thoughts are not for sale. Besides, they're too silly to be heard."

"Try me."

"Very well, but please call me Carla," she couldn't help feeling a little flirtatious. "I'll share the ones I can," then more seriously. "I appreciate the kindness you've shown toward my son.

And he does too, I know. He has never had a father figure in his life," then added quickly, "I heard you're married. Your children must really miss you."

"I'm married. But... no children."

"Oh, I'm sorry, I just assumed ..."

Mauricio came running and called out, "Mama, Mama, its supper time, let's go."

"Would you like to join me later at the helm?" Richardson asked her.

"If you don't mind waiting. It will have to be much later. I must tend to Mrs. Briggs and the children. Perhaps ... after they settle for the night?"

"No rush. Besides, I have no place else to go," he smiled and she did too. "I'll wait for you all night if need be," he said.

After supper, Sarah remained in her cabin for the night since Sophia wanted to sleep with her. Mauricio loved sleeping on the hammock that Richardson had provided and would not trade places with his mother when she offered him the use of her berth.

"Mama," Mauricio said as she covered him with a blanket. "Mr. Richardson has been teaching me sea language. Listen, the bow is the front end of the ship. Port is the left side facing forward, starboard is the right side facing forward, and the stern is the back end of the ship."

"You're so smart; I could never remember all that. I'm so proud of you," she kissed him goodnight and then sat in the armchair reading. When everyone fell asleep, she closed the cabin door softly behind her.

Sunday, November 10

Benjamin held a 20-minute morning service starboard to the galley. In the 19th century, it wasn't unusual for captains to take on a minister's position, and he had been providing those services since his first voyage as captain. But over the last few years, his sermons had been less about religion and more about the value of friendship, respecting other people's opinions, accepting other beings regardless of their physical or religious differences, giving thanks for the good fortune of just being healthy and many other topics, he felt were productive in creating harmony between the sailors. After visiting so many foreign countries as a sea merchant, and being exposed to such a wide range of religious beliefs and cultures, he had also arrived to a better understanding of the different faiths and traditions of other nations. He still believed in Christ wholeheartedly, but no longer felt the right to impose his own faith on others. While on honeymoon to Florence, he had shared his newfound philosophy with Sarah.

"Had I been born to a Jewish family," he told her. "I would

most likely be making my prayers to their God. The same would apply if I had been born into a Hindu or a Buddhist family. It all depends on where we are born, who our parents are, and of course, the society we live in. Sometimes we have no choice but to let go of our own beliefs and assimilate to their doctrines, if we are going to survive in a hostile environment."

"I know exactly what you mean," she said. "Our American Indians are a good example of being born into strong religious beliefs and ingrained traditions that were passed from one generation to the next. That is until they were forced to abandon them and abide to our mandates for the sake of their own lives, just like the Negroes brought over from Africa. Once in America as slaves, they were forced to accept and follow their master's doctrines. May God forgive me for having these thoughts," she made the cross. "But Benj, I'm curious. What if one of those religions out there has the *real* God? I only know about Jesus."

He pointed to the ocean. "What do you see below and all around us?"

"Water and a few waves, waving at us," she smiled.

"Oh yes, of course," he couldn't help feeling amused. He kissed her cheek. "But do you see the fish below?"

"No, silly, of course not."

"But you know there are fish down there, right?"

"Yes, of that I'm sure."

"In other countries, fish may have a different name but even in their language, it's still fish. It's the same with God. You and I call out for Jesus, others call him HU, or Buddha, or Allah and so many other names ... some even believe it's a She, not a He, but in the end, it's a worldwide unanimous vote — no matter what one names it, it's still God."

"The one and almighty God of the Universe!" she exclaimed. "I understand exactly what you mean. But ..." she lowered her voice. "Our thinking could be considered a heresy. My father would not understand."

"Oh, but he does, my dear," he noticed Sarah's expression. "I know you're surprised, but he and I share the same viewpoint. But he felt no one was yet ready to hear him out, especially at a time in our lives when there is so much ignorance and malice already separating people. We swore complete secrecy to each other; but you're my other half, and I have no secrets from you."

The sailors and crew members were not required to attend the Sunday service, but most had come just to listen to their captain's positive sermons about everyone having the potential to do good for each other, and many other inspirational subjects, which left everyone with an optimistic attitude about life in general. At closing, he did use a short verse from the Bible, usually one that fitted the topic of his talk that day. With no intentions of converting anyone, his 20-minute sermons were an open invitation for everyone to appreciate the gift of life no matter what their beliefs were.

On his way to his cabin, he noticed Helmut's-stained pants as he walked by. He called out, "Helmut, you know better than caulk-off on deck."

"Nay, I didn't, Cap'n. I was standing right here, the whole time, listening to ye."

"Your clothes are stained with caulking, so why do you lie?"

"I ony rested on decke for a few minutes, while ye talk." "No one is making you attend any of my talks, as you call it. Next time, use the forecastle to slack off."

"Aye-aye Cap'n," he waited for Benjamin to be out of sight and gave him the bras d'honneur gesture.

Monday, November 11

Carla and Richardson meeting at the bridge had become a nightly event, and that day while Sarah and Sophia took a nap after dinner, Carla joined him with Mauricio. Anyone watching them would have taken them for a family at the helm of a ship, enjoying their voyage.

It was a standard well-known rule on ships that meals were always served first to the captain, and in this case, his family, Carla and Mauricio. As first mate, Richardson had the privilege of eating with them, where Andrew as second mate did not. The second mate remained on deck overseeing the rest of the crew and ate later alone, or with the sailors in the galley, still known to some as the caboose.

During dinner, Richardson mentioned how much he and the crew enjoyed Sarah's playing, as it made the days less monotonous.

"If we can have the melodeon brought outside," she

responded. "I wouldn't mind playing on deck one afternoon. A little soirée for everyone to enjoy."

"That would be wonderful. And if you'll allow me, Mrs. Briggs," Charlie said while serving a medley of chicken with rice and vegetables. "I would be very happy to sing a few pieces, like we've done in the past."

"I was hoping you'd volunteer," she smiled. "Charlie, I still remember how you sang so beautifully those German and Italian operettas, when we traveled to Florence. You're so gifted."

"Thank you, Mrs. Briggs," he couldn't hide his satisfaction. "I also know quite a few popular Irish songs. And from what I understand," he turned to Carla, "You mentioned to me that you like singing the Portuguese Fado." She shook her head but he waved one finger back and forth at her, "Now, now, Miss Carla, it's too late to back away."

"Oh," she laughed. "Very well, if you insist, you can count on me. But only one song."

"I bet some of our talented crew members would love to join us with their instruments," Charlie's voice rang with enthusiasm. "We could have a gay old-time musical revue right here onboard this wonderful ship."

"Sarah, I know you mean well, but in your condition, I don't think this is a good idea," Benjamin said. Then seeing Sarah's puckered brow, he added, "But we do have a long voyage ahead of us, and a little music would be appreciated by all, I'm sure. We'll keep it short."

"Tomorrow right after dinner, Mrs. Briggs?" Charlie said.
She nodded.
"I'll go pass the word around." And he left.

Richardson didn't mind taking a double shift so that he could spend more time with Carla. They never ran out of conversation, but later that night, neither spoke much. It felt more natural to listen to the sound of the sails swaying with a lenient westerly wind along with the sound of the swells that crushed against the hull, making the ship sway up and then roll straight down over the water with a deep thump. She brought one arm around his waist and put her head on his shoulder. He placed his hand over hers on the wheel.

Tuesday, November 12

After five full days at sea, a certain amount of anticipation ran among the men that morning. They were more than ready to take part in the "merry shanty," after dinner, as Charlie had announced. The melodeon was carried out and positioned by the main mast. Tony and Luciano brought their harmonicas. Andrew surprised everyone when he showed up with a fiddle. Given his usual serious rigid bearing, no one could imagine the second mate as having any kind of musical talent. Volkert offered to whistle along. Charlie provided Mauricio and Sophia with a small metal pan and a wood spoon, each. Boz had concocted two Jew Harps held together with wire and called it, *ma trump*. Arian brought his concertina. Richardson held under his arm a flat wood piece with ridges and a wood stick.

Helmut showed no interest in participating but stood close by, against the side railing.

Sarah walked in followed by Carla, the children and Charlie. Everyone applauded arduously, as they had been eagerly waiting for the star performers to appear.

"What did you bring?" Richardson sat next to Benjamin who flashed him a silver boatswain's pipe that hung from a silver chain around his neck.

Carla wore her usual black attire but sported a long black shawl over one shoulder. Before singing, she explained that the shawl was an essential part of her dark wardrobe because that's what Portuguese women wore after losing a close family member. The Fado spoke about fate, yearning for someone forever, impossible endless love, mourning. It was the voice of the poor people, people that lived by the sea, and lost their loved ones to it. Sarah accompanied her on the melodeon.

No one knew Portuguese, but the way Carla interpreted the Fado, it moved everyone into a deep, reflective mood. It had to be a love song for sure, the saddest most heartfelt love song anyone had ever heard, and Volkert was moved to tears. Then Charlie began singing the upbeat "Nell Flaherty's Drake," and everyone joined with their musical instruments, followed by a quick version of a stomping Irish jig, carried out by a mutual accumulation of upbeat improvisational melodies that no one could name since it had just been created.

Tony and Luciano stood and began to dance. Hitting their naked heels hard on the floor deck, they danced enthusiastically while playing their harmonicas. Even Helmut began keeping the rhythm by tapping one foot. Carla, seeing the two sailors dancing, took her shoes off and asked Mauricio to dance with her. He drew a long agonizing sigh to overexpress his sacrifice, but abided by her wish. After a few rapid turns, he felt dizzy enough to lose his balance, but his good nature had him laughing just as hard as everyone else. Sophia slipped off her father's knees and joined Carla and Mauricio, jumping up and down. Noticing that Mauricio and Sophia were busy doing their own dancing interpretation, Richardson took to dancing with Carla. Sarah couldn't be happier. She looked at Charlie who sang his heart out, nodded at him and enunciated toward him the words, *thank you.*

Benjamin was far from enjoying the afternoon's "merry shanty." He felt an overwhelming fear that if Sarah overexerted, it could put her health in jeopardy.

With his arm holding firmly around Carla's waist, Richardson managed to keep themselves twirling around without bumping into anyone. Tony, who watched them intently while playing his harmonica, handed it to Luciano and approached the twirling couple. He tapped Richardson on the shoulder. "May I take a turn with the lady?" he asked politely. Richardson moved away to allow the sailor to take his place, but Helmut walked hastily toward the couple, grabbed Tony by the neck and threw him brusquely starboard into the taffrail, barely missing Sarah playing the melodeon. Benjamin stood and blew the whistle, which stopped the chaos followed by complete silence except for Tony's moan as he held his hand over his mouth, blood dripping down his chin. Sophia ran crying to Sarah, who remained seated, shaking while staring in disbelief at Tony's bloody face and then at Helmut. Carla lifted Sophia in her arms and grabbing Sarah's arm, she ordered Mauricio to follow them to their cabin.

"Helmut," Benjamin pointed at him. "Stay exactly where you are. Mr. Gillings, see that the melodeon is returned to my wife's cabin." He walked up to Tony who sat against the mast staring at the front tooth in his hand.

"Are you well?" he asked. Tony nodded.

"I won't allow this behavior on my ship," Benjamin said to Helmut. "You apologize to Mr. Esposito immediately."

Helmut stretched his hand out to Tony and pulled him up. "I'm very sorry, mate. I was wrong to allow my feelings to take the best of me, but when I saw her dancing with ye, I couldn't help myself."

"That's not an acceptable excuse," Benjamin said. "You have been a sailor long enough to know by now that your behavior is enough for me to put you in irons. If anything like this happens again, and I mean anything, you'll be severely punished. Are we understanding each other?"

"Aye, aye, my Cap'n," Helmut put his right hand on his chest. "I swow pon my mother's grave that this will never happen again. I swow, my Cap'n. I swow!"

Benjamin signaled for him to leave. Charlie took Tony to the galley to help him with the bleeding. Richardson remained on deck with Benjamin. Neither had expected such disturbance.

Benjamin broke the silence, "It's completely my fault. I knew Helmut to be nothing but trouble, but I hired him anyway."

"Don't blame yourself, you did what you had to do. Look, I'll keep an eye on him, don't worry. Your wife needs you. Go ahead, it's been a long day."

Benjamin knocked at his wife's cabin. Carla opened the door, "She's in your cabin, sir. Sophia is staying the night with me and Mauricio."

He found Sarah in bed and lay next to her taking special care not to disturb her in case she was sleeping. She put her arm around him and said, "I'm so sorry about what happened. How is Tony?"

"He is doing swell, my love, all is well."

Wednesday, November 13

Still shaken by the previous day, Sarah decided to spend the day in her cabin with Sophia. Mauricio awoke with the sniffles, and Carla had him stay indoors. He was content practicing the different sea knots he had learned from Richardson, playing with Sophia her favorite games, *Hide the Thimble,* and *Jumping Jack Doll,* and reading aloud from her children's books. Carla diligently brought their meals and spent the rest of the time helping Sarah with sewing.

Since the first night that Carla and Richardson spent their time together at the helm, the men had tagged them as *the couple,* and they openly blamed Tony for trying to cut in on them.

That night, the crew's love connection prediction came true, when Carla and Richardson, standing by the wheel, kissed for the first time, two shadows barely lit by a slivery moon, and the darkness of Helmut's hateful gaze. He wasn't going to allow things to go awry from the original plan. She needed to be reminded of her obligations, and since she was growing soft on Richardson, as well as everybody else, he would have to take care of matters on his own. On his way to the forecastle, he bumped into Luciano, and proceeded to tell him in a more than explicit manner what he had witnessed between Carla and Richardson. He finished his story with, "She does not belong to the first mate; she belongs to all of us equally, ye agree?"

"Aye-Aye," said the young sailor. "I agree, we have the same rights."

"Then go for it, mate!"

"Really?"

Helmut put an arm over Luciano's shoulder and pushed him into the shadow of the nearest mast, "She's still up there with him at the wheel, but if ye wait here for her, when she returns to her cabin, I bet she'll invite ye in."

"Ye believe she fancies me?"

"More than that. I've had my way with women like her many times, and I know the type. Ye'r young and virile, a lot better than the old goat she's with. I bet ye, she'll jump on ye before ye even ask."

"And if she doesn't?"

"Ye take control. She only knows the first mate a few days and is already in his pants. Ye go and show her what a real man is all about." He walked away.

Luciano remained still like a statue on the same spot, not quite sure as to what to do if she did walk up to him. All those days on board, they had not even exchanged a word, but he had been more than aware of her presence, the way she laughed when she walked with Mrs. Briggs or the children, was like music to his ears and then the day before, when she danced and had twirled her skirt, it had gone up enough for him to see her dainty white ankles. If what Helmut said was true, then maybe she had done that on purpose to make him ache for her. He saw Carla coming his way, but as she came closer, he turned his back as she walked by, his heart pounding so hard he thought for a moment that he was going to pass out.

Helmut heard him enter their cabin. "What happened, ye lost yer nerve?" he turned over and mumbled, loud enough to be heard, "Flapdoodle."

Luciano did not answer and climbed into his hammock. He had not been with a woman since he had left New York, and under normal circumstances, it would be no problem for him, until Helmut had fired up his emotions. He remained the rest of the night thinking about the rewards of Carla's company, while plotting his next move.

Thursday, November 14

The continuous misty cold rain through the night remained through the morning causing the deck to be slippery. As per Benjamin's orders, his family was to remain indoors on days like that since they could not afford to catch a chill. Carla brought them meals and kept them company, but allowed Mauricio, now recovered from the sniffles, to join Richardson on deck and later at the galley. Sarah made plans to sleep in her husband's cabin that night since Sophia didn't really mind when she was away. Carla allowed her to stay up as long as she liked. After supper, Richardson walked Mauricio back to his cabin and then went to tend the wheel. Before bedtime, the children liked to play their usual games, but once Sophia started to cough, she had to have her cough medicine and soon afterward, she would fall asleep.

Mauricio put on his nightclothes and laid in his hammock. "Mama," he said. "Can I ask Mr. Richardson to be my father?"

"Son, you already have a father," she tucked him in with his blanket.

"Where? Where is my father?"

"Soon, very soon you'll see him again and ..."

"Mr. Richardson never yells, and he's never too busy to do things with me. I'll miss Mr. Richardson terribly, if after this trip we don't see him anymore." He cried.

"I know what you mean meu, pequenino," she patted his cheek. "How about if I sing your favorite song, and then, who knows, maybe a miracle will happen." She sang softly, holding back her own tears.

Outside, Luciano waited, crouched down on the port side of the main cabin. She came out of the companionway and he stood, but just as fast as she stepped out, she went back in. He was about to walk away when she came out wearing a cape with a hood over her head.

"I have been waiting for you," he said grabbing her by the shoulders.

"What?" she tried to push him away without much success. "Take your hands off ..."

"Don't play games with me," he pulled her hood off and reached for the back of her head and neck with both hands trying to bring her face closer to his.

She kicked him in the knees and was about to slap him when he grabbed her hands behind her back.

She cried out, "Are you plumb crazy? Let me be!"

"Oh, so you think you're too good for me, eh? Only the first mate is good enough, is that it?" he brought his mouth to hers, but she turned her face away and shouted, "Somebody help me," but her voice was barely audible as if carried away by the wind.

"Luciano," said a man who Carla recognized as Tony. "Let the lady be." But Luciano wasn't ready to let go of his prey that easy. He held Carla by the front of her coat with his left hand, made a tight fist with the other hand, and struck Tony in the temple. Tony lost his balance momentarily but just as quickly delivered a punch back that caused Luciano to let go of Carla, and bring his hands to a bloody nose. He yelled out, "Dang ye!" and tackled Tony to the floor, then without a second thought he grasped from his waist pouch the paring knife he used for carving small pieces of wood. Carla saw the knife in his hand and tried to grab it away, but he used his elbow to push her away. She stumbled and fell against the main mast. Richardson and Boz appeared just as Luciano slid his knife across Tony's throat. Boz jumped on top of Luciano, who as if stupefied by his own action, did not even defend himself from Boz's frenzy beating. "What have you done?" Boz screamed as he kept punching Luciano. "You frigging packsaddle, bastard!"

Richardson ran to check on Carla, and seeing she was well, went to help Benjamin who had come running when he heard the commotion, and was trying to pull Boz away from Luciano. Carla couldn't stop crying. Benjamin asked Boz to accompany Carla to her cabin and remain outside her door. Helmut arrived followed by Andrew. The other sailors stood watching while maintaining their distance.

Andrew and Richardson escorted Luciano to the hold where they left him sitting in a corner. They didn't bother to tie him; he had no way out. Once on deck, the hatch was locked. No one could conceive any reasonable excuse for a man like Luciano known as a peaceful fellow, to be a murderer.

The deck was immediately scrubbed with a stiff-bristled brush, and a block of sandstone to remove all blood vestiges. Tony's clothes were carefully examined for any items that could be returned to his family. They found nothing except for the picture of an older couple, possibly his parents, tucked away in his pocket. Tony's naked body was wrapped temporarily in a sheet and tied to the taffrail. The knife was wiped clean, and neatly stored in a small box, as evidence of the crime committed. Benjamin and his two mates went down the companionway and found Boz still standing by Carla's door as he had been told. He apologized profusely for having lost control up on deck, and Benjamin told him to take his next shift off and use it to get some rest. Carla let them in.

"Mrs. Nunes," Benjamin said. "We need to talk," then noticing the children were sleeping, he turned to his mates. "Do you mind if we use your cabin instead?"

They entered the mates' joining cabin and closed the door.

"My wife is sleeping in my cabin, and I do not want to disturb her. She's not to be told, not now and not any day afterward." Then he turned to Carla. "What happened out there?"

"I ... I was on my way to meet with Mr. Richardson at the helm, like we always do after hours, when I was assaulted," Carla used the wall to support herself as her legs went weak. "Tony tried to stop him, but he wasn't as big as my attacker and couldn't fight back. It all happened very fast ..." she stopped to catch her breath.

"Mr. Gillings, take note of Mrs. Nunes's statements for our records," Benjamin said. "Tomorrow morning," he looked at his pocket watch, "Actually, there's not much time left. In about five hours, it will be daylight, and we'll be putting Tony to rest at sea. Mrs. Nunes, please fetch my wife from my cabin at daylight and keep her and my daughter with you. Your son too, he might be a bit young to be present when we lay Tony to rest at sea."

"I would have liked very much to attend," she cried. "Tony gave his life to save me from ..." she choked on her words. Then raised her hand to give time to catch her composure. "Sir, my son and I are at your service. I'll get your wife early in the morning and remain with your family as long as it's needed. Don't you worry. I'll do my best to keep them occupied."

Below deck, Luciano sat with his head bent over resting on his hands. Tony and he had been mates for five years. They were like brothers. He had even planned, when the next occasion came, to introduce him to Laura, his younger sister. Tony had taught him to play the harmonica, and many times, he had covered for him when he didn't feel well. The knife he used on Tony had been with him since he was 14; his grandfather had given it to him as a going away present when he first went to sea. He had never used it except for carving miniature horses and farm animals he hoped someday to own once he bought a farm. His parents, two younger brothers and his sister counted on him to someday take them out of New York City, and to Pennsylvania, where the land was bountiful and not overpriced. When he was a young lad, his uncle, who was a boxer, had taught him most of the moves, but only once had he gotten into a boxing brawl at a tavern. He had never hurt anyone and definitely never had taken advantage of a woman — women liked him. He blamed himself for allowing Helmut to twist his perception about Carla. She had the right to be with whoever she wanted.

"Are ye awake?" he heard a man's voice in the dark. "Are ye well?"

He recognized Helmut's voice. "How do you expect me to feel?" he cried. "I just killed my best friend."

"Calm down," Helmut handed him a tin cup. "Here, I thought ye would be in need o' something warm," he sat on the floor next to him and rubbed his hands briskly. "Brrr, it's darn cold down here."

Luciano just went on crying.

"Go ahead, it's good hot coffee; drink it while it's still warm," Helmut said. "Don't worry, ye acted in self-defense. After all, Tony attacked ye first. The Cap'n is a fair man, once ye explain what happened, he'll let ye free of any charges."

"True that I was defending myself, but Tony attacked me to protect the woman I intended to molest."

"Aye-aye, we know all that already, but to condemn ye won't do any good to the morale onboard the ship, awright? Just drink ye'r coffee and rest. Ye'r going to be fine."

He left and once on deck, he looked around before closing the hatch.

Friday, November 15

Neither Andrew nor Richardson could sleep. The few hours they had left before dawn were being spent talking, and tossing and turning in their berths. Finally, they agreed their time would be better used if they paid a visit to Luciano. Perhaps he had come to his senses and could explain what really happened.

They found him where they left him, seated on the floor, his head now bent slightly to the side.

"A-man," Andrew used his foot to nudge at Luciano's thigh.

"Wake up," Richardson bent over and shook Luciano's shoulders, but when he let go, Luciano fell limp to the side. A tin cup fell out of his hand. Richardson backed away. "This man is dead."

Andrew brought the cup to his nose. "It smells like coffee."

They rushed out and found Captain Briggs coming off the companionway. Richardson gave him the news.

"My wife is in my cabin getting dressed. Let's head to the galley where we can talk."

Charlie could tell from their demeanor that they were there to address something serious and excused himself. But Benjamin grabbed his arm, "Please don't go. Tell me, did anyone come over during the night to get coffee, from you?"

"No sir, if anything it was a very uneventful evening. After supper, as you know, I usually maintain some hot water going in case someone needs a cup of tea or coffee or a hot water bottle, but after midnight, I went to my corner, and if someone came into the galley, I didn't hear anything. The truth is," he lowered his voice as if ashamed. "Once I fall asleep, I'm dead to the world."

It was no secret that Luciano had killed Tony, but neither of their deaths had a rational explanation, especially Luciano's.

"My priority right now, is everybody's safety," Benjamin said. "Sounds to me like someone brought him a cup of coffee with whatever killed him. We must find the killer as soon as possible."

"What do ye propose we should do?" Andrew asked.

"For starters, it's best if my family, Carla, and Mauricio remain in the cabin at night, until we find who killed Tony," he faced Richardson. "And that includes Carla meeting you at the wheel, unless you personally accompany her to and from her cabin."

"I'll make sure of that. You know, if need be, I'll protect her with my own life."

"I know you would," Benjamin said. "And now I must share with you my major concern," he stroked his chin, as he always did when overwhelmed. "Luciano's death only proves that someone onboard is not to be trusted. As you know, one death is bad enough, but two in less than twenty-four hours is enough to bring some serious turmoil onboard our ship."

"A serious threat indeed," Andrew said. "We need to interview everybody, one by one, in private. That might give us some clue as to what happened."

"I agree, I'm going to make sure my wife is back in her own cabin, then let's meet on deck for Tony and Luciano's burial at sea.

We'll start the investigation right afterward."

Arian, Charlie, Boz and Helmut used the deceased sailors' hammocks to wrap the bodies, and before closing each aperture, they inserted a lead shot to ensure they would sink properly. Volkert was nowhere to be found, but when the men held their caps against their chests while standing over the two deceased mates, he showed up. His eyes were bloodshot. "Sorry, but my herz hurts," he pointed to his chest.

Benjamin read from the Bible, "God is our refuge and strength, a very present help in trouble. Therefore, we will not fear though the Earth gives way, though the mountains tremble at its swelling." He closed the Bible and added, "They'll now descend into the very heart of the sea ... may they join the kingdom of our Lord, Jesus Christ."

The bodies were tipped into the water feet first, followed by a prolonged silence.

Helmut was the first to be called to the Captain's cabin. He told him and the two mates that he had seen Luciano last when taken below by the first and second mates. That evening, he got busy scraping and scrubbing the poop deck before going to his cabin where he passed out exhausted. His story wasn't much different from everyone else who had done their duties and then retired or remained on deck but had not seen or heard anything suspicious.

"Luciano was most likely consumed by guilt," Andrew said. "The thought of facing the crew after what he had done, apparently was just too much for him to handle. He waited until everyone was asleep, and somehow made it to the galley, made himself a cup of hot coffee and added rat poison to it."

"And how did he get the coffee ...? You were with me when we closed the hatch," Richardson said.

"Obviously, he must have found a way out," Andrew responded adamantly.

Throughout the day, some of the sailors exchanged stories and the curses that came along with having women onboard. These discussions seemed to be a direct result from when Helmut was around.

While serving supper at the galley, Charlie overheard Helmut saying to Boz and Volkert, "Two of our mates already joined the Davy Jones Locker. I bet yer all wondering who'll be next on account of the dames onboard, hey?"

"Ye arrr oll a bunch of disgraceful lubbers, if ye fall for this kind of gobbledygook," Charlie yelled out. "Do ye really believe that if yer mothers were on t'is ship ye would all perish because they're dames? By jings, women give life, not death." He grabbed the hot stew pot from the stove, and holding it by the handle like a weapon, he addressed Helmut. "Ye, better knock it off, ye ignorant scuttlebutt! If ye insist on spreading malice of any kind in ma' galley, I'll pour t's boiling slumgullion casserole on top of yer thick skull!"

Picking up dialects as well as spitting out a sailor's vocabulary had always come easy for Charlie, principally when anger got the best of him.

Saturday, November 16

Sophia awoke early in the morning coughing. She cried out, "Mommy, mommy, look," she held up the blood-stained hand, "Boo-boo," and brought her hands to her chest.

"Mama will kiss your *boo-boo,* give you some medicine and then you'll feel all better," she wiped the stained hands with a wet handkerchief, kissed Sophia's chest and then went to the fetch her cough medicine. The key hung from the tiny hook on the wall, but the glass door to the top shelf of the cupboard was unlocked. *I must have forgotten to close it,* but as she reached for the syrup, she noticed the two deadly vials missing. They were to be used only when all hope was gone, their contents destined to make death less lengthy and hopefully more comfortable.

She called out for Carla, "I don't recall leaving the cabinet unlocked ... the glass vials are gone. How can they be gone?"

"Maybe you took them out and put them someplace else."

"No, I would never do that. Sophia is still very young, but she's in the curiosity phase, and just in case she could get up here on a stool, I purposely put them way in the back behind the cough medicine. I'll have to tell my husband when I see him."

"I advise you not to do that, Mrs. Briggs. He's a good man, your husband. Most likely, he removed them because he was concerned you might take them by mistake and then forgot to lock the cabinet afterward. Don't worry about it, I bet that's what happened. How about you and Sophia stay here in the cabin and wait for me to collect your breakfast. Mauricio," she called out, "Get your coat on and come with me."

Sarah proceeded to give Sophia a teaspoon of cough medicine, a lower dosage than the usual tablespoon since she was worried that they would run out of it before arriving in France. Then sat on her berth and took a sigh of relief. The disappearance of the two vials brought her a peaceful feeling. They represented the end of life, and now that they were gone, she felt an omen of recovery, the promise of hope, a new start. *Carla is right; Benjamin took the vials and forgot to lock the cupboard.*

When Carla returned with breakfast, she noticed Sarah and Sophia were dressed. "What a wonderful surprise; you must be feeling better."

"Yes, we are. Even though Sophia did cough a little blood this morning, she and I are definitely getting better," she spread some orange jam on her toast. "The sea air is very good for us."

"Yes," Carla said. "It must be the sea air."

Sophia ate two small spoons of oatmeal, curled up on her mother's berth and fell asleep almost instantaneously. An hour later, she awoke and began playing house with her ragdoll. Sarah spent most of the morning playing the melodeon and then did some sewing. But when Carla brought their dinner, Sarah was too tired to eat and laid down for a nap. Sophia joined her. Neither awoke until the evening when Carla and Mauricio were getting ready to go to the galley to collect their supper.

"Tonight, I'm staying here in our cabin," Sarah told her. "In case Sophia needs me like she did this morning."

"You know that if you want to stay with your husband, you can count on me to give Sophia her medicine. Besides, there's really not much more that you can do for her if you stay."

"Yes, my dearest friend, I know. But I'm glad I was here this morning. She was very scared when she coughed out some blood."

"Very well," Carla said quietly. "But if you change your mind, let me know. Our cabins are next to each other, and I can always call you if needed."

"As always, you're right," she sighed. "I do worry about my husband. He's carrying so much on his shoulders. I feel that he needs me now more than ever, to be by his side. If you see him, let him know that if he wants, he can come by and take me with him."

Carla found Captain Briggs and Richardson in the galley about to have supper.

"Momma, momma, can I stay and eat with Mr. Richardson, please, please?" Mauricio asked.

She shook her head. "Mrs. Briggs and little Sophie are expecting us to return with their meal and for us to join them." And she gave Sarah's message to Captain Briggs.

"Let her know that I'll stop over in half an hour. Better yet," he said mischievously. "Don't say anything; it will be a surprise."

"Carla, you can leave Mauricio here," Richardson said. "I'll take him to your cabin after we are done." He stood when Charlie handed Carla the carry-on basket with the food. "Mauricio, I'm going to take your mom back to her cabin, and I'll be right back."

They walked briskly, and neither spoke. But before entering the walkway to her cabin, she said, "I really need to talk to you, can you come back later tonight?"

"Your tone ... is something wrong?"

"I'm afraid so. But I can't leave until the children are asleep."

"Very well, then when I return with Mauricio, we can make arrangements to talk."

Sarah and Sophia did not touch their food but were exuberant when Benjamin stopped by. Sophia ran toward him, "Papa, my

Papa," she hugged his knees and he lifted her in the air as she chuckled with delight. Finally, she had called him Papa! He played with her for a while and then left with Sarah just as Richardson arrived with Mauricio.

I'll be back, after I'm done at the wheel," he told Carla before leaving.

Carla followed her nightly routine of giving Sophia her medicine before tucking her in and then reading aloud from one of her favorite books, <u>A Little Pretty Pocket-Book, Intended for the Instruction and Amusement of Little Master Tommy, and Pretty Miss Polly. With Two Letters from Jack the Giant Killer</u>, by Isaiah Thomas. Sophia had one favorite chapter, "Select Proverbs for the Use of Children." It always put her to sleep before reaching the ninth proverb, "Birds of a Feather will flock together," but that night she was a bit restless and wanted Mauricio to play doctor with her. Carla caught up on some sewing while they played. When Mauricio decided he was ready for bed, Sophia insisted on lying on the hammock next to Mauricio.

"Mama," he said. "Mr. Richardson has been teaching me all kinds of rigging knots. Today he taught me the king of all, the bowline. It's one of the most useful sailor's knots, and it's very easy to make a fixed "eye" at the end of the rope. Look Mama, look Sophie. The bowline forms a strong loop at the end of the rope, like this and does not slip or bind, and it's easy to untie under any weather condition."

She pulled a chair and sat next to them. "I'm very impressed by your sailor skills. How do you remember all that?" she asked.

"It's easy. Mr. Richardson gives me clues to help memorize the steps," he showed off his newly learned skill by describing it once again, but super slowly. "The rabbit comes out of his hole ... see? Then runs around the tree ... and then ... goes back down its hole."

"My, oh my, that sounds a lot like the story of "Alice's Adventures in Wonderland," she laughed.

"Mama, when I grow up, I want to be a sailor just like Mr. Richardson."

"Me too, me too," Sophia said.

"Mama, sing us a song about the sea, please."

She covered them with the blanket and sang softly in Portuguese, a breeze of gentle words. When they were finally asleep, she carefully lifted Sophia from the hammock and put her in Sarah's berth, kneeled next to it and held the child's hand. She cried. Then realizing that Richardson would be able to tell she had been weeping, she decided to step out for some fresh air but stay close to the companionway entrance.

As she stepped on deck, Helmut stood facing her.

"Ye and I need to talk," he seized her wrist.

She pulled her arm away. "I told you already, there's nothing for us to talk about. I hate you."

"Ye hate me, and what else is new. Ye have a new gull, eh? Ye better stay focused on why we're here before ye mess up everything we worked so hard for."

"Someone is coming. We cannot be seen together, you better go," she rushed back into the companionway and into her cabin.

Richardson had caught the two silhouettes near the companionway entrance, but in the darkness of the night they were indistinguishable. He found Helmut pulling a broom.

"Helmut, who was here with you?"

"Nay one sir. As ye can see, I'm alone," he walked away mumbling about always being picked on.

Richardson knocked at Carla's door, which she opened immediately.

"Were you on deck just now?" he remained outside.

"Of course not," she said. "I have been inside with the children," she put a finger to her lips. "Shhh, you'll wake them."

She stepped out, closed the door and stood against it. "I wanted to talk to you because some of Mrs. Briggs' bottles of medicine disappeared from the cupboard in our cabin."

"Maybe she took them out and forgot where she put them."

"I told Mrs. Briggs the same thing, but after I thought about it, that's impossible. She's extremely careful at keeping it away from Sophia's reach. The medication I'm speaking of was inside two glass bottles and looked quite different from the others. She wanted to tell her husband about their disappearance, but I strongly suggested that she don't do that, it would make him uncomfortable to have to admit he hid them from her. It's very possible he felt it was wiser to remove them, just in case she was to take them by accident."

"You're probably right," his face softened. "You did good, Carla."

The door opened, and Mauricio stood in the doorway in his nightdress and rubbing his eyes. "Mr. Richardson, it's you!"

Richardson lifted the boy and carried him to the hammock. "Go to sleep, sailor," he stroked his forehead. "You and I have a lot of work to do in the morning."

Mauricio dozed off, but his hands remained clenched close to his chest. Some children get attached to a small blanket or a toy they hold dear to their hearts. Mauricio's security blanket had become the bowline rope.

Carla stood watching the two people she most loved, her son and the man she wished could be in her life forever. She put aside the incident with Helmut and the missing medicine. Nothing else seemed to matter at that moment, and she knew Richardson felt the same.

Sunday, November 17

"Much like you," Captain Briggs announced to those who had come to Sunday's sermon. "I feel an immense sorrow within from the loss of our good mates, Luciano and Tony. It's important that we remember them for the good men they were and not for their sins. There is no sermon today; use the time as you see fit."

The men gathered on deck with Arian playing his concertina, and they sang a few sad chantey tunes with Charlie as their lead vocalist.

Captain Briggs had complete confidence in his mates to oversee the sailors, and except for being at the wheel for four hours, he spent most of that day in his cabin with his wife and daughter. Carla brought their meals, and at the end of the day, she came to check if Sarah needed anything, and took Sophia with her.

That night, Benjamin could not sleep. He sat on a chair and watched his wife sleeping. In all the years of seafaring, he had never had anyone die on board — all his sea voyages were known for the most part as being unremarkable. What if something else happened to his crew and slowed down their journey, what would happen to his family? The two dead sailors and his wife and daughter juggled back and forth like a sideshow of pictures of disproportional sizes, but as he tried to piece the images together, they melted in his hands. He awoke to the sound of heavy pounding on his door and so did Sarah. His pocket-watch read three in the morning.

"Captain Briggs ..." Richardson came in out of breath. "There's an odd, rather large light facing our ship. You need to take a look."

Benjamin asked Sarah to remain in the cabin as he would surely be back soon. He followed Richardson starboard where Andrew stood facing the bow, waiting for them. Sitting on the horizon line, an enormous well-defined yellowish half-moon shape light blinked at them on and off. According to Andrew, who had been at the helm when it first appeared, it had come up as a round silver object, which kept growing in intensity until it turned into the shape they now witnessed. The rest of the crew had stopped their work and stared at it in wonder.

"It's too huge to be a lighthouse," Richardson pointed at it. "But I would like to play with the idea that perhaps we're looking at a huge dioptric light caused by concentrated prisms or lenses."

"Well, Mr. Richardson," Andrew said. "That's all good and dandy, but we're in the middle of the ocean, with no land in sight."

"Maybe it's the moon," Volkert said. "She lost her notion of time and space, and cannot find her celestial path."

"Brother, ye'r far from being a common tar. Ye're a poet!" Boz said.

"Definitely not the moon, or the sun," Benjamin said. "Our Creator has taken care of putting the stars and planets in their correct places, and there's no deviation of his work."

"The way I see it, our Creator is cutting a shine on us and left us to tend for ourselves." Helmut said.

"You'll notice the light facing us is strong, but does not

detract us from enjoying the stars above." All eyes turned to Sarah, wrapped in a blanket, standing against the taffrail. Her voice was serene but loud enough for everyone to hear. She pointed to the sky. "They're a friendly reminder that it's still night, but they're watching over us. If there was any danger, we would not be able to stand here and talk about it. Something would have happened by now." Benjamin walked up to her and she held firmly to her husband's arm. Lately she'd been experiencing issues with maintaining her balance while standing or walking. Yet, she felt spiritually strong from within, and that's what had given her the strength to be present. *Maybe it has something to do with the way I was born*, she thought. *I'm always bringing up the positive side of everything even when it looks catastrophic to everyone else.* It also crossed her thoughts that she was going mad since she could hear children's voices and their unrecognizable language coming from the direction of the light. Or maybe, just maybe, she heard the voices because of her illness, and it was perfectly normal. She held on a little tighter to Benjamin's arm. Becoming aware of her hold, he moved her in front of him and put his arms around her waist to give her better support while attempting to keep her warm. His wife's words had just taken away some of the fear the men might be feeling, and he realized that was the perfect time to reinforce her comments.

"I believe I might know what it is," he announced as solemnly as he could. "What we're witnessing is most likely the effect of an underwater volcanic eruption, since the atmosphere above is covered with the gases provoked from the explosion below, it doesn't allow the flames to expand as they would normally on land, as such what we see is a condensation of such explosion."

"I'm sorry, Captain," Andrew said. "Perhaps I forgot to mention, but in the beginning, when I first saw it, it came across as a soft apparition — there was nothing violent about it. It started along the horizon and if anything, it conveyed a serene energy … which I confess I couldn't help enjoying. How do ye explain that?"

he smiled. Something he rarely did.

"Very good observation and question too, Mr. Gillings," Benjamin's voice remained calm, which surprised him. "Has anyone witnessed an underwater volcano before it goes off?" No one answered, which meant to him that no one had, and that included himself. "Well, let me tell you when a volcano explodes, it usually starts by blowing off the top then the top can go flat or round depending on the size of the explosion. In our case here, since it came from under the ocean, as it reached the top of the water, it cooled off rapidly and just as quickly it became flat, and then … developed into the shape we see now."

"Don't ye think, Cap'n," Helmut's scornful tone could not be ignored by anyone listening. "If it was a volcano eruption like ye say, the sea would be agitated and our ship would have turned over by now?"

Aware of everyone's questioning eyes, he decided to ignore Helmut's comment. "Andrew, let's back alee away from the light and use the sails to back and fill, and then resume our original route."

"Aye-aye, sir!" Andrew responded, and then to the crew, "Ye heard the Cap'n, bear-a-hand!" And he ran back to the helm while the others went filling and backing the sails.

"Look!" Boz pointed to the horizon. The moon-shaped object blinked a few times and then disappeared as if a wall had stood between them. Everyone stopped to stare at the dark horizon.

"Night light, night light," Volkert said. "Will you come back and shine your light on us, once again?"

"I miss it too," Boz added. "I know it's strange, but I actually miss the darn volcano …"

"If indeed it was a volcano as he says," Helmut pointed to Benjamin. "It wouldn't disappear instantly in midair."

"You could be right," Charlie said. "But, like Boz, I didn't feel frightened either, quite contrary. So why you worry?"

"Well, ye should," Helmut said loud enough for everyone to

hear him. "Anyone with any sense in their head knows we're still in danger. Hey man, even I'm worried," and he yelled out from the top of his lungs, "Hey, Cap'n, we want to know the truth."

Anger, a queer feeling Captain Briggs rarely experienced, caused his voice to rise as he addressed Helmut and those who now stood staring in his direction. "If it's not an underwater volcano, what do you think it is? You don't have an answer, eh? If you really believe we're in danger, would you like to hide in the hold of the ship? What in God's name do you want me to do?" Then his voice took a turn; it became softer, more condescending, "I do understand your frustration. We lost two of our mates, your working hours increased, and now this happens out of the blue."

The men listening maintained their silence, and Sarah moved a few steps away to stand against the nearest mast for support. "True that in the high sea we should have continued to see the light from any direction," he went on. "What do you want me to say; I'm sorry to disappoint you? Maybe it was a volcano, maybe it was an island produced by the volcano, maybe it was a corposant caused by static electricity due to the atmospheric conditions in this part of the world, and maybe it's none of those things. Obviously, at night everything looks a lot more mysterious than in daylight, and now what? Are we going to spend the rest of the night bickering like scared little rabbits, or get this ship going without further ado?"

Hearing her husband speak, Sarah had to control herself from clapping her hands like Sophia did when she liked something. The sailors and crew dispersed, except for Helmut who remained facing the captain with a chew stick sticking out from the corner of his mouth. "Cap'n, don't ye reckon we should navigate toward the light and see what the heck t'is."

"No!" Benjamin said emphatically. "I'm not risking the life of everyone onboard to go on a wild chase. The subject is closed," he drew a deep breath in and out and his voice took on a calming, soothing tone as if speaking to a child, "Helmut, your behavior leaves much to be desired, and I've had just about enough of your garrulous blateration. You need to get some sleep, maybe that will help you to think more clearly and less ill-regulated in the morning."

Helmut left mumbling under his breath.

"Benjamin, Captain Briggs, my friend, you did great," Richardson shook his hand. "And now I'm going to relieve Andrew at the wheel."

Benjamin put an arm around Sarah's waist as they walked away.

"You don't really believe we just experienced a volcanic explosion, do you?" she said.

"No, Sarah, I don't. But I couldn't allow anyone to fear the worst. Some ships have disappeared in these same waters with no man left to tell, and those few who survived, returned with some strange, terrifying stories."

"Do you think we're in danger, like Helmut said?"

"To be honest, that was my first impulse. But it didn't last long — my fears quickly dissipated and instead, I felt certain ... unexplainable comfort. Most of the men must have sensed the same gay feeling as you and I did. They were definitely disappointed when the light vanished."

"I can't even imagine what kind of phenomenon can cause such positive influence over people. I mean, after all that has been happening in the last few days, much like you, I'm concerned about the men having too much to contend with."

"What do you mean?" he opened the door to his cabin.

"I'm sorry, Benj. I know you tried keeping from me what happened to Tony and Luciano, but this ship is too small for secrets," she laid her blanket on the chair, then took off her coat. "Your two mates came here to talk to you, and you followed them out. I did not need to hear anything to know something serious had happened. When I saw Carla crying the following morning, it confirmed my suspicion. At first, she refused to share anything with me, but finally broke down and told me what had happened, including the deaths of the two sailors. I cried with Carla and then we prayed for Tony and Luciano's souls. Benj, my love, I know how much you worry about my health, but I don't want my illness to stop you from sharing your life with me. I'm your wife and friend for better or worse, and when something bothers you, I want to be there for you, and help you like you have always done for me," she faced him and used her arms around his waist to bring her body closer to him. They held the close hug as if magnetized to each other, neither wanting to let go, until he removed the hairpins holding her hair up. He moved her gently away to look at her face. He loved her smile and that her brown eyes, of such gentle nature, always lit up when she looked at him. "I'm such a lucky man to have you as my wife and best friend. Thank you for joining me out there. You're truly my lifesaver, my only one." He looked into her eyes, acknowledging more than ever what she meant to him. "Sarah, I love you with all my heart," he kissed her tenderly on the lips and began removing her nightdress, never leaving his gaze from her face. He lifted her in his arms and laid her gently on the bed, making sure a pillow was tucked under her head. He took his time kissing every corner of her body, his hands caressing her, as in his mind, she was the goddess of the sea.

After making love, they held each other without speaking and remained awake until the first ray of the morning sun.

Monday, November 18

Sailors and crew questioned if what they had witnessed the night before had actually happened. Their captain was right, daytime made everything more balanced and a lot less problematic. Carla heard about the details of the prior night from Sarah. She and the children had slept through it all.

Benjamin wrote in his journal, "... I really don't know what that was all about except for the fact that we are getting closer to the Azores Islands where the sea is known for creating some phenomena occurrences as reported by those who witnessed them. I do not believe in supernatural forces, only in God's will, but last night has me utterly puzzled." To him, the ocean was like a wild animal, when tired, it allowed to be subjugated, but as soon as it gained its natural vigor in partnership with the moon, its harshness knew no limits of destruction. He recalled when still very young, witnessing for the first time, a serious sea storm onboard his father's ship. His father had grasped his arm just in time to pull him into safety as he watched another sailor being swiped off the deck like a sardine by a colossal wave that threw him into the enraged sea, never to be found.

Carla convinced Sarah and Sophia to come to the galley for a late breakfast, but once there, neither was interested in eating. Sophia seemed a bit sluggish and only wanted to be held. Sarah had a cup of tea, and Carla, who seemed quieter than usual, only took a small sip from her tea cup. Richardson asked if she was well.

"What? "Carla responded absently. "Oh, yes, I'm fine, just concerned about Sophie's tiredness."

Mauricio offered his mother a bite of his toast, but she excused herself to take Sophia and Sarah back to their cabin. She laid Sophia in Mauricio's hammock and rocked her softly back and forth, and when the little one fell asleep, she quietly took on the task of embroidering the tablecloth she and Sarah had started at the beginning of their voyage. Sarah slept maybe half an hour before she awoke coughing. She took some cough medicine and sat at the melodeon — the closed top worked great as a desk — and got busy writing a short letter to send home once they arrived at Genoa. She had also brought along a *new* diary but had yet to start writing. The *old* diary, which was more like a journal she'd started at 12 years old, had grown over the years into two intimate chronicles of her joys and troublesome times growing up, but before leaving Marion, she burned them in one of the fireplaces. She had nothing to hide, but felt her words carried too much of the pain she had endured from losing her babies, family members and friends. She did not want anyone to read it and be reminded of their own anguish from losing their loved ones from consumption and other sicknesses. *This voyage, can very well be my last one with Benj,* she reminded herself. She carefully wet the tip of her pen into the inkwell and began her *new* diary with what could be considered more like a prayer. "When I coughed today, there was once again blood on my handkerchief, very much like Sophia has been experiencing. Please, dear God, I would like to die only after

Sophia comes to rest in Your arms. But if that's not possible, then take us both at the same time, so we can hold hands when we meet You, and if I may ask just one more favor, I know it won't be easy for Benj, so please take care of him, for the sake of our son Arthur who will need his father. Thank you, dear Jesus." She lay next to Sophia and closed her eyes.

She awoke two hours later, opened her larger steamer trunk and took out the flowery flannel fabric she had bought in New York. *While there is life, there is hope*, she told herself. And then to Carla who had just come in with Mauricio, carrying their dinner in a basket. "Sophia needs a new skirt."

"Very well," Carla said. "How about I give you a hand with the sewing machine, right after we eat?" and she awoke Sophia, saying, "Would you like to play with Mauricio?"

Of course, the answer was a bright yes.

"Very well, my little one, but first you must have dinner with us," Carla said.

"I know what you're doing," Sarah winked at Carla. "Thank you, my friend. I don't know what I would do without you."

After dinner, Carla laid a blanket on the floor as she always did for the children to sit and play doctor. Mauricio used his magnifying glass to diagnose little Reggie (Sarah's doll) problems, who coughed too much as told by Sophie, her mommy. Playing doctor didn't last long since Mauricio would rather be assistant junior mate to Richardson. He tied a few ropes around little Reggie's chest to help her with coughing and left to look for Richardson. He felt especially important when Richardson sent him with a message to Captain Briggs and brought back a response. Neither spoke about his father, but a silent understanding existed that, given the choice, they would love to be related. Mauricio was a child, but he had enough insight to recognize that Richardson and his mother cared for each other. The faint possibility that Richardson could become his *real* father made him wish their voyage would never end.

That evening, Carla offered to help Charlie with washing the dishes after supper, like she had done in the past. Not only did she find it relaxing, but also took much pleasure in watching Charlie's eagerness at jotting down the regional Portuguese recipes she shared with him. She told him about the Portuguese method of preserving cod fish by dry salting, and prior to using it, soaking it in water for 24 hours, to bring back its natural plumpness. Dried salt cod fish was the Portuguese main staple food besides bread, olives, cheese, and of course, wine, she told him. He intended to stock a few dried salty cod fish fillets for the next voyage.

He still had enough collard greens, and planned on following Carla's recipe for making *Caldo Verde* (Green Soup) for dinner the next day. Besides collard greens, the recipe called for potatoes, onions, garlic and olive oil, and he had plenty of that.

Fresh vegetables and fruit would soon be depleted, but he didn't mind using canned provisions, peas, carrots, green beans, peaches and much more. His admiration for Nicolas Appert, "The father of canning," was immense, but Robert Yates was his hero. In 1855, Robert had invented the can opener, and he really appreciated not having to use a hammer and chisel to open a tin can.

Tuesday, November 19

At noon, Carla stopped at the galley to pick up Sarah and Sophia's dinner and took a taste of the *Caldo Verde* soup on the stove. "Charlie, you have accomplished a masterpiece — it's absolutely delicious."

"Oh well," his face flushed with the compliment. "I just followed your instructions, that's all. Cutting the collard greens julienne style like you showed me, was very helpful." He told her about his plan to make Shepherd's Pie for supper, and she offered to make the dessert, the famous Portuguese rice pudding.

He was smitten by her Portuguese culinary experience and intriguing beauty, which would have made him uncomfortable working in such narrow space if it wasn't for her pleasant mannerism, not of a grand lady but more of an equal.

"What makes the Portuguese rice pudding so special?" he did his best to keep the tone of his voice relaxed enough to disguise his curiosity, while putting one of the small beef chunks he had cut, into the hand-powered meat grinder.

"The rice is cooked with salted water, that's the secret. Then we add the hot milk, sugar, butter, vanilla, egg yolks and the lemon rinds, and of course, it is a must to decorate the pudding with lots of fresh cinnamon. I'll be back later, after Mrs. Briggs and Sophia have their dinner."

She entered their cabin with a joyful smile. "I have a wonderful surprise for the two of you." She set the soup terrine on the table and served herself a small bowl from which she ate a spoonful. "Yummy *Caldo Verde* soup, and so much fun too!" She smiled at them. Neither Sarah nor Sophia could hold their laughter. Carla's front teeth were covered with a mixture of chopped collard greens and mashed potato.

"Me want soup too, I like *cadovede* soup," Sophia clapped her hands.

Carla showed them how to suck the broth through the front teeth like a strainer and after swallowing it, show off the blend of collard greens and mashed potato in the least ladylike manner. They laughed heartily after each spoonful they took, and there was no soup left when she went to join Charlie in the galley.

That evening, Mauricio accompanied his mother to the galley, but once in the galley, he wanted to stay. Since Richardson wasn't there, Charlie offered to take Mauricio back. Arian had just finished his second helping of pudding and left after he praised Carla's dessert. Helmut ate his plate clean from Shepherd's Pie. It was always everyone's favorite and guaranteed Charlie no leftovers. The same was happening with the rice pudding Carla had made. Helmut suggested that from that day on, Carla should be in charge of making the sweets. "Don't even go there," Charlie responded with a tiny grin that covered what one might call culinary jealousy. "In a few days, ye would be so fat that the ship would sink with yer fat arse."

"If ye ask me, it sounds more like ye afraid of losing yer job," Helmut pushed away his dessert. "There ye go, Charlie. Ye can have my rice." He patted his belly. "I'm full." He walked away chuckling.

"Mama, after I finish my meal, can I have his rice?" Mauricio pointed to Helmut's plate.

"My goodness, son you have such a sweet tooth. That belongs to Charlie."

"That's fine, Carla. He's young, and I need to keep my figure." He began to take his apron off. "I'll walk you to the companionway."

"It's fine, Charlie. It's still light outside." She left with supper in her carry-on basket.

Sarah and Sophia weren't in her cabin, and she checked next door. The captain's cabin door had been left slightly ajar. She carefully pushed the door open and found Sarah seated on their berth crocheting and Captain Briggs seated across from her, rocking their sleepy daughter in his arms. His eyes were on his wife who looked at him smiling. Even though Benjamin projected a certain austerity during his function as captain, his true self came across when in the company of his wife and daughter. *This is what a real family looks like when united by love.* These thoughts were followed by the proximity of their inevitable end, since nothing good ever lasts forever. A dead weight squeezed her chest and throat. "Excuse me, Mrs. Briggs, your dinner is here, I ... I have to get some air, please excuse me," she left hastily. On the way out of the companionway, she bumped into Richardson.

"Oh, I'm sorry," she said a bit flushed.

"What's the matter?"

"Richardson, I need to be alone, that's all. Nothing personal."

"Very well, but remember it's not wise to walk alone on deck. It will be dark soon."

"Don't worry. I promise to stay right here by the companionway — a few minutes of fresh air and I'll be fine."

"Very well, I have been tending the wheel until now and haven't had supper. I'm going to the galley and then I'll stop by."

"Good, Mauricio is there and he'll be happy to see you."

The gentle, cool breeze and calm sea was conducive to promoting her mind to wonder. She walked to the taffrail, looking at the ocean while fighting within herself, a whirlwind of thoughts that provoked contradictory feelings clouding all reasoning. Her original motives when she first had come aboard had deteriorated once she grew to know the Briggs family. The wholesomeness of their love for each other and the way they treated her and Mauricio made her feel that if anything, she had to protect them. And then she had met Richardson. Yes, she knew he was married, and at first, she had not expected more than their casual encounters, but everything had changed — even her son loved Richardson. *I'm ready to start anew about everything in life.* Then noticing how quickly it had gotten dark, she made haste toward the galley. *I must talk to Richardson right away. I'll tell him everything, and if he truly loves me, he'll understand my past and present predicament.* She heard the sound of a blow, then a brief groan followed by silence. She stopped and waited to hear more, but all she heard was the sound of the waves rippling against the hull. *My imagination has no limits,* she started walking again and almost tripped over a body that laid face down with blood gorging out from his skull, a wood beam laid next to his head.

"Oh my God," she cried out. "Oh, meu Deus! Oh, my God!"

"Calm down, woman," Helmut appeared. "Now, let's see who it is," he turned the body over. "Oh, it's the second mate."

"You mean Mr. Gillings?" she cried out.

"It does look like him, hmm? Most likely he's been drinking, and when he walked on deck drunk, he got hit by a wood beam the wind blew in his direction."

"Helmut, you must think I'm an idiot," she pointed toward the sky. "There is no wind, and Andrew does not drink. You ... You killed him!"

"Go, bugger off," he lowered his voice. "Go below to yer cabin and shut pan, or I'll do the same to ye."

She ran straight to the galley.

"Mr. Richardson is not here," Charlie said. "By the way, Mauricio wasn't feeling good, and he took him to your cabin." She rushed out past the main hatch where the yawl sat and almost missed Richardson on the port side.

"Carla ..." he called her attention. She fell into his arms sobbing and told him where she had found Andrew dead, bleeding from his head.

"Are you sure?" he asked.

She couldn't stop crying. "I saw him ... I saw him with my own eyes, I swear and ..."

"We need to find Captain Briggs," he held her hand as they rushed down the companionway. "Mauricio wasn't feeling too good, and I didn't want to leave him alone in your cabin, so I left him with the Captain and his wife, and then came looking for you."

"Captain Briggs, I need a word with you outside," Richardson said as soon as he walked in.

Carla found Mauricio curled up in the armchair with his arms crisscross over his stomach. "Mama, my tummy hurts a lot."

"That's because you ate too much rice pudding, my little sugar plump," she kissed his forehead. "The next time you want to eat more than one bowl, remember what you're suffering now." She turned to Sarah, "It's my fault for allowing him to eat Charlie's portion. I should use more discipline on him."

"Go ahead, Carla," Sarah said. "Take him to our cabin, and once lying down, maybe a hot water bottle to hold against his tummy will help ease the discomfort."

"Good idea. Yes, that always helps. I'll be back soon to see if you need anything else. Oh, have you had a chance to try the pudding I made?"

"No, I'm sorry Carla. Sophia and I truly enjoyed the *Caldo Verde* soup for dinner and weren't hungry for supper. But we'll definitely save the rice for breakfast tomorrow."

Carla helped Mauricio to lay in his hammock and tried to cover him with a blanket, but he was running cold sweats.

"Mauricio, I'm going to get you a hot water bottle. You be a good boy and wait here. It will take me just a few minutes to get back."

She ran as quickly as she could to the galley, but when she returned with the hot water bottle, Mauricio was not in the cabin. She knocked at the Captain's door, but Sarah had not seen him. She knocked at Richardson's door, but there was no answer. She came up on deck, and seeing Benjamin and Richardson walking toward her, she ran to meet them.

They had not seen him, and they had also checked the spot where Carla had last seen Andrew and found no vestiges of him or the blood.

"No! That's impossible. I saw him dead, right over there, bleeding from his head, over there, by the yawl." Her eyes opened wide as she let out a terrorized scream and took off running, calling for her son. Maybe he had fallen overboard. She climbed over the side ready to dive into the ocean. Richardson managed to hold her down, as she struggled to get loose from him.

"Meu filho, my son!" she cried out. "Mauricio, Mauricio!" She fainted.

Richardson carried her to the captain's cabin, and Sarah placed a cold towel over Carla's forehead. When she came around, she started to laugh, "I know what happened to Mauricio. He's hiding, don't you see? He's hiding. He's playing with me," she laughed but also cried. "He's such a playful little boy; he wants me to go find him. I have to go look for him." She tried to stand, but Sarah put her arms around her. "Carla, you must listen. Most likely he's hiding, like you said, but it's dark out there, and it's best for you to remain here."

"Yes, Carla we're going to look for Mauricio right now," Richardson said.

Just then, they heard a hurried knock at the door. It was Arian. "Cap'n, I need to see ye, right away, please."

Benjamin stepped out with Richardson.

"Arian, you really look under the weather," Captain Briggs said.

"Aye Cap'n, not feeling well, not well at all, since supper. I just want to tell ye that I was coming out of the forecastle hoping to puke over the side, but the stomach pain was so bad that I fell on my knees. I finally got up to get some help from Charlie, and that's when I saw Helmut carrying over his shoulders Mr. Gillings ... the second mate. Oh, Gawd!" he moaned. "Oh, Gawd ..." He bent over and then straightened out again. "Sorry Cap'n, but I'm in a lot of pain," he took in several short breaths as he motioned his body back and forth while holding his hands against his stomach. "Helmut threw Mr. Gillings overboard and Mauricio ... Mauricio stood there facing Helmut. The boy was crying, and I heard him say, "Stop that. What you're doing is not nice." Arian went down on his knees once again and moaned.

Richardson seized him by the shoulders and lifted him up. "You saw Mauricio? Where is he?"

"The boy ran," Arian cried out. "And Helmut ran after him. He called out for his mother, and I couldn't do anything except roll on the floor from the pain ... oh crap!"

"Then you didn't really see what happened to Mauricio, right?" Richardson said. "He could have gotten away and ..."

"Nay, Mauricio is gone ... I'm afraid the boy is ..." Arian's voice became barely audible. He bent forward and went into a fetal position, shaking, and when he stopped, he tumbled sideways.

Captain Briggs bent over and placed two fingers on Arian's side of the neck. "Dear God, he's dead!" He stood and made the cross. "We need to stop Helmut, right now."

"Exactly, but he might be armed."

"We must proceed with caution. I'll need my sword."

"I'll go get my sidearm."

They both rushed to enter the companionway as Charlie was coming up.

"Mind the grease," Richardson said apologetically.

Charlie moved to the side. "No problem, Mr. Richardson, go ahead. Captain Briggs, what's all the rush? I came to check on Mauricio, but he's nowhere to be found. What's going on?"

"Charlie, listen, we need your help. Bring some rope and meet us back here as soon as possible," he brought a finger to his lips. "Be very quiet, and if you see Helmut, just stay away from him."

In his cabin, Benjamin proceeded to take down his sword from the wall hanger.

"Benjamin, what're you doing?" Sarah asked. "What're you going to do with that sword?" Seeing the food basket on the table, he gasped in terror. "Have you eaten any?"

"No, I'm sorry, but Sophia and I weren't hungry."

"Thank God! Carla, please listen to me. Richardson and I have to take care of very important matters, and we're also going to look further for Mauricio. I need you to stay here with my family. Can I count on you?"

She nodded silently.

"Benjamin, please tell me, what do you need the sword for?" Sarah insisted.

"Sarah, there's no time for me to explain anything right now," he grabbed the food basket, and before leaving, he said, "This door must remain locked until I return. I'll be back soon, I promise."

Once on deck, he threw the basket and its contents overboard. With Charlie and Richardson on each side, they went straight to the forecastle where they found Volkert lying in his hammock, groaning.

"Have you seen Helmut or Mauricio, by any chance?" Richardson asked.

"No, I have not seen anybody," he went on groaning. "Boz was here, but he left to throw up."

"Very well," Benjamin said. "You need to get up immediately and do the same."

Noticing that Volkert wasn't moving, Richardson shouted, "You heard your Captain, now do as you're told, right now. It's an order!"

They found Helmut standing at the bow. He faced them with one hand on his hip. "Blimey! It's about time ye showed up. I was getting tired of waiting to see who was still around. So ... it's just the two of ye, eh?" He smirked. "Ye don't think ye can take me, do ye?" He pointed to Charlie. "Oh, ye brought the old man along. What happened to the German brothers — are they indisposed?" he let out an animated laugh.

Richardson reached for the revolver in his holster and pointed it at Helmut, "You scurvy dog, what did you do to Mauricio? You better answer me, or I'll shoot you right now. Where is the boy?"

Helmut remained motionless at the sight of the gun. "Wow, ye finally show some balls, but ye don't scare me. Besides, I have no idea what happened to him."

"You're a rotten liar!"

"What do ye take me for, his keeper? Go ask his mother."

"You, miserable scalawag of a coward," Richardson kept the gun pointed at Helmut. "Arian witnessed Mauricio talking to you when you threw the second mate overboard. Now, you tell me what happened to Mauricio, or I shoot your brains off right now."

"Richardson, don't do it," Captain Briggs put a hand on Richardson's forearm. "We need him alive if we're going to get anything out of him. Charlie, use the rope to tie Helmut's hands behind his back."

Not knowing exactly what the circumstances were, Charlie vacillated as he approached Helmut, who found it to be the perfect opportunity to grab Charlie and use him as a shield, but Benjamin caught on to the maneuver, and as soon as Helmut brought his right arm across Charlie's neck, Benjamin branded his sword in a rapid precise move toward Helmut's right forearm, cutting deep into the flesh. He let go of Charlie with a screeching yell. "Tarnation seize me!" he cried out and, grabbing the bleeding arm, staggered back while staring at them with a stupefied look on his face.

"I'll repeat once again, Charlie tie his hands behind his back," then to Helmut, "You're lucky that my family is onboard or I would hang you myself right now from the yard arm. You'll be put below until we reach land, and then the authorities will decide your fate."

Charlie tied Helmut's hands and then pulled his apron off and wrapped it tight around Helmut's open wound.

"Sorry Captain, I can't stand the sight of blood,"

"I understand. Charlie, you have been a great help. We'll take it from here."

"Very well then. I'll get back to the galley, and please let me know when you find Mauricio." With Helmut walking in front of them, Benjamin and Richardson took him down to the hold and had him sit against a wood beam. Richardson tied Helmut's ankles and then reinforced the wrists behind his back with extra rope and tied the extra rope's length to one of the metal hooks hanging from the wood beam above Helmut's head. He yanked it to make sure the knot was secured. "I'm going to ask you for the last time. What happened to Mauricio?" Helmut didn't answer, and he yanked harder on the rope making him groan. "I already told ye, I'm not his keeper."

They closed the fore hatch and proceeded to search for Mauricio once again, but after looking in every possible corner where he could be hiding, they had to admit he was nowhere on the ship.

"Richardson, this is very hard for me to say, but I believe that Arian witnessed more than what he was able to describe to us. If Mauricio saw Helmut throwing Andrew overboard, like Arian told us, I'm afraid he may have killed him ..."

"I know, but I can't accept it. He was just an innocent child. How could anyone commit such a horrendous crime? Benjamin, the very thought that he's gone is too unbearable for me to endure." He wept.

They were next to the galley and went in. They found the

Lorenzen brothers seated at the table drinking from their tin tumblers.

"I found them here. They looked like ghosts," Charlie said.

"At first, Volkert refused to come with me," Boz said. "But finally, I convinced him that we should seek Charlie's help."

"I gave them a good amount of powerful syrup made by an apothecary friend of mine who felt every cook should carry it in their ditty bag, in case the meal they made had gone astray, and their customers needed a little expelling help ... Which, in this case," he pointed to Boz and Volkert. "They really needed to get it all out as soon as possible. They have been throwing up after each mug of the boiled syrup, and after I watched them out there, the stink made me throw up too. Here, drink some more." The brothers willingly slugged it all in, and then ran out just as fast to the side of the ship.

"I don't understand, we all ate the same food!" Charlie said.

"Well, I have not had supper, and luckily for my wife and daughter, they were not hungry."

"I had a good portion of the Shepherd's pie but didn't get the dessert. Once Mauricio started feeling sick, I took him back to his cabin, and then everything just rolled over one thing after another," Richardson said.

"My brother and I had Shepherd's pie," Boz said as he walked in followed by Volkert. "We had double portions of it, and with all the bread we ate with it, we only had room to share a small bowl of the rice pudding and then left to tend to the ship."

"Arian ate supper and then took two large servings of rice pudding for dessert," Charlie said. "I took a taste of it earlier in the day ... but I hate cinnamon and spit it out. You think it was the rice pudding?"

"The rice pudding, that's it!" Benjamin said. "Only those who ate it ... Which reminds me, Carla made the dessert. We need to speak to her."

"Yes, she did make it," Richardson said defensively. "But she had nothing to do with it being bad. She would not have allowed her son to eat it."

"Mauricio ate his serving, and then I gave him Helmut's. Oh my God! What have I done?" Charlie held his head between his hands. "Someone poisoned the rice. Who could have done it?"

"Helmut!" Captain Briggs and Richardson responded simultaneously.

"He figured if he poisoned everyone," Richardson said. "He wouldn't have to bother killing each of us individually like he has been doing."

"But why?" Charlie asked. "What is he going to do with the ship when there is no one onboard to run it, except himself?"

"Maybe he's gone crazy, and in his madness, he doesn't realize what he's doing," Benjamin said. "I mean what kind of cold-hearted man would kill a child, unless he was out of his mind? I'm afraid we need to tell Carla about her son ..."

"I'll do that Captain, if you don't mind. I believe it's my responsibility. Mauricio meant a lot to me," Richardson said.

Charlie gave an analytical look at Boz and Volkert, "I believe these men are going to be fine. But they could use some time off to rest here a while longer. Captain, you know I can tend to the wheel, right?"

"Yes, Charlie, please do that. Thank you."

Benjamin returned to his cabin followed by Richardson, and Sarah opened the door once she heard his voice. Seeing her husband's sword marred with blood, she backed away. "Benjamin, what happened?" Then moved toward him, "Are you hurt?"

"I'm fine, Sarah," he wiped the blood off the sword with his handkerchief and put the sword back on the wall hanger. "I had to use it to stop Helmut from hurting Charlie, and in the process, I wounded his arm with it. Richardson and I have him securely tied in the hold, and he won't be hurting anyone else anymore."

"Thank God you're both well. Did you find Mauricio?" she asked Richardson. Carla sat stiffly in a chair as if at attention.

Richardson's lack of response made Carla take a rapid glance at him and then refocused her transfixed gaze back at the wall across from her.

"I better go relieve Charlie at the wheel so he can go check on Boz and Volkert," Benjamin said. "Richardson," he shook his hand. "I thank the Lord for having you with us." He kissed Sarah on the cheek and took another step over to Carla. He touched her shoulder lightly. She did not respond. He left.

"Carla," Richardson said.

She raised her hand, "You don't have to tell me. Your eyes can't hide the pain you feel." she stood. "Mrs. Briggs, if you don't mind, I need to go to my cabin and be by myself. May I leave Sophie here with you just for tonight?" She left hurriedly.

Richardson followed her, and stood outside her cabin until the morning.

Wednesday, November 20

Captain Briggs, Richardson, Charlie, and the Lorenzen brothers' health now recovered, gathered to put Arian to rest at sea. Volkert held Arian's book <u>Gulliver's Travels,</u> against his chest. He was the only one who knew of Arian's harsh childhood and how *Gulliver* had given Arian the strength to continue to endure in a world of prejudice and cruelty. It wasn't until he had joined Captain Briggs and his crew that he had finally felt like a man. Volkert inserted the book inside the hammock before they covered Arian's body and tied it. He took his cap off, went down on one knee and brought his right hand to his heart. Everyone did the same. He looked at Captain Briggs who responded by nodding. "Thank you, Cap'n, for allowing me to speak. Mate Arian, you were the tallest friend I ever had, your giant heart was appreciated by all of us, and we will miss you. God be with you." Then he added in German. "Gott sei mit dir."

They tipped him feet first into the ocean. A moment of silence followed.

Richardson stood over the taffrail and murmured, "Mauricio, son of my heart, these are for you so that you may continue to practice making sea knots in Heaven," he held three small ropes in his hands. "Someday, God willing and if I'm lucky enough, I'll join you."

Carla had been standing the whole time on the port side holding to her chest Mauricio's magnifying glass. She watched Richardson drop the ropes over the side and into the ocean. She brought the magnifying glass to her lips and kissed it before dropping it over the taffrail. Then she returned to her cabin and curled into the hammock where her son used to sleep.

Benjamin and Richardson met with Charlie, Boz and Volkert at the galley to organize a working schedule. Everyone would take turns at the helm and the basic chores to keep the ship on going. Charlie still did the cooking but no longer spent time preparing fancy meals. Simplicity meant more time to help his fellow mates. Five men to run the ship to Genoa wasn't going to be an easy task, but they were determined to do it.

The women could not be accounted for any type of manual labor — one was too weak and sick just like her child. The other wasn't much better.

Richardson knocked at Carla's door. Getting no answer, he left the dinner tray on the floor by her door, with a note, "If you need a friend, let me know. Yours, Richardson."

When he returned with supper, the note was gone but the food remained outside.

Holding on to her husband's arm while he carried Sophia, they joined Charlie for supper in the galley, but Sophia had a serious coughing spell, and once she began to cry, they had to leave. He took them to his cabin and then headed starboard. Bending his head and upper body against the taffrail, his vision became blurred with tears. *Dear God, how can you allow this to happen? I have given you my complete devotion, and in exchange, what have I ever demanded or asked from you, except my family's health?* He looked up at the sky, but there were no stars that night, or a merciful God looking down upon him, only the thick fog that had swallowed the ship mercilessly. *How dare you abandon us, how dare you allow Mauricio, a child, to die? And my men. What could they have done to deserve such harsh end? Where is your divine justice? I beseech thee, O lord! My family is dying. I'm only begging you to let them live, that's all I ask from Thee!* A feeling of guilt came over his thoughts. He kneeled, his hands together in prayer. *Please forgive me, dear Father in Heaven, I didn't mean to offend you in any way. You're a merciful God, so please, if my wife and daughter must perish before we reach our final destination, please allow them to join you in Heaven without further suffering here on Earth.* He made the cross and stood. He entered his cabin and found Sarah and Sophia sleeping in his berth.

He closed the door softly behind him and went to relieve Richardson at the helm.

Thursday, November 21

The sequence of the latest fateful events had caused more than an emotional impact on everyone. Without Mauricio, Andrew, Arian, Luciano and Tony, the ship had become a ghost vessel of dark schemes and shadows, accented by the constant cold mist, which, like osmosis, had penetrated gradually into their bones' marrow. The men were definitely used to worse weather, but now, an unusual sense of doom had taken possession of their spirits. They could feel Helmut's presence below deck, a monstrous piece of lead pulling their once joyous spirits down and under. If given a chance, they would have taken justice into their own hands, but in accord with Captain Briggs religious beliefs, they did their best to distance themselves from such thought. Charlie was chosen to take on the job of feeding and keeping him clean, until they arrived at Genoa.

Carla had been spending the days and nights in her cabin since Mauricio was gone. The woman who had embarked for the purpose of caring for two ailing people was the one in need of much compassion. Sarah did not want to disturb her, but that evening, she brought her hot tea and then sat quietly in the corner chair, reading a book. She knew the pain of losing her own babies, and her heart felt for Carla. The silence between the two women prevailed until Sophia, who until then, had been playing with her ragdoll, walked up to Carla. "Calla," she said. "Where is Mauri?"

"I'm so sorry, Carla," Sarah stood and put the book on the side table. "I should have known better than bring Sophie with me. We'll leave you alone."

"No, Mrs. Briggs, please stay. It's a perfectly normal question. My dearest child," she turned to Sophia. "Let me show you where Mauricio is," she pointed to her chest. "Mauri is inside here. Go ahead. Put your ear next to it and you'll hear his heart beating, next to mine."

Sophia climbed on Carla's lap and put her ear on her chest. She clapped her hands, "I hear him, I hear him, tick, tack, tick, tack ..." then giving it a second thought, "But ... but when will he come out to play with me?"

Carla began to cry. Sophia put her hand on Carla's chest. "Don't cry. Mauri can stay there with you; you don't have to cry anymore. Mama, can I stay with Calla?"

"Mrs. Briggs, please let Sophie stay," Carla implored. "She's very young, but she has the soul of a wise spirit and brings me much comfort."

Friday, November 22

Early that morning, Benjamin and Richardson paid a visit to Helmut. First, they tried Benjamin's way, by showing clemency and even understanding if he explained the reason for his killing spree. But Helmut showed no desire of collaborating and remained silent.

"You either answer our questions," Richardson said. "Or I swear, we'll hang you right here, and no one will be the wisest." Helmut remained unyielding. Richardson grabbed him by the neck. "You're not deaf. I want an answer right now. What happened to Mauricio? What did you do to him?"

Helmut remained impenetrable except for crying out when Richardson kicked him in the ribs. Benjamin had to pull Richardson away or he would have killed him.

Much like Benjamin, Richardson went on with scarcely any sleep, but he still found a few minutes, twice a day, to check on Sarah, Sophia and the woman he loved.

Charlie balanced his duties between the kitchen, taking care of Helmut, and lending a helping hand to Boz and Volkert.

There was a mutual purpose onboard, a unified objective: Get the *Mary Celeste* to its destination as soon as possible.

"I depend on God and you to help deliver our cargo to Genoa," Benjamin had told them. "The faster we get there, the sooner we can make it to France. My family is in need of urgent medical care. But if we work together and the weather holds up, our chances of making it are very promising."

They believed him, but in his heart, he didn't. He did not share his torment with anyone, not even Richardson. Each morning that he found his family alive, he counted his blessings.

Even though he barely had any time off — as he worked side by side with his men — he made sure to stop and check on his family several times a day.

Saturday, November 23

Sophia ran a light temperature all night, but in the morning, the fever broke, and she even ate one of the bunny's ear and tail of a small hoecake Charlie made just for her.

Later that morning, while Sophia slept, Sarah offered to read to Carla from one of her poetry books she had brough along, but Carla preferred free verse over the carefully monotonous rhythm of the classical styles. But she did pay special attention to Sarah's comment that music was God's way of establishing a heart-to-heart language with him.

"There is one particular song that I would love to sing directly to God," she told Sarah.

"What's the name?"

"'A Mother's Prayer' ... A Portuguese song, of course."

"Maybe I can accompany you on the melodeon ..."

"Oh, my sweet Mrs. Briggs. For this song, I would prefer to sing without any musical accompaniment, so God can really hear my words."

Veronica Esagui

Charlie was going by the companionway when he heard Carla's lyrics. He had befriended a few Portuguese sailors while traveling in the Mediterranean with Benjamin, and since he had a natural gift for learning languages, he recognized the words enough to understand the cursing chant of a mad woman filled with the delight of a violent revenge against the man that had killed her child. Carla cried copiously after she finished "A Mother's Prayer."

"Don't worry," she told Sarah. "Singing that song has made me feel a lot better."

Sunday, November 24

The previous night's thick fog had dissipated for the most part, and the ship moved now at a steady pace of 10 knots through the surrounding calmness of a dark grayish blue ocean.

Sunday's early morning gathering was postponed because there were not enough hands on board. "I'm sure God will understand if we go on with our chores and skip today's services," Benjamin said. "May the great Lord above bless us and keep the rest of us safe." They all hurried to their posts.

In her cabin, Sarah let her fingers run softly over the keys of the melodeon as she played "Nocturne op.9 no.2" one of her favorite Chopin melodies. Sophia slept in Carla's arms, who sat in the corner chair, her eyes staring into space like an owl watching beyond what anyone else could see in the dark.

On deck, Charlie was busy rolling a thick, long rope when he became aware of a musical echo, an exact copy of the mesmerizing music Sarah played on the melodeon. He stood to pay better attention to what seemed to be coming from the horizon, then gazed around hoping to find someone who, like him, could hear it too. Charlie was quite familiar with the echo effect, the reflection of sound arriving after shouting inside an empty room, but the notes he heard bouncing back played in a lower key than Sarah's music. He looked up at Boz at the wheel, and since he did not seem to be aware of anything going on, he bent over again to finish rolling the rope. *I've been at sea too long.*

"Hey Charlie, you hear that?" Boz called out.

"You bet I do," he stood immediately. "For a moment, I thought I had lost my mind," he laughed with contentment.

"I'd say, Mrs. Briggs' music sounds even better when played in double," he laughed with Charlie.

"You two are mighty gay this morning," Richardson said as he walked by. "Everything orl korrect?"

Boz and Charlie responded in unison, *orl korrect,* but the swooshing echo of their voices just augmented their laughter. Richardson had no idea of what was so funny, but he found himself laughing along. Hearing the ongoing laughter not far from him, Volkert walked away from their direction, *Even my brother has gone mad; ja everybody in this ship is going crackers. We're doomed.*

Sarah stopped playing and so did the echo, just as sudden. Boz and Charlie looked dumbfounded at each other and then at Richardson. "Mr. Richardson, so you heard it too, eh?" Charlie said.

"I heard you laughing, and I guess I did a bit myself. Hey we all need a good laugh after what we've been through."

"No, before that," Boz said. "Mrs. Briggs' music was echoing from across the horizon and back at us. You ... didn't hear it?"

"I only heard you laughing, which got me laughing too," he let out a short chuckle. "With all respect, maybe you're suffering from exhaustion. We all are, that's for sure."

"Are you telling us, we suffer from exhaustion, and as such, our minds can hear the same sounds?" Charlie protested. "It's like saying we're all experiencing the same dream."

"Very well, maybe you're right. Men, now listen. How about we keep this occurrence between us. I don't see any reason to bother the Captain over such trifles. He already has enough to contend with. Are we in agreement?"

"I agree," Charlie said. "If Mrs. Briggs finds out, she might not want to play the melodeon anymore, and we need music onboard; it does well for our spirits."

"My lips are sealed," Boz said.

Each went their own way, but Volkert had returned in time to hear them. He crouched down on the port side of the forecastle and cried. *I'll never see my hinterland or my mother again. Most likely she died, since she was already old and ill when we left. I should never have gone to America. I should never have become a sailor.* He heard footsteps and wiped his tears rapidly on his sleeves. There was no way he was going to allow anyone to call him a milksop. He spotted Captain Briggs and walked in the opposite direction, but his thoughts continued to batter him. *We're cursed, cursed between the devil in the hull below us and the surrounding cold and dark ocean where we'll soon be food for the fish.*

Charlie rang the wall brass bell hanging outside the galley. At the start of their voyage, it had always come across as the sound of "come and get it while it's hot," but now that the crew had diminished considerably, and the work had more than tripled, the bell had become more like a church bell calling for their faithful members. Eating together had become a ritual of emotional support, a reassurance of their own survival. Boz, a positive, energetic man, couldn't help but sympathize with his brother's hopeless feelings. Losing most of their mates under such drastic measures and the vanishing of Mauricio had caused everyone a stupor of the senses. Benjamin and Richardson felt that sharing their meals with the two brothers was now an important part of keeping up the morale, and as such, they took turns being there. It was also a special treat when the women joined them at the galley.

Sarah had a knack for bringing out a positive conversation, and even though the signs of her illness showed in her sunken cheeks and pale complexion, they appreciated her effort to be present. When she didn't come to the galley, Carla didn't either. Richardson took the responsibility of taking meals to their cabin, since he knew most likely either Sarah and or Sophia were not doing well that day.

To everyone's surprise, Sarah, Carla and Sophia showed up at the galley for supper. The child sat on Carla's lap, but seemed lethargic and wasn't even tempted to taste the chocolate pudding Charlie made just for her. Carla excused herself and took Sophia back to their cabin.

Charlie propped a pot of hot lamb stew in the center of the table, and Benjamin offered thanks for the dinner they were about to partake in. He used the wood ladle to serve Sarah the first serving, but she motioned none for her. He served himself. Volkert held his bowl high in his hand and filled it to the very top. The ship shook unexpectedly, causing him to drop the bowl, which rolled in Boz's direction and onto his lap, causing him to start swearin' and dancin' as if possessed by a rowdy evil.

"What in God's name!" Benjamin ran out with Charlie, and Boz followed them still swearin'.

Sarah turned to Volkert who sat staring at the stew mess. "Mr. Lorenzen, if you give me your arm, I could use your help to get me out on deck."

Richardson called out from the helm, "Captain Briggs, so glad to see you, it looks like we hit something."

"Another ship?"

"No sir. No vessels of any kind that I can see."

"We're at high sea, so it's impossible that we hit land or even an iceberg at this latitude." He brought his monocular tight against his right eye. Except for the slight glow of the sun half hidden by clouds, giving the water a transparent green glow, there wasn't much to see above the surface. He walked diligently from one side to the other looking out each time.

"It was a light tap, but we definitely hit something, that's for sure," Boz brushed vigorously his stained pants.

"Wait," Benjamin brought his left hand up as he looked attentively through the monocular. "Quick," he waved his hand up and down. "We must control forward motion until we identify what this is. He pointed at what appeared to be a thick green pasture surrounding the ship."

"I see it now," Richardson pointed to the sides of the ship. "It's all around us; I'll go get the lead line to measure the depth." He returned quickly and started lowering the lead weight attached to a hemp line.

"Green monsters," Volkert said as he arrived with Sarah, who let go of his arm to stand against the taffrail. He began biting whatever fingernails he had left while walking in circles. "They'll slide up our ship and after sucking out our blood, they'll pull us into the water to drown. Most likely they already made a hole in the hull so that our ship can submerge faster. We're all kaput."

"Mr. Lorenzen, you have such an interesting, fertile imagination," Sarah wore her usual confident smile. "Be a dear and please go to my cabin and check on Sophia and Carla, then come back and let me know how they're doing."

He left, and Benjamin stood next to her as they watched the line slipping down between Richardson's fingers.

Sarah borrowed the monocular from her husband and bent over the taffrail to look down. *This has to be the most beautiful green color I have ever seen.* But she quickly backed away when she recognized the same children's voices she had heard before. She still did not understand what they were saying and blamed the unfamiliar intonations on the ongoing fever. Getting a grip on her emotions by telling herself that, like her son Arthur who was afraid of the dark when there was really nothing to fear, she bent over the side once again to look and listen more closely. She could still see the green below but the voices could no longer be heard.

She handed the monocular back to her husband. Meanwhile, the line had reached its full length, and Richardson pulled the rope up slowly hoping to find something adhering to it, but the line came up as clean as when he dropped it. "Don't look like anything solid," he said. "Perhaps it's just grass, or ... seaweed."

"Maybe we should attach a bucket to the end of the rope and that way, we might be able to grab something from the top," Boz said. "Go ahead, tie me to the rope and lower me down."

"You're a good man, Boz," Richardson said. "But it's too much of a risk."

"Mrs. Briggs," Volkert said. "Mrs. Nunes told me to tell ye and the Cap'n that Sophia is sleeping and they're doing well, but I'm afraid she's not doing well at all, for all I know, she could be dying."

"Volkert," Benjamin said. "I have a very important task for you to do. Check inside the cabins, the deck and all around us for any water damage. And Volkert, take your time," he watched him walk away. "Poor man, he really needs help. Mr. Richardson, please stay at the helm and watch for any other disparities you might find floating around us. As you already know, the ocean in this region is at its deepest and ideal for sailing, thus it's completely irrational to even think we rammed into anything solid. I'm going to take my wife back to my cabin and go over the charts." He lifted Sarah in his arms and headed to the companionway.

He pulled out a chart from his top desk drawer and opened it over his desk, conscientiously smoothing it down with his hands. The ship stirred once again, and Sarah was glad to be sitting.

Charlie knocked at their door but entered without waiting for an answer. "Captain, did you feel this next vibration?" he didn't wait for his answer. "We agreed not to tell you anything, so you'd not worry, but with these late developments coming onto us, I feel you need to know."

"What are you trying to say, Charlie?"

"This morning, when Mrs. Briggs was playing the melodeon in her cabin, Boz and I heard her music being played, like an echo … a soft, muffled echo, note per note. Mr. Richardson was close by, but he did not hear anything."

"So something like that happens onboard my ship, and no one tells me about it," he left in the direction of his first mate.

"Mr. Richardson," he called out for him. "Why was I not immediately informed about my wife's music being heard this morning, coming from … from out there?"

"Like you, I did not hear it, and at the time, I did not find it to be much of a concern for us to worry about when you already have so much to cope with."

"Mr. Richardson, you need to put our friendship aside when it comes to matters of safety onboard our ship. It's not up to you to make such decision as to what is important or not. As first mate, I depend on you to keep me posted of everything that happens. If we're going to survive any further setbacks, it's most urgent that we work together as a unit, and I mean all of us."

"Captain," Richardson reached out to shake Benjamin's hand, "I apologize. You're absolutely right; we must work together if we're going to make it."

On witnessing the strong bond of friendship between Benjamin and Richardson, Charlie followed the example and shook hands with Boz. Volkert arrived in time to see them shaking hands, and when Boz extended his hand to him, he backed away with a terrified look on his face. "Why is everyone shaking hands, are we saying auf wiedersehen?" Then he added, "I saw no damage to the ship, but that doesn't mean anything, I may have missed something serious."

"No damage, you say," Benjamin held a hand to his chin and paced a few feet, then as if suddenly he'd seen the answer, "Everyone follow me," and he rushed to his cabin. He found Sarah lying down. He knelt next to her and took her hands in his. "My dearest, I know you're very weak and not feeling well, but I need you to play on deck the same tune you did this morning." Seeing the look of wonder on her face, he added, "It's very important that we do that right now." Then to the others, "The only way to find out if there's any logic to my thinking is to repeat the same circumstances of this morning, but make it even better. Let's bring the melodeon and a seat, out to the bow." Carla opened the door of her cabin to inquire about all the commotion. She didn't want to wake up Sophia and would remain indoors with her.

Once situated on deck, Benjamin and the men stood next to Sarah, like watchdogs, focusing their eyes between the surrounding ocean and the horizon. Sarah began playing, and the music could be heard back from the horizon, except for the tone quality having such rich tone that Sarah couldn't help saying, "*Their* music seems to be coming from a very different and powerful musical instrument." She continued to play.

"This is what you two heard earlier today?" Richardson said.

"Aye-aye, Mr. Richardson, but now it's definitely a lot clearer and louder than when Charlie and I heard it earlier." Boz said.

"It makes sense," Benjamin said. "When Sarah played inside the cabin, it wasn't loud enough to make an impact on the ocean waves. That's the only explanation ... the ocean acts as a sound spreader ..." Just as Sarah finished playing, they became aware of the sudden surrounding silence.

"This was such an amazing grand moment in my life," she couldn't help being excited. "So many times I wondered what it would be like to play a musical instrument with the capacity of projecting each note loud enough to be heard from one home to another, from one city to another and even all around the world." She had just disclosed a bit too much, concerning the mere possibility of something that couldn't possibly exist.

"Most likely you doubt my sanity at this moment, but please allow me to expand my imagination as I see the amazing possibilities of the future, now that I have encountered a close glimpse of what I always dreamed about."

"My dearest, you don't have to apologize. When considering God's power and the intelligence he has bestowed upon us, nothing is impossible for men to create. In the last century, we have had, including the present one, the development of several major inventions that were not even conceivable, like the steam engine, the locomotive, the self-winding mechanism for pocket watches …"

"The can opener, condensed milk," Charlie said.

"And let's not forget," Richardson said. "Vulcanized rubber pneumatic tires for bikes …"

"The stapler …" Boz said.

"Elevators built with safety breaks," Volkert said to everyone's surprise. Then he added, "That's what they say, I wouldn't trust them …"

"Gentlemen," Sarah said. "I'm very tired and I must retire now, but let me tell you that with all these historical inventions at hand, don't be surprised if soon we discover how to make a machine that can carry us across the sky," she took Volkert's arm and walked away smiling as she knew she had just provided an impossible concept for anyone to grasp.

Even Charlie couldn't help laughing out loud.

"Let's bring our sails back up and put to good use the wind we're now experiencing," Benjamin said.

When he returned to his cabin, Sarah was still awake. "Come, husband, lie next to me. I miss hearing your heartbeat next to mine." She rested her head on his shoulder, "A lot has been happening, but I'm not afraid when you're near me."

He kissed her forehead. "Sarah, I keep thinking that perhaps we should have never left home," he sighed. "But if we didn't …" he stopped for a few seconds. "But if we hadn't …" No, he wasn't going to finish that sentence; it would be like admitting defeat, it would mean that there was nothing left, no hope, nothing to live for. He let his heart speak for him. "This very instant that I hold you close to me, I want it to last forever. I dare not think of my life without you," he caressed her face and took his time stroking her head softly with his fingers through her hair. He rocked her slowly, very slowly in his arms just like the first time he had held their son Arthur. He held her until she fell asleep, and after listening to the pounding rain on the skylight above their heads for a few minutes longer, he left the cabin to take the night shift at the wheel.

The *Mary Celeste* moved steadily at 9 knots until 7:00 p.m. when, with freshening wind, her speed increased to 10 knots.

At 8:00 p.m., her royal and topgallant sails were taken in. By 9:00 p.m. her speed dropped to 8 knots, at which she continued until midnight. Back in his cabin Benjamin entered in the log, "Knots, 8: Course, E. by S; Wind, west: stormy conditions prevailing over the Azores, November 24." Then he laid next to his wife.

Monday, November 25

According to hourly entries in the log between 1:00 and 4:00 a.m., the *Mary Celeste* continued at 8 knots. At the break of dawn, an entry was made on the log-slate, "At 5, made the island of Santa Maria bearing ESE." A similar entry was posted at 6:00 a.m. Benjamin observed Ponta Cabra, the northwestern extremity of Santa Maria Island at an approximate latitude of 37°0' slightly further north than its position at noon the previous day. He entered on the ship's log slate, "8:00 a.m. 25 November 1872. Eastern Point bears SSW, 6 miles distant ..." He stopped when Sarah awoke to a bloody coughing spell. Carla walked into their cabin, carrying a silver tray with a small jug of water and several towels. The disarray of her long hair, and the red eyes sent a clear testimonial of her grief. "Don't worry, Captain, I know you have chores to do. I'll stay and care for your wife," she said.

Charlie had spent the night working on deck and had caught about an hour of sleep that morning when he awoke crying. In his dream, Mauricio was crying out for help as the ocean waves engulfed him and took him under. He felt obliged to prepare a nourishing breakfast for whoever came to the galley and even managed to make some flat bread, but no matter how busy he got, Mauricio's plea for help kept haunting him. It was time to take some food to Helmut. He opened the hatch half way, and then just as quickly, he closed it down hard. *Let him wait.* He put the tray of food on the floor and went to offer Boz some help on deck.

Volkert found Richardson in the galley with a coffee mug in hand. "Mr. Volkert, as you can see, we don't have much of a show-up for breakfast," he stood. "We better get back on deck with the others."

"Very well, Mr. Richardson, but if you don't mind, I'll eat first, or my hands will shake and I won't be able to think straight."

"Well, we can't have that, can we? You go ahead and eat something," he left.

Volkert took three hoecakes from the stove and drowned them in maple syrup. He ate them while gulping the black coffee from his mug, then he grabbed a flat bread and stuffed it with two pickled eggs and a chunk of cheese and drank a second refill of coffee before leaving. He followed up with assiduously scrubbing the wooden-planked starboard deck with a bristle brush and salt water.

Charlie had honestly forgotten about Helmut. If it weren't that on his way back to the galley, he tripped over the food tray, splattering it all over. "Darn it, what else can go wrong?" he hurriedly mopped the floor and just as quickly hurried to the galley where he found Volkert stuffing his mouth with bread. "Nosh, is the only thing that gives me some kind of comfort," and he took another flat bread with him.

Charlie couldn't stand wasting food and decided to put together a large plate of everything on hand and bring it to Helmut. He was about to open the hatch when he heard the frantic voices of Boz and Richardson coming from the helm. "What's happening?" he asked Captain Briggs and Volkert who were running toward the helm.

"Wish I knew," Benjamin said. "All I know is that the ship is moving way too fast."

Charlie put the plate down next to the hatch and followed them. When they reached the helm, Captain Briggs had the same question as Charlie, but Richardson seemed to be at a loss for an answer. "Go ahead, Boz, you'll be better at explaining."

"I had just taken hold of the wheel when suddenly I had no control over the steering. Cap'n, it was as if the rudder had been disconnected. As you'll notice, the sails are down, and if I don't have control of the ship, then what? It's as if an underwater current is taking us to who knows where."

Benjamin tried to turn the wheel, but no matter how hard he tried, it didn't budge. Without the wheel to control the ship, he was afraid the direction in which the ship seemed to be going would take them away from the one and only way to Genoa.

The ship suddenly slowed down, and Boz tried once again to turn the wheel. He cried out, "I'm still unable to control the ship."

"I remember reading in "Buys Ballot's Law," concerning variants of atmospheric pressure ..." Benjamin said. "Perhaps we are at the center of a storm. I still have the book, perhaps ... I can find an answer. I'll be right back."

Richardson followed him.

Benjamin pulled "Buys Ballot's Law" from his wall cabinet, opened to the first page, and then began flipping through it absentmindedly. "I'm so frustrated," he laid the book on his desk next to the open chart and used his fist to pound the top of his desk.

"In the name of God, what is going on? Richardson, I'm scared for my family — an hour lost from arriving in time, can be too late for them ..."

"I know exactly how you feel, my friend. But the ship has slowed down, and that's good ... Meanwhile, I'm going to check the connection to the rudder and see what can be done to fix it," he patted Benjamin on the shoulder. "You'll see, everything is going to be fine, and we'll continue on our way, and later, we can look back at all this and have a good laugh about it." But he knew there was nothing to joke about, considering the lives that had already been lost. Benjamin nodded his head and put the compass back in the box.

Charlie finally made it down into the hull to feed Helmut, who immediately asked, "What in 'ell is going on up there?"

"Oh, nothing really, just a little commotion between Boz and Volkert. You know how brothers can act. Nothing for you to be worried about," he put the tray of food on the floor and brought his hands to his chest.

"What's the matter with ye?"

"I don't know. I have been getting this pressure over my chest lately, probably indigestion, most likely, no thanks to you." He rubbed his left arm briskly and then sat across from Helmut. He filled a spoon with porridge from the bowl. "Open your mouth, if you want to eat," he said. Not able to conceal his hard feelings toward Helmut, he tried not to look straight at him.

"Ye reckon I killed the kid, right? Well, I tell ye. He was playing around climbing the ropes and aloft he went, even after I repeatedly told him to get down. But he wouldn't listen, and when I turned around, he was gone. I swow on my mother's grave that I'm telling ye the truth."

"Oh yeah. Then what about the men? Were they also playing with the ropes when they died? I know you already told me you had nothing to do with the rice pudding getting almost everyone killed …

"Ye don't accept as true that I did not kill the kid, why would ye believe that I didn't have anything to do with the rice being bad? Look, if ye're the man I have always considered as a fair person, ye know that I could never hurt anyone. I have to agree that I'm ill-tempered as ye have seen in the past, but that don't make me no murderer."

Much like Captain Briggs, who was always willing to give

everyone the benefit of the doubt until proven guilty, Charlie felt the same way. Helmut had to control himself to keep a straight face, as he thought, *this idiot will believe anything I tell him; if he wasn't such a good cook, I would have killed him from the start.* He looked at Charlie with teary eyes, and his voice took on an imploring tone, "Please don't take away the little pride I still have. Let me eat the food with my own hands. Let me enjoy yer delicious food, like a man and not like a slave tied up."

"Sorry but I have told you several times that I can't disobey the captain's orders."

"Charlie, my pal, look, we're in the middle of the ocean, where can I go, where can I hide? I'm inside this 'ell hole with nay way out. There's nothing to fear from me. Man, leave me with some dignity, and at least the use of my hands to eat with. I promise that I'll remain here. After all, ye have the key."

"Do you want some bread? I made it fresh just this morning," Charlie said.

"Blimey! What d'ye think? Nobody makes bread like ye," and he chewed slowly, making small moaning sounds of pleasure, and licked his lips as if not to lose a single crumb. "Thank ye, Charlie, ye'r the best," he said as if talking to a close friend. "I understand how ye feel, I really understand, but can ye free my hands, so I can eat? Ye can come back later and tie me up again; just let me prove to ye that I'm not the scoundrel ye think I am."

Without a second thought, Charlie freed Helmut's hands. "Go ahead and eat your food. I'll be back." On the way out, he locked the door and then the hatch.

In his cabin, Benjamin and Richardson were going over the charts when they heard a knock on the door. "You better come, Captain Briggs. It's happening again," Volkert's voice came across so calm that Benjamin and Richardson exchanged a concerned glance. "The boat is speeding along on its own once again, but there's more," Volkert maintained a beaming smile. "The water is very beautiful, very beautiful, indeed."

Benjamin could not help pushing Volkert out of his way, as he rushed out with Richardson. Charlie and Boz waved, encouraging them to join them at the bow. Their eyes met the landscape of water and neither could utter a word. It wasn't just green; it was beyond green. It was beyond the green pastures they had ever seen, or the green emerald colors of the oceanic seas they had crossed. Not a single cloud obstructed the heavenly blue skies over such immaculate green. There was light, but no sun rays to attribute such visual euphoria of well-being, and the wind had stopped as if paying attention not to disturb such smooth pasture of waveless ocean. *So this is where God lives* was the first thought that crossed Benjamin's mind. *Thank you, God, for bringing us to your home, thank you.*

"Charlie, please go with Volkert and bring my family and Carla here. Tell them to come as they are, no need to bring anything with them."

"I'll go with Volkert," Richardson said, as he couldn't wait to see Carla.

Richardson returned, carrying Sophia in one arm and Sarah holding on to his other arm with Carla helping from the other side as the illness had taken away Sarah's ability to stand on her own. Sophia, even though only 2 years old, showed the closing of death as her emaciation produced a precocious old-age look, immensely grotesque when she smiled. At the far horizon, a see-through glass globe-like structure came into view. The *Mary Celeste* continued moving steadily toward it as everyone stared in awe at the strange structural apparition growing before their eyes. As they came closer, its see-through walls moved away, revealing an aperture that grew wider and wider. An invisible force pulled them into its midst, and the see-through walls closed slowly behind them.

PART III
Limitlessness

Below and Beyond

The *Mary Celeste* continued to move forward toward an inviting shimmering light. Passengers and crew remained close to each other, covered by an intense feeling of wellness, except Benjamin, who also felt a blissful feeling like everyone else, but couldn't help thinking, *what if it isn't God's house, what if this ship is taking us to our death?* Then he rationalized, *even if it's not God's house, and we crash into whatever is ahead of us, I have no way of stopping our fate. But looking on the bright side, at least I'll be next to my wife and daughter. All of us will be together, before God.* His gaze fell on Sarah who looked at him with the loving tenderness she had always felt for him, the man who just 10 years prior, she had given her heart at the altar.

"The God who is ready to separate us here on Earth will have us united in Heaven," he held his listless child against his chest and used the other arm to hold Sarah against him.

Richardson and Carla held hands. Everyone remained

motionless as if hypnotized by the same force that had drawn the ship into the bubble-like sphere.

"We've arrived," Boz pointed at an island with tiny minuscule waves washing against the shore of sparkly white sand. A noticeable wide pathway surrounded by lush green vegetation led up a steep hill. On top of that hill stood some kind of flat, round building, its style not anything they were familiar with.

"Ah, ja, my brother we have," Volkert put an arm over his brother's shoulders and the other over Charlie's, who stood next to him.

Benjamin continued to struggle with a diversity of thoughts. Perhaps their ship would suffer the same end of the schooner *Sea Gull* on a rocky lee shore near Cape Horn, where she had last been seen with everyone onboard. Perhaps the structure on the top of the island was a lighthouse, even though it had a peculiar form. He recalled how in April 1851, during a memorable storm on the coast of Massachusetts, Minot's Ledge Lighthouse had been carried away and its keepers lost. Maybe what seemed to be a tiny, odd-looking island happened to be the result of a catastrophic waterspout that tugged it out from its original place and dropped it in the middle of the ocean, right in front of them. *No, I'm not allowing myself to think such absurdities; I accept our voyage here wholeheartedly.* The ship came to a soft stop a few hundred feet from the shore.

"The coast seems to be friendly," Richardson commented. "But we shouldn't take a chance of getting marooned on some rocks if the ship starts moving forward again. Let's drop anchor."

Benjamin pointed to the lush green bed of grass surrounding them, thick enough and high enough to halt any ship. "I don't believe we need an anchor. Like Boz said, we've arrived."

"Now what?" Charlie didn't expect an answer.

"Now ..." Benjamin pointed at the island. "Now, we go ashore."

"Aye, Captain," Richardson said. "Boz, Volkert, Charlie give me a hand with the yawl."

They eagerly loosened and cut the ropes that held the yawl over the main hatch, and soon were ready to launch the yawl.

"Captain Briggs," Richardson said. "With all respect, maybe it would be a good idea to send someone to the island to make sure it's safe."

"Richardson, I have come to the conclusion that there's no use to oppose our destiny, as such, I cannot leave anyone behind. We are all in this together."

"Very well, Captain, then I must ask you to allow me to remain onboard until everyone is inside the yawl."

"You know very well that as the Captain, I'm the last one to abandon ship."

"Yes sir, but we're not abandoning ship, and as such, it's more important that you're with your family, as we all make a little excursion to this delightful island," noticing Benjamin's indecision he added quickly, "As your first mate and friend it would be an honor."

Benjamin looked swiftly at his wife, then at Sophia and nodded his head. Boz and Volkert used the two thick ropes attached to the davits to secure the yawl from dropping too rapidly, and it landed softly on the smooth surrounding grass sea. He used the rope ladder and carried Sarah over his shoulder. Charlie carried Sophia in the same manner. Carla descended next, followed by Boz and Volkert and finally Richardson, who carried a hatchet, joined them. He cut the two ropes holding the yawl with a swift blow and threw it into the green ocean. "Off with instruments that symbolize violence or bad thoughts."

"Oh, shiver me timber, Mr. Richardson, what if we need to cut down a tree to make a fire tonight?" Charlie said.

Everybody laughed, including Richardson, who winked at him.

Volkert and Boz took to rowing hard toward their destination — no one looked back at the *Mary Celeste* — their eyes focused on the island that called each by their names, like an oasis in the middle of the Sahara Desert.

They didn't have to row more than a few yards. Volkert and Boz were the first to jump off and began pulling the yawl ashore until it stopped, a prisoner of the surrounding sand, and safe enough for everyone to step out. The sand that at first seemed so white from afar possessed now a glittering silver color, and its warm, soft texture invited them to take their shoes off. They sat on the sand like children admiring the way the sand slipped off the palms of their hands. Above them, the immense sky was covered with stars, tiny mini stars provided daylight like brightness, the kind of light they imagined only existing in Heaven, calming, soothing and refreshing.

They didn't experience hunger or thirst.

An almost non-existent breeze moved the air they breathed, and as they parted their lips, they took in the nourishment, unaware of such delicate mechanism. The grass-like ocean they had seen from the ship had disappeared as well as the *Mary Celeste*. The flat like round structure on the hill they had observed from the ship had also vanished. No one cared to question these transformations — at that precise moment, they were content to just sit on the warm silver sand, feeling sheltered from harm. Benjamin was the only one standing. He held Sophia in his arms, his gaze upon the surroundings, not quite sure what to look for. His attention was drawn to Sarah, who upon holding a handful of sand, allowed it to slip from her fingers. "Husband, this is such a delicious feeling; come and join me."

He sat next to her and placed Sophia between them, who remained motionless except for extending one hand to gather a pink crystal in the shape of a small rectangle. "Present," she handed it to her father.

He turned it on both sides. "Looks like a professional stone sculptor went through a lot of work to cut, grind and polish this stone. It's truly a masterpiece," he passed it to Richardson.

"Losing one of these anywhere in the world would be considered a painful loss to their owners," Richardson held it in the palm of his open hand. "What in the world is it doing on this island, in the middle of nowhere?"

Volkert called out, "I found a yellow one," he went around showing everyone his precious find.

"Where there are two, there must be others," Charlie announced, "Let's scope the rest of this beach."

Among the camaraderie that had developed further in the last few days, it was easy to turn such mission into a treasure hunt, but Carla walked away. She stopped at the edge of what had once been grass-like water and now had changed into a calming turquoise glow. "Mauricio …" she whispered. Tears ran down her cheeks. "I deserved to lose you but not at the cost of your life, my son." She brought her hands together to pray, but just then, she felt something sharp under one of her feet and bent over to see it was a bright red crystal. She held the stone in her hand and stared at it, *Fire! Fire and blood from the hell I was created from.* She squeezed it as hard as she could. *Go ahead, take my blood, take all my red blood and give it to my son, instead, so he may live.* She was startled when Richardson touched her shoulder.

"Yours is red, like a rose, and mine is blue. A very fitting color for me, since that's the way I feel when I'm not with you." She responded by putting her arms around his neck and resting her head against his chest.

Sarah had remained seated and continued to watch each handful of sand slipping between her fingers, then as she reached once again for the sand, she found a stone that displayed a crystal-like transparency. Each had found their precious stone. They were all different in color but identical in size and cut with two facets, one side embedded with a group of concentric circles cut by linear lines gathered at the center and then extending through tiny circles formed an enigmatic labyrinth. Around it, a narrow border, displayed tiny peculiar symbols.

"Aye mates, let's continue to look for more treasures," Boz began digging with both hands. "We'll be rich beyond our imagination. C'mon, everybody, start digging." But as soon as he took a handful of sand, the space would fill in just as quickly.

"Brother," Volkert laughed. "You look like a dog digging for a bone. You already have your green stone, what more do you want?" And he sat between Benjamin and Richardson. "Quite odd, that we found exactly eight crystals, don't you think?" he held his on the open palm of his hand. "One for each of us; it's just too much to be a coincidence. It's a setup. I would not be surprised if each stone had our names engraved in them. I mean, just look at this seashore, it's perfect, too perfect in my humble opinion."

"That's right, it is faultless, and we're wrong to remove these crystal-like stones," Benjamin put his down on the sand. "They don't belong to us. I suggest we put them back where we found them."

"I'm sorry, Benjamin," Richardson said. "But like Volkert, I also believe they're meant for us. Our ship was drawn here by some mysterious power, and then this island appeared out of thin air ..."

"I'm torn by the idea that if we take the stones, we might disturb the natural harmony of this environment of peace and beauty," Benjamin said. "But I see Volkert's point and yours. And if that's true, then we need to find out why we're brought here."

"I love the way it makes me feel," Sarah stroked her stone in the same loving way she used to stroke her pet turtle as a child. She stood on her own. "I would like to keep it," her voice was clear, strong. She brought it to her heart.

Like everyone else, Benjamin eyed her in disbelief. The woman standing before him was no longer the one he had carried into the yawl, what seemed to be a few minutes ago. He stood, lifted her in his arms, and twirled her joyfully around and around. "My love," he exclaimed, unable to contain his delight. "You ... you're well. This is a miracle!"

"Put me down, husband of mine. Everyone is staring," she said a bit flushed, but smiling.

"Mrs. Briggs," Carla said. "You're not coughing and ... you look healthy, really good."

"This is truly a miracle," Benjamin couldn't help repeating. "But how can it be possible?"

Sarah stared at the crystal in her hand. "Maybe ... something to do with it?"

"It's just a crystal, a stone," Benjamin said.

"I believe it's more than that. It drew me to caress it, like a medium, a pathway toward what I most needed, my health, and my life." She glanced at Sophia who lay in the sand as if sleeping. Her pink crystal had rolled out of her hand into the sand. She rushed to her daughter's side and lifted her up, urging her husband, "Quick, give me her crystal, she's dying," she slipped the stone between the child's hands and guided her daughter's hand to brush it gently. "Live, my little one," she said. "Live and smile again."

Sophia opened her eyes and chuckled as if something had tickled her hand. There was no question in anybody's mind; the crystals possessed the power of life.

"I feel fine," Boz said. "But I'm going to ask my stone to help me to be in the best of health too." He didn't seem to be any different afterward, and they assumed the reason for that was that he wasn't dying. Still, like Charlie said, before stroking his orange crystal, it wouldn't hurt if everyone followed Boz's example. Afterward, they sat in a circle. Charlie was the first to speak, "My friends, it looks like we have found the secret talisman of life ... maybe even eternity," he wore a joyous smile.

"If we can go back and take these stones with us, we can save so many lives," Sarah closed her eyes for a moment. "Imagine, no more sickness to take our loved ones away."

"This isn't real," Boz rubbed his eyes with both knuckles. "After the nightmare we experienced onboard the *Mary Celeste,* we're dreaming all of this."

"Brother, we're all awake," Volkert pinched Boz's arm, and he let out a cry. "If it was a dream, you wouldn't have felt that, now would you?"

"We could be experiencing an illusion," Richardson said. "But illusions I believe are also singularly experienced much like madness, and we can't possibly all be crazy."

"It's a bottom fact, no question about it that my little girl and I were dying before we came here, now look at us," Sarah said. "Look at her rosy cheeks; she's a bundle of energy." Sophia was busy jumping up and down, like any other 2-year-old.

"This is all very real," Carla stood. "We've been given a second chance so that we can mend our ways," her eyes became noticeably bright as her words vibrated throughout her being like a tuning fork. "We're not imagining anything. From the moment we arrived to this island, I felt its magical powers," she touched her bosom with a closed fist and sat back on the sand. "My son is in a better place."

"Yes," Benjamin said. "He's in Heaven with our Lord Jesus."

"No, Captain Briggs, my son is not with Jesus. He's somewhere safe, and hopefully soon, I'll be given the chance to fix the wrongdoings I made in the past," she stood again. "Mrs. Briggs, please forgive me if I lied to you about who I am; you too, Richardson. I never meant to hurt anyone, and what I'm going to tell you is not in any way an excuse for what I've done. As much as I believe my son is in a better place, I also know that I'll never see him again, and that's what hurts so much," she crossed her hands over her heart. "I do not want your pity, just your forgiveness, and please don't take away the friendship you have shown toward me. You're the only true friends I ever had, and I can no longer allow you to continue believing the lies I told you onboard the *Mary Celeste*." She sat.

"I was born in Lisbon, Portugal, not the islands of Azores, as I told you, Mrs. Briggs. My father worked in a factory as a brick-maker and spent his earnings on booze. My mother never lasted more than three weeks to a month as a maid, just enough time to discover where the lady of the house kept her jewelry and other valuables. When I saw my mother coming into our shack in the middle of the night carrying over her shoulders two large bedsheets folded and tied like sacks, I knew that with the money she would get at a pawn shop, it would be enough to carry us for a month or even two, depending on the value of the loot. My three older brothers did well with begging and pickpocketing in Lisbon, until the oldest got caught and put in jail for mugging a French diplomat and his wife. We never saw him again. My two other brothers began dividing their time between pickpocketing and breaking into homes. When they broke into homes, I remained outside. My job, as their lookout, was to whistle like a bird if they were in jeopardy of getting caught. I was also the "carrier" of their smaller but more precious stolen goods, since at 11 years old, I was quite agile at outrunning the police. At 12, they decided I was old enough to start my pickpocketing career in the streets of Lisbon. The first time I tried to get my hand into a lady's purse, she caught me by the ear and smacked me so hard that I went home with a bloody nose. The second time, the police were called. They put me in a dingy, dark cell by myself, and one of the guards made me strip, and with a long leather belt, he whipped me until I fainted. I came to when he threw a metal bucket of icy water over me. "'Girl,'" he said. "'I have a daughter your age, so I'll be good to you. But you come back again for stealing, and you'll be sent to Angola to rot in an African jail,'" he pointed to my wet clothes lying in a puddle. "'Now, get the hell out of here, if you know what's good for you.'"

"I refused to continue working with my brothers even after they beat me, so my mother made me their servant, cooking, cleaning, washing and ironing their clothes, but that wasn't as bad as when my father beat me if the soup wasn't to his liking, or he simply beat me because he had nothing else to do. When I turned 13, my brothers and my mother trained me as their *fish bait*. All I had to do was offer men my smile and the promise of a good time.

They followed me to an alley, and my brothers took care of knocking them unconscious and robbing them. A year later, my mother decided it was time for me to make a *real* living. She had me dressed in a nightdress and applied make-up on my face to make me look older. "I'm counting on you to please this man no matter what it takes. Do you understand?" Her dark eyes always told me what words didn't, as she opened the front door to Mr. Rodrigo da Silva Nunes. He could tell I was scared, and my knowledge of how to please a man had much to be desired. But he took his time with me, and considering that I didn't have a choice but to obey my mother, I did appreciate he was patient and didn't beat me. He called me "his little girl," and I felt loved for the first time. My mother kept the money he paid her, but let me keep the fresh flowers he brought me. When I heard my parents plotting to extort more money from Mr. Nunes by telling his wife of his infidelity, I feared they might kill him if they didn't get what they wanted. I told him about their plan. He paid someone to act as a policeman to come to our home and take me away from them. They were told that if they ever tried to get in touch with me, he would have them and my brothers jailed for theft and prostitution. Mr. Nunes furnished an apartment in the most modern part of Lisbon and told me all I had to do was live there and wait for him on Tuesday nights. He hired a private teacher to teach me to write Portuguese, English, math, and also voice lessons. Besides being a very successful businessman, Mr. Nunes could not take a chance of us being seen together unless we were in a foreign country. Twice a year, he took me to cities like London, Paris, Rome and Barcelona, and he would buy me beautiful clothes and jewelry, which I could only wear when we traveled." She sighed deeply before going on. "Four years later, on a cold Tuesday evening in November, I waited and waited in vain for Mr. Nunes. A week later, still no word, and my first thought was that he had found another "little girl." For the next month, I used the money he had given me to cover for groceries and other necessities. And then I received a personal visit from the landlord. The rent for December was due. I was to either pay or get out. I went to Mr. Nunes' house and acted like I was looking for employment as a servant. His widow informed me that her husband had died peacefully in his sleep three weeks prior, and she wasn't hiring. There was no way in Heaven that I was going to return to my family. I sold all the furnishings in the apartment, the jewelry and my clothes, and together with what I had been saving, I bought a steamship ticket to Brazil," she cried.

"My sweet, dearest friend," Sarah sat next to Carla and held her hands in hers. "I can understand why you held all this from us, but from now on, you no longer have to keep secrets. We love you very much and consider you an important member of our family."

"Thank you. You can't imagine how much your words mean to me."

Sophia reached out with one finger and touched one of Carla's tears. "Boo-boo?" she kissed Carla's wet cheek.

"Thank you, Sophie. You're a little angel; did you know that?" But Sophia was already running back to play in the sand.

"I'm glad you shared your story with us," Richardson said to Carla. "But I assure you that my feelings toward you have not changed. Our past is like dust in the wind, gone forever. And I agree that it's distressing that we had to make so many mistakes in our lives in order to become who we are, and Carla, I love who you've become."

"Thank you, Richardson. I love you too, with all my heart, but I still have more to tell you, and …"

He put a finger to her lips, "You don't have to do that right now, my darling, let's focus instead on what we have together, and what the future will bring our way."

Benjamin made a gesture with his head for Richardson to follow him. They stood not far from the group. "Richardson, what's your take on our situation here?"

"I don't know. I'm as baffled as you."

"Richardson, I have not encountered anything like this in the Bible, and I do not know what to make of it," he removed his black stone from his coat pocket and held it up. "But I have been looking and analyzing every angle and noticed a light pattern inside characterized by ridges that enter on one side and then exit on the opposite side. Look at yours; do you see what I'm describing?"

Richardson looked attentively at his stone. "Yes, I see it, now that you mention."

"Well ... when I first met Mauricio, I gave him a magnifying glass," he stopped, overwhelmed by emotion and had to clear his throat. "The first thing he did was to examine the palm of his hands and fingers, and his response was one of pure wonder. Later that day, I sat in my cabin to investigate what had amazed the lad, and that's when I discovered an intriguing pattern of loops, whorls and arches on the palm of my hands, fingers and thumb. I found that Sarah and Sophia have them too. I even examined Charlie's hands and made some drawings. I was planning on checking everyone else on board, but with everything that started happening on the ship, I had to abandon the project. The ridges on my stone remind me of the fingers and palms of my hands ..."

Richardson squinted attentively at his fingers. "You are telling me the lines in our hands are the same as in the crystals? I mean ... that has to be a coincidence. Have you considered that maybe, just maybe, they were produced by the ocean's underwater currents?" he looked at Benjamin and added, "I see you're serious, but even if it's true what you're saying, then what? What are you suggesting?"

"I don't know. Let's run this by the others and listen to their responses."

Everyone began to look for similarities in the patterns between their stone and their hands. Sophia was busy covering her crystal with sand and then looking for it, astonished for always finding it in the same spot.

"These stones have given us the gift of life, and I see them as the answer to our future," Sarah said. "I could be wrong, but if they match the lines on our fingers or our thumbs as you say, then … they could be coded … like a knob on a safe … a key to a door …" she knew she had gone beyond any common sense when Charlie said, "With all respect, Mrs. Briggs, I see no doors." A profound but short-lived silence followed.

"Cap'n," Boz said. "We're all in agreement that these crystals may have been placed here for us. Well, in that case, what Mrs. Briggs says makes a lot of sense. Throughout my life, I have studied and examined many plants and their leaves, and I found that the leaves were usually compatible only with their own vegetation. What if these crystals that were here waiting for us, possess the unique pattern that identifies each of us … I'm just thinking out loud, of course. But I can't help thinking that these stones could very well be our identity leaves, they identify us," he looked at the stone in the palm of his hand. "This crystal stone is my leaf, my identity key!"

"And the door?" Charlie insisted.

"Not a door, as we know," Boz said. "More like … a systematic identity pathway."

"I know exactly what my brother is saying," Volkert said. "The first recorded image of hand and finger images were uniformly taken for identification purposes about 14 years ago by a man named Sir William Herschel, who worked for the Civil Service of India. He insisted on recording a handprint on the back of a contract for each worker to distinguish employees from others who might claim to be employees when payday arrived."

Everyone stared at him.

"Golly, Brother! You sure know a lot more than I ever gave you credit for."

"I don't talk much, but I read a lot, Boz."

Sarah held her stone up to eye level. "When we use a key," she said, "we position the handle between our thumb and the side of our first finger. The thumb plays the role of acting like a fulcrum to rotate the key into the keyhole …"

"Sarah, my darling, you may have something there," Benjamin said pensively. "So if we were to use our thumb, let's say, on the flat side of each stone ..."

"With the intent of moving on through what Boz calls a systematic identity pathway," Volkert said. "We might have as a group, a master key to move forward."

"From the moment we were faced with leaving the ship," Benjamin said, "I felt we're all in this together for better or for worse. But I just want to make sure that everyone is in agreement with taking the next step."

"I like it here," Carla said. "But I'm ready to move on."

Everyone agreed they felt the same way.

"The worst that can happen is nothing happens," Sarah said. "And we'll have to put our thinking caps back on once again."

Benjamin signaled for all to come closer. They made a circle around Sophia, and faced each other.

"Sophie," Benjamin bent down with Sarah to their child's level. "Mommy and Daddy are going to help you play a wonderful game with your right hand, are you ready?" he lifted her up. She flashed one of her upbeat smiles. She was ready to play.

"Ladies and gentleman, and you too, Sophie," he gave her a kiss on the cheek. "Hold the stone in your left hand with the flat side up. Very good, Sophie. Now show me your right thumb," he said. "We have all agreed that we're ready to move on with our lives." He took a deep breath in and let it out slowly as if conjuring his inner strength to follow through. "I'll count to three, and when I say three, we'll press our right thumb on the center of our stones all at the same time. Wait!" He counted a beat. "Are you ready? One, two, three!"

Ωελχομε

They spontaneously closed their eyes during the split instant of darkness that took over them to find themselves in the same position, but now saw that they stood on a wide plateau of land covered with dainty white daises at their feet, facing a vast valley of luscious greenery that resembled more like a well-cared for and manicured garden. Their senses awoke to a soft melodic tune in the distance, and the sweet scent of lilacs and sweet pea. The men turned their heads cautiously, evaluating their new environment, but the two women smiled at each other: Nothing could be more perfect.

Benjamin took an evaluating look at the group. "Good, we're all here," he lifted Sophia onto his shoulders, and she clapped her hands as she always did when she was happy. "Let's go," he took hold of Sarah's hand, and everyone walked toward the continuing wide trail of white daisies facing them.

"I wonder what kind of musical instrument is playing such exquisite melody. Benj, it reminds me of the same tone quality we heard when I played the melodeon on the ship."

"My very thoughts."

"Mrs. Briggs, if there's a Heaven, this is it," Carla pointed to the surrounding vegetation.

Boz had fallen behind. He stood motionless, unable to close his wide-open mouth. He called out, "Has anyone ever seen orchids like these?" They stopped and went back to get a closer look with him.

Orchids of all colors, sizes and shapes, draped from the branches of lemon and orange trees, and clusters of strawberries and raspberries sprouted wildly from large planters held by hooks on golden posts. Some trees were easy to recognize, such as the Cherry Blossom in full bloom and a flowering Dogwood. He zigzagged from one tree to another along the pathway, expressing his enchantment with several loud shouts of pleasure. "This is a Rainbow Eucalyptus, also known as the Mindanao Gum or Rainbow Gum because of the rainbow-like colors you see, and over there," he ran to the other side of the pathway, "This is a Baobab tree, known as the Corn Tree or Monkey Tamarind from Guinea in West Africa. I've seen it drawn in books. Follow me, follow me," he said excitedly. "Over here is the Royal Poinciana, a native of Madagascar, and ... and," he couldn't speak fast enough. "Oh, my goodness, looks like a Blue Jacaranda, a native of south-central South America. Can't miss its long-lasting pale indigo flowers; I recognize them from the colored drawings in the same book."

No one could resist sitting under a very large ginkgo tree with a surrounding field of yellow leaves. Richardson pointed to a tree not that far from them, with its branches going every which way and stretching nearly 17,200 square feet. "I confess that I don't know much about trees, but I do recognize the Angel Oak tree. I saw it once in Charleston, South Carolina. Just look at those branches!"

"Boz, how can so many plant species," Charlie asked, "from

every corner of the world, needing a very specific weather to thrive, be living here in such close harmony?"

"Mother Nature takes care of her children," Boz replied as if he were part of Nature's family.

They were in no rush as they walked across the valley admiring the large assortment of vegetation. From her father's shoulders, Sophia caught sight of several segmented waterfalls ahead. "Papa, white rain," she clapped.

As they drew closer, the sound of the music they had been hearing was unquestionably coming from the waterfalls. The huge pool made by the main waterfall gave way to several smaller ponds. They stopped to listen while admiring the trickling motion of the water falling over a variety of colorful striated rocks and then tiering into multiple-sized drops, each ringing a musical note as it hit the rocks along the way and into the turquoise water below. "This is the source of the music we heard onboard the *Mary Celeste*," Sarah observed, and then to herself, *I wonder where the children are.*

As if answering her question, Sophia caught sight of *them* in the distance. "Papa, Papa, look," she pointed to several as young as she and as old as 5 or 6 years old, playing in one of the smaller ponds, on the extreme side away from them. They were topless and all wore short silvery loin cloths, resembling a sort of nappy. Some had dark skin, others were green, orange, white, and there were those covered with scales or hair like fur, but they all had one thing in common, they acted no different from other children their age, jumping into the water and laughing as they splashed at each other. Some used the wide, thick leaves from the surrounding trees as water slides while others chose to jump in from the surrounding trees. Sophia couldn't think of anything more delightful than to join them. "Happy, me," she waved at them.

The passengers and crew of the *Mary Celeste* must have been quite a sight in their odd-looking worn-out attire, because the youngsters, taking notice of their presence, stopped frolicking and stared at them much like deer facing a headlight. A young, light brown woman in her mid-20s, wearing a white tunic and silver sandals came out from behind one of the smaller waterfalls. They gathered in clusters around her, pointing at the strangers. She lifted two of the smaller ones in her arms, and after kissing them, she put them down and addressed the other children in a language that was foreign to Benjamin and his group. Two of the oldest children, one with light blue skin and extremely large eyes and the other of a dark maroon color, also with large eyes but curly silver hair that grew out from two pairs of earlobes, followed her obediently as they walked up the path toward the intruders. The others remained behind showing their adorable smiles and waving back.

As the woman walked toward them, Charlie took a step behind Richardson. "For all we know, those two innocent looking nippers could be little cannibals in training."

The trio stopped about six feet from them, put their hands together as if about to pray, and nodded their heads. She spoke with a melodic dialect. Boz stared shamelessly at her shoulder-length light brown hair with silver highlights, parted to the side, and held by what he believed to be the rarest flower in the whole world, a Middlemist red Camellia.

"I'm sorry," Benjamin used the same greeting manner with his hands. "But we don't understand your language."

She took a few moments as if interpreting his words and then responded, "My name is Sol. I was telling the young ones back there to behave, but I remained in my idiom when I spoke to you. I can understand your confusion." She mentioned to the two children to go back to the water, and they ran down the hill. "They consider these ponds a playground, but in reality, this water guarantees their immunity from any foreign microorganism that could affect their health while attending school on our beautiful planet Earth."

"Oh good, we're still on Earth," Benjamin said. "We were all wondering ..."

"I imagine you have many questions, but for now, I would like to personally invite you to enter the ponds for your own purification before meeting the *Elders*."

Volkert began to undress, but Sol motioned to him, "No, please. Everyone must enter the water fully clothed, so that your skin and clothes can be purified from any microscopic organism that can negatively disturb our environment."

He diligently put his clothes back on and was still the first to jump in the water. His head came up and one hand waved back at the others as he yelled out, "Come on in, the water is perfect," and he let out a joyful laugh as he splashed around. Boz and Charlie went in followed by Carla and Richardson. Benjamin with Sophia in his arms and Sarah by his side, entered the water cautiously. Benjamin held Sophia for as long as possible, but soon, he had to give up on it, as the little one wiggled herself free and swam like a fish toward the other children.

"I declare, how is that possible?" Sarah looked at Benjamin. He shrugged his shoulders, just as stunned.

"We're in the greatest playground of the world, of the whole entire world; there's nothing better," exclaimed Volkert as he swam on his back and then rolled over and over like a seal. Boz laughed at his brother's aquatic abilities and then, out of habit, he squeezed his nose between two fingers and let himself submerge until his feet touched the bottom. There he found Volkert sitting on a rock staring at him with a broad smile. They could breathe underwater. They hugged each other.

A little farther away from the brothers, Charlie sat under a leafy plant, his eyes tearing with a happiness he never knew existed. "I never heard of a place like this on Earth. We must have heard her wrong."

Benjamin and Sarah walked hand in hand admiring the surrounding underwater flora as if they were taking a leisurely walk at home, on Spring Street back in Marion. Carla and Richardson took turns immersing gently up and down, and as they came up, they exchanged smiles. Richardson could tell that Carla had something else on her mind. He reasoned her positive outburst on the island had been a tactical way of putting on appearances, to cover the agony she felt with the loss of her son. He missed Mauricio terribly and could only imagine what it was like to lose one's own child. He decided it would be best not to intrude and instead, allow her the time to mourn.

The rapid progression of understanding the children's language happened in a way that they weren't even aware of. They had simply acquired the meaning of each word. Carla could swear the two little boys by her side addressed her in Portuguese, while Volkert and Boz understood them in what sounded like German, and to everyone else it was English at its best. They now spoke in the same melodic tone as the children, and it felt natural, as if they had lived there all their lives.

Ωελχομε sang the children. And they understood from that one word, that they were in a community of knowledge, a world where love, friendship and goodwill lived side by side.

Turel and Biola

After their underwater walk, Benjamin and Sarah came up to look around, and that's when they noticed a couple probably in their late 40s — standing next to Sol. They wore white tunics and sandals much like Sol's attire, but theirs shimmered like silk. One wore the shoulder-length hair in a box braided style; its gold strands matched the beard with a single braid. The other's hair, also the same color and shoulder-length, was combed back straight and smooth. Each wore a gold necklace with a crystal pendant, similar to the ones they had found on the island, but smaller. It seemed like the couple had been watching them, and when their eyes met, they greeted Benjamin and Sarah by bringing their hands together like Sol had done. Benjamin asked Richardson and Carla to gather Sophia and the others, but Sophia was already swimming toward them. Perhaps as a result of their recent experiences, they were not surprised that when they came out of the water they were as dry as if they had just taken a walk in a park, on a spring day.

The couple greeted them again, and the one with the beard

said, "Welcome, dear brothers and sisters. My name is Turel and this is my wife Biola," he pointed to the woman next to him, who smiled at them, and then bent over to lift Sophia in her arms.

"Pretty," Sophia said as she ran her fingers gently through Biola's smooth, straight hair.

"My wife and I are the permanent members of the Ancient Committee of the Sacred City of Atlantis," he motioned to the children still playing in the water. "I see that you already met a few of our youngest Atlanteans, including some from the planets of ..."

"Did you say Atlantis?" Benjamin said.

"Plato, the Ancient Greek philosopher told the story of Atlantis," Sarah said. "Its founders were half god and half human ..."

"A tall tale, no question about it," Turel wore an amused smile.

"I have to agree with that," Benjamin said, just as tickled. "With all respect, who are you? And ... where are we?"

"Come," Biola said, still holding Sophia, who had snuggled with an arm around her neck. "You must all be very tired. We live close by, and after you rest and join us for a meal, we can answer your questions."

Turel touched a large metallic flat panel behind him. It slid open sideways, and he motioned for everyone to enter. Inside, he pointed to the cushioned seats positioned to one side of a half-moon-shaped, flat metallic board, that he sat next to. The inside walls were smooth like glass. There were no windows. As if she could read their minds, Biola said, "This vessel will transport us home safely, I promise. But meanwhile, let me serve you something cool and rejuvenating."

Next to each seat, a round column arose from the floor. An iridescent pearl color seashell sat on top of each column.

Trying to be polite, they did the same as Biola, they held the shell in the palm of their hands and waited to see what to do next.

"It's a Nautilus Seashell — look," Sol demonstrated by

bringing it to her lips and silently took in its fluid. Everyone tried and agreed that the purple liquid was very refreshing, and the taste resembled fresh grape juice. As they finished drinking, they put their shell on its respective receptacle. Sophia, trying to imitate the adults, did the same, even though she had not yet finished hers. When her seashell and column withdrew into the floor like the others, she had a meltdown.

"Mine, mine," she cried out. Sol, seated next to her, retracted Sophia's drink. To her parents' surprise, Sophia said thank you.

Benjamin felt the need to explain their own behavior. "You must be surprised about us acting so childlike in the water. I'm sorry …"

"You did what came naturally," Turel interrupted. "There is no need to apologize for being human. We have arrived."

"We have?" Charlie asked. "It didn't feel like we were moving."

"Our newest autonomic traveling vessels, within and outside our city limits, have achieved maximum computerized velocity with minimum movement felt, of which our engineers are very proud. With longer distances than this, especially interplanetary, then we use our split-second transportation system."

Neither Charlie nor the others were going to ask Turel to explain what he meant by split-second transportation. Their previous forms of traveling prior to boarding the *Mary Celeste* were already a far cry from what they had experienced since leaving their ship. They left the so-called *vessel* and willingly followed their hosts across a wide stone porch on a hill.

"Wow, my, oh my, we're surrounded by diamonds everywhere," Boz stopped to acknowledge the effect of the sparkly bright lights coming from gigantic tall buildings, streets, bridges and round, flat machines sweeping through the air. They had seen four story buildings in New York City, and the Trinity Church with its whopping 281 feet, but now they were staring at structures 50 and 60 floors high, not including the gardens in between the different floor levels. Richardson couldn't help asking, "How do you manage to carry the water up so high into the gardens?"

"Our water comes from above, after being treated to remove the salt and other chemical particles," Turel responded.

"Of course, from above," and then to himself, *that was a stupid question.* He added, "The *city* seems to be round from up here."

"Yes, and on the other side of this hill, the land-dwelling continues as far and beyond what the eye can see," Turel said. "By the way, the small vessels you see flying around are like the ones we used to get here."

"Bumblebees," Sophia remarked.

"That's exactly what we call them, excellent observation," Turel said to her. "And the others below are narrow and elongated to drive on the streets, and in the water canals. We call them *barracudas*, because of their shape, and their pilots tend to speed a bit, even though they have a choice of being run automated," he chuckled before going on. "All vessels are individually owned. First, one becomes a master at driving on the roads, and you can see how much traffic is out there. Then we learn how to navigate through the canals, and finally, we graduate to air cruising, which is my favorite of all three. Once we are licensed in all forms of navigation, we graduate into outer space traveling, which is a must to learn in order to reach the other planets."

Once again, Benjamin and everyone else just listened. It was no use to try to understand so many incomprehensible impossibilities. Somehow it made more sense to accept they were in Atlantis, a more than likely fairy tale, than to accept they were still on Earth.

"A few of the taller buildings are equipped with a bright beacon light on the very top," Biola pointed out. "They work in unison with the surrounding buildings to keep the whole city lit. They draw from each other the energy needed to remain continuously operational. The lower buildings along the canals have less intense lights but strong enough to light the streets and over the bridges. These lights collect enough energy that even when turned off, they still provide a comfortable temperature, like you are experiencing now."

"We could have used those lights onboard the *Mary Celeste,*" Volkert rubbed his hands together. "Those chilling nights and days will remain engraved forever in my memory."

Everyone stood together baffled as they looked at the city and its surroundings.

"Captain Briggs," Turel finally broke their silence. "Biola and I will be very happy to make you comfortable in our home, and once you get a chance to rest and eat, I promise to answer all queries. We understand none of you are familiar with our way of life, but soon enough, I know you will have a better understanding of the world you find yourselves in," he opened his arms to four young individuals walking at a fast pace toward them.

"These are our children," Biola's eyes brightened. "Our son, Ares."

"So glad to make your acquaintance," said the handsomely fit, 14-year-old with long half black and half white braided hair down to his waist. He had no eyebrows or lashes, and his big, dark round eyes stared bluntly at the newcomers.

"Our older daughters, Gorgeia and Margaritari, and our youngest one, Okeanos," Biola said.

"It is a pleasure to meet you!" the sisters said in unison. They couldn't be more than 20 years old and looked like an exact copy of each other. To see one beautiful woman was always a treat for Boz and Volkert, but to be greeted by two mirror images went beyond their expectations.

"We are twins, identical twins," said one of them.

"I look forward to being your friend," Okeanos said to Sophia. She was a mini copy of her mother and couldn't be much older than Sophia.

"Our daughters will show Charlie, Carla and Mr. Richardson

to their accommodations," Turel ignored the disappointed look in his daughters' faces and on the two sailors. "Ares, please take Boz and Volkert to their respective chambers."

Biola turned to Okeanos, "How about you and me showing Mr. and Mrs. Briggs and their daughter Sophia their rooms?"

"Yes, dear mother, your wish is my own too," she responded. Okeanos mature behavior caught Sophia's attention, and she copied her new friend's steadily paced steps as they stepped into a large building and followed the adults.

"Sophia," Biola stopped walking and turned toward her. "With your index finger, yes your second finger," she said noticing that Sophia stared at her right fingers. "Go ahead, touch this door." The opaque glass door opened, and they entered a large room with light bluish-green walls and tiny dark blue lights encased in the ceiling over a large bed covered with an emerald green cover that matched the pillows. To one side was a full-size mirror with a dark blue glass door on each side. From one shelf, a delicate variety of colorful flowers and ferns grew out of a fish tank with two goldfish.

"This is your quarters, and over there through that smaller door, is Sophia's bedroom. Children's rooms are smaller like them, a lot more fun that way. But much the same furnishings as yours, pink and purple décor for girls who seem to have a preference for those colors, and blues and reds for boys. But there are also other colors available for those of a different gender or who express a desire to create their own unique signature style. Would you mind if Okeanos shows Sophia her room?" Neither Benjamin nor Sarah objected, and the girls went in giggling.

"I hope you will find the bed comfortable. The mattress and the pillows are filled with ocean water, and these buttons on the headboard can control how soft you want it to be, and the one in the middle, what kind of music you would like to hear. The other buttons have more apps, but you will discover their use little by little." She called their attention to a small glass panel. "You can drop in here your present clothes, and they will be returned mended and clean." She walked over to a glass table. "Over here ... is a computer and screen. I know you are not familiar with this type of technology, but soon, even Sophia will be able to use the one in her room, not only for studying but also for entertainment. In Atlantis, computers are our way of life, and they have been in use for a long, long time," she turned their attention to the wall-to-wall window. "A grand view of the city from this window, but when you want to sleep, just touch the glass over here, and all the light from outside will be gone." She turned and faced one of the two large opaque glass doors at the corner of the room, it opened automatically, and they followed her in. "These are your bathrooms. Sophia has her own. The toilets work by sensory. They are programmed to take care of themselves once you move away from it ... When it comes to bathing at home, we prefer showers to baths, and in this shower space, the walls can sense your body temperature as you step in, so the water will be according to your comfort zone, but you can still make it hotter or colder, if you so desire." She showed them the control panel. "The soap is made to work for your hair as well as your skin type. The mirror here above the sink is especially nice for the ladies," she smiled. "Think how you would like your hair to be styled and your thoughts will be projected into reality. Works great when you are in a hurry," she winked at Sarah. "Your new attire is already set up in your adjoining dressing rooms. Everything else will lend to itself as you learn to master your surroundings. Don't be afraid to touch, nothing can go wrong, and if it does, there is a saying, *without err, how can you learn?* So please take your time to explore, and I will see you later for our meal." She knocked at Sophia's door. "Okeanos, we need to leave."

A Lifestyle Yonder

As long as they could remember, Charlie, Boz and Volkert had always slept with one or two family members, and later as sailors, they had shared their cabin with their fellow mates. It was a way of life they had been accustomed to and thought nothing of it. Their lives had always been about back-breaking work and taking care of others. But now, having their own private bedroom and bathroom surrounded by such unimaginable luxury in a world of such magical wonders, made each wonder, if they had died after all. But it couldn't be Heaven, they reasoned; they had not seen any angels flying around, and when it came to meeting God, they were happy not having to face him. For most of their lives, they had behaved the best they knew how, but they could have been a lot nicer. Maybe the Bible had omitted this place called Atlantis so that no one would commit suicide to get there sooner. None of them felt they deserved it more than their friends, who had died at the hands of a madman.

A man wasn't supposed to cry or let out his feelings of sorrow, unless there was no one around to hear him. Once in his room, Charlie went down on his knees, "Dear God, I would have traded my life for the child." His pain was unanimously felt by the others.

Richardson and Carla were not married, but the significance of putting them together in the same room meant their hosts knew about their relationship.

As soon as Margaritari left their room, Richardson attempted to hug Carla, but she pushed him away.

"Carla, what's the matter, why do you run from me?"

"I'm not. I just prefer that you don't hold me right now."

"Why? We're alone. Nobody can see us," he said playfully.

"How do you know that nobody can see us?" she used his words to make a point.

"The problem is not that you're afraid someone can see us, is it?" he held her by the shoulders. "No, I don't believe that. What are you really afraid of?"

Tears rolled down her cheeks, and her voice trembled, "Please, Richardson, let go of me."

"I completely understand how you feel losing Mauricio, but on the island …. you seemed to come to terms with our relationship and were ready to face the future, together. Did I do or say something wrong? Please tell me."

"Richardson, you're everything I wished for, all my life. But right now, I find it impossible to accept any of the love you offer me," she used her hands to cover her face, wet with tears. "Richardson, I do not deserve your affection, that's all I can say."

He protested by pacing back and forth. "How can you say that? There's nothing, absolutely nothing, to stop us from being happy."

"Please, Richardson, don't be angry. Later, you'll know everything, I promise you."

"Later, when, and why not now? You know you can talk to me."

"For the last time, I'm begging you, if you truly love me, you must respect my wishes and don't ask me any further questions. When I'm ready, I'll tell you." She went into the bathroom, and the glass door closed behind her.

Sarah had to bend over to enter Sophia's room. She couldn't help smiling when she saw her child sleeping peacefully spread out on the bed, like a bear rug. *Dear God, my little girl is alive, and I'm here to see it,* she couldn't help giggling as she admired the fully furnished tiny room. *Truly a doll house, I would have loved something like this when I was her age.*

She tiptoed out of her room and found her husband standing with an enigmatic look on his face by their glass desk.

"When I touched the top of the glass, a light came on, and it asked me what I wanted to see, and I said jokingly of course, show me New York City. And the same voice asked me what year and day. I was so overwhelmed that I said, never mind, show me a map of Atlantis ... And this map came up. Can you believe it? I need to see what's on the other side." He crawled under the glass table. She bent forward to watch him and was about to join him when he came out, shaking his head.

"Nothing underneath the desk, I really don't know how a map can be made without paper. This new science called computer is beyond my understanding. Sarah, I feel like an old dinosaur that has been dug out alive, and transported into the future."

"I feel the same way as you. But at the same time, I love everything we have experienced thus far. Benj, I truly believe we have a promising future here for all of us."

"How is Sophie?" he sat on their bed.

"Asleep. It was definitely past her bedtime."

"Have you ever seen anything like this?" Benjamin bounced up and down, while still seated on the mattress.

She sat next to him and bounced along. "So much nicer than our old corn husk mattress, and so big too," she laughed and tumbled back. Lying in each other's arms, they kissed, and then rolled on the bed from one side to the other like children on an amusement ride. They kissed once again, and just as they started undressing, a familiar little voice caught their attention, "Mama, Papa, me hungry."

They stood as rapidly as they could and did their best to gain their composure. "I believe we should get cleaned up and dressed," Sarah buttoned her shirt and brushed her fingers through her disheveled hair.

It was easier than they thought to get the showers to work. Sarah used hers with Sophia, and they sang out a storm while lathering themselves, "It's raining inside, it's raining inside," Sophia repeated after her mother and they sang, "We'll shine clean and sparkly like the big, huge moon above, the big, huge moon above." In the other shower, Benjamin whistled along.

The white tunics and footwear provided for them were very similar to the ones they had seen Sol and their hosts wearing. In his dressing room, Benjamin found a long gold chain next to his tunic. Sarah saw two gold chains, one shorter than the other, next to their clothes, and assumed the smaller one was meant for Sophia. Each chain had an empty pendant holder, and they inserted their stone into it; the sound of a snap demonstrated that it was safely latched. Sarah took full advantage of the bathroom mirror. She combed her hair down smoothly and held it to the side with a braid.

"Oh my, you both look so fine!" Benjamin said when his wife and daughter came into the room.

"Dear husband. You look swell yourself," she kissed him on the cheek. "This tunic is so comfortable," and she twirled with delight as Sophia imitated her. Then catching her inner thoughts, she took on a solemn look, "I miss Arthur. I wish our son was here with us."

"Me too," he hugged her.

A two-tone melodic ringing brought their attention to opening the door. They were greeted by Sol, Carla and the crew. They all wore white tunics except Sol's was a light green color, matching the green stone in the single strand tiara on her head. They followed her into a large chamber occupied by about 40 unique-looking individuals sitting on large pillows strategically set in small half circles facing a two-foot elevated stage where eight oversized seats in the shape and color of sunflowers, stood in the center. Sophia was the first to notice the see-through glass ceiling offering an impressive view of colorful fishes of all sizes and shapes swimming above.

"Mama, Papa look up!" she clapped.

Biola acknowledged them with a friendly smile, and with her eyes and a gesture of her hands, motioned them to sit on the pillows next to her. The pillows took on their body shape, providing excellent support and comfort.

Boz couldn't take his eyes off the stage. "The color and shape of those chairs in the middle of the stage," he said to Biola. "Are the same as the helianthus annus," and to himself, *sunflowers, who would have thought ..."*

Biola interrupted his thoughts, "Yes, and like the sunflower, they stand for dignity, glory and passion. Throughout the centuries, the *Elders* have been our mentors and our guiding light; those seats are a reminder of our beginnings and lasting brotherhood. The *Elders* are the only ones privileged to use them," she smiled. "A long, long time ago, we used those flowers for making biodiesel," noticing the look on their faces she added. "A type of fuel to make things run. Where you came from, it will not be discovered for another 40 or more years of your time. We don't use it for fuel anymore — just about everything now runs from a specific motherboard, programmed to address anything we need from A to Z. But we still grow the sunflowers in the nursery, as an important, healthy addition to our food production."

The twins arrived, followed by Ares and Okeanos, who asked permission for Sophia to join her with the children on the other side of the room. They left holding hands. The Lorenzen brothers immediately made space for the sisters to sit next to them.

"I'm Korallion," she sat next to Boz. "Named after the Pacific elkhorn coral because my skin color takes on a bright golden tan in the dark."

"I'm Margaritari," she sat next to Volkert. "Because like the Akoya pearl, my eyes can shift between green, blue and violet. You are brothers and look much alike, but the colors of your eyes let us know that you are Volkert and not your brother. If you look closely, you will also see other tiny differences between us. My hair has a few reddish highlights, and Korallion's displays more of a golden tone."

Both couples became involved talking to each other, and Ares moved his pillow closer to Benjamin to ask him about the *Mary Celeste*, the ship that ran without any automated device.

Someone whispered "The *Elders* had arrived," and the room became silent. Everyone stood, including the children, who until then, could be heard laughing and talking.

The Elders and Humanity

Turel walked on stage with the *Elders*, who wore long, black hooded robes with long sleeves like his and a flat mini crystal hanging from their thin but long neck chain. Except two of the *Elders*, who exhibited luminous figures without any particular shape, they moved side by side without wearing anything but their own brightness. They all took their assigned sunflower chairs except for Turel, who remained standing to the side facing the crowd. His voice rang joyfully, "Dear brothers and sisters, we are here tonight to celebrate the presence of our beloved *Elders*, Ragor, and his wife Quynh, from the planet Zarzgoon, brothers Adalius and Bevan, sisters Alaina and Declan, from our parallel Universes and Hesed and Ahava, from Or, the place of light."

Benjamin and Richardson stared at each other, so there was more than one *Universe*, who would have known?

Ragor, and Quynh stood and removed their hoods, and after making the now familiar hand greeting, let out a radiant smile, causing everyone to respond in the same manner. They looked like ordinary folks, perhaps in their mid- to late-50s. Their black skin contrasted with their short, tightly waved snow-white hair tied to one side by a very short braid. They sat, and Adalius and Bevan stood and removed their hoods, showing remarkably elongated shiny skulls, their length possibly exaggerated by their lack of hair, tiny round eyes and small narrow lips. They nodded their heads several times. A pleasant wide-ranging tone came across with each nod, and everyone responded by nodding back. Once Adalius and Bevan sat, everyone's attention drew to Alaina and Declan, who remained seated with their hoods on and lacked any facial expression, as if their features had been sprayed with lacquer, except for their two upper extremities, each with several digits protruding from the sides of their tunics, that gracefully interlaced back and forth like mini ballerinas. Their message caused a roaring applause from some of those attending as well as a few who used the dexterity of their own multiple fingers to respond their affectionate feelings to the *Elders.*

The room went dark when Hesed and Ahava began to project from their seats a radiance that slowly transformed itself into a multitude of single beams and spoke to each person individually, before retracting back. The room lit up, and everyone brought their hands together, bowed their heads, and responded unanimously, "We thank you for your precious enlightenment." Turel observed a few beats of silence before saying, "Let's also give a warm welcome to our new brothers and sisters from the land above."

"You are home with us," was heard across the room. Turel left the stage and sat next to Biola. He turned to Benjamin and his group, "Your arrival has coincided with the visit of the *Elders,* and they asked me to tell you that they can't think of anything more pleasant than celebrating old friendships along with the start of new ones. They also look forward to meeting with you personally the next time."

Benjamin and his group responded by putting their hands together and nodded as they had learned its meaning to be also a way of saying the feeling was mutual. They refrained from asking questions. In due time, they would get the answers they sought, hopefully after their meal, as it had been promised.

"I don't know how old the first ancient couple is," Charlie said. "But I hope to look that good when I'm considered an antique." He always laughed at his own witticisms.

"Can you tell us a little more about the *Elders*?" Benjamin asked Turel.

"So much to tell you. It's impossible for me to provide you right now with a short, simple answer. Let's just say that they have always been part of our lives. Brother Ragor and Quynh are the original leaders of the Ancient Committee of the Third Reigning Atlantis in Zarzgoon, 20.7 billion miles from the Earth. The other four *Elders* with them are chief members of the Universal Unity Committee and high functionaries in their respective planets Platra and Zuybri, and then there's Hesed and Ahava, from the place Or. Their degree of mercy, love and wisdom is something that the *Elders* from every Universe have been working very hard trying to reach, and yet much needs to be achieved still before we can grasp such degree of purity. Hesed and Ahava, come from far, far away, but we have always felt like they are our next-door neighbors, always present … The others you see down here sitting among us, are my own family, some which you have met, and also close friends and dignitaries of this city where I have had the honor of presiding for more than three of your centuries."

"He must've meant three of our years …" Richardson said to Benjamin.

"I can't help wondering …" Benjamin said pensively.

They had come from a Victorian era of prejudice and preconceived rules and laws, where the average life expectancy was 45 years old, if lucky. They had personally witnessed the remarkable recovery of Sarah and Sophia, much like Lazarus rising from his grave. They could have easily perished like the others onboard the *Mary Celeste*, and yet they had been brought over not only by the most inconceivable forms of transportation but also into a world where all forms of life were respected and cherished. An overall feeling of gratitude toward their hosts was felt deep within their hearts. Only Carla seemed unimpressed — maybe the best description would be to say that she was mentally absent from her surroundings. Richardson kept an eye on her while trying to figure out what could be wrong, but respecting her request not to ask any questions, he remained silent by her side. Turel announced the meal would be starting.

The floor space closest to each seated group opened, and a table top surfaced with an array of small bowls and dishes filled with a variety of geometric shaped food. There was nothing that resembled what they had eaten in the past. Everything had a different taste and its own vibrant color. It was like eating pieces from a rainbow and drinking the colorful nectar of the gods. The tables rotated, and everyone had a chance to try a little of everything with the use of a seashell spoon that matched their seashell plate. Soft background music exuded from the surrounding silvery glass walls, and from the very center of the room, a pleasant, warm sensation swept over the guests.

"I see no wood burning," Volkert said to Margaritari. "Perhaps, an invisible fireplace?"

"Yes, you could describe it as invisible," she smiled. "We use the inner core of the Earth to our advantage, by using the constant change of the molecules within the outer core around the center core, to regulate the temperature everywhere, like … like a thermostat."

"Thermostat?" Volkert and Boz asked in unison.

"Oh, sorry I keep forgetting the period you came from. If I'm not wrong from my studies of past and future events on Earth, it will be another 11 years from now, your time of course, when a teacher will figure a way of maintaining heat at a certain temperature in his classroom, during the cold months. The room where he teaches is heated by a basement furnace, but he will get tired of being dependent on having to call the janitor to take care of the furnace, so he invents the first thermostat, which includes a bell to ring as a signal for the janitor to adjust the furnace damper in the basement — basically the very start of the thermostat."

"130 years later," Korallion said. "The United States and other countries will have something a lot better than that, still a bit primitive but you can program it to turn on or shut off the heat, including a cooling down mechanism, they will name, air conditioner."

"How do you know all this?" Boz interrupted her.

"Our computers provide us with historical images and information concerning the past, as well as the future."

"I know I'm asking a silly question, but … the music we hear," Volkert said. "Computers?"

"Musicians and computers," Margaritari said.

"Computers, eh? These computers, really arouse my interest. I would love to learn more about them."

"I can teach you. It's not that difficult once you understand the basics. Then if still interested, you can attend one of our universities for more advanced learning."

"I must ask you something," Boz said to Korallion. "When we arrived, I saw trees that I recognized as not being fruit bearing, but different fruits and vegetables grew from their branches, and the orchids … I mean, Sol wore a Middlemist Camellia in her hair, as if they were a dime a dozen, I mean ... How can that be possible? I'm completely flabbergasted by the plant life here."

"Ah, a subject very close to my heart. You may even call me a horticulturist of sorts," she smiled, and her skin color took on a bright golden tan, her eyes bright with joy. "A long time ago, we discovered how to create a root web between fruit trees and non-fruit trees that were open to being surrogate to fruit bearing. They exchanged information about each other's DNA through their root system, and they are able to flourish and pass it on to the next tree. You might say some of the species you saw were intertwined with each other, in perfect DNA harmony."

"Dee ann a?"

"Yes, the molecular basis of all life. We studied its function, growth and reproduction from bacteria to yeast, to plants and animals, and were able to even build mini sustainable gardens between each apartment floor in the city. Children are delegated at a very young age on how to take care of them. No one goes hungry here. Boz, it's going to be a pleasure to teach you."

The food was light but fulfilling. The best part of their meal was to taste each morsel like a palate adventure.

While Boz and Volkert continued to enjoy the charms of their female companions, Charles did the same with Sol, but every time he took a bite of one of the mouthwatering delicacies, he couldn't help thinking how much he would love to meet at least one of the chefs, for he was sure there had to be more than one. "Excuse me, Sol. But curiosity takes the best of me. The cooks who prepared the food, what do they do with the leftovers? And ... where is their kitchen, it must be very, very large."

"Not as big as you think, and there are no leftovers. All the food is perfectly quantified for each of us. The Universal Health Care Organization, UHCO, has mastered the science of producing the correct amount of a healthy balanced diet for each individual, and that leaves us without the need to indulge."

"The science of cooking! I always thought it was more of an art, but I see your point, we have to mix the correct ingredients to make sure we always get the same results. I would call the presentation of this delicious meal a perfect example of the science and art of cooking."

"I like that description better too, even though in about 128 years from now up there," she moved her thumb upwards. "Food will be scientifically engineered for profit regardless of its lack of nourishment and compatibility with the human body, and obesity will become a widespread health issue in the United States," she noticed his puzzled look and added. "Obesity, means overweight, like a person of your height may weigh 50 to 100 lbs., or more, than you."

"How will they move around with all that mass?" he laughed. "What will be the cause of such aberration called obesity?"

"They will become addicted to the engineered food. Which is made for profit with lots of fat, sugar and salt. As they indulge in overeating, they get bigger and bigger and movement becomes limited. Children will be following the same bad habits as the adults and later developing diabetes and heart disease among other health problems, which will be erroneously treated with drugs and surgery, instead of addressing the cause."

"That's so sad. I would love to develop my cooking skills to a healthier level."

"That's easy, Charlie. You can sign up as a student at our Culinary University where you will meet, for starters, a few of the most outstanding chefs in this Universe," she smiled when his eyes lit up. "They are always looking for individuals like you with a culinary passion. I'm sure they will be thrilled to share their knowledge."

Benjamin sat back watching his wife, who was busy talking with Biola about the music she had heard onboard the *Mary Celeste* and then by the waterfalls.

"We used the waterfalls to reproduce and transmit your music back," Biola said. "It was a way of making you aware of our presence and that we meant you no harm. The young ones you heard speaking were very excited to be part of the project."

"I truly appreciate your kindness; we were going through a very traumatic time onboard the *Mary Celeste*," she sighed. "The waterfalls are also a musical instrument?"

"Yes, one could even compare them to the old-time carillon with its dozens of bells or a large pipe organ since they were played by striking a keyboard to form a melody or simultaneously to sound a chord. But these particular waterfalls are a little different. They use each rock below like keys on a keyboard, and each water drop works just like when you used your fingertips on your melodeon, to create a musical composition. It also possesses a recording device that can reach and capture music from anywhere on Earth and then transmit it for our listening pleasure. Everything is programmed and controlled by musical engineers — musicians like yourself who love playing not only on the waterfalls' motherboard but also other significantly unique musical instruments that I know you, as a talented musician, will enjoy exploring and playing."

Ragor and Quynh stood from their chairs, and the room went silent once again. "My brothers and sisters," Ragor said, "May the Truth always illuminate your paths." Quynh added, "And may we all continue to enjoy the benefits of *your* light," she opened her arms toward Hesed and Ahava, who responded by changing colors from green to soft blue.

Adalius and Bevan stood and nodded, projecting to everyone in the room the élan ringing of their auditory communication. "The period we spent here," their nodding rang in complete harmony. "Has been with most favorable results as we studied with our brothers Turel and Biola, and their committee the present Earth's issues. We would like to announce that we have successfully put together an outline to help HUmanity from self-destruction, before reaching their year of 2050." Alaina and Declan also stood, and the rapid interchanging movement of their many fingers, caused everyone listening, including Benjamin and his group, to feel deeply moved.

Ragor turned toward Benjamin's group. "Thanks to the cosmogyral peregrinations of galaxies, which by following the simple physical laws, allow us to travel at the speed of light between Zarzgoon and the Earth, we bid you goodbye for now, but look forward to meeting you again, on a more personal level."

The *Elders* left the stage, and the tables retracted back into the floor space.

"Make yourselves comfortable in your seats," Turel said.

"You may want to lie back to better enjoy the view from above."

Sophia came over and nestled between her parents. Okeanos joined hers.

Turel touched the crystal on his chain and the ceiling opened to what seemed to be the sky of a summer night, only stars. Little by little, the stars began to move rapidly toward them like snow speckles crossing their vision. Had they been lifted into the skies above? They couldn't help expressing wonder as a few "oohs" and "ahhs" were heard from Benjamin's group, and when one of the stars started expanding and getting closer and closer, some brought their hands up to shield their faces while others used their forearms to fence off an approaching ball of fire.

"That star became the planet Earth, around 4.54 billion years ago," Turel's familiar voice soothed them enough to draw away their fears. They sat back. "Notice the changes, the cooling down as we move rapidly through time and witness the Earth being created as the third planet from the sun," he used a thin beam of light from his handheld stone to circle around his points of reference. "These are the North and South America continents; this region across the Atlantic Ocean is Europe and Asia, which we like to refer to as Eurasia. Asia is the largest continent, and over here is Africa, the world's second-largest continent. Just to give you an idea for reference's sake, our Atlantis stood here amidst the Atlantic Ocean, sandwiched between North America and Northwest Africa." Turel's voice took on a tone of solemnity, "I know it looks like a large continent, but actually we were just a small outpost, a center for studies when compared in size to the other quarter of a million Atlantis, spread throughout the Universes."

"It was during this time when HU-573b, a particular planet very similar to the Earth came to our attention. Due to the ill practices of its inhabitants, HU, as we called it for short, became depleted of all its natural resources. Along with a high rise in pollution and deadly viruses, the people of HU were rapidly dying, and it was common knowledge that they would be extinct before the next generation. Through an expansion program that had been created specifically to help populate planets that were suitable for life, the *Elders* immediately offered them the opportunity of commencing a new life on Earth. As scientists, we had reached the *Wisdom of the Ages* thanks to the enlightened relationship with the *Elders,* and we could not ask for a more exciting study. Our principal focus in Atlantis was to observe our HU brothers' progress as human beings on Earth and hopefully, they would stop their natural tendencies toward self-destruction. But all of this is too much to cover right now. I'll cut it short, our first two million years here were called the *Golden Age.* We had no need for possessions, and money had no value, gold was used to create outstanding works of art and incorporated into the architectural designs of our buildings. Around 928 B.C. to give you an idea of your time, a few of the humans on Earth began expanding their travels from one continent to another, and since we allowed them to cross our land when needed, they soon became aware of the riches available in Atlantis. As the word spread, we knew from watching the result of their unrestrained greed that caused them to take over other countries and even kill their own brothers, that we would have to make arrangements as soon as possible to either leave Atlantis or defend our post, which, by then, had grown into a small nation." Turel looked at his wife, "Biola, go ahead, my dear."

She stood. "We contacted the *Elders,* whom you met earlier, but to our surprise, we learned that we were facing a much worse enemy. Atlantis was going to succumb to a voracious composite volcano at an earlier date than we had anticipated, and the energy of such massive explosion would cause our land to submerge with all its inhabitants. Most of us were immediately transported home, to the original Atlantis on planet 50164, except for those who volunteered to stay and help build under the *Elder*'s guidance a strong enough glass structure to cover our beloved land, and withstand the enormous pressure to which it would soon be put through. We could not save the entire continent, but what we saved was well orchestrated down to every infinitesimal detail. Very much like you, Captain Briggs, the way you mastered the tools you had to know to keep your ship out of harm's way during a storm, we use our technology to detect any abnormal movement below or above us that can affect the stability of Atlantis, and we became proficient at moving our position under water while keeping its inhabitants safe. As you can see it now in fast motion, when the volcanic eruption happened, it provided the false impression to a few witnesses that Atlantis as it was already known, had dissipated completely from existence. Mythology took over, with all kinds of stories left to mankind's imagination."

"An interesting note here," Turel said. "On a more updated view of the Earth in your time, you'll notice the occidental side of Europe and Africa and the oriental side of the Americas north and south if brought together, could fit like puzzle pieces. And if someone was to take on the project of investigating some of the fauna and flora of both sides facing the Atlantic Ocean, believe me, it's no coincidence that animals and plants have so much in common."

"Please excuse my ignorance," Richardson said. "I don't mean to be rude, but are you saying that Atlantis is under a huge glass bowl?"

"You have an interesting way of analyzing structures," Turel chuckled. "We like to call it an underwater dome. But now that you mention, it could be described as a glass bowl — a very, very large bowl. Actually, we live under several of them, each programmed on a regular basis to reach into the ocean's surface and extract, within a few seconds, enough solar energy to run all our needs, as well as keep enough in reserve, if, for any reason, we were to need more."

Benjamin raised his hand, "I notice that everyone here refers to time ... as if it lacks any importance or ... doesn't exist. You have spoken of things that happened thousands of years ago as if they just happened yesterday."

"Time as you are used to referring to it," Biola said. "is simply a registry of the speed of life related to your daily living on Earth. The mayflies are a good example — they only live 24 hours but they enjoy a full lifespan, procreate at a very rapid rate and still find time to form groups to dance together on all available surfaces they find. Also, jellyfish are biologically immortal since they can revert back to their premature state, but sadly they don't live forever because they can get injured or eaten by other animals. So, even though here in Atlantis as well as those on other planets can be considered immortal, we are no different from the jellyfish that stops existing if put in harm's way. But putting all that aside, since time is endless for us, our technology has advanced tenfold with each passing of your centuries, and we have acquired the tools to foresee the future and stop many catastrophic events, like the one that almost destroyed Atlantis and its people."

"But that's absolutely wonderful," Sarah said. "We can warn humanity ahead of time and stop wars and major calamities and ..."

"My dear, dear sister Sarah," Turel said. "Believe me, we've done that several times, more than we can account for. We sent messengers to spread the word of love, and you already know what happened to them. We sent scientists to provide knowledge for better living conditions in impoverished countries, and their ideas were stolen and used for profit. We showed how to grow a better crop, how to create transportation without the need of gas and produce less pollution, but once again major corporations took over. We sent doctors to teach holistic care, but the pharmaceutical companies shut them down," he looked down and saw that Sophia had nodded off. "We have a lot more to tell you, but let's wait until you catch some sleep, and then we'll talk some more."

Choices

It had to be the next morning, the aroma of hot chocolate awoke Benjamin and Sarah. They could not resist drinking the smooth, dark liquid from the glass-like seashell lying on their small side tables next to their beds. They felt revitalized and ready for whatever was coming their way. They heard a soft knock coming from Sophia's bedroom door. She came in wearing a chocolate mustache, and when they signaled for her to join them, she laid between them.

"Mama, Papa, me happy here. Can I go to school with sister Okeanos?"

"School? Oh ... of course," Benjamin exchanged a surprised glance with Sarah. "I don't see why not."

"Good, I go to my room and get ready," Sophia kissed them and left.

"Can you believe what she just said?" Sarah felt overwhelmed by emotion.

"Yes, my love, I heard," he wiped her tears with his fingers.

"Our little girl is growing up."

"We also need to get ready, if we're going to keep up with her," she laughed, and he followed her to the shower.

Sarah had just finished tidying their bed when Turel's announcement was heard in their room, "A very good start to you," said the familiar voice even though he was nowhere in sight. "I would like to invite you all to meet me in the hallway, whenever you're ready."

Sarah opened the door and put her head out, and the doors to the other rooms opened simultaneously. Laughter ran rampant. Benjamin and Sophia joined her to see what was so funny.

"Our lives are so intertwined with each other," she explained. "That we all opened the doors at the same time. Isn't that remarkable?"

Okeanos came running, made her usual gracious greeting, took Sophia's hand and off they went.

Turel waved at Benjamin and his group from down the hall.

"Welcome to my study," he said. "Have a seat, make yourselves comfortable."

The five walls in the oval-shaped room were covered from floor to ceiling with softly lit multicolor narrow discs. He stood next to a square glass table in the center of the room and pointed at the walls, "In case you're wondering, those are my books. The younger brothers and sisters rather use their 3D mini-chips for reading but I'm a bit old fashioned to give these up. Anyway, my friends, you must have noticed that once you arrived in Atlantis you developed the faculties to understand our language, right?" Everyone nodded and he went on. "Our language is the universal idiom, and it will come in handy if you ever decide to travel to other planets, since our idiom transforms itself to translating itself into any other foreign language, the very reason you were able to understand the *Elders* earlier on. You must have also noticed that at present none of you suffers from any further health ailments. And as long as you remain with us, your health status will remain as it is. Sister Sarah and Sophia are completely recovered. Volkert recovered from his chronic depression, and Charlie, you are fine too," noticing his questionable look, he added. "Yes, my brother, one of the valves to your heart was close to failing."

"Oh, so that's why I wasn't feeling well onboard the ship. Thank you, thank you, brother Turel," he stood to shake his hand, but then backed away. "Sorry, I've noticed no one in Atlantis shakes hands. Old habits are hard to break."

"No reason to thank me. Health is a born right to be enjoyed while living," he smiled. "And you are correct, we acknowledge each other without the need to shake hands, something we learned from witnessing how deadly viruses spread by hand contact," he brought his hands together and bowed. Charlie did the same and then sat back next to Boz and Volkert. "So here in Atlantis, no one gets sick," Sarah still wondered how that could be possible.

"Let's put it this way, no one dies from being sick, and if someone does get sick, which is quite rare, it is treated immediately. The illnesses you are so familiar with were eliminated awhile back. But we still take precautions."

"If no one gets sick," Richardson said. "And we don't get old, I mean really old, what about population overgrowth? How do you control that?"

"I didn't want to go that deep into it, but since you ask, let's just say that one dies only when that person has achieved the satisfaction and understanding that their mission for living has been accomplished, but so far, I have not met anyone who came to that conclusion. With so many universes and over 700 quintillion planets in each universe, believe me, there's a lot to keep us occupied, including our struggling planet here and its inhabitants. They are quite a handful," he nodded. "The only reason we have not given up or left them to be exterminated on their own, is because about 50% of them have shown great potential to do good, and the *Elders* feel we would be doing wrong to abandon them." He waited a moment before continuing. "I'm afraid that humanity as you know now, will change drastically in the next few years, and so will the Earth. Some will go on a crusade to save the planet, like what happened in HU, but what they don't realize is that the planet will survive fine, what they need to do is to mend their ways in order to save themselves. As you heard before during our first meal together, we are working very hard at finding a solution to save HUmanity once again, the *Elders* feel they are worth saving, mostly because of the ones living amongst them who we classify as truly human beings ... we feel very optimistic about it. Still, we will be meeting once more, to make sure that our intervention will be successful without jeopardizing our own lives. Once again, too much to tell you at this point."

"Why did you take us in? Why did you help us?" Sarah asked.

"Yes, what can we possibly offer you that you don't already have?" Benjamin said.

"You are not the first ones we have saved from their ill fate. We have several rescue committees, and they follow very strict rules when it comes to putting our world into peril of any kind. For example, our Sea Rescue Committee's mission is to analyze from their monitors the events happening onboard ships and then respond accordingly. Your inner strength in a time of defeat touched the hearts of our *Elders* in Or, and since we knew that if we didn't interfere, you would all perish, we voted to bring you into safety. But in all fairness, you took the initiative to get into the yawl and roam away from the *Mary Celeste* and toward the *Island of Initiation,* one of our entry ports. We are sure that once your lives are enriched by knowledge, you will find your purpose for being here."

"On the island you speak of," Carla said. "I momentarily felt like my son was alive, but ... he was too far from me, too far...."

Turel tried to interrupt her. "Sister Carla ..."

"Knowing that I'll never see my son again has taken away my soul. I must pay for what I did to him, the crew and Captain Briggs' family. The only way I can do that is to go back to the

Mary Celeste and face the consequences of my wrongdoings."

"Sister Carla, please listen, if you return to the *Mary Celeste,* it means your death."

"My life is already meaningless, but as long as I have breath within my lungs, I know I can at least try to make a difference. Brother Turel, you told us you can look into the future, so you know I must stop what's about to happen. If I don't, a lot more innocent people will die. Please help me, I need to return to the ship and stop them from putting *their* plan into action."

"Carla," Richardson said. "What's going on?"

"Do I still have time?" she put her hands together and bowed to Turel.

"Yes, you do. And I would like to add that the crystal you found in the sand when you first arrived is a personalized microcomputer," he raised his hand to stop Richardson from interrupting. "Another hundred years or so and people around the world will have at least one or two extremely primitive forms of these per household and carry them everywhere they go before they find a way to insert them into their bodies," he shook his head. "Sorry, I tend to easily deviate away from matters at hand, especially when I know the historical outcome. To your question, yes, you can return to your ship, but you'll be facing the dangers you faced before joining us."

"Carla, why do you want to go back? You can't possibly be serious," Richardson said.

"I'm very serious," she said.

"Perhaps I should share with you some facts first," Turel said. "And then each of you can make a better educated choice, if you still want to return to the *Mary Celeste* or stay."

"We would like to stay," Volkert glanced quickly at his brother, to confirm. Then went on, "I look forward to learn more about computers. I'm fascinated by what it has to offer."

"Yes," Boz nodded. "I would love to stay and become a horticulturist like Korallion."

"I'm no coward, but I would rather stay as well, if I may. I don't need much persuasion to know that here is the beginning of my new life," Charlie said.

Benjamin reached for Sarah's hand, "I would also like to stay in Atlantis with my wife and child."

"Good, very good, I was hoping everyone would say that," Turel said. "But it seems that Sister Carla and Brother Richardson have not quite made up their minds," his voice showed concern. "If you return to the ship, there is no future for either of you, but it's still your choice, of course. I'm going to show you some indisputable facts, and then you will understand my apprehension about going back," Turel pointed the stone on his chain to the glass table at the center of the room, and the *Mary Celeste* came into full view, getting rained upon while bobbing up and down in the middle of a sea storm. The Lorenzen brothers and Charlie grasped each other, their eyes and mouths open wide as if they were staring at a ghost. Sarah hid her face in her husband's shoulder, and Carla brought her hands to her face and sobbed. Richardson, sitting next to her, put his arm over her shoulders, "Don't look at it. It's best not to look at it, it can only bring you pain."

"I must apologize," Turel turned off the image. "I'm so used to seeing historical films of the past and future, that for a moment, I took for granted that I could share with you what the future brings to the *Mary Celeste*. Very well, I'll tell you instead. Carla, if you return to the *Mary Celeste,* a group of pirates plans to take over the ship, and they will not leave any witnesses behind."

"Pirates?" Benjamin stood. "Why would they want to take over the *Mary Celeste?* The denatured alcohol?" he couldn't contain his laughter. "That doesn't make much sense. Who are these pirates?"

Carla stood. "I'll tell you who the pirates are, since I was one of them." Richardson remained seated and stared at her in disbelief. She went on, "Helmut worked for Captain Morehouse and his gang. Not wanting to arouse any suspicions, they waited five days in New York before following a parallel route to ours. Captain Morehouse is the one who arranged for the murder of Mr. Gottschalk so that Helmut could take his place. Getting me onboard was easy under the pretense of being a nurse, and a companion for Mrs. Briggs and her infant daughter. My job was to keep Helmut informed about their health. They hoped the disease would kill them before they took over the *Mary Celeste,* to remove their clandestine material."

"What clandestine material? You were a spy for Morehouse? You?" Benjamin raised his hands above his head and stared at her shaking his head. "You were waiting for my family to die?" he sat back as if drained of all bodily strength.

"I thought ..." Sarah cried.

"I'm very, very sorry, Mrs. Briggs. I was following Morehouse's orders, but once I met you and your family, I could no longer go along as planned. You're the closest I have ever come to having a family," she faced Richardson. "Helmut was infuriated when I told him I no longer wanted to be part of the plan. He must have heard me talking to Charlie about making the rice pudding because he asked me to leave the door to the kitchen open when Charlie wasn't in the galley, so he would be the first to taste the dessert. I swear, I had no idea that he was planning to add poison to it."

"That dirty scallywag, I should have forced the rice pudding down his throat when I had a chance," Charlie used his hands in a gesture he had learned in Italy when a cook asked him for the recipe of his chicken stew.

"I have no one to blame but myself," Carla went on. "Helmut admitted to killing Mr. Gillings, and I should have warned Mr. Richardson and Captain Briggs right then. But everything was going too fast, and by the time I came to my senses, it was too late," she cried. "Being stupid does not excuse me from being an accomplice, and I paid the price with my son's life ..." she couldn't stop crying.

"Mauricio witnessed Helmut throwing the second mate overboard," Turel said. "And he wasn't going to allow the boy to tell anyone. He ran after him with his knife. Mauricio climbed one of the ropes until he reached one of the sails, but Helmut followed him, grasped the sail, and proceeded to shake it. Mauricio held on as long as he could, but by then, the poison had seriously taken over his body, and as Helmut kept tugging at the sail, he couldn't hold much longer and had to let go. Luckily, he fell in the water, and I immediately sent help, like we have done for so many others in the past. We had him transported to urgent care on planet Gea where they are equipped to handle the effects of poison and accidental drowning at high seas. He is still there, in critical condition."

Richardson, who had not moved from his seat, still trying to assimilate what his beloved had just confessed, caught her as she slumped over.

"Don't worry," Turel said. "She just fainted. She will be fine," then turning to Benjamin. "One of Helmut's missions was to bring onboard 20 barrels with dynamite."

"Helmut substituted 20 barrels of alcohol for dynamite?" Benjamin said.

"He did not substitute the barrels already onboard. There was plenty of space below."

"Captain Morehouse was the father of my son," Carla sat up with Richardson's help. Morehouse's name echoed like thunder out of everyone's mouth.

She stood. "Captain Briggs and Mrs. Briggs, I don't blame you if you'll never forgive me. When Captain Morehouse invited you to dinner a few days before leaving New York, he was well aware of what had happened to Mr. Gottschalk, and the predicament he had put you in. He knew Helmut had worked for you in the past, and you would not be happy with his suggestion, but he also knew you were in a bind for time and would feel obliged to take Helmut to cover the loss of one of your men. He can be very persuasive," she wiped her tears with the back of her hands. "He arranged everything well in advance. Helmut's job was to bring the dynamite aboard. My job was to keep Richardson distracted and out of the way, leaving Helmut to do his dirty work without anyone being the wisest." Richardson moved away from her. "I didn't know you. I didn't know I would fall in love with you. Richardson, I swear to you that I'm not the same person I used to be before I met you. When I said I loved you, I was telling you the truth." She cried inconsolably.

"Captain Morehouse knew Captain Briggs had an understanding with his men," Turel said. "And that the crew knew better than to attempt to open one of the alcohol barrels. He needed someone to sabotage the *Mary Celeste,* and Helmut was the only one he trusted to get rid of everyone so that when the *Dei Gratia* caught up with your ship, he could take it over without any hassles. He also planned on doing a double business deal, take the dynamite barrels, which he had a buyer for, and then collect the salvage award for finding the so-called "abandoned" *Mary Celeste.* As we speak now, I'm afraid the *Dei Gratia* is getting closer to your ship."

"Brother Turel, I'm ready to leave," Carla said.

"No Carla, you can't go back. I won't let you," Richardson tried to hold her.

"How can you still want me after all I have done?" she pushed him away.

"It's all in the past, Carla. Like you said, you're not the same person, and my love for you has not changed. If you keep insisting on going back, I'm going with you, and I will help you with whatever you hope to accomplish."

"Richardson, this is my problem, not yours. I cannot allow you to risk your life for me. I need to get back before Morehouse arrives. If the dynamite reaches its destination, a lot of people will be hurt, and I must put a stop to it. Besides, Helmut is tied down. I'm not in any danger."

"Actually ..." Charlie stared at his fingernails, unable to look anyone in the eyes. "I untied his hands so he could eat the porridge I made the morning we left. I can't stand food being wasted. I ... I was in a hurry to leave with everybody and ... I didn't realize until later that I had left without tying back his hands."

"It doesn't matter," she said. "He doesn't scare me. Richardson, I'm going alone."

"No, and that's all there is to it. Brother Turel, I'm going with Carla."

"You and Carla, return to your rooms and change back into the clothes you wore before arriving. I'll wait here for you."

"Mrs. Briggs, it was an honor to be part of your family, even if only for the short duration we had together." She turned in the direction of Boz, Volkert and Charlie, "I'm very, very sorry, I didn't mean to hurt you or your mates." She ran out of the room.

"Richardson," Benjamin called out. "I wish you and Carla the best of luck."

"Me too, Richardson. Please take care," Sarah said.

"I speak for the three of us," Charlie said. "If you get a chance, let Carla know that we forgive her; meanwhile, we'll pray for her safe return with you."

Richardson left and so did the sailors.

"Benj, I'm so happy you decided to stay with me and Sophie," Sarah said.

"I could never leave you, Sarah. You mean the world to me," he held her close in his arms.

"I understand you miss your son, but anytime you want to see him," Turel said, "there is a computer in your room, and once you learn how to operate it, you will be able to see him, just like you saw the *Mary Celeste* a little while ago. You won't be able to communicate with him, but you will be able to follow him as he grows up. He will be making you both very proud." They left, and Turel turned the screen back on. The *Mary Celeste* could be seen once again in its full spectrum.

Pirates

Richardson and Carla sat across from Turel.

"Even though you have your minds made up, let me ask you just one more time. Are you sure you want to go back?" Turel said.

Carla said yes and so did Richardson.

Turel pointed to the crystals hanging from the chains on their necks. "You can remove those; you will need something a lot more powerful," he took the crystal off from his chain and handed it to Richardson. "This one has 58 processing facets, each working in unison to borrow directly from our motherboard the quantum energy you will need to be transported over and back. Take good care of it, you both will need it to be able to return to Atlantis if you are successful in your mission. For that to happen, it's imperative that you dispose of the dynamite and leave the ship before Helmut sees you and the pirates' arrival. Since you will be changing the future by going back in time, everything is dependent on how quickly you move. To get to the ship, place this crystal in the palm of your hands, either of you, it doesn't matter. I have it programmed so that when the other side of the crystal is covered by the other's hand, when you state your wish to board the yawl, which is close by the *Mary Celeste,* you will both be transported there. Once you accomplish your undertaking, follow the same procedure for returning to Atlantis," he paused momentarily and then added, "According to the segment I just watched, today is Thursday, December 5th, and Helmut is standing at the bow with a monocular, expecting the arrival of the *Dei Gratia.* Make sure to row the yawl to the stern of the ship by the davits. I saw two long ropes dangling from it, and you will need them to climb onto the ship. Hopefully, Helmut will remain focused at the bow watching for the *Dei Gratia,* and there will be less of a chance for him to see you."

"We're infinitely grateful for everything you have done for us," Carla said.

"I will be following you from my screen, but like I said, the outcome is completely dependent on your success to carry forward your intentions as fast as you can."

"We understand," Richardson held the crystal from his chain, in the palm of his hand. "Are you ready?" he asked Carla. She nodded and placed the palm of her hand over the crystal. Holding it firmly, they closed their eyes and voiced their destination.

Using the two oars on the yawl, Richardson rowed closer toward the stern and proceeded to quickly fasten the yawl to one of the manropes. With her long skirts, ascending the side ladder was a lot more difficult than descending. She quickly discarded the heavy dress, lifted her lightweight cotton undergarment skirt and tucked it around the waist.

Once onboard, they took a brief look at their immediate surroundings. Helmut was nowhere in sight. They noticed the fore-upper-topsail and foresail had been blown away, and the fore-lower-top-sail had been ripped from its fastenings along the yard held by its four corners. Richardson shook his head and whispered,

"Looks like this ship has been battling a storm; we better hurry." They loosened the battens, securing the edges of the tarpaulin that covered the main hatch to the hold below. He went down the ladder followed by Carla. Once below, he stared at her. "What are we going to do, open all the barrels? How do we know which have the dynamite?"

"Helmut marked the top of the barrels with a tiny cross, so they could be easily identified."

"We need to get them on deck," he tried picking one up, but it was heavier than he thought. Using the ropes hanging from a beam above, he harnessed a pulley to lift one barrel up the steps.

Once on deck, he handed her a clawhammer. "Just give a good blow to each barrel I bring up, that way we're guaranteed that once we throw them overboard, their contents will spill out in the water. Will you be able to take care of that?" he asked.

She picked up the clawhammer like a Joan of Arc ready to strike for the cause. "Dear, dear Richardson, you'll never know how good this makes me feel," she flung a blow that split the top off the barrel, like a lightning volt.

Preoccupied with their tasks, they forgot about Helmut.

"Only two more barrels left and we're finished here," Richardson said.

"Look," she pulled on his sleeve and pointed to the frightful sight far in the distance. A two-mast vessel with a fully square-rigged foremast appeared on the horizon. Even with the hull down due to the curvature of the Earth, they had no doubt in their minds as to whom that brigantine belonged to.

"Don't worry. We can do it. I'll hurry up," Richardson hurried below, but when he reached the last step, someone hit the back of his head with a beetle mallet. He let out a groan and fell face down.

Standing by the open hatch, Carla cried out, "Richardson ..." But as she started to take the first step, she backed away. Standing over Richardson, Helmut motioned the mallet toward her, "And now it's ye turn, ma lovely," he yelled out. "I'm a climbing

Jacob's Ladder. Ye and me, have a lot to catch up on." His usual raucous laughter went on as he took his time climbing each step like a spider crawling toward his web-trapped victim. Carla grabbed a bundle of boltrope next to her and threw it at him. Not knowing what was coming at him, he got caught off guard and fell backward. She ran to the captain's cabin. But once she reached the companionway, her instincts dictated that she would be better off on deck, where she would not feel so confined.

The ship being at the mercy of strong winds and with no one at the wheel, dipped up and down and wavered in all directions. Squalls of wind and rain coming in at short intervals and the noise of the growling masts quivering like tall giants about to crumble on deck, augmented the violence of the breaking seas. A breach broke across the deck knocking her down and carried her against the taffrail where she managed to hold on, as she caught sight of Helmut stumbling on the port side and coming in her direction. She crawled toward the main cabin, only 18 inches above deck, and laid flat against its side. Her heart throbbing like a steady drum beat was the only thing that kept her mind from shutting down as she held still what felt like an eternity. Suddenly the skylight over the captain's cabin popped up and so did Helmut's head, a hideous Jack in the Box. His bulging black eyes glared directly at her. "Oh, there ye arr, ma beauty!" His wide-open mouth exposed the two decayed teeth he had left. She let out a terrorized scream.

"I'm a-coming forr ye," he said before retracting inward like a snake.

She ran starboard and then toward the forecastle and crouched next to it, watching as he came out of the companionway. He stretched his arms out yawning and then walked aft. He used the mallet to yank out the lazarette hatch, looked in and said, "Nay, she's not here." The sea had calmed enough that he walked leisurely starboard. He climbed on top of the forecastle and noticing the scuttle latch was missing. He took a quick peek inside the opening and repeated, "Nay, she's not here." He slipped on the wet top and lost his balance but landed on his feet. His exasperation finally surfaced, "Dern, I had enough. Woman, the longer ye hide, the angrier I get, and the angrier I get, the more ye going to," he sang out the next word, "sufferr," with an emphasis on *err*.

She laid as flat as possible against the side of the forecastle.

He stopped a few feet from her, facing the port railing, his back to her. She dared not breathe, as tears rolled out in silence.

"So ye think ye smarter than me, hmm?" he said, maintaining his back turned. Then knowing well in advance where she laid, he turned quickly on his heels and let out a triumphant hoot. When she tried to stand, he used the wood mallet like a sword, pressing it on her chest and pinning her down.

"Yer lover is dead and ye arr next. But first I take ye like the whore ye arr, do ye hear me?" He threw the mallet to the side and dropped on top of her, his big calloused hands tearing at her bodice. He bit her naked breasts and then forced his tongue into her mouth. She responded by biting his tongue as hard as she could while trying to reach for his eyes with her fingernails. He backed off with a bloody mouth, momentarily stunned. He slapped her across the face and then proceeded to choke her with both hands. About to pass out, she gave up struggling, but when he held himself up to open the front buttons on his pants, she used the opportunity to kick her right knee into his groin. As he rolled to the side with a moan, she pulled herself free, but did not run far before tripping over the fore hatch that laid unexpectedly on the side.

He stood over her once again, "Ye arr not worth it. It's time for ye to croak."

She closed her eyes and crossed her hands over her face. When she felt a pair of hands grab her by the shoulders, it took some time before she stopped kicking and screaming — it was Richardson. She cried as they briefly hugged. Helmut laid face down on deck after being knocked over the head with the mallet.

"We can't take a chance if he's still alive," Richardson said.

"We need to get him off this ship." They tied Helmut's hands and feet and threw him overboard.

"We still have two barrels to get rid of. Let's finish what we came here to do," he said.

The *Dei Graia* accosted the *Mary Celeste* just as the last barrel got axed and thrown into the ocean.

"Give me your hand, Carla, it's time for us to leave."

"No, you go. I still have business to take care of with Morehouse."

"Are you out of your mind? You heard Turel, Morehouse will kill you!"

"I don't care. I lost my son because of him, and he's going to pay for it."

Before he could stop her, she grabbed the clawhammer lying on the deck and ran starboard.

To Carla's surprise, Morehouse was already onboard with five of his men, but that did not discourage her. "You filho da puta! You killed our son!" she tried to hit him with the clawhammer, but she was no match for him. He grasped her wrist and twisted it until she dropped it. She proceeded to hit him with her fists, but one of his men pulled her off Morehouse and held her back.

"Calm down, woman, what're ye saying? Where's the boy?"

"You put Helmut, a murderer like you, on this ship, to kill everyone onboard, and Mauricio became one of his victims."

Morehouse took a look at Richardson who had put up a good fight but had finally succumbed to the three men who had him pinned down on the deck with their feet. "Oh, I see," he nodded his head repeatedly, "Ye were too busy to be a mother and watch over my boy, is that it? Where were ye when all that happened — let me guess, in bed with this *merda*, eh?" he slapped her across the face hard enough to cut her bottom lip.

"Meet Mr. Richardson, the only "real" father Mauricio ever knew," she said.

He made a fist to punch her when one of his men called out,

"Captain, our dynamite is gone."

"What in sam hill is going on here?" he turned to Richardson, who was now being held next to Carla. "Come to think o' it, where's Helmut?"

"Wouldn't you like to know," Carla said, taking his attention away from Richardson.

Morehouse grabbed her by the chin with one hand. "I can easily crush yer face. Ye better tell me exactly what happened onboard this cursed ship."

"We're all planning to escape from Helmut, but he caught us before we could get into the yawl. He killed Captain Briggs and his family, and the few men who were still alive, he threw them overboard. But in the end, he got what he deserved — he's at the bottom of the ocean along with your cursed dynamite."

"How convenient. Only the two o' ye survived, eh?"

"I curse you," she shouted back at him. "I curse you until the day you die, when you become a crippled old man with maggots growing in your guts. Yes, I want you to live for a long time so you can be cursed by a thousand deaths, and when you finally die, you'll burn in hell for what you did to my child," she spit at him.

He wiped his face on his sleeve. "Ye are the one who's cursed. Ye're the one going to 'ell, deep down into its bottomless pit," he punched her in the chest, and the men had to hold her up as she bent backward from the blow. Richardson struggled to free himself, but the men had him well secured. Morehouse made another fist and hit Richardson in the jaw.

"Get 'em in the yawl. I want 'em to feel the agony o' knowing they're going to drown and nothing can save 'em."

Seated close to each other in the yawl, Richardson and Carla heard the demonic laughter of Morehouse and his men.

"Do you still have the crystal?" she asked Richardson.

He touched his chest, "Yes, under my shirt."

Captain Morehouse used the small ax he carried on his waist belt to remove the cleats holding the box from the roof of the aft deckhouse. All its contents fell out.

Morehouse bent over the taffrail, "I have a going away present for ye," he threw the broken sextant and chronometer overboard, then pulled out a pistol from his belt pocket. "Now, let's see how well t'is Army pistol works," he cocked the hammer and slid the breech back for easy cartridge insertion. Then he moved the block forward before pulling the trigger to shoot twice in their direction. The first bullet cut the rope attached to the yawl. "Wow," he yelled out. "I'm impressed. Ye must agree that I'm good at shooting, eh?"

The second shot made a hole in the bottom of the yawl. "Hey, Carla, tell the Devil I sent him my best!"

He pointed at them once again and fired. The bullet hit Richardson on the left shoulder, making him drop forward from the pain.

Carla bent over Richardson and used her upper body to cover the maneuver of bringing out the crystal from under his shirt without attracting attention. "It's time for us to go home," she whispered. Keeping the crystal in the palm of her hand, she positioned Richardson's right hand over it, and they voiced their wish in unison.

Captain Morehouse and his men could swear Carla and Richardson had suddenly vanished just before the yawl submerged, but they were never going to admit such a ridiculous thing. It was well known that when staring at anything on a foggy rainy evening out in the middle of the ocean, it could produce all kinds of visual disturbances.

Ten days later, Captain Morehouse and his crew arrived at Gibraltar, after towing the Mary Celeste for 800 miles and tried to collect $46,000 from the ship's insurance.

A salvage hearing was summoned by Attorney General Frederick Solly-Flood, who suspected Captain Morehouse and crew of foul play. They were charged with piracy and conspiracy to carry out insurance or salvage fraud.

Three months later, and not having found proof of their guilt, the court awarded one-sixth of the $46,000 for which the ship and cargo had been insured, suggesting that the authorities were not entirely convinced of the Dei Gratia crew's innocence.

Thank you

Dear Reader, if you enjoyed this book, you can leave a review on Amazon.com. It will be much appreciated, and hopefully an incentive for other readers who enjoy historical fiction, or other publications by the same author.

www.veronicaesagui.com

Other books by Dr. Veronica Esagui
(Available at all book stores, Amazon.com and Kindle)

 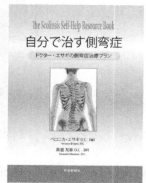

The Scoliosis Self-Help Resource Book
(English and Japanese)

Includes the illustrated step-by-step approach to TESP (The Esagui Scoliosis Protocol), a very specific group of exercises for the spine. Through this book, a person with scoliosis will discover that they may have options other than drugs or surgery. "If by writing this book, I can shed some light onto scoliosis management that is more proactive than waiting under observation, then people will understand their options and I will have done my best as a chiropractor and educator."

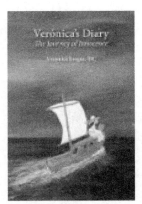

Verónica's Diary - The Journey of Innocence
(1944–1962)

Describes in the most candid manner the first 18 years of Veronica's life growing up in Portugal, until a pre-arranged marriage with her cousin brings her to the USA in 1962.

Veronica's Diary II - Braving the New World
(1962–1988)

Follows her trailblazing accomplishments as a music teacher, performer, news reporter, theatre director, playwright, owner of three music centers, theatre producer and owner of the only American dinner theatre in the world in a Japanese restaurant.

Veronica's Diary III - Awakening the Women Within
(1988–1994)

Her children are now grown up; her ex-husband is still her friend, but her lovers don't fit the role model of the romance novels she used to read as a young girl.

Veronica's Diary IV – Angels Among Us
(1994–1996)

Experiencing the darkest days of her life, Veronica is thankful for the angels along her path, some of whom were still exorcising their ghostly pasts as they strived to earn their wings.

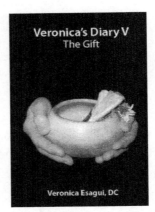

Veronica's Diary V - The Gift
(1996–2003)

A stranger follows Veronica into a supermarket and hands her a small pottery, insisting that the gift is meant only for her. She accepts it. Veronica's rich life experiences as a time traveler have finally taught her to recognize that her quest for happiness has finally been granted.

by **Veronica Esagui**
and
Linda Kuhlmann

Aged to Perfection — A comedy play —

"A merry exploration of what shapes our definition of love and family." Mary Lyne Monroe, Portland Book Review

"I have never seen such an original idea on stage or screen."
— Thomas Snethen, Oregon Writers's Colony

***

Script can be ordered directly from Papyrus Press, LLC
Handson13@hotmail.com

The following are available from Amazon.com

Moments Before Midnight *and* **Terra Incognita**
Oregon Poets Write for Ecological, Social, Political, and Economic Justice.
www.bobhillpublishing.com

Now we heal – An Anthology of Hope
Writing participant with 18 other authors
Wellworth Publishing